Acclaim for
Of Giants and Other Men:

'A beautifully realized novel that doesn't shy away from describing the horrors of war as well as life's moments of beauty.'

'Author Peek manages to weave the 20th century history of Nicaragua together with a moving story of betrayal and redemption, without sacrificing the tale's descriptive beauty.'

Kirkus Reviews

'*Of Giants and Other Men* is a sleeping giant, in and of itself. It promises much, evolves its plot slowly and carefully.'

'…a sweeping epic covering some 50 years of modern Nicaraguan history as seen through the eyes and experiences of ordinary people experiencing war, death, conflict, and social change. Peek's focus on the nucleus of a family and how it's affected by these events creates the perfect macrocosm of experience that narrows the lens even to a father/son relationship.'

Midwest Book Review

'*Of Giants and Other Men* has plenty of charm to it, as well as compelling dialogue and beautiful descriptions. It is a book that sticks.'

Portland Book Review

'*Of Giants and Other Men* begins and ends with an untimely death, but the middle is where the reader is well, and truly, hooked.'

'Most memorable is Peek's unique talent for capturing surroundings through the most under-referenced of senses: scent. (…) These elements are where Peek shows the most potential to become a great writer.'

'Recommended for fans of literary fiction.'

San Francisco Book Review

Of Giants and Other Men

A Novel

Caspar Peek

Tumbleweed Books
New York, NY 10003

First print edition, 2015

ISBN: 978-1-942591-00-9

Cover design: Katya Tabakova

www.tumbleweedbooks.org

For Leila

Of Giants and Other Men

Chapter 1

"Dead people," Tomás said on the day he was put in charge of the morgue, "have been part of my life for as long as I can remember."

It was 1931 when his father, Raúl, returned home to the small Nicaraguan town of León after spending three weeks in the mountains of Las Segovias, in the country's far northern reaches. Victoria, his wife, had locked herself in her room, and he slept in the study that night, the coldness of his pistol numbing his cheek through the thin fabric of a cotton shawl, while his boots were being cleaned by a quiet maid, and placed at his feet, ready for use. They were polished to a shine, with no traces left of vomit or blood.

The pitapat of small feet woke him, and when he opened his eyes he saw his son standing in the doorway, a sagging diaper hugging his thighs.

"Come here, Tomás," he said, waving the boy towards him.

"Baba," the boy babbled.

"When I last saw you, you could neither walk nor talk," Raúl said when the boy had walked half the distance. "And look at you now." His cowlick falling over his left eye, the boy advanced, steadily, holding his arms in front of him as if he were sleepwalking. Raúl came off the sofa and knelt down on the floor, stretching out both arms.

"You can do it. Be brave. I'll meet you halfway."

When the boy fell over, his father caught him. Tomás reached for his father's boots, scuffed but shiny, and when he got hold of one he tried to sink all of his six teeth into it. The taste of leather and wax filled his mouth, and he grimaced.

"Not so tasty, right?" his father said, laughing. "They're not for eating, really. But why don't you try them on your feet?" He lifted the boy and lowered him into the boots, all the way down until he was in up to his thighs.

"Looking good, soldier!" Raúl exclaimed, holding his son steady. "Just give it some time, and they will fit you just perfectly. Time," he said once more, nodding. "And you still have so much of it."

When his father let go of him, Tomás fell over and started crying.

"Shhh," Raúl said, but it was too late. A key ground its way through a lock, and Victoria rushed in, dressed in her nightgown.

"What are you doing?" she said, lifting the boy. "Sofía, come and help me!"

"Just showing him," Raúl sputtered, but when her brow furrowed into a frown, he shrugged and said no more. After the nanny had carried the crying boy away, Victoria turned back at her husband.

"Don't do this, Raúl. I can't stop you from putting your own life in danger, but leave the boy out of it. I will not let you take him away from me."

He noticed that her face looked paler than he remembered. "Of course not," he said, and hugged her. "Why would I?"

He stayed one week. Victoria told the maid to hide his boots, and he did not ask for them. When Tomás climbed onto his parents' bed and wriggled in between them, they both laughed. He kicked them until he had driven a wedge between their bodies, and snuggled up against them both.

"Strong boy," Raúl said, but she hushed him.

"Don't start again, Raúl," she said. "You promised to leave him out of this." He kissed her, and life was good for six days.

At dinner he told her.

"I will be leaving tomorrow," he said.

She closed her eyes and bit her lip.

"Don't go," she said. "If you go now you will lose your son. And you will lose me."

"I don't want to lose you. Or my son."

"Then don't go. It's simple, and it's in your hands."

"Why do you ask me to choose?" he said. "Why can't you accept that I need to do this? That I cannot stand by idly while our country is being plundered?"

"What's it to us?" she said. Slowly, emphasizing each word. "They're peasants, and this is not your fight. Let them fight their own war." She set down her glass, hard, and it shattered when it hit the table. A trickle of blood welled from her hand as she closed it into a fist.

"Let me," he said. He opened his napkin and tied it around her hand, making a knot to silence the knuckles that pointed at him with rage and defiance.

"Why can't you live your life?" she said. "Why do you need to live someone else's life? You're not one of them. Why can't you think of us? Of your son?"

"That's what I am doing," he said. "I am thinking of my son – I know that there will be no future for him here unless there is a future for all of us. Can't you accept that this is how I want to live my life?"

She shook her head. "It no longer is your life. You have a son, you should think about his life, too. You will lose him, and worse than that, he will lose you. Is this what you want?"

He took her hand, held it to his face.

"Victoria," he pleaded. "Please try to understand."

"No," she said. "I love you, Raúl, but love has its limits."

It was the emptiness of the bed that woke her. The contours of his body were still imprinted on the mattress, and the pillow next to her head smelled of him: a deep musk that had drawn her into a treacherous sleep. *Too late*, she thought, *why didn't I hear him?*

"He just left," Sofía said. "Two men came for him."

"The car," Victoria snapped. "Tell the driver to crank up the car, fast. Where did they go?"

"I heard them talk about the river," Sofía said. "The Rio Chiquito."

She saw them across the river. They had climbed down the embankment and were walking towards a small boat moored to a *pochote* tree.

"Stop," she yelled at the driver. "Stop here and let me out!"

She screamed at him, a single word. He turned around when he heard his name, and looked up at her from across the river. Tall and light-skinned, he stood out from his companions, three peasant men wearing straw hats and sandals. He waved at her, and smiled.

She could not move. Leaning over the low stone wall, she felt the dizziness that comes with both victory and defeat. *This is where he dies*, she thought. *This is where he stops being part of my life.*

One of his companions pulled at his sleeve, motioning for him to get into the boat, and he nodded.

"I love you, Victoria," he shouted. "And tell my son I love him, too. Nothing else matters." He turned and got into the boat. The eddies pulled at it, impatiently and making it swirl without direction at first. But then the current caught it and soon it drifted out of view. He looked back, once, and raised his hand.

There were no letters, and then he was killed. Not in a fight, not even in an ambush. It was when he left the presidential palace with Sandino, the guerrilla leader, after a gentlemanly talk with the President. Just the three of them, over dinner: steak with figs and a shot of rum to patch things up and seal the peace. But that did not suit Somoza, the Commander of the National Guard. Men like Delacorte and Sandino would be a menace forever, stirring up trouble. So just before going off to attend a poetry recital, Somoza gave orders to capture the rebels as they left the palace, and take them to an airfield where they were to be shot point-blank. There was to be no discussion. No pleas, no bribing.

When Sandino made the Mason sign of distress, the captain of the Guard called Somoza.

"What is it?" Somoza barked. "I'm having dinner here, what's the matter?"

"He made the sign," the captain said. "Now what do I do?"

"I'm eating, goddamnit," Somoza yelled. "Right now I'm eating, and when I'm eating I'm not a Mason. Just do as you were told, carry out your orders!" He slammed the phone back on the hook.

"What was that?" his wife said.

"Have to do everything myself," he growled.

The guardsman hung up and turned to the prisoners.

"No more words," he said. "Just stop yapping already, no more words." There was a round of bullets: two in the heart and one in the head.

"That ought to do it," the captain said. When the President was informed of the execution he was incensed, but the damage was done.

"This is not what I asked you to do, *Comandante*," he hissed at Somoza. "These were not my orders!"

The comandante shrugged it off: "Can't get the shit back in the horse, Señor *Presidente*," he said. "Might as well end it now."

And that's what they did, although the President knew that by bloodying his hands there would be no going back. The *Guardia* raided Sandino's cooperatives in the North, and within a month they were all dead. Men, women, even the children.

"Everyone understands death," Somoza told his men. "Why waste efforts on subtleties?"

The President gave orders to dig up Raúl's body. It was because he had come from a good family, when such things still mattered. He had "known the young man's grandfather," he explained to his wife, as he climbed into the baldachined presidential bed.

"I owe it to him," he said. "This was all a big mistake." His wife shook her head at the thought of all the people who had paid with their lives for the mistakes made by others.

On the morning that Tomás's father came home, Victoria and her cousin Pilar were sipping coffee on the patio. Pilar was a potted plant in a big flowery dress, bookish-looking with her horn-rimmed spectacles. Victoria, however, was a leopard stretching before the run, with cheekbones that pushed up her eyes until they were drawn-out slits resting under her eyelashes.

A car pulled up to the house, and the maid announced the visitors: "Doña Victoria, it is Don Emilio, with a soldier." The two men were led into the sitting room, and waited for Victoria to appear. As she walked in, accompanied by Pilar, both men stood up, and she kissed the one announced as Don Emilio on the cheek.

"Hello, cousin," she said. "To what do I owe the honor of this early visit?"

"Good morning, Victoria," he said. "We are sorry to disturb you at this hour." He pulled at his starchy shirt collar, not used to wearing a suit and tie, but the occasion had clearly called for them. He straightened the flowery tie and scraped his throat.

"I am here in my official capacity as vice mayor," he said, "and this is Captain Andrade." The captain smiled faintly, but did not salute. He was carrying a round object in a brown paper bag, and once they sat down he balanced it on his knees with two gloved hands.

Victoria did not know that Tomás was listening to the conversation. He was in the bathroom down the hallway, the door ajar to make sure he would not get trapped inside. Here, sitting on the toilet with his shorts dropped to his ankles, was where and how Tomás learned of his father's death. He learned of his death before he had learned of his birth. Or even his life.

The vice mayor hemmed and hawed and scraped his throat a little to gain some time, but at one point there was no more escaping the reason for his visit. He thought, *how on earth am I going to tell my cousin that her husband has been shot like a dog? And that only because of his last name, his body was not left to rot inside a tar pit, but was burned instead? Such things are best left unsaid,* the vice mayor thought, and so he just said: "We are bringing your husband home."

At that moment, the captain opened the paper bag, and out came a clay urn, which he held up with both hands. His immaculate gloves turned a streaky reddish-brown, which he ignored. Instead, he looked at the vice mayor and raised his eyebrows. The vice mayor shook his head, just barely, and closed his eyes for a second. Then the captain put the urn on the coffee table and pushed it resolutely towards Victoria, seemingly glad to be rid of it.

Victoria had not moved a muscle while her cousin spoke, nor did she acknowledge the urn. In truth, she had been expecting the visit. And in truth also, if there were such a thing, to her the conversation was over before it had begun. *There,* was all she could think, *there, it's finally out, death foretold, finally become reality.* She did not blame the cousin-twice-removed; she did not even blame the words he had spoken. The arrival of this urn was the moment when her options had irrevocably turned into immutable facts. For one second she thought, *what if I refuse to accept this urn?* But of course it did not matter anymore. She had let go of the man long before his body was brought home. Just like the words her cousin had spoken, the urn was only that: a message confirming what had already become fact and now needed to be stored away alongside all the other things that had stopped being possibilities, so they would no longer seek to introduce doubts into anyone's life ever again.

She looked at the urn from the corner of her eye as it sat on the table, the way she would size up a beggar, expecting it to jump at her if she let down her guard. It stood earth-colored against the whitewashed wicker, out of place in her home, and unwilling to leave. It was sealed with thick red wax, as if containing something contaminating, something with the power to upset delicate balances and bring about repeated mistakes. But she brushed aside those thoughts, and decided that they would not become part of her life.

"Thank you, cousin," she said, "thank you for coming yourself."

The cousin forced a smile, awkward and wry. "I'm sorry, Victoria," he said. "I wish…"

"It's all right," she interrupted him, "it's all right, cousin. I understand. Thank you for coming." The cousin was relieved, and it showed in his face. While Pilar accompanied the two men to the door Victoria went to her room, and only the urn stayed behind in the living room.

When the voices had died away the bathroom door opened, and a small boy walked slowly towards the sitting room, expecting to find the father who had been brought home. But there was only an urn. He was puzzled by the absence of the tall man whose picture he had seen on his mother's night table. *Maybe there is a genie in the bottle,* he thought, trying to peer through the clay. But he saw nothing.

Touch it, he thought. *My father must be in there. I'll let him out.* He started peeling away the wax. It was soft still, and came off in thick bands. Soon his fingers were resting on the cork, a round sliver of tree bark that had come all the way from Portugal to seal a destiny. He tried to pry it open, but it had been wedged in with force and purpose, and his hands were no match for those. Lifting the urn with both hands, he shook it up and down. His arms could barely make it around, and he huffed while his face turned red.

"Holy Virgin Jesus Mary," Pilar screamed as she walked in. Tomás froze and almost dropped the urn.

"Victoria, Sofía!" Pilar yelled, sinking back against the wall. When Victoria ran in she was met by the glorious sight of her son standing naked from the waist down, holding the urn pressed against his belly like a giant balloon.

"Sofía!" she shouted, but there was no need for shouting, as the nanny had been right behind her.

"Come now, Tomás," Sofía said, prying his fingers away. He fought and screamed, but in the end the urn fell on the floor and rolled away, and that was that.

"This boy!" Aunt Pilar gasped. "Nothing good will ever come of him!" Victoria shook her head and left the room without saying a word.

She decided that the urn should be kept out of sight. Everything had its place in the world, and the place for an urn was a dark cave, a suitcase, or a rattan trunk. So it was left in the storage room in back of the house, all the way behind the servants' quarters. But Tomás did not forget about it. He looked for it, lifting the lid of every trunk and suitcase he came upon. The suitcases for the masters were made of cowhide in those days, while those for the maids and nannies were made of cardboard. They had names written on them, and "LEÓN" in large letters splashed in white paint, which gave them a sense of finality, as if they belonged to elephants who were being reminded where their final journey would take them. It was not until two years later that he found the urn in the garden shed. He was hanging over the side of a rattan trunk, trying to pull out the urn with both hands, when Sofía walked in.

"What are you looking for, little man?" she said. He pointed down.

"*Aisa*," he said. "Father."

Sofía shook her head and clicked her tongue. "So let me help you with that." She leaned into the trunk as well.

"Now that's one dusty-looking bottle you got there, little one. Would you like me to clean that for you?" She lifted the lower hem of her dress and started polishing the clay vessel.

"*Ala ala*," Tomás protested, pulling at her dress.

"Fine, so we won't clean it," she said.

He put the urn at the bottom of his big mahogany armoire, which had a flaming red groove on its front that looked like a burning spear. The urn stayed there for many years, while he took it out from time to time to caress it the way a mother caresses the stomach of a child that has fallen ill, "so so," with smooth and deliberate movements of the palm of her hand, as if to shove out all the evil spirits that inhabited a tummy. Standing in front of the mirror, he would shake it and listen to the rustling sound inside. *It sounds like the sea,* he thought, *like the sea in a conch shell.* And when he listened more closely, he heard a voice. *As if someone were speaking underwater,* he thought, *breathing and speaking underwater.* He pressed his ear to the urn until it hurt, until his hands and face were stained with red clay dust.

One day he told his cousin Fausto about the urn in his armoire. Fausto was one year older, and tall for his age.

"What do you two talk about?" he said.

"Things. He has asked me to do something."

"Like what?"

Tomás hesitated. "I can't tell you," he said. "I promised I would not tell anyone."

"Can I listen?" Fausto said. "I would like to listen to your father, too. My father has told me about him."

"What did he say?"

"He said your father was brave but stupid!"

"You're a liar!"

"Am not. That's what he said."

Tomás bit his tongue until he tasted the sweetness of blood on his palate.

"Then I won't show him to you," he said.

"Fine," Fausto said. "Dead people should be in the ground anyway, not in a soup cup in your closet."

Tomás did not take out the urn for weeks after that, while he thought about his cousin's comments. He had many questions to ask of his father, but the urn remained silent after that day.

"Nuunik antuka" is what Sofía called him, "my sun and moon," because she was with him day and night. Sofía had been Tomás's nanny for as long as he could remember. She came from Nicaragua's Caribbean coast, and had prominent Miskito features: almond-shaped eyes, high-set cheekbones, and thin sleek hair tied up in a knot. Her fingers were long and slender, and seemed to go on forever. She had come to live with his family before he was born, even before his father had left, which made her part of the few people-who-had-known-his-father, but she never spoke of him. Victoria had left her son in the care of his nanny, and spent little time with him: hers was a busy world, of parties and funerals, and shopping trips to Managua. So Tomás spent his earliest days in the company of his nanny, and did not learn to speak until the age of three. At least, this is what everyone thought. When he was almost two years old, he started making sounds that no one could make sense of. The few times Victoria asked him a question, he did not seem to understand.

"Child, say something!" she would say, but after several tries she shrugged and sighed, thinking *if he's not mute he must be an idiot.*

It was not until Aunt Pilar came visiting one day that the mystery was solved. They were sitting in the dining room drinking Jerez wine, and Pilar's curiosity was roused by the strange words coming from the boy's room.

"Victoria, how come this boy does not speak yet?" she said. "He's almost three years old now; is he mute?"

"I don't know," Victoria replied. "But Sofía seems to be able to make sense out of his grunts; why don't you ask her?" They called Sofía, who had just finished giving Tomás a bath and brought him along into the dining room.

"Say hello to your Aunt Pilar, Tomás," his mother said.

The boy did not move. Instead, he started babbling.

"See," Victoria said, "I think he's retarded. Definitely not mute."

"Hello, little man," Aunt Pilar said, sticking out her big red nose until it hovered over the boy. Tomás looked up and smiled.

"Tuktan nani aisika bani pa," he rattled off.

"God almighty, what is this?" Pilar squinted. "Sofía, what is the boy saying? And how is it that Doña Victoria says you understand his grunts?"

"But, Doña Pilar, the child, he does speak," Sofía said. "He speaks Miskito with me, all the time. He speaks very well!"

Aunt Pilar did not move. But she did turn paler than a doorpost.

"He speaks what?" she gasped.

"Miskito, ma'am. My language. I have been speaking to him all along. He speaks very well!"

Doña Pilar almost exploded that day.

"Spanish!" she croaked, "Spanish! Only Spanish from now on! And you, Victoria, say something please!"

Victoria shrugged. But Pilar did not let up, and so it was in fact agreed that Tomás should be given proper schooling as soon as possible. From that day on, he was taken to his mother's family's mansion every day, and Sofía was under strict orders to no longer speak Miskito to him.

When Tomás was five years old, a little boy with straight silky hair and eyes the color of caramel, he told his mother he would marry her.

"Of course, little man," she said. "You just grow up first, and then we'll see."

"I will take care of you, *Yapti*," he said.

"Still speaking Miskito, eh?" She laughed.

"I need to go now, little man," she said as she undid his fingers form her dress. "Someone is expecting me in Managua; I will see you again tomorrow."

He told Sofía later that day, sitting on the cot in her room where she was folding clothes.

"But you can't," she said. "Boys can't marry their mothers."

"*Mami* said I could," he said. "She said I should grow up first."

"But she'll be old when you are grown up."

"Doesn't matter," he said. "Old people can still get married, no?"

She shook her head. "She'll still be your mother."

"Why is she away so often?"

Sofía sighed. "Your mother has many friends," she said, "and needs time to visit them."

"I will make her stay with me when I grow up."

She ruffled his hair.

"Sofía," he said, "I want you to tell me a story."

"Well," she said, turning around and sitting down next to him, her great, warm body giving off heat like a steam engine. "I will tell you the story of *Aimayapa*." It was near nightfall, which arrives without warning in the tropics, and leaves little time for twilight.

"In a time so far away that we barely remember it, the skies once opened up and all their waters came pouring down. Soon the whole world was starting to fill up with sky water, and many people drowned. Now, there were two children, a brother and a sister who went by the name Aimayapa, and they climbed up a tall tree on top of a hill. When they reached the crown they held on to each other and looked around, but by now all they saw was water, as far as the eye could reach. They sat in that tree for many days, until one day it stopped raining. They heard only silence, because the water had nothing to brush against except the one tree where they were sitting. The silence was so deep that the sea and the sky seemed to be one, and the earth was covered with darkness. The earth was windless and cloudless. There was only silence.

"On the sixth day, they saw how the sun had returned to the skies, and then the waters sank, and after a while they saw the land once more. They remembered that they were hungry, and started looking around for something to eat. But there were no bushes, no trees, and no other people. Then they saw a flock of pelicans. They waited for someone to come and bring them food. However, no one came, and when their hunger had become so great that they thought they would faint, they climbed down the tree.

"Wan Aisa felt sorry for the children. So he dropped a yucca tree, and then a *quequisque* shrub, and finally two plantain shoots and a banana tree. The children planted the trees and shrubs and when they woke up the next day, they saw that they were already bearing fruit. The sister picked a fruit and gave it to her brother, and they felt good for the first time in many days.

"And the brother and sister grew up, but they found the earth a lonely place. And so they lived like husband and wife, because there were no others like them. They had children, and the earth became filled with people once more, and happiness returned. They often told the Story of the Water and the Tall Tree to their children, and to their children's children. And when the Aimayapa brother and sister died, the Story of the Water and the Tall Tree had become a story, no more. Wan Aisa whisked them away and made them into stars, and these are the stars we call Aimayapa."

It was dark when she stopped talking, and he could no longer see her. But when he reached out he felt her arm, warm and soft. He raised his voice over the sound of the starlings circling the evening sky.

"I liked the story."

"Yes."

"I've heard it before, haven't I?"

"Many times."

Chapter 2

The lawn that surrounded the Cortés mansion was a sea of carefully manicured green. The meticulously trimmed lawn grew on carefully evened soil – no knolls, no molehills, nothing that might distract from the endless levelness that allowed the Cortés family to see clearly, and far.

Two boys dressed in sailor outfits ran out of the house, chasing each other. The one being chased was taller and dressed in mock fatigues. His tan gave away the hours he had spent in the sun. The other boy was pale-skinned, his hair long and wavy, and clinging to his forehead while he gave chase. They ran into the shrub forest behind the mansion, until they reached a dark pond. There they sat side by side, looking at the pond and the long strands of Spanish moss that seemed to have been draped over the trees by giants. Fausto pointed towards a green speck, only slightly brighter than its surroundings.

"See, there's one of them," he said. Tomás peered through the undergrowth and saw the puffed-up crest under the scaly head. He picked up a rock and threw it at the lizard, which jumped off the rock and quickly ran towards the water's edge. There was a faint splish-splash of water being pushed aside by the nimblest of dancing feet, and then it was gone. Tomás picked up another rock, and then another and another. He cleaned them on his shirt and counted them, passing them from one hand into the other, and piling them up beside him.

"You need to give it spin," Fausto said. "Like this!" He picked up a flat, slim rock and weighed it in his hand, then lifted one leg and launched the rock. It ricocheted twice and disappeared in the water where the basilisk had been moments before.

"See," he said, "just practice more, cousin."

Tomás said nothing, and instead threw the largest rock he could find in the pond. It made a splash, and big ripples, and then more rocks followed. Fausto pulled out a knife from his belt and looked at his reflection in the blade. The handle was made of deer antler and had Fausto's name on it, inlaid in cork.

"Did your dad give you that knife?" Tomás said, looking at the shiny blade.

"Yes," Fausto said. "He says a knife is a man's best friend."

Tomás thought for a moment.

"I wished someone gave me a knife," he said.

Fausto shrugged. "My father is not always so nice," he said, his mouth turning down. "Maybe you're better off not having one."

Tomás found this difficult to understand. "Why?" he said. "How can it be better to not have a father?"

Fausto kept turning the blade around, noticing how the reflection of his face grew longer when he held the blade at a certain angle.

"He never stops giving me orders. He says I'm disobedient, that I need to grow up." He kept the knife poised now, balancing it on the palm of his hand.

"Your father is always nice to me," Tomás said.

Fausto's expression did not change.

"Lucky you," he said. "Lucky you, because your uncle loves you more than he loves his own son." Tomás wanted to protest, but before he could open his mouth, his cousin had straightened his back and assumed a stern face. Lowering his voice, he said: "Discipline. Discipline and consequences." Tomás burst out laughing, but Fausto was not amused.

"Always these rules of his," he said. "This rule, that rule. Rules for treating the servants, rules for riding a horse. Rules for Saturday, rules for Sunday. Why do we need so many rules?"

Tomás raised his shoulders. "Everybody has them," he said. "You think my mother doesn't boss me around?" Fausto did not answer. He was looking at his reflection in the blade of his knife, and liked what he saw: dark eyes, a straight nose, and the beginnings of a square jaw.

"The features girls fall for," his aunts had told him. He turned the knife and held it up the way bullfighter's aides do before taking aim.

"Your mother's never there to boss you around. My dad says she goes to see men in Managua," he said, lowering the knife. "He says that's why she's never here."

Tomás felt his cheeks grow fiery. "You're lying. Your father would never say that, you know that."

Fausto shrugged. "This is what he told me," he said. "Whether you believe it or not." Tomás tried to imagine his uncle saying this about his mother. He was ashamed at the thought of his mother being with strange men.

"You're a liar, Fausto, a big fat liar telling big fat lies." He stamped his feet and turned to leave. Fausto patted the sheath dangling from his belt, and quickly slid behind his cousin. Slinging his arm over the other boy's shoulder, he flashed the knife in front of his eyes.

"Discipline!" he shouted. "Discipline and consequences!" Startled by the gleaming knife, Tomás jerked his head backwards, knocking his cousin in the forehead.

"Ouch!" Fausto screamed, and dropped the knife. "What did you do that for?"

"Are you crazy?" Tomás's voice was hoarse, and he was panting. "I thought you were going to kill me!"

Fausto started laughing. "Just a joke," he said. "It was just a joke, Tomás."

"I don't like your jokes. They're stupid."

Fausto was rubbing his forehead, which showed a large, red spot.

"Where's my knife?" he said. "Where did it go?" Tomás spotted the knife floating in the pond beneath the low-hanging branch of a cedar tree, slowly drifting away from the shore.

"Help me get it!" Fausto said. "It's your fault I dropped it! If I don't get it back my father will kill me!" He stepped into the water, holding on to the cedar branch. The knife was so close, but it was as if something were tugging at it, pulling it towards the center of the pond. Fausto was groaning, straining himself to reach his knife. Then, with a dry snap, the branch broke off, and Fausto fell headlong into the water. The pond was shallow, its bottom a carpet of thick mud sucking at his shoes.

"I'm sinking, Tomás!" he screamed. "I'm sinking, get me out of here!"

Tomás bit his lip. "Only if you admit you were lying," he said.

"What?" Fausto said. "I'm drowning, who cares what I said about your mother!" But Tomás made no move, so Fausto relented and spoke the words.

"Much better," Tomás said. "Now, what did you want me to do?"

"Find something. A stick, a vine, anything. Hurry!" He was waist-deep into the water, and each time he pulled out one leg the other one was sucked in deeper. Tomás started pulling at a thick sarsaparilla vine dangling from a blackened ficus tree.

"Hurry!" Fausto shouted. "Hurry, I'm sinking." The water had climbed to his chest, and he could no longer lift his legs. He raised his arms, as if this would help him escape the mud sucking at his feet.

Finally, Tomás managed to twist off the vine.

"Wrap it around the tree," Fausto yelled. "Wrap it around and make a knot in it, then throw me the other end! Hurry, Tomás!" Tomás did as his cousin told him, and when they were both holding the vine, he started pulling, his heels digging deep into the mud. He pulled hard, and felt the muscles of his arms tensing until they were sore. But Fausto was still stuck in the mud.

"It's no good, Fausto," Tomás said. "We must get help. Let me go get help."

"No!" Fausto said. "No, my father must not see me like this. Try again, you can do it." He leaned forward as much as he could, until his chin was under water. "I'll try to float; I'll make it easier for you. Please try again, cousin."

Inch by inch Tomás pulled the vine around the tree trunk, until he himself had almost reached the water's edge. He started coughing, but ignored it. He kicked and dug in until he felt his feet sink into the soil, and his cousin was lying in the mud beside him, barefoot and gasping. Suddenly Fausto grabbed his cousin's leg and started laughing. Loudly and uncontrollably at first, until it turned into a low-pitched wheeze.

"That was close," he said when the wheezing stopped. He pulled himself up further and slapped his cousin on the back. "That was close, wasn't it, cousin? But fun, right?"

"I don't think it was fun," Tomás said. "It was stupid. If you hadn't put that knife in my face this wouldn't have happened."

Fausto was still snickering. "Calm down, cousin," he said. "Just take it easy. No need getting all worked up over something like this. It's all a game, you know." He looked out towards the pond again. "Now let's go get my knife."

On the other side of the pond, the knife had ended up floating peacefully among the water lilies. While Fausto pulled it out and cleaned it on his pants, Tomás felt something warm running down his hand, and as he lifted his arm, he saw blood where the vine had chafed and cut his palms.

"I cut myself," he said, showing Fausto.

"It will close by itself," Fausto said, and shrugged. "You're not afraid of blood, are you? I can't be friends with a coward."

"Don't be ridiculous, Fausto. Of course I'm not afraid of blood!"

"Then prove it to me! I will drink your blood and you will drink mine. We will be blood brothers." He stretched out his wrists and held them together tightly.

"We need something to catch the blood," he said. "Look, we'll use that plantain leaf out there for a cup. Now let me see that hand!" He pressed on Tomás's palm, but the wound had already closed.

"I'll have to bind off your arm," he said.

"Can't you get some blood from my wound?"

Fausto shook his head. "No, cousin. New wounds are better. Now take off that kerchief and tie up your arm." Tomás undid the knot that held the kerchief tied around his neck.

"How's that?" Fausto asked, as he finished tying the knot.

"It feels like my arm is going to explode."

"Good, that's how it should feel!" Fausto pulled out his knife and slid the blade between his index finger and thumb. As he pulled it away, a thin red line appeared on his finger.

"It's just been whetted," he said. "Are you ready?

"Yes," Tomás nodded, swallowing hard. The blade resting against his arm felt cool, almost soothing. There was a sting as the metal sliced through his skin. When he looked down, he saw the blood running down his hand again, dripping onto the plantain leaf. It had not hurt, or not as much as he had expected. Some of the blood had spilled on the ground, but it had been soaked up so fast he found it hard to spot where exactly it had gone.

"I'm going to take off the handkerchief, and then you are going to tie my arm in turn," Fausto said. Tomás struggled to tighten the knot, and when it was done, Fausto handed him the knife. "Here, you do it. Just like I did to you!"

Tomás looked at the knife and felt his blood leave his face. "But...I..."

"Tomás, you must do it, quick!"

Clumsily, Tomás pushed the tip of the knife against his cousin's skin.

"No, not like that," Fausto said. "You have to cut, didn't you pay attention?"

Tomás held the blade against Fausto's arm, and Fausto clenched his teeth in anticipation.

"OK," he said. "Do it! Now!" Tomás pushed down on the knife, making a back-and-forth movement until he felt the skin rupture. It reminded him of cutting through the sheep intestine that held sausage together. Blood started dripping onto the plantain leaf, where his own blood had already started clotting. Fausto took off the handkerchief but kept his arm clenched against his chest.

"All right, now we must pledge," he said. He took the folded leaf and held it up before him.

"Let's drink each other's blood," he said. "Repeat after me: I hereby seal our friendship in blood."

"I hereby seal our friendship in blood."

"I shall not fail my brother, ever."

"I shall not fail my brother, ever."

Fausto dipped his finger in the sticky mixture and stirred it before handing the leaf to Tomás. It smelled sweet, almost like Mass wine. He gulped when it clung to his palate, and at once the distinct flavor of metal filled his nostrils. Fausto took the leaf from him and licked off what was left, carefully, so as not to waste any. Tomás watched his cousin's throat expand and contract as he swallowed.

"You first, me first," Fausto said. "That's how it will be. We will always put each other first." Tomás nodded, and then they washed their arms and legs in the pond and sat waiting for their wounds to close and their clothes to dry.

"How will you walk back?" Tomás said. "You lost your shoes."

Fausto thought for a while. "Let me borrow yours," he said. "I will sneak into my room to get another pair, and come back here. No one will notice."

Tomás took off his shoes and watched as his cousin trudged away, clumsily and noisily, his feet trying to adjust to shoes that were too small for him. When he could no longer see him, Tomás heard the sounds of the forest return. He tried to make out the call of the macaw and that of the toucan, and just as he thought he had identified all the noises, and given them the names of their owners, he heard the silvery sound of patter on the water: splish-splash splish-splash. Not far from the shore, right above the spot where he guessed Fausto's shoes were buried for all of eternity, he saw a basilisk running across the waters. He no longer heard the toucan or the macaw. He only heard the basilisk, its crystal pitapat creating ripples larger than any that could have been caused by a rock.

He was startled when his shoes were plunked down beside him. When he looked up he saw his cousin looming over him, grinning, his sunburned face flushed.

"Discipline," he said. "I managed to sneak in and out without anyone noticing. Discipline."

That night, when Sofía put Tomás to sleep, she noticed the cuts on his arm and hand.

"What happened here?" she said. "Did you cut yourself?"

"A briar," he said.

She looked a bit longer. "No, let's see, this is a knife wound, too sharp and clean for any thorn bush. No briar could have done this. Did you do this to yourself, Tomás?" Her eyes seemed to see right through him. She suffered from strabismus, which made it seem that she was always staring at him from the corner of one of her eyes, even when she was not.

"Yes," he said, and looked away. "Yes, I was playing with a sickle I found in the tool shed." Sofía looked at him and shook her head.

"Tsk, tsk, tsk," she said. "You can fool your mama but you can't fool me, young man. You didn't do this to yourself. Someone did it to you. Have you been fighting?" There was no use in lying to Sofía.

"Your cousin Fausto?"

"I did it myself," he sputtered.

"Don't waste my time, young man," she said. "I don't have that much left of it."

Chapter 3

The great mansion built by the first Cortés, who had arrived in Nicaragua in the mid-1800s, was imposing. It had five wings stretched out like fingers on a hand, and it had all been built in one shot. No additions, no alterations, and no modifications, as if the old patriarch had known exactly how many branches of Cortéses would one day need to be accommodated. Yet the size of the mansion was nothing compared to the geography of smells that ruled it. There were camphorwood cabinets to stem the rot of worms and termites, deeply furrowed and carefully buffed to release the smell of sassafras. In the bedrooms of married couples, the deep smell of cocoa was a constant reminder of the first Cortés imperative, to go forth and multiply.

From room to room, the house was a giant, multi-chambered womb, where the incessant hum of its denizens drowned out all still sounds, leaving only creeping murmurs, secret whispers, and the sound of turning pages while bedside stories were being read. The house seemed to breathe; it seemed to shiver, shrink, and swell with each page being turned, every breath of air inhaled, and every puff of spent oxygen sent back out into the world. A blind man might have mistaken it for a whale beached far from the sea: gasping, bloated, and utterly unaware of its inescapable nakedness.

There was always someone being born in the Cortés family. Generations spread out along twenty, sometime thirty years of childbearing, and it was not uncommon for mothers and daughters to be pregnant at the same time. The scorekeeper was Tomás's aunt, Doña Elvira, whom everyone asked about family history: who had been married to whom and who had been born to whom, and where and when and what he or she had done. There were always curious great-grandchildren and now even great-great-grandchildren of Don Pablo Cortés God-rest-his-soul who had not yet heard the story of how the forefather had arrived. Because although the greatness of the Cortéses had started with Don Pablo, "he himself," she told them, "he himself had been the scion of a long and distinguished line of Cortéses whose roots went all the way back to Roland the Hornblower, and was that distinguished enough for you children or what?"

On top of that big, wobbly pyramid of Cortéses sat Mama Mica. That was short for Michaela, but everyone called her Mama Mica. At what point that had happened no one knew, but it must have been shortly after her husband had died. Don Pablo had been her senior by many years, marrying her after his first wife died of typhoid fever without bearing him any children. Mama Mica made up for this during the ten years they were married, as if to erase from the forefather's memory the years that he had vainly labored the rocky soil of his first conjugal acre. So when Don Pablo died, he left behind eight children. Dressing only in black from that day onward, Mama Mica was a mountain of wrinkled flesh and black lace that seldom moved. She rarely left her cavernous quarters, which smelled of hyacinth and jasmine.

She was the great mammalian foremother, more breast than body, and family lore had it that she had suckled her children, her grandchildren, and even some of her great-grandchildren. She also knew more about leaves and roots, and what they could do to people, than anyone wanted to admit. She was the first port of call when a child got sick, a heart was broken, or a husband was too tired to sleep with his wife. As was becoming of an oracle, Mama Mica stayed largely out of sight, speaking instead through her oldest granddaughter Elvira, who was now a grandmother herself.

Not marrying was not an option for female Cortéses, and not producing offspring much less so.

"The ancestor did his duty to God and Country, and in that order," Doña Elvira proclaimed to the small fry assembled for Cortés Sunday school, "but most importantly, he went forth and multiplied, and so ensured the continued survival and glorious existence of the house of Cortés!"

Rafaela, Victoria's cousin, was twenty-five years old when she broke with this, the first of Cortés directives. Rafaela was short and stocky, and had always preferred cars to ragdolls. She had been in love only once, everyone said, and had no intention of marrying a man she did not love.

"Don't you worry, love will come after," her aunts told her. "How do you think the lot of us got married?" They laughed, but Rafaela did not think that love was a laughing matter. So she hatched a plan.

"I want to take care of Mama Mica," she said at Sunday dinner. Where before there had been the clatter of tens of forks and knives, there was now sudden silence.

"What?" her mother said. "What did you say?"

"I said: 'I want to take care of Mama Mica.'"

"But," said her mother, flustered. "But that's my job; you can't take care of her."

"Why not?" Rafaela said.

Elvira turned around to her twin sister with eyes that were about to fall out of their sockets and walk out of the house all on their own.

"Lili, say something!" she said. "Tell her to come to her senses."

Lili mulled it over, and said: "Come now, Payita, what is this talk of taking care of Mama Mica? When your time comes, yes, perhaps, but right now, you're much too young for that. Why, you're not even married yet – you're practically still a child!"

"I don't want to get married," Rafaela said. "I'll be happy to take care of Mama Mica."

"Taking care of Mama Mica" was a hallowed task in the Cortés house. In fact, it was more than a task: it was an honor for which all of the female Cortéses would gladly give up their left hand. That Mama Mica might one day pass away had not occurred to anyone. It was such an utterly unthinkable possibility that it was ignored to the point where it no longer existed.

"Out of the question," Lili said.

"Then let's ask Mama Mica," Rafaela contested.

"Child, stop being obnoxious now," her mother chimed in. "This has gone quite far enough."

"I'm serious, Mother," Rafaela said. "And I think I'll be much more useful to Mama Mica than anyone else here."

"I won't hear another word about it," Elvira said. She fluttered a nervous hand to the maids to start serving dessert.

No one saw Rafaela sneak into Mama Mica's room that day, nor the day after, carrying with her a small bag of herbs. The week after, Elvira fell ill.

"It's a woman's thing," Lili said when the men inquired. That was usually enough to make the men disperse. Elvira locked herself up in her room when she found out what the problem was.

"At my age?" she yelled at the doctor.

"Why not?" he said. "Who told you it was too late?"

Her husband was happy. "Still functioning well, that old shotgun, eh, boys?" he said, and grinned the widest grin ever.

"Now who's going take care of Mama Mica?" Lili said to her sister. They looked at each other and raised one eyebrow each, which looked like a shot from a freak show taken in the mirror labyrinth.

They asked Mama Mica.

"So you're pregnant again," she said, before Elvira could open her mouth.

"Yes," Elvira said. "I didn't think that I could still be."

"Haaah," Mama Mica spat. "We Cortés women can go on giving birth right up until the day we die. You should have known better."

She thought for a while.

"And I take it you're here to ask me who should replace you?"

"Yes, Mama," Lili said. "Elvira can't take care of you in her condition." Mama Mica hummed and closed one eye, and the sisters bit their tongues because they knew where their own eye twitching had come from.

"Rafaela," Mama Mica said. "Rafaela will do."

The sisters were flabbergasted. "But," Elvira started, "but Mama Mica, Rafaela is too young!"

"Nonsense," Mama Mica cut in, "and besides, what makes you think I want to be surrounded by old women all day long?" And that was really that. Elvira could do little more than accept the decision. There was never any more questioning Rafaela's role of caregiver. She never took a day off, and never fell sick. When her mother gave birth, she was the one who told Mama Mica, and she was the one who took the baby to the old lemurian to be blessed and suckled. An unspoken bond held the two women together: the mammalian foremother and the childless descendant.

"We both made choices in life," Mama Mica told her once, "this is why we understand each other. Life does not happen to us. We happen to life instead."

Tomás lived in the house his father had built. It was a modern house, in the center of town. In his house, there were women only: his mother and Sofía, Juanita who cooked, and Maria Juana, the cleaning lady. So rarely did a man come into his house that Tomás believed for many years that men and women lived separate lives altogether. Not even a portrait of his father was to be found, as Victoria had ordered them removed shortly after Raúl's final homecoming.

"It was cleaner that way," she had told herself. "Nothing to remind me of loss, and when there are no reminders, loss itself will be lost one day." But Raúl was always there. *Not as a ghost or an accusing finger,* she thought, *although God knows he would have been jealous.* He was there as a reminder that time was the cruelest of poisons, and that she had been left to face life by herself. *You left me, Raúl,* she thought. *Not for a woman, and not for money. Not even for glory. You left me for an idea. How could you?*

Her life became a string of shopping sprees and parties, yet none of the men she met became part of her life. *And how much easier it has become,* she thought, *now that there are only needs and wants to be filled with variables, eternally changing variables.* There was only now, the inexorable, slow-creeping now that occupied her days. She had stored the memories of the past out of sight. Tomorrow would be nothing but another today.

Though his mother thought she was discreet about her escapades, Tomás knew. There were small things: a notebook, a comb, a pen with engravings.

"Whom does this belong to, Mother?" he asked her when he found the pen. "Did this belong to my father?"

She looked at him, sharply.

"No," she said. "There is nothing left in this house that belonged to your father. Except you of course." She took the pen from him and put it in her handbag. "Must have fallen out," she said."

Once, when he was ten years old, he saw her with a man. The man was short and bald, and poorly dressed. He saw them from a distance, across the Rio Chiquito, which had almost dried up and smelled of rotting cornhusk. They were holding hands, and he saw how the man leaned into her and held her by the waist, pulling her towards him. She could not have seen her son standing behind a pochote tree. He saw how her back arched until her hips thrust out towards the balding man. He saw how the man reached for her hair and pulled her in. He heard her laugh across the rotting corn. Then they got into a small car and drove away, quickly, as if time were running out on them.

When he saw her the next day he could not shake off the image of the short man. Everywhere she went he imagined the man with her – at the dinner table, on the porch where she read her magazines. In his mind's eye he saw himself sneaking up on the man. They were almost the same height; his hands could reach the man's shoulder blades without effort. He pushed him into the river and watched how a strong current dragged him away, hauled him over the spiky trees and craggy rocks littering the riverbed. When he looked at his mother again, he saw her alone, without the bald man, and she was smiling at him.

"What were you thinking about, Tomás?" she said.

He took her hand. "You," he said. "You, Mother."

Whatever happens, he will not follow in his father's footsteps, Victoria had promised herself. *I'll have a live coward before I have another dead hero.* She shielded him in every way she could: he was not allowed to mingle with the boys in the street, not even with the children of the maids, and when her brother offered to give Tomás a knife, she refused.

"No need for this, Rogelio," she said. "I don't want him to grow up and become like his father."

"But," Rogelio said, "every boy his age gets a knife from his father. You can't take that away from him."

Her jawline tightened. "I didn't take it away from him," she said. "His father did."

Tomás stuck his nose into his uncle's study.

"Is Fausto here, Uncle?"

"He's not here, Tomás," Rogelio said. "But why don't you sit with me while you wait for him?"

Rogelio's study had no windows. Instead, Tomás saw the heads of game animals hanging from all four walls: deer, a boar, and larger ones he did not recognize.

"Did you shoot those yourself, *Tío*?" he said.

"All of them," Rogelio said. "A man should only be proud of the things he has done himself. Don't steal from others, not even words, and don't pretend to be what you are not." Tomás played with his marbles, dropping them back into the small bag he was holding.

"Your father was a great hunter," Rogelio said.

Tomás was surprised. No one ever spoke of this father.

"I knew your father well," Rogelio continued. "He was younger, but in many ways he was older than me."

"How so, Tío?" Tomás said.

Rogelio pursed his lips. "He knew what he wanted. But his vision was so clear that it blinded him."

Tomás continued dropping the marbles.

"Let me show you something," Rogelio said. He opened a photo book, leafed through it until his finger came to rest on a dog-eared picture with serrated edges, as if a saw had zigzagged around it.

"There," Rogelio said. "That's you, with your father."

Tomás looked intently, spying the man in the center of the photograph. He was tall, yet he did not make the other men appear short. He was leaning into Rogelio, his body signaling trust the way brothers trust each other – not by what they say, but by what they have lived through together. The tall man was looking down at the small bundle he was holding in his arms.

"That's you," Rogelio said. "You were part of this family from the day you were born."

Peering at the picture, Tomás felt perspiration dripping down his forehead and nose.

"This?" he said. "This is me?"

"Yes. He wanted everyone to see you; he said the day you were born was the happiest day of his life. 'My first-born,' he said. 'I will have many more children, but my first-born is special.'" The picture was grainy, yet Tomás could clearly discern the outlines of a small head appearing under his father's chin. *So close I could have smelled his breath,* he thought. *Why is it that I do not remember him?*

"Why did he leave us?"

"He did not leave you. He just never came back, but not because he did not want to."

"Did he no longer love my mother? Or me?"

Rogelio shook his head. "Oh no. After he got married he never looked at another woman in his life. The problem was that he loved you too much. And your mother. He loved everyone."

Tomás sat with his head bent, until he felt his uncle's hand on his crown.

"Don't think too much about it, Tomás. These things belong to the past."

"And the men who killed him? If you say that my father was a good man, then what are they?"

"These things are complicated. Life is not all blacks and whites."

"But were they punished?"

Rogelio sighed. "Don't think about these things. They will only make you unhappy."

"I don't understand, Uncle. These people killed my father."

Rogelio shrugged. "Me neither, to tell you the truth. But this is how life is — and we all make choices." He looked at his nephew, who continued staring at the picture.

"Your life is different; will be different. Be smart and learn to live in the world you have. Your father did not want that. But it got him killed."

Tomás rolled his hands into fists. He felt Rogelio's hand bear down on him, more heavily this time, until it hurt his shoulder.

"Nothing can bring back the past, Tomás — the dead are dead. And killing people doesn't bring back the dead."

"Read your books," his mother told him. "No need for curiosity — it kills."

In the weeks before Christmas, when the rains subside and thunderstorms no longer bring relief from the heat, the streets of León turn into a stage where hundreds of giant puppets parade. Under each puppet's skirts a man curses his bad luck for having to strut through the blazing streets with all that womanly weight on his shoulders. The puppets are effigies of Spanish women from colonial times: glassy blue eyes, a powdery pink complexion, and wildly flying flaxen hair — everything the brown-skinned mestizos are not. She is the *Gigantona*, the Giant One. She dances her mad dance and sways her long and gangly arms while a young boy beats the drum and whirls ahead of her:

La Gigantona, la Gigantona
Va por las calles de León
Con sus tambores y trovadores

When Tomás heard the frenetic rhythm of the drums, he rushed to the window to see her. Tens of children were screaming: "*La Gigantona* is coming, *la Gigantona* is coming!"

"I want to go out, Sofía," he shouted. "I want to go and see the Gigantona!"

But before Sofía could answer, Victoria's voice sounded from the back of the house.

"No, Sofía, he cannot go out to see that despicable puppet!" The music grew louder, announcing the arrival of *lira* and drums and wild maracas made from dried *jícaro* shells filled with dried beans. It took all of three minutes for the cloud of children to turn the corner and fill the street. Tomás's heart stood still when he saw the giant towering ten feet tall, and the shiny eyes that he thought were staring at him alone. She danced and whirled with the sound of the drums, with outstretched arms that swayed like the colored fringes hanging from the maypole.

And all around her was the *enano cabezón*, the water head dwarf. He was everywhere, he guessed her every move. As if on cue, the Gigantona and the dwarf stopped in front of Tomás's house. He pressed his head against the rusty metal grid when the dwarf started reciting his poem: "*Bomba, bomba,*" he chanted, "I am the dwarf with the giant head, I am forever in love with you, and if loving you is a sin, so a sinner I will be. You are the most beautiful of flowers, God willing one day you will arrive at the door to my heart, which loved you before it even knew about dreaming. But I am but a simple sinner, an admirer of your beauty, and you are a princess who travels far from my dreams."

When the dwarf finished, the drums fell silent, and everyone stood in front of the window, staring at Tomás. The dwarf waggled forward, careful not to trip over his much-too-long garb. Tomás smelled the dwarf's sweat. *As if salt water had been mixed with frying fat,* he thought.

"Do you love her?" the dwarf bellowed. "Do you love her as much as I do?" Tomás glanced behind the dwarf and saw the silent Gigantona, saw her glassy eyes staring at him. He swallowed.

"Yes," he said. "Yes, I do."

The dwarf turned around. "He says he does!" he shouted. The crowd started laughing. Then the dwarf lowered his head and whispered so that only Tomás could hear him: "Words mean nothing, boy. You must mean them. And you must make them mean something."

A thunderclap tore through the silence. Startled, Tomás fell out of the windowsill, and when he climbed back up, the dwarf was gone, pulled back to into the whirlwind of colors and drumbeats.

"*Bomba, bomba, soy el enano cabezón,*" he heard the dwarf yell at the top of his lungs, and at these words the whole procession turned and walked away.

That night he put his ear to the urn. He had not taken it out in a long time, and the rustle inside sounded like a storm, pent up and angry.

"They will pay, all of them," he said. "One day I will kill them all."

Chapter 4

Ana was Tomás's favorite cousin, and they were born two years and three days apart. She had come to live with the other Cortéses when she was seven, and the threat of war in Europe had made her parents decide to come back to Nicaragua. It was a Sunday afternoon when they first met. He had been sleeping in the hammock, after a meal of *nacatamales* that had left his stomach heavy and painful. The hammock made screeching sounds as the big metal ring tying all the rope together ground against the hooks screwed into the walls. He was nine years old at the time, small for his age and barely starting to learn the names of trees and cities, of countries and the familiar subdivisions of a flat earth cut up in conveniently sized squares. He was reciting the countries in his head when someone stirred the hammock, and when he opened his eyes he saw Ana.

"Bonjour," she said, and sent the tassels hanging from the sides flying. When he saw her face, flanked by thick brown tresses, he thought she was an angel standing over him.

"Who are you?" he said, because he had never seen her at the mansion before.

"I'm Ana," she said, "and who are you?"

"Tomás. Tomás Raúl Delacorte Cortés." He had been taught to use his full names when introducing himself.

"My cousin Tomás!" she exclaimed, clapping her hands. "Nice to meet you, cousin."

He was surprised. "I've never seen you before," he said. "Who says you are my cousin?"

"But I've heard about you, cousin Tomás!"

His mother's cousin Jaime came in and said: "Ah, there are you are, my darling," before patting her hand. Then he shook Tomás's hand as well and said: "Tomás, this is my daughter Ana, your cousin. Everyone says she looks just like your mother when she was Ana's age."

And that made it official. So he got up to look at his new cousin, curiously taking in the narrow shoulders, the long neck and spindly legs sticking out from under the dress.

"Could you show Ana around, Tomás?" his uncle said. He nodded without taking his eyes off her.

"Yes," he said, "yes, I will show her everything."

Would it be too much to say that they became inseparable? Then let it not be said. They looked so unlike, the lanky boy with glasses who recited the names of countries and knew the periodic table by heart; and the wide-eyed girl who loved singing, dancing, and the smell of recently blown out candles. She teased him about his wayward hair, the locks that hid his eyes from her when he bent down to read or pick up a pencil she had dropped.

"More hair than a girl!" she crowed.

It did not bother him.

It was the dry season, before the dusty houses in Poneloya could be stirred by rain. In Poneloya, the well-heeled citizens of León maintained beach houses almost as large as the ones in town. The children spent all of their school vacation here, enjoying the long succession of sun and misty mornings. Ana and Tomás raised a stash of straw and hay up into the rafters of the barn, hoping that some birds might build their nest there. How surprised they were when, one day, a pelican took up quarters in the lonely cedar tree standing in the front yard instead.

She spotted it first. Tomás was still asleep when she burst into the boys' room and dragged him out of bed.

"Come with me!" she insisted. "You won't believe what I just saw!" They stood looking at the nest from below, seeing how the male had made room for the female, and how straw and twigs were being moved here and there, as if being tweaked for a homecoming.

They watched for weeks as the two brown birds flew in and out, and stomped about the nest. They forgot about the straw they had raised up into the rafters. And with no one tending to it, the straw blades came unstuck, one by one. Until one day, a mouse climbed up against the walls and brushed the wisp of straw with its tail. When it slid between the rafters the wisp came undone into one hundred blades of straw that floated down, like feathers, and noiselessly landed on the terracotta floor.

Ana was startled when the May rains broke. They were lying at opposite ends of the hammock, their legs and feet entangled in the middle. They were slowly swinging the hammock and watching the curtain of water that stretched before their eyes.

"When does fall come?" she said, peering at the water, at the mists that made it that much harder to see the trees and the mountains behind them.

"We have no fall," he said. "We have no summer, no winter. We only have rain or sun." Her mouth turned down. She missed the red and yellow flames covering the pathways in Luxembourg Gardens, as she missed the smell of mushrooms and new earth slowly forming inside chestnuts and pinecones. She reached out and felt his foot. Holding it with one slim hand, she tickled him with the other.

"Will you take me back to Paris one day?" she said.

"Paris," he repeated, "Paris, capital of France. It takes more than one month to get there from here." She tickled him again. He tried to shake loose but she held him firmly, and when he looked at her, he saw her jaw muscles tighten. Her whole face was soft except for her jaw, where her stubbornness hid.

"OK," he said. "OK, I will take you there."

She let go of his foot. "Now say it again," she said.

He reached for his foot, expecting her to take hold of it again. But she did not. She just sat there, waiting.

"Yes," he said. "Yes, I will take you to Paris."

When the rain stopped, the earth started sizzling. As if all the heat that had been chased underground was finding its way back to the surface. The hammock was no longer swinging. They were both still, listening to the sizzle of wet earth, and the patter of traipsing ants lost in a landscape changed by the rain. Or perhaps they only thought so. Perhaps the ants knew where they were going, and why.

He would read to her every day, even when she learned to read Spanish herself. She brought him all her favorite books to read — stories from Mexico, Madrid, Rome, and Paris. She cried when he read the stories from Paris, because she could smell the wet streets, the lavender tones of Paulownia blossoms, and the sweet scent of yeast lingering in the *boulangeries*. She closed her eyes and heard the echoes of a bandoneon disappearing into a rainy night, and the flinty sound of pebbles, unyielding to her feet as she walked in the Luxembourg Gardens.

Many May rains came and went, and each year they would lie in the hammock together. Each year their legs and arms grew a little more, and one day they could no longer fit from opposite ends.

"Move over, Tomás," she said, and snuggled in beside him. It took some getting used to, until all the spindly arms and legs had found their place. And for the first time they were lying side by side.

"Read me another story," she said. She reached over to the side, where her schoolbag was sitting on a chair, and steadied herself on his chest, her hair tickling his face.

"But you read better than I now!" he exclaimed. "Faster and better! You should be reading to me!"

She laughed. "Just this one time then," she said. "But don't get any strange ideas! Just this one time." He stretched his arms behind him until his left arm was under her head, yet his right arm did not embrace her. She opened the book, and read to him. He imagined them like this forever. And so it was, for many rains to come.

It must have been the god of May rains playing a trick on them. The rains arrived early that day, before nightfall, and the strong gusts of wind circling the house coaxed the fruit trees into giving up their smells, and carried them onto the porch, as if they had been magi sent to deliver their gifts to a boy and a girl reading stories in a hammock. Tomás smelled soursop and lemon, the tangy scent that was mango. And then there was the smell of vanilla.

"Vanilla," he said, "do we grow vanilla in the garden?"

"Rafaela gave it to me," she said. As a birthday gift."

He inhaled deeply now, feeling how the scent tickled his nostrils. He felt dizzy as it filled his lungs.

"Like ice cream," he said.

"What?" She pushed him away and he fell out of the hammock, onto the tile floor.

"Ouch" he said. "That hurt."

"It's French vanilla perfume, not cheap vanilla ice cream!" He was flabbergasted, but when he looked up he saw that she was laughing, her teeth gleaming, and her tongue timid yet visible, like a tiny animal.

"You need to learn how to speak to a lady, Tomás. How else will you ever find a girl and get married?" He clambered to his feet and stood over her. He saw her head tilting towards him, her hair pushed back so it uncovered her neck. He no longer smelled soursop or lemon. There was only vanilla, pure and strong, and he drank.

"I don't need to learn those things," he said. "I already know where to find this girl." He blushed, surprised at his own words, and took a deep breath.

Her laughter turned into a smile, and then it too faded, as she closed her eyes.

"Let's go inside," she said, "the wind is blowing in too much rain." She held out her hands, and he helped her out of the hammock.

"There," he said, without letting go of her. She looked down at their hands, and then up to him.

"I'm scared."

"So am I."

The next day, when Ana was doing her homework, Rafaela sat down beside her.

"Is it hard?" she said.

"It's French. You know."

"I didn't mean the homework."

She blushed. "I don't know what to do."

"Hmm. Do you think he does?"

She smiled now. "I guess not," she said, and put down her pencil. "But I wished he did."

"Tomás is a good boy. Be patient with him."

Ana turned to face Rafaela now. "Is it always this hard?"

"I don't know. I was in love only once."

"And what happened?"

Rafaela stared out into the gardens. "It's a story," she said. "One story among many." Ana waited, looking at her aunt.

"No," Rafaela said. "You don't want to hear this. Be glad and young." But Ana kept looking at her.

"What always happens. Along comes someone else."

"But it doesn't always happen, does it?"

"Of course not. It only happens when you allow it to happen. To you. Or to him." She pulled a small cotton bag out of the pocket in her dress and slipped it to the girl. Ana inhaled deeply, getting dizzy as the scent of juniper berries nestled in her nostrils.

"Put it under your pillow," Rafaela said. "You will dream well."

She sat down in the hammock the next evening, while the clouds were gathering, and opened her book. After a long while, she heard the door being opened, but she did not look up.

"Rafaela told me you were here," he said.

She blushed. "Really?"

He shrugged. "Yes," he said. "She came to visit my mother this afternoon, for tea."

She smiled and moved to the side, putting her feet down. "Do you want to sit?" He sat next to her. *How odd*, he thought, *we have never sat in the hammock like this.*

"I've been thinking…" they both started.

"You first."

"No, you first."

He leaned in, and then she did as well. The smell of vanilla was all around him now, until her lips touched his. He felt confused by the warmth of her body, the warmth that flowed from her like a halo, a bubble he entered each time their heads or hands came near each other.

Suddenly, the door to the porch opened up. Fausto looked at them without blinking.

"What are you two doing out here?" he said. Startled, they let go of each other's hands. Ana blushed and fumbled for her shoes while Tomás rushed to unhook the hammock.

"And why do you creep up on people, Fausto?" he said.

"I don't. I just came out looking for you. Did I interrupt something?"

"Stop it, Fausto. There is nothing to be interrupted."

Fausto looked at Ana now. "I guess not," he said. "I guess not."

When they met again, the next day, their bodies seemed the same — the spindly legs that had grown, the arms that got into each other's way. And yet, it was as if they had just been introduced. Tomás now noticed the tightness of her school uniform blouse over the small mounds beneath it; the pinkness of her nails, and how her cheekbones had become more pronounced, pulling her face into a perfect diamond. Mostly, however, he thought it was the smell, the scent of vanilla that enveloped her and that he did not remember noticing before. When they had finished reciting their lessons to each other, she snuggled up against him. He closed his eyes. He sensed her chest expanding over his, and her hand moving across until it reached his arm. He tensed up, and she felt it.

"What?" she said, squeezing his arm. He shifted his body away from her, so her hand fell back on his chest.

He sent her poems on the days he could not be with her. It was easier when her arm was not on his chest, her mouth not near his ear. They were pure this way, not like his mother and the bald man, or any of the men he had not seen but imagined had been with her. Ana was pure, and he would respect her. On those days, the thought of her made him want her more, and the paper and pen made it easy to speak to her without her knee around his thigh. When she received one of his poems, she opened the paper slowly, allowing the smell of juniper to warm the air, and reading the words until they all seemed strung into a single sentence.

"Your poem has so many questions," she would tell him later, "and I cannot answer them. But it's beautiful. It tells me you love me."

Every morning Fausto waited in front of his cousin's house, so they could walk to school together. This morning, when Tomás came out and Sofía handed him his bag, he noticed that his cousin looked downcast.

"What happened?" he said. "Did something happen to you?" Fausto remained silent at first, but when Tomás insisted his face turned red and he bit his tongue.

"He wants me to become a farmer like him, but I told him I didn't want to. So he told me I either become a farmer or join the army. He says I will come to no good if I don't learn discipline." He shook his head and turned away.

"You're lucky you don't have a father," he said

"But I wish I did," Tomás said.

"Ha," Fausto scoffed, "that's what I used to think, but it's just not true. Now I think it's better to have no one than someone who is never proud of what I do." They walked silently, jumping the puddles of muddy water that had remained after last night's rain.

"I am proud of you, cousin," Tomás said.

Fausto stopped.

"You're not saying that just to make me happy, are you?"

"We're blood brothers, remember?"

Fausto cracked a thin smile. "Yes," he said. "Yes, we are. And we must stick together, cousin, come what may. Don't let anything come between us. Anything or anyone."

Now it was Tomás's turn to blush. "What do you mean, Fausto?"

Fausto shrugged. "Nothing," he said. "What would I mean?" They walked on until they reached the gate of the schoolyard, where Father Pío was standing guard, greeting each boy as they entered. Before they went to their classrooms, Fausto held his cousin back.

"Listen, Tomás," he said. "I think we should spend more time together. Do you want to go fishing again, as we used to do? We can go this afternoon."

"I am seeing Ana," Tomás said. "I promised."

"I see."

Tomás felt awkward, torn between his desire to see Ana, and his loyalty to his cousin. "Maybe tomorrow?" he said.

Fausto said nothing, and walked towards his classroom.

On impulse, Tomás ran after him. "OK," he said. "OK, we'll go fishing. I will tell her I have to study alone."

Fausto's face broke into a grin. "Yes," he exclaimed. "Yes, let's do that."

He did not have the heart to tell her. When she walked out onto the veranda he was not there, so she stepped into the hammock and opened her books. After ten minutes, Sofía arrived and gave her a note. It was carefully folded and the edges were sealed with tape. "Ana" was written in awkwardly scribbled letters that tapered off, as if the writer had felt remorse. Sofía did not move while Ana opened the note, carefully, so as to not destroy the paper. When she finished reading, Sofía was already sitting next to her in the hammock, and put her arm around her shoulder.

"It's nothing," she said. "He's very busy, it's nothing. You know boys; they need time with other boys."

Now Tomás and Fausto walked back from school every day. Tomás no longer ran home to drop off his bag and do his homework, and rush off to the Cortés house to be with Ana. Every day Fausto was waiting for him now, and there was always something exciting to be explored – hunting giant *garrobo* lizards stuck between the ceiling and the roof, or stealing mangos from someone's backyard that Fausto would skillfully peel with his fish knife.

"I even brought salt," he crowed, waving a small paper pack, shoddily folded and stapled together. Tomás admired his cousin – *so resourceful*, he thought, *always planning ahead, always knowing where the mangos are ripest.*

"Fausto," he said one day. "Why are you always fighting your father? Why are you always disagreeing with him? Maybe you should try to stop fighting him."

Fausto thought about it. "Maybe you're right," he said. "Maybe pretending to agree with him will make him like me."

"That's not enough. You must mean it."

Fausto smirked. "No, cousin," he said. "What you mean and what you say are different things. My own father taught me that. On that one at least we agree."

One day, Fausto whisked his cousin away after school, refusing to tell him what the plan was for the day.

"Shhh," he said, laying a finger over his lips. "I can't tell you yet. Don't worry about your bag; it's better you don't go home first. All those women at your house might just tell you to stay and do your homework instead." They walked to the Cortés mansion, but instead of entering through the gate, Fausto took his cousin around the wall, until they reached one of the sheds where tools and machinery were kept for the cotton harvest. The plaster had fallen off the walls in many places, and whitened straw was sticking out from the rough grout sandwiched between the bricks.

"What are we doing here, Fausto? Are we allowed in here?"

"Don't worry," Fausto said. "Nobody comes in here when it's not harvest time. Come, sit down." He pulled out two crates and patted one of them. Then he turned back and rummaged through the other boxes and crates.

"What's that smell?" Tomás said. "It stinks in here."

Fausto stuck his nose up and sniffed. "Thorn apple," he said. "What do you expect with all those cows around here?" When he climbed back from behind the crates, he was carrying a bottle of rum.

"Feel like having a drink, cousin?" He held up the bottle and shook it. "We're missing the ice but what the heck; we'll make do without it!"

"Where did you get that bottle?" Tomás said. "Did you steal it?"

"Why do you always think of me as a thief, cousin? Do I look like a thief to you?"

"No, of course not," he said, quickly. He felt bad for having suggested it. Fausto unscrewed the cap and took a gulp. He squinted and let out a deep breath, then passed the bottle to his cousin. "Your turn," he said. Tomás took the bottle and looked at it without moving.

"Come on, don't be a sissy. It won't kill you!"

Tomás set the bottle to his lips and took a sip, then another. The alcohol stung his lips and tongue, and he sloshed the rum around in his mouth, feeling the spirits tickling the insides of his nose.

Fausto was grinning. "Swallow it," he said. "You need to swallow it, how else are we going to finish the bottle?" Tomás swallowed and coughed. His eyes started watering and he felt the rum stinging his stomach. Fausto took the bottle from him and drank again. After that, he passed he bottle back, and so it went until they were both giggling. Fausto pointed at the tractor parked in the middle of the shed, covered by a large tarp.

"Cousin," he said. "Do you know how to drive?"

Tomás shook his head. "No," he said. "My mother told me not until I am sixteen."

"Ah, nonsense." Fausto made a dismissive gesture. "I say you start today." He stood up and pulled down the tarp. Two mice ran out from under the seat, in different directions. Fausto leaned in and puttered around the gearbox, sweeping aside straw entangled around the stick.

"They always leave in the key," he said. "No thieves around here, I guess. Come help me, Tomás, we're going for a ride." He climbed onto the seat and turned the key. When the gearbox screeched in protest, he cursed and stepped hard on the clutch. The engine kicked over, and Fausto made a triumphant face.

"Come, cousin," he said. "Get up here." Tomás felt his head spin when he climbed up, but for the first time in his life he felt invincible, and he did not need Fausto to push him down on his half of the driver's seat.

"Your ass is too big, cousin," Fausto said. "You're almost pushing me off." Tomás put his hands on the steering wheel, crossing arms with Fausto. The wheel felt hot and sticky.

"What do I do now?" he said.

"Just keep your hands on the wheel and put your foot down on the gas pedal when I say so. I will handle the brakes. Gas!"

As Tomás pressed down on the gas pedal he felt the engine come alive. It shuddered, like a horse. Fausto turned the steering wheel slowly, and Tomás felt the big hind wheel brushing against his pants.

"Move over, Fausto," he shouted over the sputter of the engine. "You're pushing me off this damn thing!"

"What language!" Fausto said. "If only your mother heard you now, cousin!" Tomás did not want to think of his mother now.

"Damn thing," he repeated, "goddamn damn thing!" Fausto steered the tractor through the door and they were out in the fields. One of the day laborers was looking at them from a distance, his hand shielding him from the glare, and seemingly surprised to see the cotton tractor out this time of year. The fields were muddy, but no match for the mighty wheels.

"OK," Fausto said after they had driven around in circles, "I'm letting go of the wheel, you're on your own now." When his cousin lifted his hands off the wheel, Tomás grabbed on to it with all his might. He felt how the wheel was sticking to his hands, unwilling to let go of them.

"This is fun, cousin," he shouted. Fausto laughed, too.

"Now let's go over there where the *campesinos* live," he said. "Let's drive around their houses. They drove through the fore, bumping in and out of the tracks and laughing all the way. There were six small houses leaning against each other, strung together like pearls along a dirt road. Tomás brought the tractor out of the fore and onto the dirt road, his face getting redder with the effort. There were chickens on the road scavenging for the worms that had come out after the rain, unconcerned with the noisy tractor headed their way,

"You're doing great, cousin," Fausto said. "Now just floor it!" With this, he stepped on his cousin's foot, and the tractor shot forward. The chickens ran away, and so did the dogs. But the house was not so lucky.

"No one got hurt," Don Rogelio concluded, and the campesinos were compensated for the broken wall and half-collapsed roof. He ordered his foreman to hose down the two boys with ice-cold water, in the backyard where the farmhands showered, and had them locked into separate bedrooms for two hours.

"Whose idea was this?" he barked. He was sitting in the study that had belonged to the forefather himself. Fausto was taking in the coat of arms and the deer heads hanging from the walls, while Tomás was staring at his feet.

"It was me who did it, Tío," Tomás said. "I wanted to try and drive the tractor."

"And the rum? Where did you get the rum?"

Fausto looked at his father now. "It was my fault," he said. "I got him drunk. He has never drunk before, you know that, Father."

"Discipline," Rogelio said. "Discipline is what you need, the both of you. You for setting the wrong example, and you for listening to your cousin's bad advice." He stroked his moustache with one hand while tapping the table with the other. "I hear that your Aunt Rafaela could use two pairs of hands for her herb garden and sorcery business. That will teach you. Now get out of here."

When Ana heard what had happened she was furious. "Why did you let Fausto drag you into this?" she said. "That lout! You're better than that, Tomás. Stay away from him."

"I missed you," he said. He had been repeating the words in his head for days. There had been many words at first: apologies and explanations, but they had whittled down to just a few, and in the end none of them had survived, and he just told her the ones that came to him.

"I have missed you too," she said. "What took you so long?" He thought about it, but there was no answer other than that he had needed to spend time with Fausto.

"I understand," she said. "Boys need time off with other boys, right?"

He laughed.

After they had gone back inside, one of the azalea bushes shuddered, and Fausto came out from behind it. He sniffed the air, like a dog. Then he spat, and left.

Chapter 5

There was a *genízaro* tree in front of Tomás's house. Massive and gnarled, it was known as the rain tree, and provided shade to the townspeople gathering beneath it from dawn to dusk. It was said that the Indian chief, Nicarao, had surrendered to Hernandez de Córdoba, the Conqueror, under this same tree, only to be strung up like a common thief, here in his own house. But who remembered this? Not the tree. Not even the people who gathered in its shade.

Under the great genízaro tree a horse was waiting for Tomás. Rogelio had promised his sister to take his nephew on a hunting trip to the Meseta de Estrada. It was a one-day trek, across the Cordillera de los Maribios, a stretch of desolation that skirted two active volcanoes. Most boys started accompanying their father on hunting trips by this age, so Victoria was grateful for her brother's offer. Sofía tied Tomás's knapsack to the pommel, and gave him a small pouch made of rabbit leather, with two coins inside. When he looked at the coins he saw they were old British pennies bearing the effigy of Queen Victoria. He brought them to his nose and smelled.

"Copper," Sofía said. "For good luck. Rub them when you feel lonely."

They rode up the main road and then straight towards the volcanoes, passing though high-flying cane and low-waving cotton. Malpaisillo was a new town, less than one year old. There were barely fifty houses, but the street grid that had been laid out jumped numbers until it reached three digits, preparing itself for the greatness and glory that would never come.

Don Rogelio decided that this was a good place to rest and have lunch. "Let's stop here, Juan," he told his foreman, and dismounted. "We're halfway there, boys," he said as he turned to the boys. "Let's take a break; we need to stay out of the sun for a few hours."

"How late will we be there?" Tomás said.

"We should be there by nightfall." Rogelio glanced away at Fausto, who was busy stirring up a termite's nest at the base of a tamarind tree.

"You know, son," he said. "Those termites may seem blind and stupid, but sometimes they cause more damage than a *tigrillo*, and you won't even realize it, not until it's too late."

"What's it to me?" Fausto said. He raised his shoulders without turning. "I don't climb trees."

Night had fallen when they arrived at the cabin. It was large, with several adjoining structures, and propped up by adobe walls that must have been white once. Sticks were protruding where the plaster had broken away in large chunks, exposing the rocks that held the wall together. There was so much darkness around the roof that the boys could not see where the house ended and the sky began. *Chocorrones*, large black carpenter bees, were swarming around the torches that had been staked into the ground all around the cabin. Fausto counted sixteen horses standing outside, each with its saddle and bit removed, browsing from a trough filled with hay. The horses whinnied and shuddered as the four new horses, damp with perspiration, were led past them. Fausto's horse was in estrus, and the browsing stallions stamped their feet and chafed at the bit, blowing out billowing clouds of humid air.

When the door opened, the night was suddenly filled with boisterous laughter. "Here's the master shooter," a fat and graying man shouted. His and Rogelio's bellies clashed as they hugged and tapped each other on the back. Then it was someone else's turn, and a third man's, and so on, until he had made the rounds and there were no more backs to be tapped and bellies to be clapped and rubbed against.

Rogelio turned around with a big grin and said: "You know my son, Fausto, of course. And my nephew Tomás. This will be their first hunt!" The small crowd of men came forward and saluted the two boys.

"I remember my first hunt," one said. "Best hunt ever: the rush when you capture your first piece of game, nothing compares to it." There were two other boys, who were introduced as Rubén and Arturo. When the clapping and slapping was done, everyone sat down to steaming plates of food.

"Eat now," the fat man said, "because tomorrow you will need all your strength, and you will have nothing to eat until the hunt is over."

Rogelio roused them before dawn. He was fully dressed, in hunter greens and browns, and squeezed their feet sticking out from under the covers.

"Get up, boys," he said. "Take your bath and get dressed fast; today you shall hunt with the men." He put his hand on Fausto's shoulder, but the boy shrank from his touch as if a knife had seared his flesh. Rogelio squinted and his mouth jerked, but he said nothing. The two boys walked behind the cabin, where they found two men waiting in line, while a third was splashing water over his body with a small wooden bowl. After their bath, the boys sat waiting for the rest of the men to come out, and watched how the sun climbed rapidly above the tree line. Rogelio came over and stood in front of Tomás.

"You're the only boy who does not have a knife," he said. He reached inside his pocket and pulled out a folding knife. "Take this one, and tie it to your belt. You will need it today."

When his uncle had left, Tomás looked at the knife and weighed it in his hand. *Just the right weight*, he thought. He stabbed it into the moss, hearing the fiber break as he twisted it, before pulling the knife out again. He let his fingers run over the spine, and back to the blade, counting off the serrations one by one before snapping it shut and clipping it to his belt.

The small band of men and boys left the village and followed a cow's trail for twenty minutes. Each of the boys had been given a dog on a long leash, and they struggled to keep the dogs on the path. There were briars and thorn bushes along the trail, arid undergrowth that the cows had scorned. They veered left and walked until they came to a cave from which a fast stream of water sprang. Tomás knelt down to scoop up the water with his hand. It was clear and unspoiled in his palm, a roiling fistful of liquid glass.

"We need to head west now," Juan said. "The best hunting grounds lie west of here, beyond this stream." As they walked, Tomás noticed how the landscape changed. It was lush and green now, with tall trees whose branches joined above them. Even the path was marked clearly, as the thicket seemed to have been hoed down and kicked in until it stayed behind the invisible line that separated path from greenery. The dogs had calmed down, matching their pace to that of the boys.

"Don't stay behind, boys," Rogelio said over his shoulder. "We have a lot of work to do. And you better save some energy for tonight as well!" He lowered his voice as he spoke to the man walking next to him, but Tomás could hear him nonetheless.

"My son should have made it out here last year," he heard his uncle say. "But I waited until his cousin turned sixteen, so they could go together."

"What's tonight?" Tomás asked his cousin. Fausto made a gesture with his hands, sticking one finger through a loop made by the thumb and index finger of his other hand.

"I don't understand," Tomás said. Fausto repeated the gesture. The two other boys, walking behind them, were laughing at his questions, and so were the men walking behind them.

"They already know what's coming," one of them said, and they all laughed, a solid booming laugh that could have shot a hole through the cloud cover above them. Tomás was worried. "What do they mean, Fausto?" he said.

"They mean that we're going to get laid tonight, cousin."

Tomás felt his throat choking up. "What?" he said. "No, I don't want to. It's dirty." He blushed.

Fausto shook his head. "So just tell my father you don't want to."

"Can I?"

Fausto rolled his eyes. "Do you want to upset my father?"

"No," he said. "No, of course not."

Juan looked back at them too, now. "Just keep walking," he said. "Keep walking and don't fall behind. Worry about tonight when you get there."

Rogelio halted when they reached a small clearing with a tall oak tree on one side. He raised his hand. "Form a circle around me," he said. Tomás noticed that only a few men were carrying rifles; most had only long bowie knives.

"Why is that?" he asked Juan, but the man said nothing. He pointed at Rogelio instead, who looked impatient and annoyed with the distraction.

"Juan," Rogelio said, "you take the boys and the dogs. We will drive out the buck and you bring it to bay. You know the drill.

"Now listen up, boys," he continued, turning to the boys. "When the buck comes out, you trap it. You may let the dogs attack to wear it down, but you must wait for us to come in. We respect these animals; we're hunters, not killers. Hunting is not a game, and if you want to be a man you must play by the rules. This is very important — there are always rules to everything." Tomás glanced at his cousin, and saw him roll his eyes at his father's words. Rogelio looked at each of the boys, and called out their names.

"Rubén," he said, "Rubén, Arturo." Both boys nodded, and he continued: "Tomás, Fausto." The last word ended as a question, but Fausto did not look up.

When the boys were busy greasing their whips, Rogelio came over and sat down next to his nephew.

"Tomás," he said, "I want you to keep an eye on Fausto."

Tomás looked at his uncle in surprise. Usually Fausto was told to look after him, not the other way around.

"I…" he started, "I don't understand."

Rogelio's expression was stern. "That's all right, Tomás," he said. "Just look after your cousin, that's all. Make sure he does not do any crazy things. Make sure he plays by the rules."

Easier said than done. As if I could control Fausto.

Rogelio might have read his mind. "In my mind, you're my son as much as Fausto is," he said. "You're both made of the same good, solid wood. And I appreciate that you are loyal to Fausto, but loyalty is not enough. You must also know right from wrong." He ripped off some leaves of a flowering shrub in front of them and rubbed them between his thumb and fingers.

"Smell it," he said, holding the squashed leaves under his nephew's nose. "You know what this is, right?"

"Of course, Tío. It's *yerbabuena*."

"Yes. Horsemint. And do you know what it's for?"

He hesitated. Rogelio laughed.

"Don't remember Rafaela's witches' brew classes, do you? It calms the nerves. It might even make you brave. But once you find your own courage to do what is right, you realize that you never really needed yerbabuena." He stood up and rested his hand on the boy's shoulder.

"Your father was a brave man, Tomás. He had principles and rules in life, and he lived by them. He understood that we control the rules, not the other way around." He paused to let the words sink in.

"Now I need you to help Fausto understand this." He lowered his hand, and held it out for Tomás to shake.

"What counts is what we do when no one is looking, Tomás. Just remember that." They shook hands, and Rogelio walked away. Soon all the men had left, trailing out in single file except for Juan, the four boys, and two of the scouts.

"Let's go, boys," Juan said, and started walking into the thicket.

"How do they know where we will be waiting for them?" Fausto asked.

"Simple," Juan said. "It always ends in the same place, by the water's edge. We know exactly where to wait for big game; we've been doing this for years, and nothing ever changes." The dogs were going wild, growling, howling, and foaming at the mouth. Two hours later they spotted the buck; it was midstream across a muddy brook. It made no attempt to run away, as if it had been waiting for them. Its antlers were bobbing as it stood looking at them – panting, its nostrils flaring, and its flanks heaving.

"We wait here," Juan ordered, "we wait until the others catch up with us. We'll form a circle and keep it from getting away. This is an old buck; it's finished in any case."

They led the dogs all around the deer until they formed a full circle of boys and scouts, and dogs tugging at long leashes. But the dogs were in no mood to sit back patiently. They jumped at the buck, snapping at its tender nostrils. It kicked back furiously and lowered its antlers to charge. It had nowhere to go between the thick undergrowth and the dark trees, the hissing boys upstream and the snarling dogs downstream where the water had started running red. All the exits were blocked by the beasts and the men that led them.

It took less than twenty minutes for the buck to stop kicking. One of the dogs lay whimpering on the riverbank with a gaping wound on its head while another lay still in the water. The buck no longer seemed to be seeking to flee, not even to be begging for its life, as if it knew that this was the end, foretold and inevitable. It was shivering, and its muscles stood out like thick cords pulsing under its skin. Lowering its head, it backed up into the underbrush, splashing around the watering hole, which tomorrow would be crystal-clear once more and carry no memories of the slaughter that was to be.

While the dogs were attacking, Fausto had been busy carving nicks into tree stumps. But now that the buck was showing signs of exhaustion he put his knife away and walked over to Juan.

"Give me that gun, Juan," he said. "I'll shoot it now!"

"It's your father's kill. He'll be here soon."

"I'll deal with my father; just give me the gun!"

Juan hesitated. His fingers tensed around the rifle, but in the end he handed it to Fausto. He did not say a word, except to order the dogs away, one by one. The stag stood alone now, with its front legs spread out, the velvety antlers lowered for a last stance.

Majestic, Tomás thought. *It almost feels criminal to shoot this animal.* He smelled yerbabuena in the air, coming from where the buck and the dogs had trampled mint shrubs into pulp. He remembered his uncle's words, and stepped forward.

"Fausto," he said. "You shouldn't, just leave it already. Your father…" Fausto looked at him without undoing his clasp.

"Don't argue with me, cousin," his eyes were saying, "don't argue, and don't let me down."

"You can't," Tomás tried once more. "Your father said we needed to wait for the men to come back. They told us to wait; we don't know how this is done. Can't you see – they told us to wait for a reason. We're just boys, we don't know how this is done. We're not…"

"I am a man now," Fausto interrupted. "I'm a man just like them; I've already done everything a man has done. So I don't need anyone telling me how to take down a buck."

They all looked on as Fausto hoisted the rifle. He aimed at the bulk of the animal's chest, and fired. Birds flew up from the treetops as the shot echoed between the trees and up towards the skies where it dissipated, and would one day be gathered as thunder. Tomás ducked instinctively when he heard the shot. The buck sank through its knees, slowly, like a tree being felled after long and determined hacking away at the base with blunt axes. It groaned, a deep and rattling groan, and then a wheezing. Finally, only the low yelps of the dogs were heard, mourning their dead companions. Fausto handed the gun back to Juan and looked around triumphantly, turning to look each person in the eye.

"That's how it's done," he said. "That's how we show those old men how it's done." They all looked at him, too bewildered to speak. Shaking his head, Juan cracked open the gun to pry out the empty shell.

Suddenly another noise filled the clearing as the men were upon them, breathing heavily. Large sweat spots were showing across their shirts, and they were buckling under the weight of the shotguns slung across their back, as if a giant foot were stepping on them and pinning them down. They all stared at the fallen buck, and the clearing turned silent, as if on cue. The buck was panting heavily, one dilated pupil staring into the canopy as the adrenaline was fighting to keep it alive. Rogelio looked around until his gaze came to rest on the rifle in Juan's hand.

"Who shot the buck?" he thundered.

No one spoke. Juan looked at the boys, the rifle weighing heavily in his hand. He saw Fausto looking back at him, a smile playing on his face. Rogelio looked up at the sky, and then he turned and looked at the boys standing in the undergrowth, holding back the two remaining dogs.

"Consequences," he said. "Life is nothing more than a series of consequences. And this one does not fit." He looked around with a glint in his eyes.

"So…who…shot…the…buck?" he said once more, separating each word. Fausto looked his father in the eye, and the other boys looked away. No one said a word.

"Tomás?" Rogelio inquired. Tomás shrugged and muttered something under his breath.

"Was that something I should have heard?" Rogelio's voice was stern. Tomás looked at Fausto, and was surprised to see that his cousin was not hiding his amusement at the sight of everyone's silence.

No matter what I do, he thought, *no matter what I do, I will lose a friend and make an enemy.*

"I didn't know," he said. "I'm sorry, Uncle, I didn't know."

"Didn't know what, Tomás?"

"Nothing," Tomás said. "Nothing."

Rogelio turned back to face Juan.

"So was it really you, Juan? Why do I find that hard to believe?" He peered at the other man and twisted his moustache. "Think about it, Juan," he said in a low voice. "Think about this real hard."

"It was me."
Rogelio turned around and looked at Fausto without having seen him speak the words. He did not seem surprised.
"Hmm," he said. "At least we won't need to add cowardice to disobedience. I will deal with you later." With this, he turned back to the other boys.
"We did not finish this morning's lesson," he barked. "There is a reason why we don't shoot the buck. We hunt it, and we corner it. And we stand up to it: my knife against its antlers. It gets a fair chance, because that's what life gives you – a fair chance to defend yourself." He looked around once more. "Why do you boys think we go hunting?" he said. "We don't kill for fun – we kill for a reason. We must have reasons, always. Reasons and discipline. There's a fine line between murder and execution, and if we didn't know the difference, we would be criminals ourselves. That is why we take you out here – to learn the difference. Because there's no honor in shooting a cornered animal." He walked over to the buck and pulled out his knife, a long bowie knife that gleamed when a sudden ray of sun bounced off it. When he looked down at the buck, he frowned. He seemed to have a change of mind, because he sheathed his knife again.
The buck's chest and throat were throbbing, making a rattling noise, low-pitched and hurried: the noise a man might make when he knows that he has a limited number of breaths left in him and wants to take them all in, desperately clinging to each one of them, refusing to give them up. *Like breathing under water,* Tomás thought.
The buck's tongue had fallen out and was touching the muddy waters without lapping, like a small bird that had fallen from its nest. Rogelio stood above the buck, looking into its bulging, watery eye. Then he bent over, put his knee on the deer's back, and took hold of the antlers.

Tomás had never heard the sound of a snapping neck before, and was surprised by its loudness. It sounded like the tearing of thick cloth, the kind curtains were made of. And it lasted several seconds. His whole body jumped, expecting the deer to let out one last rattle. But there was no more sound, only a splash as the big head fell back into the mud. Rogelio pulled his knife out again, and sliced off the deer's right ear.

"Just in case," he said. "*Por si las moscas.*" He dropped the ear in the small leather pouch dangling from his hip. After he cleaned his knife on the skin he walked away, and sat down under a giant mango tree.

"Come, boys," Juan said, "now is your turn." The boys stepped forward and started the skinning and gutting.

"Work fast," Juan said, "we must be done before the heat sets in." Tomás flipped open his knife and about to stick it into the deer's belly when Juan stopped him.

"Easy," he said. "There's science to this, boy. Watch me now." He watched in fascination as Juan sliced through the skin and pulled out the bladder, then the rest of the organs. *Clean*, he thought. *He knows how to do it without leaving a mess.*

They cut off the head and set it on a tree stump in front of Rogelio, who reached out to touch the antlers, then lifted the head to feel its weight, and shook his head in approval.

"A fine specimen," he said, "this truly is the best hunting domain in the whole country!" They all laughed and the men opened bottles of rum. When the deer had been skinned completely, they cut up the carcass.

"No time for smoking the meat," Juan said, so the pieces were packed in swaths of cotton, everything down to the last hoof and tail. Everyone loaded a chunk onto their shoulders, and they walked out fast, without looking back.

Chapter 6

That evening, the cabin filled up with smoke. It would have smelled of unforgiven sins, if there were such a smell. The deerskin, rubbed with salt, was soaking inside large covered barrels, and the head had been placed on sticks over a bed of coals to smoke the inside. Tomás found Fausto sitting on a log by the fire, brooding. He sat down and bent over to reach for the rake.

"Don't rake the fire," Fausto said.

Tomás pulled back his hand. "Why didn't you tell him right away?"

"Tell him what?"

"You know what I mean."

"No."

"That you were the one who shot the deer."

"And you are the one who was supposed to make sure I wouldn't, aren't you?"

"Yes. But I couldn't."

"So this was my test, and I failed. Do you think you passed yours?"

"I didn't rat you out."

Fausto shook his head. "That's true," he said. "And now you know why I waited." He stirred the embers until sparks flew up and mingled with the fireflies.

"We all lie, cousin. You're not any better than me. You think I don't know what you want to do with that knife my father gave you?"

Tomás blushed, but before he could think of an answer, there were footsteps. Juan walked up to them and plunked down between the two boys. The smell of rum was on them as he sighed long and deep. His eyelids twitched as he squinted at the deer head standing amid the cinders.

"We'll be doing some singing tonight, boys, and some other business it's time you learn about." He slapped his thighs, and Fausto started laughing. Tomás jolted and stood up quickly, clutching the coin purse hanging around his neck.

"I forgot," he said. "I forgot to tell your father that I can't do this."

Fausto had not moved. "You already disappointed him once today, cousin. Want to disappoint him a second time?"

Tomás hesitated. "It's not good," he said. "It's dirty, it's not good."

"Well, you decide," Fausto said. "If I were you I just wouldn't tell her. No one would be any the wiser, you know. And what's the deal anyway? I have already been with a girl. Nothing to it."

Tomás looked at his cousin, surprised. "This is not about Ana," he said. "You don't understand. I…"

"Then what is it about?"

Tomás stayed silent.

"And now," Juan said slowly, "now I'm going to sleep, boys." With this, he fell backward, and started snoring even before his body touched the ground.

At seven the eating started. But first there was more backslapping and belly-rubbing, as the men filed in. Tomás and the other three boys were given beer now; he drank reluctantly at first, but when his cousin pushed him he drank another bottle, and then another, until his head started spinning. At nine o'clock two of the men went outside, and when they returned some twenty minutes later, they were accompanied by five girls. They were local girls wearing cheap dresses that were meant to make them look older, and lipstick they did not need. The oldest one might have been twenty; the youngest one fourteen at most. When they came through the door, roars went up.

"Here's the best venison of all," someone screamed. Tomás did not know whether to feel sorry for the girls or hate them for their garish makeup and high-pitched laughter. The men lined up in a double wall of bulging bellies and heaving chests, and the girls were being pushed through the arbor of bawling flesh, into the back room.

"Where are the boys?" the burly leader screamed. "Bring them in, this is for the boys!" Tomás felt several hands slapping him on the back and shoulders.

"Here's one!" the man next to him shouted, and pushed him through the room. He hit his head against a doorpost and his left ear went deaf, as if it had been hit with a hammer. The pain passing from one ear to the other was excruciating, and he squinted his eyes to see rows of soundlessly shouting men egging him on towards the back room. Fausto was already at the door, screaming with the others and sipping beer from a bottle.

"It's our turn, buddy," he said, his face red and contorted. Tomás tried to read his cousin's lips.

"What?" he yelled at the top of his lungs, but he could not even hear his own voice. "What?" he yelled once more, but then the door swung open and they were both pushed inside. The mastodon who had opened the door was grinning at them.

"Now don't be afraid of these little darlings, they won't bite," he said, and shut the door behind them. Tomás and Fausto looked at each other, and then the door opened behind them once more, and the other two boys were shoved into the room as well. The girls were sitting on two large beds pushed against the walls. They were speaking, but he could not hear them. The fireplace was cold and filthy, smelling of acrid smoke and rancid beans.

Metal frames, Tomás thought. *How strange that they have metal beds in this place. Not wooden. Metal.*

One of the village girls said something – he saw her mouth move, and then the sound came back to his ears.

"...been with a girl before? Maybe just with a cow?" All the girls giggled.

"Come over here, boys, we won't bite," the older one said. Tomás saw how the three other boys shuffled towards the beds, nervously chuckling and casting sideway glances at their companions. The kerosene lamps on the night table and dresser flickered and cast shadows on the walls that were larger than life.

This one looks like Ana's hand, he thought when one of the shadows fell on his arm. He made no movement, thinking he could sit it out now that the men were gone. From outside the room the brawl continued, and the noise became rhythmic as the men started singing drinking songs. One of the girls, the youngest-looking one, got up from the bed and sat down on a chair against the wall.

"What's with her?" Fausto said.

"She's here to watch," the older girl replied. "So she can learn."

"This is not right," Tomás said. "I don't want to do this..."

"Hey!" the other three boys exclaimed. "If you don't want it, get out of here, sissy. We're not going anywhere." They laughed and elbowed each other. Fausto grabbed his cousin by the arm.

"You're not going to chicken out on me, are you, *primo?*" he said. Tomás shook his head in a way that meant neither yes nor no. He looked at the young girl sitting on the chair, nervous and scared.

She probably does not know what will happen to her one day, he thought. The other girls took off their blouses, then their skirts, folding them up neatly and putting them on the chairs standing against the walls.

"We're ready now," the older one said, and the four of them lay down on the beds. The boys peered nervously at the dark aureoles, the nipples made erect by the cold mountain air, and the pubic mounds standing out against the flatness of their bellies. The boys shuffled about the room, wordlessly, and eventually each found a place. Fausto pushed his cousin until he found himself on one side of the bed, while the tall boy from Rivas ended up on the other side. He saw Fausto from the corner of his eye on the other bed, naked but for the knife he had left strapped to his shin. The moon cast shadows on the far wall, as if the boys were actors being pulled up and dropped again by an invisible puppeteer, with just enough slack to move a leg here, an arm there. He heard the moaning of the boy next to him, and felt the bed rocking back and forth with the creaking sound of metal springs.

"Do it, Tomás," he heard his cousin say. "Damnit, be a man." He slung the rabbit pouch around his back and closed his eyes, forcing himself not to think of Ana. Gritting his teeth, he entered the girl beneath him. Her body gasped and pulled away, then relaxed and pushed back at him. He wanted to gag, but his body did not let him. Soon he started perspiring, and felt how the coins in the rabbit pouch sent their coldness through the leather as it stuck to his skin. A trickle of sweat had started running down his nose, and a drop fell on the girl's breast. He followed it with his gaze and stared at the dark nipple, intrigued by its erect fullness, and the way the tissue rippled and bulged. He avoided her face, although she was moaning and pulling him closer to her. Suddenly, the door was thrown open and two men came in holding leafy eucalyptus branches. They were drunk, and laughing loudly. One by one, they lashed the boys across the buttocks with the eucalyptus branches, and the boys laughed, too, except Tomás. Then they threw the branches in a corner and grabbed the girl sitting on the chair.

"Enough learning," one of them said, and between them they threw the girl on the bed, next to Tomás. She screamed and fought as they ripped off her dress, but the other girls made no attempt to interfere.

"You!" the man said as he pointed at Tomás. "You're the runt here, so you might as well go with this one."

"She's only a girl," he protested, but the man pulled him away and pushed him down onto her.

He heard Fausto's voice from across the room: "Just do it!" he said. "Stop arguing, Tomás, just do it!" One of the men kept the girl pinned to the bed while the other pressed down on Tomás's back. When the girl was no longer able to move her body, the man let go of her and instead started hitting Tomás with the eucalyptus branches. Each time he felt the branches lash his buttocks he bit back the pain and pushed harder, pressing down on the girl, locking her in until she moved along with the heaving bed. She scratched his arms and tried to bite him, until the men held her arms down as well.

I don't want this, was all he could think, but his body soon stopped resisting, and then he no longer needed the men to push him down on the crying girl. They let go of him and laughed as he grunted and ground down on the girl in a steady rhythm.

Anger came over him, pouring into every thrust of his loins. Anger at not being able to control himself; anger at not being able to resist the pleasure that gripped him as if he were a rabbit being held by the ears.

"It's your fault," he groaned. "It's your own fault, why did you come here? Now you're getting what you asked for."

Finally, the girl stopped fighting, and then she stopped crying and moving altogether. She was looking at the wall, while the moon lit half her face. He could not make out the other half that was absorbed by darkness. The eye he could see was wide open, but it was looking away, not at him. When they saw that the girl had stopped moving, the men pushed him down one last time and threw away the eucalyptus branches.

"You don't mind if we take this one, do you, boy?" one of them said, taking the older girl by the arm. "We can see you're a young bull ready for breeding, but surely one is enough for you, right?" They laughed and left the room with the other girl, who giggled and cooed. Tomás gagged and pushed himself up, away from the clamminess of the girl's skin against his chest. Feeling dizzy, he watched the ceiling, and listened to the continuing groans of the other three boys, and how

one by one their moaning stopped. One of the girls giggled, and then
there was only a low mumble left.

A chocorrón had landed on the girl's shoulder. She shuddered,
fluttered her hand to brush it off. It fell on its back with fully closed
wings, a gleaming scarab with a pronged antenna. Beyond the brown
naked shoulder Tomás looked out the window, saw rows of flowering
eucalyptus trees, the ones that grow between rocks and on the flanks of
extinct volcanoes.

It's all lost, he thought. *How can I go back to her now?*

Chapter 7

He stopped making room for her in the hammock. She climbed in and snuggled up to him, holding his hand and letting her other hand rest on his chest. His body tensed and froze, and he undid her clasp. He no longer smelled the vanilla that danced around her hair. Instead, there was eucalyptus, always eucalyptus, and hints of mint and pepper that made him wince. His lip trembled, and he withdrew. She felt how his body tensed, and let go of his arms.

"I need some time," he said.

She looked at him, surprised "Can you tell me about it?"

He shook his head. "It's…I'm confused," he said.

"About me? Is there something I have done?" She put her hand back on his arm, and he cringed.

"No! I mean, no, there's nothing you have done. I just need some time, please give me some time."

She withdrew her hand, and he saw tears rolling down her cheeks.

"Don't you love me anymore, Tomás?"

He felt like hitting himself even more. "No," he said. "I mean, yes, I do. It's just so complicated."

"What is?"

I just need time, he thought. *I just need time to forget, and feel clean again.*

She wiped her face, and looked back at him. "*Está bien,* Tomás," she said. "We can wait." She caressed his cheek and gave him one more kiss.

"Rafaela tells me you're no longer making time for Ana," his mother said. He was surprised that his mother would ask.

"School," he said. "I have so much to study." He buried his nose back in the book.

"Strange," she said. "I thought the two of you liked each other. A lot."

"We do," he said. "But I need to study."

"I hear Ana cries a lot. She says you don't like her anymore." His mother lit a cigarette, and instantly the smoke was near him, entering his nose and lungs. He started coughing.

"I will go outside," he said. "I can't breathe while you're smoking in here."

She blew out another ring of smoke. "I keep forgetting," she said, stamping out the cigarette. "This will be the last one, I promise."

"I am going outside," he said. He stood up briskly.

"Has something happened?" She moved towards the door, faster than he could.

"No," he said. "Nothing has happened."

"Something happened, I know. You've been strange ever since you came back from that hunting party." He felt the blood rise to his cheeks and his skin starting to tingle.

"Nothing," he said. "Just your imagination, Mother."

"My imagination? You think I don't know what happens on those hunting trips? You really think all women are idiots just because we don't bring up certain things?" He jerked his head back and looked at her from the corners of his eyes.

Did she know? How could she? She put her hand on his but he withdrew, quickly.

"Whatever it was, get over it. Don't let it ruin your life; it's too short for that. People are practical, especially men."

Why doesn't she care? he thought. *She should be angry, instead of telling me to forget about it.*

"You don't know anything," he said. "You just hear things, that's all." She leaned back, and played with a sliver of tobacco stuck to her tongue.

"Maybe," she said, "but that doesn't mean they can't be true."

He took up swimming, and endured endless cold showers. He scrubbed his hands until they were bleeding, but the smell of eucalyptus was in his nose, refusing to leave. He smelled it on his fingers, his hands. It was there, and the longer he held his hands pressed against his nose the more pungent it became. *Like smoke*, he thought, *like smoke that stays inside your lungs.*

"Why are you always smelling your hands?" Fausto asked him. "You look like a spider monkey, what's wrong with you?"

It was true, Tomás realized. He remembered a big and strong specimen with golden eye rings and a long muscular tail. It had been kept on a leash in the backyard, where children threw stale tortillas at it. One day, one of the children wrapped cow dung inside a tortilla, and the monkey picked it up and held it under its nose. And ever since that day, it had been rubbing its hands, smelling them incessantly and refusing to eat. The children stopped coming, bored by the sight of a monkey lying coiled up in the dirt and refusing to perform any more tricks. But Tomás had come in every day, after school, holding out fresh bananas and *jocotes*. The monkey had refused to take them, and when he passed by one day the maids told him the animal had died.

"It died of disgust," they told him. *Is that possible?* he remembered thinking.

"What did they do with the body?" he asked them, and the maids pointed to a pile of chicken bones and buzzing flies in the far corner of the courtyard. *Its face had looked anguished*, he remembered. *Almost human, the way those piercing eyes continued to stare at me.*

On a Sunday evening, when the family had packed up and was ready to go back to León, he stayed behind at the beach house.

"But what if your asthma plays up?" Victoria said. "Who will give you the injection?"

He shook his head. "Not the season, and no pollen on the beach anyways."

"Make sure you carry the injection with you," she said as she got into the car. He nodded and patted the pocket of his jacket.

"I'll be back tomorrow, Mother," he said, "don't worry about me." He waited until it was dark, and the hawkers and fishermen had gone home. The moon was a pale sliver of light bouncing off the stillness of the ocean.

He walked south. A mile, perhaps more, until he reached the mouth of the Rio Chiquito where it flowed into the ocean. The sand felt wet and cool under his feet. Digging until his hands were sore and his fingernails had been pushed back into his skin, he made a shallow hole in the shape of a cross. The ocean waves started lapping at his feet, and he saw gleaming leatherback turtles being washed ashore by the tide. He took off his clothes and lay down into the hole, stretching out his arms. The sand was cold and dense; he felt the water seeping in from below. *Cleanse*, he thought, *I will be cleansed now. The ocean will wash it all away. And then I will love Ana.*

The tide came in quickly now. He felt the water rush over his feet and legs, then his groin and torso. He closed his eyes, waiting for the water.

It washed over his face, and he felt some of it trickling its way into his ears. His nose stung, and he coughed when the waves receded, but he did not move. The next wave was stronger, heavier, lashing him as it moved up across his body, and covering him with froth as it rolled back. Again and again, until the waters no longer rolled back, and he felt as if he were floating under water. He held his breath, sensing the water that pooled and eddied around his ankles and wrists, tugging at his hair as if it were a wicker coracle. Holding his breath, he felt his heartbeat slowing down, and marveled at how it sought to synchronize with the waves washing over him.

I can breathe here, he thought. *No noise here, just water and moonlight. If I stay here, I can learn to breathe under water.* But soon his pulse quickened, and he felt the blood rushing to his head, the air in his lungs swelling his throat – bursting, looking for a way out. He opened his eyes and panicked when he saw a dark form moving above him. Then the turtle was thrust ahead by the tide, and the moon was back.

Gasping, he sat up, and a new wave hit him in the face, stinging his eyes and nose. He coughed and crawled out of the hole, up to where the sand was dry and warm. He crouched and could not tell whether the salt he tasted on his tongue was the ocean's or his own. *Life*, he thought, *I must live life. My life.* His breath became longer, until his heartbeat slowed down and his skin relaxed, and pulled itself away from his bones.

When he came back to the beach house he scooped up water from the deep tiled sink and let it run down his head and back. He used up a full bar of soap, and when he was done he sat down in a rocking chair on the porch and slowly rocked back and forth. The grains of sand wedged under the rockers made a squealing sound each time they were being squashed, as if pigs were being dragged into the slaughterhouse by their curled-up corkscrew tails. He smelled his hands, and for the first time in many months, the smell of eucalyptus was not there.

When he saw Ana again he felt as though a weight had finally been lifted. They laughed, and Ana did not ask him what had happened. *I am happy he has come back to me,* she thought. *This is all that matters.* He watched her from a distance as she walked home, the way he had watched his mother and the bald man. *I love her,* he thought. *And I know that she loves me.* He shivered again at the thought of himself on top of the girl in the woods. *Ana must never know.*

Soon after the rains stopped, Ana turned fifteen. All her cousins, aunts, and uncles had been invited to her *quinceañero,* including relatives in the third degree who rarely entered the Cortés mansion. On this occasion, Mama Mica herself had come out to join the festivities. Seated under an avocado tree, she almost appeared to be competing with her great-great-granddaughter, greeting the widows and widowers of relatives who had long since died. Rafaela stood beside her, clutching a wicker basket from which she occasionally picked some leaves or sprigs, whenever Mama Mica leaned back and whispered something in her ear.

Fausto and Tomás were standing in line to give their present to Ana when Tomás spotted Rafaela waving at him.

"Me?" he said out loud, pointing at himself. She nodded, but he was too far to hear her voice. Again she beckoned for him to come over.

"*Tía* Rafaela is asking me to go see her," he said.

"Really?" Fausto said. "So let's go see what she wants."

When they got to her, Mama Mica was asleep.

"Does she ever wake up?" Fausto said.

Rafaela looked at him sternly.

"I'm serious," Fausto continued. "How do you know she's not dead? I mean, maybe she swallowed some bad grapes, you know." He poked his elbow in Tomás's side, but his cousin ignored him.

"I want to talk to *you,*" Rafaela said, emphasizing the last word. Fausto stopped poking his cousin and looked at Rafaela, his head slightly cocked.

"Am I unwanted here?" he said. When Rafaela said nothing he turned. Tomás reached behind him.

"Fausto," he said, "just wait for me, I'll be right there." But Fausto walked away fast, without looking back.

"Do you love Ana?" Rafaela said.

Tomás was taken aback.

"Why are you asking?" he said. "Why is that your business?"

Rafaela laughed. "You're family," she said. "And so is she. That makes it my business."

He shook his head. "I still don't see…"

"You're what now…seventeen?"

"Yes."

"Ana says you have never tried to kiss her."

He opened his mouth to say something, but thought the better of it. *Nothing can be kept a secret in this house*, he thought.

"Yes," she said, "you're right; there are no secrets in this house. Didn't you know that? Girls need to feel loved, Tomás."

"It's none of your business," he said. "We're just kids – we play, and then we stop playing." He glanced at Mama Mica. He did not get to see a lot of her. But for Ana's quinceañero she had come out. *And what for?* he thought. He bent down and touched her hand. It felt dry and thin, like the parchment rolls that all the Cortés children were shown in Sunday school, with the ancestor's coat of arms, and letters written in a script no one alive could still write. Her hand twitched when he touched it, and he withdrew his hand, afraid of waking her. But she had already opened her eyes. Not slowly, as most old women did, but quickly rather, and steadily, the way a rosebud opens.

My mother's eyes, he thought, *and Ana's*. Before he could say anything, Mama Mica gestured for Rafaela to bend down. She whispered something in her ear, without taking her eyes off Tomás. Rafaela rummaged through her bag; she took out one small cotton bag after another, smelling them all.

"This one," she said, holding it out for Tomás to take. "It's a gift from Mama Mica, Tomás, for you to give to Ana." He took the package and held it under his nose. It smelled of apricots, with a hint of cardamom.

"But I already have a present for her," he said.

"Never mind, give her this one as well. Girls love presents, you know that. The more the better."

He nodded. *Best to just agree with her*, he thought.

"Fine," he said. "I will give it to her."

Mama Mica had stopped looking at him now. He noticed how she was dozing off again. He put the package in his bag with the other gift he had brought, and walked away. When he looked back he saw the two women almost as a single figure against the quickly setting sun.

Someone bumped into him from behind and threw him to the ground. When he looked up, he saw Fausto. They both shook off the dust on their suits and picked up their bags. Fausto looked into his and made a face.

"It's broken," he said. "It was my present for Ana."

"What was it?" Tomás said.

"A bamboo cage," Fausto sighed. "With a crystal bird inside. Now what do I do? Ana doesn't like me much to start with, but if I don't give her a gift she'll never forgive me. Where am I going to get another gift so fast?" Tomás looked behind him, and was relieved to see that Rafaela and Mama Mica had gone back inside.

"I..." he started.

"What?"

"I have two gifts."

Fausto looked surprised. "Why?" he said. "Why did you bring two gifts?" Tomás decided it was too much to explain, so he mumbled something and opened his bag. The deep smell of ripe apricots greeted him, as if honey had been spilled on a bale of fresh hay. *Which one?* he thought. *Perfume, or a book about Paris?* He looked at the two presents in his bag. *Paris, I will take her to Paris. When we grow up, I will take her there. Ana is too young for perfume anyway.* He took out the small bag and gave it to his cousin.

"Here," he said. "It's already wrapped; all you have to do is give it to her."

"Thank you, cousin," Fausto said. "You're the best friend I'll ever have." They hugged and walked to the central courtyard where Ana was sitting on a brightly painted chair. The aunts, uncles, and cousins walked up to her, one by one, and put presents in her lap.

"You go first, cousin," Fausto said. Tomás walked up to Ana, holding the present in front of him. She smiled at him, and he noticed that her eyelashes had grown.

"Hmm," she said. "It smells of apricots. Is that what it is, Tomás? Did you bring me essence of apricot?" She clapped her hands.

He blushed. "No," he said. "It's…well I think there might have been some apricots in the bag before."

"Oh," she said. "You think so, yes?" He fumbled for his bag. His hands felt big and awkward, and he had the urge to go and wash them. She pursed her lips but said nothing else, although he thought she wanted to. She stretched out her hand and let it rest on his arm.

"Oh, Tomás," she said when she had unwrapped the book, "thank you so much, this means so much to me."

She kissed him, and he blushed.

"For now," he said. "It's just a book for now. We will go to Paris when we grow up. It's a promise."

She squeezed his arm. "I can't wait to grow up," she said, "and I know you will keep your promise." He kissed her, and walked away.

"And?" Fausto said as they brushed shoulders. "Did she like it?"

"Of course. All girls like books, don't they?"

"Hmm," Fausto said, grinning. "I'm not so sure about that."

"Here," he told Ana. "I brought you a gift." He held out the bag to her, and she took it. The smell of apricots was in her nose again, and she looked up, surprised.

"What's this?" she said. "Did you also have your gift mixed in with apricots?"

"No," he said. "I don't mix things. I am made of one piece, one mind. This is what I bring you." She put her nose against the bag and inhaled, deeply. Opening it, she was surprised to see the small flask, delicately wrapped in an embroidered kerchief.

"So nice of you, Fausto," she said. "I never expected you to bring me this… Not at all like you."

"Me neither," he said. "But you know what they say, 'don't judge a book by its color.'"

She laughed. "Cover," she said. "Don't judge a book by its cover."

"Well, you know what I mean. I don't read much, so they all look the same to me." She opened the flask and smelled it.

"Hmm," she said. "Apricot essence, divine! Smell it, Fausto!" She held the flask up for him to smell, and it hit him without warning. It tickled his nose and quickly traveled up to his throat and eyes. He drew back when he felt the impulse to cough.

"Strong," he said, "stronger than rum! Could make a bull cry, I bet." She smelled again, holding the flask away from her nose.

"Yes," she said. "It is very strong indeed. Thank you, Fausto."

That summer, Fausto and Tomás were lounging on the beach.

"So what's with you and Ana?" Fausto said.

"What do you mean, what's with me and Ana?"

"You know, are the two of you...?" He made a gesture with his fingers.

"Of course not!" Tomás exclaimed. "We're too young."

"Too young, eh?" Fausto raised his eyebrows while Tomás bit his lips.

"I want to wait," he said. "And I want her to wait for me."

"Well, she's not the only girl in the world, you know." Fausto laughed and raised his bottle in a toast. "Plenty of fish in the sea, and they don't all think they're 'too young.'" He laughed again and handed his cousin a bottle of beer.

Chapter 8

Fausto entered the Military Academy. The decision had been his father's.

"To teach me discipline," he told Tomás the day he left León for Managua. His father's blue Cadillac was humming impatiently as the two boys said goodbye.

"You know I was never going to be anything else, right, cousin?"

Tomás laughed. "Yes, you were always playing with knives. I guess it is the right place for you."

Fausto grinned. "And even if it weren't...I figured out that you were right, cousin."

Tomás was surprised. "How?" he said.

"No use always fighting my father. I guess I should just go with the flow, right?"

Tomás raised his shoulders. "I am really the last person to ask," he said. "I wish..." Fausto straightened his back, and let his hand rest on Tomás's shoulder.

"Until next time, cousin," he said.

Tomás decided to become a doctor, but his decision came only weeks before enrollment closed. For a long time he had not known what he wanted to do, but when Doctor López invited him to his clinic one day, he ended up fascinated by the fetuses and brains floating in jars of formalin.

"When left in formalin, the brain takes on the consistency of an avocado," Doctor López said. "Isn't that amazing?"

"How can it be conserved for so long, Doctor?" Tomás said.

"See," Doctor López said. "Once you drop a body part in formalin, it becomes suspended in time. No more decay, and no more loss. No more pain. Just suspension in time. Of course you won't bring them back to life. Nothing can do that. But you can study the things that are dead, and by studying them we don't forget them."

Two weeks later Tomás entered medical school. In those days it was easy – few people could read or write, and fewer yet had the time, or desire, to spend years memorizing chemical formulas and counting bones. But these were the things Tomás enjoyed most. It was the sense of timelessness, he realized. The sense that a body, no matter how weak and fragile it might appear, followed rules older than any human being could remember, and no human being could change. The circuits, the wiring, the ever-expanding and contracting organs, the unyielding strength of skulls and bones that only fire or acid could break.

Tomás was reading on the porch of the beach house in Poneloya, and had not heard his cousin's footsteps. The hand that suddenly came to rest on his shoulder made him jump.

"Stop reading, cousin." Fausto's voice was lower than usual, and Tomás smelled the rum on his breath.

"Why do you always have your nose in books?"

Tomás put his book down and looked back over his shoulder. "I like books," he sputtered.

"Yes, and the smellier the better, I guess." Fausto bent over and stuck his nose inside the book. "Just as I thought," he said. "Smelly old books. Why don't you come with me tonight? I'm meeting this girl, met her this morning." He flashed a long grin.

"What girl?" Tomás said.

Fausto shrugged. "Some girl from down here," he said. "Juanita. Josefa. Something."

"I'll stay here," Tomás said. "I don't feel like going out. And I'm with Ana, you know that."

"She'll bring a friend."

"No," Tomás said. "No, I'm fine."

Fausto's grin was gone. "What's the matter with you?" he said. "These girls are looking for it, don't you know? They are all looking for it, like dogs in heat. Some may not show it, but they're all the same. I don't see why you're making a problem out of this! If it's not me it'll be some other guy, what's the difference?"

"Not me and Ana," Tomás said. "We're different."

"You liked it when they took us to those girls, didn't you? You liked it as much as I did."

"No, I didn't. I hated myself for it. And I still do." He dropped his head.

"They're all the same," Fausto said. "Just wait and see; in the end they're all the same. Take it from me."

When Tomás kept silent, Fausto raised his shoulders and stomped away.

Zenzontle birds were circling the mango tree in the yard when the aunts and cousins gathered on the porch that evening.

"Who wants to go for a walk?" Ana said. "It's a cool evening and there's a full moon. Anyone want to come?" Four of the younger cousins raised their hands.

Ana looked at Tomás. "Will you come too, Tomás?" she said. They walked down the beach towards the lagoon, greeting neighbors sitting in front of their beach houses. The tide was low, and the channel leading to the lagoon was almost empty, allowing them to cross. There were no houses on the other side, only tall saw grass stretching inland from the beach. Two of the cousins had run ahead to look for conch shells when Ana heard low noises coming from the grass.

"What's that?" she said, perching her ear. "Did you hear that, Tomás?"

"No," he said. "Must be the wind, there's a lot more wind on this part of the beach."

"Enough wind to beach a whale!" one of the cousins crowed.

"I will go and check; perhaps someone is wounded or needs help. Just stay here and mind the children," she said.

"Ana, don't," he said. "This isn't safe, just let it be." But she was already heading for the expanse of waving grass. It was bending down and lifting up again, flayed by the wind but following no rule. The noise became louder now, and when she came closer she could distinguish a low voice and one that was slightly higher – the voice of a girl used to smoking. She bent aside the leaves and spied between them. The moon cast its light on a clutch of arms and legs entangled with clothing – shorts, a skirt – as if the two had not had the time or patience to take them off. The wind picked up, and when she bent back the leaves, they stayed flattened, hugging the ground. She saw the two writhing and grinding bodies, the girl's heaving to meet the boy's in an unspoken rhythm, like a wave of ocean water that ebbed and swelled. They were consumed by a drive Ana could only guess.

They do not tire, she thought as she heard their groaning become deeper and lower. The girl was clawing the boy's back, and Ana saw how his skin retracted when the girl's nails dug in. But he did not stop, did not pull away. Instead, he renewed his thrusts, and his grunting became louder. Ana touched her chest, felt how her own heart had started beating faster, as if seeking to synchronize itself with the boy's. Suddenly Tomás's voice ran out over the wind. It was faint but clear:

"Ana? Ana, come back. Where are you, Ana?"

The boy stopped moving, and turned his head. She tried to pull up the grass in front of her to hide behind, but the wind did not let up. The girl pushed the boy off her and reached for her clothes, but he did not.

He saw Ana as she saw him. Her eyes widened as she saw his face, then his body.

Fausto looked at Ana without moving, as if he had expected her to be there all along. Again she heard Tomás's voice: "Ana, where are you? Come back, Ana."

She turned and ran, and when she reached him she was breathless and flustered, but the moonlight was too pale for him to see it.

"Let's go back to the house," she said, before he could ask her what she had seen. "Too much wind, we should not have come out this far."

She could not sleep that night. The image of two writhing bodies grinding against each other was stuck in her head, and she saw the scene unfold over and over, stopping each time where Tomás's voice ran out to her. A piece of clapboard had come undone near the window, and each time the night breeze lifted it and slammed it back against the house her belly muscles contracted. A faint smell of apricots filled her nostrils as she pushed her face deep into the pillow.

She imagined the soreness of Fausto's skin where the girl's passion had marked him. She squeezed her arm, and then embraced herself to pinch the skin on her back. Her nails raked her shoulders, the tender skin beneath her armpits. Slowly at first, then faster, until her skin tingled and burned. Each time the clapboard banged against the house she gasped and stopped moving, feeling the burning sensation spread across her skin.

It was late when Fausto arrived. She heard him mumbling to the guardsman at the gate, heard their muffled laughter. The next morning, when she saw him at breakfast, she said nothing, and neither did he. She was surprised herself that she was not shocked by what she had witnessed, or revolted by it. Each time her dress brushed against the soreness of her shoulders that day, she was reminded of the absence of apologies.

Chapter 9

Fausto was polishing his boots in the refectory. He had not heard the footsteps that passed the doorway, and how the room had slightly darkened. In the reflection of his boot he saw a shape standing ten feet away from him, and dropped the can of polish. It ran away from him, spinning like a top. A boot came down on it, and when it lifted, Fausto looked up to see a face studying him from behind dark glasses. Anastasio Somoza, the younger of the President's two sons, looked just like his portrait hanging on the walls of the Academy. The body attached to the face had a gleaming belt around it that looked to Fausto like a hoop straining to hold a barrel together.

He jumped to his feet to salute.

"At ease, Corporal," the major said. "And sit down." Fausto pulled two chairs from the wall and waited for the major to be seated.

"Corporal," Somoza started, "you are Corporal Cortés, aren't you?"

"Yes, sir, Major, Corporal Fausto Cortés, sir, Major," Fausto shouted. The major took a pack of cigarettes from his chest pocket. Lucky Strikes, short ones without filter. He tore off the foil tab and shook the pack against the palm of his hand until three cigarettes came sliding out. He lit one and let it dangle from his lip.

"You smoke, soldier?" He held out the pack to Fausto.

"No, sir, I don't smoke, sir," Fausto replied. His hand trembled; it wanted to run away, and he squeezed the horsehair shoe brush harder to control his hand. Somoza smiled. A curt smile, more a reflex than an expression. Behind the rimmed glasses, Fausto saw nothing.

"Corporal, I was told that you are the best marksman in the Academy. They told me you never miss your shot. Now I need a good marksman to accompany me this Sunday. Someone to have my back, if you get my drift." He left a silence there, like a composer writing a score, measuring the length of notes and half notes: a quaver here, a pause there. Fausto felt how his lungs drew in less air, as if the air itself had become rarified.

"Yes, sir, I am a good marksman, sir," he blurted.

"Good!" the young Somoza said, uncrossing his legs. "But good is not good enough. I need someone better than good!" Fausto saw himself reflected in the major's shiny boots.

"Can you be that man, Corporal?"

Fausto hesitated. He wondered what the major wanted from him. What business could there be on a Sunday that could not wait until Monday? But this young Somoza, barely ten years his senior, spoke like a person who was not used to giving explanations to anyone.

"Yes," he said, "yes, sir, Major, I can be that man."

"That's settled then. Report to the Main Gate on Sunday. Eight hundred hours. Sharp." He stood up, and Fausto snapped to attention.

"As you are, Corporal," Somoza told him over his shoulder. He threw the cigarette butt in the patio as he walked out. However, he had barely taken six more steps when he stopped, and turned around.

"Oh, and one more thing, Corporal."

Fausto did not move.

"You better be as good with your gun as you say you are. If there's one thing I detest it's a liar."

On the Sunday that followed he was at the Main Gate fifteen minutes early. At eight o'clock sharp, a jeep came rolling towards the gate; Somoza was in the backseat, flashing a wide grin.

"Get your ass in here, soldier!" Fausto got into the front seat, next to the driver. A sudden movement behind him caught his eye, and he noticed how a long stick seemed to grow out of the major's hand, which he used to tap the driver on the shoulder every so often. Left shoulder, right shoulder, and other taps in the middle, meant perhaps to indicate faster and slower, or stop and go. Soon they had left the barracks behind them, and all throughout their ride there was the concert of taps that left a patchwork of pricks and scratches on the driver's shirt, as if to ensure the existence of a written record of their itinerary. Once they had left the city, they turned onto the Pan-American Highway and soon arrived at Tipitapa, where the country's main prison was located. When the soldier standing guard recognized the visitor, he spoke into a telephone, fast and nervously, and opened the gate.

"I never tell my drivers where I go," Somoza said as they got out of the car. "Security above all." He crossed his arms behind his back while they walked towards the main building.

"Let me tell you why we're here, soldier," he said. "We are going to witness an execution today. Have you ever seen an execution, soldier?"

"No, Major," Fausto replied. "Never, sir." Somoza stopped in his tracks and looked back at him, squinting his eyes in disbelief, it seemed. Then he pulled out the extra arm from behind his back and let it rest on Fausto's chest.

"I need to know where you stand, Corporal," he said. "Squeamish men have no place in the Guard."

"Yes, sir," Fausto said. The stick resting on his chest made him feel singled out and suspect, called to answer for deeds before they had been committed.

"That's why we're here today, Corporal, and that's what we are going to find out today."

A captain came to meet them. He was in his early thirties, not much older than Somoza himself, and his hedgehog hair slightly lifted the officer's hat, which seemed to be floating. The captain saluted, then shook the young Somoza's hand and leaned forward while he whispered things in the other man's ear. Somoza shook his head several times, a curt jerking of his jawbones, as if he were swallowing something, some words perhaps the other man had said and that were particularly distasteful to him. His wattle bulged as he spoke. The captain nodded in the direction of the courtyard, and they both walked that way. Fausto followed on their heels.

After crossing the courtyard, they stopped in front of the perimeter fence, which was made of barbed wire strung along tall concrete posts. A wooden post was pitched in the mud, and guarded by a bored-looking soldier.

"Open up, soldier," the captain said. The man shouldered his gun and pulled the pole out of the mud. It made a slithering sound.

"All right then," the captain said, and the three of them stepped through and walked out towards the riverbank, where four more soldiers were waiting. Two of them were smoking, and hastily threw away their cigarettes when they saw officers approach.

"At ease, boys," the captain said, turning around to his guest.

"OK, *muchachos,* where are our guys?" Somoza said.

"Right here, Major." One of the soldiers pointed over his shoulder, towards the lake. Everyone walked up the grassy knoll, and looked down the other side. Under the watchful eye of a sergeant, a boy and a young man were crouching on the riverbed, where the river threw itself into the lake. Barefoot and with tattered shirts and pants, they looked like nothing more than two peasants huddling on a stretch of mud before herding the donkeys home.

"Corporal!" Somoza beckoned for Fausto to come forward. He had pulled out his stick and pointed at the two peasants.

"Do you want to know what they are guilty of, Corporal?"

"No, sir, Major."

"I'm going tell you even so. Conspiracy, Corporal. Conspiracy to overthrow the government. Nothing more and nothing less. Remnants of that scoundrel Sandino's army of bandits. No matter how hard we try, the vermin keep coming out of the woodwork. Like termites. But today is reckoning day, Corporal, you understand me?"

"Yes, sir, Major."

"Today we will make our country a little safer for democracy. We are making Nicaragua safer one traitor at a time! REMEMBER THAT, CORPORAL!"

"YES, SIR, MAJOR!"

The captain made a sign to one of the soldiers, who walked towards the prisoners and kicked the younger one in the legs.

"You, get up! Come on, stand up, *hijueputa!*" The boy looked around, unsure what to do, so the soldier kicked him once more.

"You think we are going to help you up or what? You think that's what we're for, to help up traitors like you, human garbage?" The other soldiers laughed. Fausto watched, aware that his hands were trembling. *This boy is barely older than I am*, he thought. The soldier pushed the boy with his gun until he had regained his footing. Then he pulled out a big hunting knife and cut loose the rope that was tying his wrists together. The boy looked surprised. He looked from his untied hands to the two officers, and then back at the soldiers standing behind them. Somoza made a movement with his stick. A dismissive movement, a fly-swatting movement.

"Get the hell out of here," he said. "Go!"

The boy stared at him but did not move.

"Corporal," Somoza said, "is your gun loaded?"

"Yes, sir, Major," Fausto said.

"Then I want you to take aim in exactly thirty seconds."

"Sir?"

"You heard me, Corporal. Twenty-five." He had not turned to look at Fausto.

"Run, sonofabitch!" Somoza yelled at the prisoner. "Get out of here! It's your only chance!"

The boy turned and ran, his shirt fluttering behind him like a ragtag flag, towards the tree line that was an impossible twenty seconds away. Somoza turned to face Fausto and tapped him on the chest with his driver stick while unbuttoning the clasp over his pistol with his other hand.

"Shoot him, Corporal. Show me what wood you're made of." Fausto's eyes opened up wide now, and his jaw dropped. He looked at the other soldiers, as if to ask them to tell him whether this was a joke or a test. But they were busy taking bets. Dirty banknotes changed hands, banknotes with the face of the President's daughter on them.

"Fifteen," he heard Somoza bark. He felt the stick counting the measures against his chest, a metronome of impeccable precision. *And what if I don't?* he thought. *Will he shoot this poor bastard himself if I don't?*

"Ten, Corporal."

Somoza's eyes were empty. Not nervous, and not excited. Empty. *He doesn't care. He doesn't care either way. What choice do I have?*

"Five."

The boy fell. He was close to the tree line, and wavered, as if he had changed his mind and wanted to negotiate. Somoza said nothing. He nodded and pouted his lips as Fausto lowered his gun, and then he walked away. Fausto was breathing heavily. His head was bursting, and he felt something acid climbing up his esophagus. Forcing it back, he leaned on his gun, and waited for his heartbeat to slow down again.

"Hey, you," one of the soldiers said. "That was a pretty good shot. You know, if you hadn't pulled the trigger the Man would have shot you instead. You know that, right?"

"What?" Fausto said. "Why would he...?"

"The Man never accepts no for an answer," the soldier said. "But you did good, boy, you did good." He winked at him, showing his blackened teeth.

"Goddamn this," Fausto mumbled to himself. "Goddamn this, what's the point of this? Shooting some poor bastard in the back, how does that add up to anything? Kill for no reason?" He shouldered his gun and followed Somoza. The soldiers were busy swapping banknotes as he walked past them.

When he had almost reached the barracks, he heard a shot. Instinctively, he ducked. Another shot followed; a lighter sound, as from a handgun. He turned and looked out at the distant tree line. The boy's body was still lying where it had fallen, and three *zopilotes* were circling above it. The soldiers were laughing on the other side of the ditch, and he heard a splash, as if a bag of cornmeal had fallen into the river.

Somoza was already sitting in the backseat of the jeep. He shook hands with the captain, and Fausto saw how the stick arm had started crawling up the driver's back again.

"Let's go, Corporal," Somoza said, "let's get out of this shithole and have a drink."

They took the road back to Managua, but after fifteen minutes Somoza tapped the driver's back to the right, and they veered off the highway, onto a dirt road towards the lake. The stick went tap-tap left, right, right, left, right all along the way, until they reached Punto Hueto. A cantina was wrapped around a guanacaste tree, hugging it like a randy lover. An older man was sitting at one of the smudgy tables with a young woman, but when they saw the military jeep dusting its way up to the cantina they got into their car, fast, and drove away. Somoza and Fausto sat down, and the barkeeper came over to take their order. Wearing a sleeveless undershirt, he was sweating in spite of the breeze.

"What may I offer you, Don?" he said.

"A beer," Somoza said. "Give me an ice-cold beer. *Una Victoria bien heladita, oiste?* And one for the corporal too." He drummed the table with his fingers while the tree house owner brought the beers.

"I need an aide-de-camp, Corporal," Somoza said, plunking the bottle down with a bang. "Someone to have my back, if you know what I mean. Someone with *cojones!*" He peered at Fausto through his thick horn-rimmed glasses, and his fingers split in pairs as he pushed them down on the table. "Someone who is not afraid of breaking eggs from time to time," he continued. "Hell, you gotta break eggs from time to time if you want to get things done. Do you know anything about breaking eggs, soldier?"

Fausto nodded.

"You see," Somoza said, clenching his hand into a fist. "You see, I need someone who sees possibilities where other people see limits. Are you a person who sees possibilities, Corporal?" Fausto stared at his beer and raised his eyebrows. Somoza leaned back until the plastic chair started shaking.

"Now, do you want to ask me any questions about what happened today?"

Fausto saw the running boy, the fluttering shirt against the row of beckoning trees.

"I was wondering why we needed to set him loose first, Major," he said. "I thought we put criminals in front of a squad."

Somoza looked amused. "I like your thinking, Corporal," he said. "Asking a few questions makes a soldier smart. Asking many questions, however, makes a soldier dead. So let me tell you the answer, because I don't need a dead aide-de-camp." He took out a kerchief from his back pocket and started patting his forehead.

"You see, we give them a chance."

"But..." Fausto started.

Somoza raised a hand. "Wait," he said. "We give them a chance, but only one. We don't do second chances in the Guard; you ought to know that. So the guy gets to run away, and we give him thirty seconds. Fair's fair, no?" He chuckled, his head turning redder yet. "Why go through a stinking court case – we already know they're guilty, that's not the point." He patted the back of his neck now, quickly turning the kerchief into a wet brown rag.

"You see," he continued, "someone's going to get it no matter what. If my marksman is good, the scumbag gets it right there. And if he does escape...well, if he does escape he will spread the word that in the Guardia we don't fuck around. *No andamos con mierda!*" He laughed out loud, and lifted the bottle to down the last of the beer. But before he put the bottle to his mouth he paused to look straight at Fausto.

"What did the other guys tell you?"

"Which other guys, Major?"

"There's your answer, Corporal. Just so you know they were right." He drank and slammed down the empty bottle.

"Any other questions, Corporal?"

Fausto raised his shoulder. "No sir," he said. "No questions, sir." Somoza grinned and leaned back.

"Very good, Corporal." He squeezed his kerchief into a wet ball and threw it at the dogs waiting at a distance. They sniffed at it and looked back at him, as if expecting more. Somoza pushed back the plastic chair, scraping it against the rough concrete floor. He got up and threw some damp banknotes on the table, then pointed his finger at Fausto.

"You'll go far if you keep this up, Corporal. Mind my words, you'll go far!"

Chapter 10

The young Somoza took Fausto to a family gathering, where he was introduced to the President and his wife, an elegant lady who barely spoke Spanish but instinctively knew the difference between *bon* and *mauvais goût*. Somoza the elder took a liking to Fausto, so when he finished his two years at the Academy, the President arranged for him to be assigned to his Presidential Guard, with a lieutenant's commission. He was often sent out to far-flung corners of the country, accompanying the younger Somoza on "special inspections."

One of these took him to the Atlantic Coast, where the President had "picked up" farmland during the war, not too far from Puerto Cabezas, in the middle of the Mosquito Coast. There were eight farms in total that had once belonged to Moravian missionaries and German settlers. However, when Nicaragua declared war on Germany, all properties held by Germans, no matter how long they had lived in the country, were confiscated for reasons of national security. The only way to reach some of the formerly German properties on the Caribbean coast was by taking the mud road leading from Jinotega to Puerto Cabezas, all three hundred miles of it. Somoza Junior, two accountants, and a military escort set out from Managua early in the morning: three jeeps of men in good spirits. They were handpicked, because Somoza was paranoid about security.

"I need guys who will have my back," he told each one, "and I'm only going to tell you once. With me, there are no second chances. Anyone who thinks there are second chances has been smoking weird shit." They all laughed. Somoza did take care of his men. There was always food and rum aplenty. Women, too, as the Somoza business interests extended to the network of brothels that kept Managua swinging at night.

They took the road north, reaching Jinotega just before nightfall. A mountain town built with uniform slabs of gray concrete, Jinotega was the last town before descending into the jungle going west, and there would be nothing resembling a town for two whole days, only farmhouses and huts with leaky roofs and dirty children splashing in muddy streams. For two days they followed the dirt road, crossing the rivers Tuma and Prinzapolka where they had widened to create fordable shallows. The last town before arriving at the farm was Rosita, a trading post so ugly that no priest had been convinced to stay there for more than two months. La Rosita was little more than a collection of warehouses for miners and stores selling 80-proof rum. Gold-diggers from out West would come in to trade with merchants out of Puerto Cabezas. It was the true border of Nicaragua, where the Pacific and the Atlantic regions of the country parted ways. The only things that seemed to unite them were the rum and the prostitutes milling about the rum shop.

A full day out of Rosita the headlights of the jeep beamed onto a wooden cross that had been pulled down and bent into a makeshift milestone. "*Lamer5ed*" it read in clumsily drawn letters. Somoza tapped the driver on the arm and pointed with his finger, screaming above the noise of the engine: "That's it, the sign there."

The farm they entered was different from any farm Fausto had ever seen. It had none of the usual Moorish layout: no courtyard patio with shady trees, and no servant quarters. On this farm, Fausto noticed as they walked through the main building, all the rooms were the same. Somoza seemed to read his thoughts. "German," he nodded, pointing towards a wooden shield hanging from the wall of the living room.
"*Über allem die Liebe*" it read. Fausto tried to pronounce the words, but the strange sequence of letters felt awkward to his mouth.
"What does it mean, Major?" he asked when he had finished tasting the words. Somoza's eyes looked larger than usual through the thick glasses. Fishlike, as if the glasses themselves had been filled with water. "It's German, Lieutenant, who cares what it means! The Germans lost the war, that's all that matters. Who cares what they wrote on their walls!"
They spent four days on the farm. It had thick walls made of bamboo and sisal, with layers of adobe cemented between the bamboo trunks. The rooms were cool in spite of the heat, and the caretaker was quick to pump up cool water from the well. Somoza sent the men out

in the morning to survey the land and tally the cattle and water sources, and the accountants wrote everything up in neatly kept ledgers. In the afternoon, they pulled out the boxes and crates they had found in the storage room.

"Separate, boys," Somoza said. "Separate all the tools, the rest you can pile up outside."

At night they played cards, and drank the beer they had brought with them.

On the last evening, Somoza ordered the pile of garbage to be burned, as part of the general cleaning of his father's new property.

"What about this trunk, Major?" Fausto said. He pointed to an old leather trunk covered with a blooming mold.

"What's in it?"

"Books, it seems, but they've been eaten by termites." He pulled out a crumbling stack of papers held together by a leather spine. Somoza gestured, and the men hauled the trunk to the edge of the pyre, turning it inside out. Sifting through the dusty paper mass with a stick, Fausto felt something solid. Shaking off the dirt, he pulled out a book that had survived the onslaught of termites and time. The calf hide was intact, feeling taut and glass-like, and held in place by a metal clasp that kept the covers tightly squeezed together.

It was a diary, written in regular strokes on neatly trimmed pages that belied the years it had spent in the belly of a jungle, while countless blind termites had made their home nearby. It was as if they had never smelled it, had not noticed its presence among the pile of books that had been turned back into mindless cellulose. Fausto shrugged and closed the book, brushing the dirt off the front cover.

Something for Tomás, he thought. *Always has his nose inside a book, and the smellier the better.* He slid it inside his bag, and joined the others.

In the early hours of the fifth day, Fausto felt someone kicking him in the soles of his feet.

"Get up, Fausto, and be quiet!" Somoza hissed. He looked up to see the major with naked torso, pistol in hand and pants held up by a suspender belt. Outside, the moon shone with a pale round face, while the new day timidly dawned over the horizon, coloring the sky with pastel colors.

"Look there now, Fausto, see those beggars stealing my water?" Fausto rubbed his eyes once more as he peered through the window. The "beggars" were village women, five of them: an old woman, two women half her age, and two young girls. They were walking towards the well, apprehensive and alert, like deer suspecting an ambush. In their hands were plastic buckets that had once been bright yellow. Slowly they cranked up the lever and started pumping water, the sound of metal grinding against metal, mixed with that of slow-moving water carried far by the thin air of an early morning. The old woman gestured to the others to not make noise.

"Can't have these Indians stealing my water," the major hissed. "*Indios jodidos*, I'll give them water." He pulled the door wide open and ran out into the pale morning sun. "Follow me, men," he shouted.

Startled, the girl who was cranking the pump let go of the force rod. It shot up in the air, knocking her back, and a trickle of blood welled up from the left corner of her mouth. The two women rushed to her and lifted her head, shook it left and right, but her arms had gone limp against her body. The younger of the two women started sobbing and rubbing the girl's face, smearing blood and dirt into her nose and eyes. The old woman sat motionless. She looked up at Somoza who had stopped six feet away from her, hands akimbo. Suddenly she reached behind her and pulled out a short, broad knife, a knife for gutting fish. She came to her feet fast, much faster than anyone would have expected from a woman her age, and lurched forward, the knife traveling ahead of her. Had the major not had his pistol ready, the old woman would surely have stuck the knife in his potbelly.

As it was, however, Somoza had time to fire two shots: one at her head, and one at her heart. It was as if he had been waiting for her, as if this were shooting practice. He looked back at Fausto and winked, as if to say: "This is how it's done: clean and simple, no second thoughts." He beckoned with his pistol: a short, jerking movement of the hand, as if he were a conductor directing an orchestra of bodies, moving them from one place to another, and only he knew the whole partita – when one instrument would fall silent and others would need to join in.

"Tell them to take the water to the bathroom, Lieutenant," he said, pointing to the women and girl huddling behind the well. "And if they want water, we'll give them water!" He trained his pistol on one of the women and laughed, before holstering it again. The soldiers led the women away; they were screaming words that none of the men understood.

"Damn Indians," one of the soldiers yelled as he slapped her in the face, "when are you going to learn Spanish, when are you going to realize that you live in Nicaragua?" Fausto stooped to check the fallen girl's neck, but one look at her eyes was enough to see that she was dead. When he rolled her over, he saw the bulging outline of her body. Something stirred inside it. Something trapped and slowly dying. He imagined small feet kicking, small fists punching against the walls of the uterus, a voiceless cry, eyes that had not yet opened looking for light, and then the ebbing away of oxygen, the slow death that comes from stagnant blood trapped inside chambers and arteries.

"Major," he said. "This girl was pregnant!"

Somoza looked at the girl, then at Fausto, and wagged a finger.

"Don't try to pin that one on me, Fausto," he laughed. "First time I see this girl, swear to God!" The other men laughed, too, and then they all turned around and went back into the house, pushing the women ahead of them.

Fausto looked back at the body of the girl lying before him; her belly had stopped moving now.

"It's over," he said to himself. "So what good does it do to mention it? Did I think I could have saved this girl? There's nothing I could have done. This man doesn't take no for an answer." He bent over and closed the girl's eyes.

On the way back, they stopped in Siuna. The jeeps had gotten stuck several times, and the traction board had broken in two under the wheels that were idling in the soupy mud.

"Termites," the sergeant concluded, "we should have checked it when we had time. We won't make it to Jinotega, *jefe*," he said, "We'll make it to Siuna, that's the best we can do." There was no garrison in Siuna. In fact, there was only one guesthouse, a ramshackle building made of breezeblocks with a tavern attached to it, the very last house on the paved road that went from Managua as far as Siuna.

Somoza beckoned for Fausto to join him.

"Sit, Fausto," he said, "sit with me and have a drink." Fausto plucked up a chair and set it next to the major's, who pushed the bottle of rum his way.

"Let's have a drink, Fausto, I think we deserve it!" Their glasses touched lightly. The major made slurping noises, trying to get the chicken meat out from between his teeth. When he was finished he clicked his tongue and swallowed. Fausto remained silent. He sloshed around the rum in his glass without looking at the major.

"What's eating you, soldier?" Somoza said. He scratched his belly and belched.

"I was thinking about what happened back on that farm, Major."

"That was self-defense, Lieutenant," Somoza said with a straight face. "You saw how that old Indian goat came jumping at my throat with a knife. All self-defense, and on my own property to boot! She was trespassing! Look here, Fausto, you either eat or are eaten. Look at nature; look at the tigrillo, the boa, any predator. They all know that when you stop eating you become prey yourself. We are a pack of wolves, but when we stand still long enough, we will be hauled away by ants, and hollowed out by roaches, termites, and grasshoppers, all the stinking vermin!" He brought down his fist as he spoke the last words.

"Too much old wives' talk around here," he said, "too much trying to be nice to people, we all know that shit doesn't work. Are you with me, Fausto?"

He saw a rippling stomach, and a fluttering shirt that stained red even before he had lowered his gun. *It's a job,* he thought. *They order me, and I do the job. I ask no questions.*

"Yes, Major," he said. "I'm with you, Major." He clamped down his teeth until his jaws hurt, while Somoza served another round of rum and pushed the glass back to him.

"I don't force people, Lieutenant. Everybody here knows what they are expected to do. No surprises."

"Yes, Major," he said again. "I understand, Major."

The trip back to Managua was uneventful. Everyone was quiet, and not even Somoza could muster the energy to draw circles and lines on the jacket of the driver in front of him. Fausto stuck the diary in his locker at the barracks, and slowly it got covered with other things. And then one day, when he was about to go back to León on leave, he rummaged through his locker and found it again. He looked at it, smelled it, and winced. He took it home with him, if only because there was no place for books in the barracks. He left it at his parents' house, where it was forgotten once more, and ended up inside a rusty metal trunk.

One day he accompanied his boss on a trip north, to Chinandega. Once they had left León behind them, the road passed through cotton fields on both sides. Somoza was humming.

"You know anything about cotton, Fausto?"

"A little, Major," Fausto replied. "My family…"

"Ah, yes, your family. So what do you think of this cotton here?"

"Impressive," Fausto said. "Everything looks squeaky clean."

"Exactly," Somoza snapped. "Squeaky clean is the word. So let's go visit the owner, shall we?" He tapped the driver on the back when the fields were interrupted by a wall, and then a gate, and soon they entered the driveway that opened up to a large mansion. The planter was surprised to see the President's son on his driveway, and instantly stiffened. But when Fausto introduced himself, he relaxed.

"So you're Rogelio's boy?" he said. "Why don't you two come in and have a drink?"

They settled in on rocking chairs behind the house, near the pool where children were playing.

"How's the cotton?" Somoza said. "Doing well this year?"

"Can't complain," the planter answered. Fausto was listening from a distance. He was sitting to the side, as he had learned by now, listening in on the conversation with one ear, while keeping the other one open for spotting trouble.

"Have you considered teaming up with us?" Somoza said. "We could help out with some facilities perhaps." The planter was an old man, and could easily have been Somoza's grandfather.

"Look here, boy," he said. "I've been running this farm for many years now, and have two sons to help me. It's nice of you to offer, but we're doing just fine here."

"No problem," Somoza said. "We're here to help, you know. Just let us know if you change your mind."

They visited tens of farms during the trip, and Fausto noticed how the major kept meticulous records in a small notebook.

"Curious, eh, Lieutenant?" Somoza said when he saw Fausto glance at his notebook. "You're wondering what the hell is going on here, right?" Fausto smiled sheepishly.

"Good thing you're not asking too many questions." Somoza scraped his throat and scratched his belly before continuing: "We're taking stock," he said. "We're taking care of this country, making sure it lives up to its potential." Fausto raised his eyebrows, and Somoza winked. "Some of these of guys are stuck in the past," he said. "Small holdings, nothing mechanized, bad pest management, you name it. So we're taking stock."

One month later, they went up north again. The three jeeps whirled forward over the highway, but this time the cotton looked brown and diseased. Somoza kept looking at him, but Fausto kept mum.

"Damn, Fausto, what do you say of that, eh?" Somoza said at last. "Looks like something nasty hit the cotton here, what say you?"

"A bug," Fausto said. "Must have been a bug – but how, and so fast?" Somoza chuckled but said nothing.

They did not turn into the driveway of the old planter's house this time. Instead, they went straight into town. The bank was housed in a small building with paint that had long faded, and two soldiers standing guard.

"Two of our guys," Somoza gestured to Fausto as he walked past the soldiers. "We provide them as protection against bank robbers. For a fee of course, ha-ha! None of these banks gets robbed when our guys are standing guard, believe you me!" Somoza went into a small office with one of the bank managers, and Fausto saw through a window that the bank manager showed his boss some papers. Somoza shoved the papers away, impatiently. The whole discussion took less than five minutes, and when his boss came out Fausto knew that he was not happy.

"They forget who their friends are," Somoza grumbled when they were back in the car. "Ungrateful bunch, they keep sticking up for these damn bourgeois landowners. My father is right. But we'll see who laughs last. We'll see."

Not too long after, Fausto was sent on a trip to Chinandega by himself.

"Go do this for me, Lieutenant," Somoza said as he lit up a cigarette. "I am going to trust you on this."

The banker gave him an envelope.

"Open it," he said. "I want you sign for this." When Fausto looked at the paper, he saw it was the deed to the cotton farm.

"What's this?" he said.

"What does it look like?" the banker said. "Seems someone put in a winning bid on a foreclosed cotton farm. Poor sod," he went on, "terrible blight attacking out of nowhere. No reserves and the whole farm put up as security for their loan. This farm has been in their family for more than half a century, but what can I do? I run a bank, not a charity."

"Does this happen a lot?" Fausto said.

"The blight or the foreclosing?"

Fausto blinked.

"Where do I sign?" he said.

The banker read back his signature: "Cortés?" he said. "Are you a Cortés? From León?

"Yes, something wrong with that?"

The banker raised his shoulders. "Who am I to say if there's something wrong with that?"

Chapter 11

Anatomy, he thought, peering at the bones laid out on the table. *The perfect machine.* He liked the lab: the quiet, the order. The constancy of temperature and light. He spent long days and evenings dissecting corpses, marveling at their silent and never-ending complexity.

"Our bodies have not changed in thousands of years," he told his classmate Manolo. "Just think how marvelous that is. All these parts — exactly the way Hippocrates described them to us."

"You can't look at body parts as separate from people, Tomás," Manolo laughed. "Doesn't work like that. It's not a pair of shoes you're talking about; it's a person."

"Of course," Tomás said. "I understand that."

"Do you really, Tomás? Sometimes I think you talk about body parts as if they were persons. As if they could substitute for them. And why do you spend so much time with these cadavers? I can't stand the smell of pickles that hangs around them."

Tomás looked up, genuinely surprised. "I don't smell anything," he said.

He explained to Ana the long bones and the short bones, and the others, the ones that could not be properly categorized.

"Only two types then?" she said, snuggling up to him.

He told her about a boy one day, a boy who had died of tuberculosis.

"What was his name?" she said. He did not know, although he remembered that a name had been scribbled on a cardboard tag tied to a big toe.

"So small," he said, "this boy should have been almost my size, but he weighed almost nothing."

"So sad," she said, "his mother must have suffered. It would be very difficult to lose a child, don't you think?"

"I don't know," he said. "I cannot imagine having children."

She froze. "What do you mean, Tomás?"

"I'm not sure I want to have children."

"I want children," Ana said, "I love children, don't you?

"Of course," he said. "Of course I do."

She stared at him with wide-open eyes. "I don't understand," she said.

How can I have children? he thought. *It's a cruel world, and who says I will be a better father than my own father was? An accidental father, is that what I want to be?*

Rafaela found in her in the garden, alone.

"What is happening, Ana?" she said, taking the chewed-up cinnamon stick out of her mouth.

Ana shrugged. "Girls don't go to school, you know that."

"Hmmm. Would you want to go to school?"

"Why ask the question?"

"Because you need to know what you want in life."

"Did you want to go to school when you were young?"

Rafaela looked away. A breeze came into the garden, and she felt how it landed on her arms, lifting the down, then flattening it against her skin once more.

"I don't want to become a lonely woman, *Tía*," Ana said. Then she saw her aunt's face, and regretted her words.

"There are many ways to be happy," Rafaela said. "And you're too young to think about loneliness."

"I don't think Tomás wants to have children."

"Has he told you that?"

She shook her head. "He says he's not sure."

"Is it him you want, or children?"

She tilted her head, and thought about the question.

"Why do I need to choose?"

"You don't. But you need to know what's more important to you. And so does he."

One day, there were no more long bones and short bones to be shown and explained. He came to her from class, wearing his lab coat still, although no stethoscope. She leaned into him and breathed in deeply, as she always did, expecting the scent of juniper that had surrounded him for as long as she could remember. But it was gone.

Panic struck her, so she inhaled again, but the tanginess that reminded her of lemons and apples, and carried within it a hint of bitterness; the smell that had enchanted her when she was young, had faded. And now that it was gone, she saw only a boy. No longer the promise of a man, he was just a boy who had not grown up; a boy who had exchanged one toy for another. And she realized that her happiness would not come from him.

Fausto shot himself in the leg while cleaning his pistol, and was sent home for two months.

"Better than languishing in the military hospital," the doctor said.

Somoza came to see him before he went home to León. "Stupid thing to do, Fausto," he said. "Always make sure you know whether your gun is loaded before you do anything with it."

The aunts were delighted to have a young lieutenant at home. He had started growing a moustache that hid his lopsided smile.

"Dashing!" the aunts said, except for Rafaela.

"He looks so much like the ancestor," they said. "The same commanding looks, those ears lying flat against his head like a wolf's!" Every pore in his skin screamed "conquest," and if there was anything his uniform did, it was drive home the message that he was cut out for things so great that the whole Cortés family might very well be swallowed by them one day, as if by a giant fish, and that nothing would remain of its name, its ancestors, or any of the glorious lore that each generation of Cortéses had passed on to the next, throughout a century of blinding certainty.

"You need to exercise that leg," Doctor López had told him, so he started long walks around the grounds. He hated the crutches, but there was no other way. Every day he got up at dawn and walked for one hour, and then again before nightfall. Some of the children were up early, and played with his crutches when he let them.

"I am the Gigantona," a small girl crowed as she climbed on top of one of the crutches, while two boys were holding it steady. Fausto laughed, and let the children play with his crutches, and with him.

Ana saw. She saw what Fausto himself did not see. She saw how he was not paralyzed by doubts or guilt. *He frightens me*, she thought, as she watched him from behind her bedroom window. Below, she saw him chase two boys and a girl running away with his crutches. He was limping, but his face showed excitement only.

Fausto spun the knife lying on the table in front of him. Like a top, it swirled with clockwork pace, perfectly balanced on the glass eye riveted into the bolster.

I'm screwed, he thought, *no matter what I do, I'm screwed one way or the other.* He let his fist come down on the knife, stopping it dead. *These doubts, I need to put them behind me, or else they'll slow me down. I will leave my doubts here, in my home. The boss is right: there is no place for doubters in the Guard.*

He ran his finger over the blade. He tasted the iron through his pores until he reached the jagged roughness that promised pain.

I need a place to come back to, he thought. *If I do what they ask of me, I must know where to come back and find myself again. Why can't I be like Tomás? He can doubt all he wants; no one asks him to stop doubting. I must keep him close to me; I cannot afford to lose him. Not to Ana, and not to anyone else.* He rubbed his finger back and forth over the blade, and did not stop when his skin broke and blood dripped down onto the bandage on his thigh. *I am my own blood brother now,* he thought, and held the knife under his nose. *Sweet, sweet and mine alone. Now I know what to do.*

She was a girl still, barely eighteen, when Fausto asked her out. For the first time she felt that a man wanted her as a man wants a woman. Neither one had ever mentioned what had happened in the tall saw grass that night on the beach. She preferred for him to not remember it. She had watched him as he flirted with girls selling fruit and tortillas. It did not matter to her. The more he flirted, the more she desired him. She had fallen in love with Fausto without knowing why. *It was his manliness,* she decided. *The absence of hesitation, of doubts. He seems so certain, so sure...*

He wanted Ana because she helped him come back to the life he thought had slipped from him. When he was with her, it was as if that other life, the life with the Guardia, did not exist. As if it could be thought out of existence for a day, or an hour. He did not tell her what it was he needed to do, or how. Her presence was enough for him, he told her. *And Tomás will never leave Ana. He will stay with her, and with me. I know that Ana will bind him to me.*

The day she told him that she was seeing Fausto, Tomás felt as if he had been hit by a truck. But he was angry with himself, not with her. *Stupid,* he thought, *I am stupid, and Fausto is not. Does she not see that he is as unclean as I am? But what can I offer her? I cannot give her what she wants: a family, children. They are all abandoned, eventually.*

"Doesn't it bother you that Fausto is dating Ana?" his mother said.

He shrugged. "Why should it? We were just kids, that doesn't count."

"I started dating your father when I was eighteen," she said. "I didn't think we were just kids." He was surprised by her comment. She never mentioned his father, or even the life that she had lived before he was born.

"So what are you saying?"

"I am saying that there is never anything innocent about a boy and a girl seeing each other. Ask Sofía how old she was when she had her first child." She raised her voice: "Sofía, come for a moment, will you?" Sofía pulled her dress in place and stood behind Tomás's chair. When she put her hand on his shoulder, a lock of her hair fell against his face.

"Yes, Doña Victoria?" she said. "What did you want?"

"Sofía, can you tell Tomás here how old you were when you met your husband?" She nodded at him: "You wait and see," she seemed to tell him.

"I was fourteen, Doña Victoria," Sofía said. "And my first child was born when I was fifteen. We had five children together."

"And did you have a boyfriend before that?" Victoria continued.

"No, Doña Victoria, with my people we don't have boyfriends, we meet each other and we get married."

"Thank you, Sofía."

"There," she said when Sofía was beyond earshot. "Even Sofía, who is practically a saint, got caught up in the boy-girl game before she had even learned to write her name! What do you say to that?"

"What's the matter with you?" he said. "She decided she wants to be with him, what part of that is so hard to understand?"

"You'll regret it," she said. "You'll regret this for the rest of your life. And so will she. It's not too late. Go to her. Talk to her, and you'll see she'll rethink this whole business."

He didn't. But he did keep a picture of Ana in his room for months. He looked at her face, her smile. He looked for a sign that would deliver him, something that would tell him he had been right. It never came.

Fausto decided to ask his cousin to be his best man.

"You can't do that, Fausto," Ana said, but he laughed it off.

"Why not?" he said. "I know Tomás; he'll just brush it off with some rational argument." She felt sorry for Tomás, but he insisted.

"Better pick someone else," Tomás told him. "I don't think I can escape from the lab."

Fausto looked disappointed, but he shook his hand and said: "I understand, cousin. Duty, right?"

"Yes," Tomás said. "I made a promise."

He told himself that he would lock himself up in the lab that day. But when his mother told him that the President would attend the wedding, he closed the door of his room and pulled out the drawer of his desk. Shoving aside pens and rulers, matchbooks and playing cards, he eventually found the things time had pushed towards the bottom of the drawer.

The switchblade knife and the rabbit pouch were tangled up in a thick and moldy leather cord.

"There you are," he said. "I knew you would be waiting for me, both of you."

On the day Ana and Fausto were to get married, Tomás drove to the mansion. The wedding had all the pomp expected of a major Cortés event, with hundreds of people milling about the front lawn. Fausto looked handsome in his gala uniform, tanned and with a full black mustachio. When Tomás saw Ana standing next to Fausto, a corsage made of apricot blossom pinned to her dress, he swallowed deep. *Too bad*, he thought. *You are leaving me no choice. It must be done, and it must be done now.*

He was surprised to see so many cousins, many of whom he had not seen in years. Cousins twice removed, cousins three times removed; after four generations it was only at weddings and funerals that all of Don Pablo's offspring found reasons to meet. Tomás shook hands, all the while keeping his left hand lodged inside his pocket, where the blade was resting and gradually growing warmer against his hand. He started sweating, and moved into the house.

When the President arrived, the guests rushed into the courtyard. Somoza stood on the side step of his Cadillac and waved, taking in the cheers, while his son shook hands with Fausto. The guest of honor, the President was soon seated at the head table. He was in a good mood; he had plenty of reasons to be happy, as he was now the richest man in the country.

"It's official," he had told his sons. He was chatting with Rogelio – nothing serious, no business. Tomás walked towards the head table, slowly, clasping the knife and looking down to avoid seeing cousins whose hands he did not want to shake. He felt the shortness of breath come over him, like a fist clenching his throat. With his free hand he touched his breast pocket, looking for the pouch that contained the syringe and the vial of adrenaline. *Not now*, he thought, *just a little more, almost there.*

The hand on his throat tightened its grip, and his head was near bursting. He sat down on a chair against the wall and tried to control his breathing. At that moment someone slapped him on the back, hard. He gasped for air, but it was the slap, he realized, not the asthma. He relaxed when he saw that the only people looking at him were third-degree cousins.

"Tomás, I thought you couldn't make it!" Fausto exclaimed, crouching beside him. "And what just happened to you? Did you swallow a bone?" He grinned. "Did I just save your life?" he said. "Don't tell me I just saved your life, cousin!" Tomas clasped the knife even harder, and his hand tore through the thin lining of his pocket.

"What's that in your hand?" Fausto said. "Your syringe?"

"No," Tomás said, "no, it's nothing. Just something I had in my pocket."

Fausto kept looking at him, but the grin was gone.

"Just something, eh?" he said. "So why don't you show it to me?"

"It's nothing. Something I was going to give away."

Fausto wagged a finger at him. "Ah," he said, "you always were a good gift-giver, cousin. But come now; let me introduce you to the general. I'm sure that's why you came, no?"

Tomás fluttered his hand as they both stood up.

"I know what it's in your pocket, cousin," Fausto whispered. "If you want I can introduce you to him. You'll get real close."

"No need," Tomás said, "I'm done here; I don't feel too well." But it was too late: Fausto was waiving at his father, who was busy presenting new members of the Cortés clan to the President, who gave a lukewarm hand to the boys and a peck on the cheek to the ladies.

"Good," he said, approvingly. "You are taking care of the future, Rogelio, we need large families." He saw Fausto waving across the room, and pointed at him.

"Who's that young man over there, standing by your son?" he said. "He looks familiar, but I can't place him."

"My nephew, general," Rogelio said. "My sister Victoria's son." Somoza continued looking at Tomás, searching for something that would jog his memory.

"Your sister Victoria? There's something about him that…what's his name?"

Rogelio swallowed. "Delacorte, Señor Presidente, Tomás Delacorte Cortés." He had tried to slur the first part, but there was nothing to be done. The words had been heard.

"Ah." The general's face remained expressionless, and then again: "Ah, I see. The widow's son." Perhaps the sight of Tomás brought back memories he might have preferred buried forever. He watched as Fausto tried to drag his cousin towards the head table, but then the other boy broke loose and ran away. Somoza nodded and raised his glass: "Let's toast, old friend. To friendship and long life!"

"To friendship and long life," Rogelio repeated. But his efforts to keep the general animated fell flat from there. Somoza seemed to have retreated into himself, a brooding tortoise who only looked up from time to time to take in the sight of young people dancing. Just before dinner, something happened that changed the old sourpuss's mood: a young girl was brought to the podium to sing. She was four or five perhaps, slender and with deep-set eyes and thick wiry hair that had resisted combing. Just a girl in a swirling pink dress singing songs for a newlywed couple.

The President was pleased with the singing. He started tapping the table and humming along. When the girl finished singing, he asked for an encore.

"Sing me 'Volver,' *chiquita*," he said. She looked aside to her mother, an elegant woman in a tight polka-dot dress. Her mother took her hand and started humming the lines, and the girl fell in, timidly at first, and then, as the orchestra came in, with more verve.

"Bravo," the general said as she finished singing. He held up his glass for another whiskey to be poured and slapped his knee.

"What's your name?" he said. Somoza asked for everyone's name, all the time. He was legendary for remembering names, and facts connected to the names.

"Faces are not my strong suit," he quipped to his lieutenants, "but names I never forget, got them all written up in the big ledger," and he pointed at his forehead. His lieutenants laughed, but meanwhile were thinking: *Am I in that ledger? What could the old coot possibly have written up about me?*

"I keep track of everyone worth keeping track of," he told his sons. "That's what you get from owning an insurance business. You two had better remember that, because when you forget a name you're in deep shit. Names run this place, more than money!"

"Will you take me to Paris?" she said.

"Of course!" Fausto said. "Paris it is!"

But it did not happen. "Orders," he said. "I have received orders to leave for Ocotal." She cried, and he was quick to tell her that Paris would come later. He took her on outings instead: the Social Club, a military parade, the weddings of other cousins. She enjoyed the visits, the dances and the parades, the people she was meeting. *Paris*, she thought, *almost Paris.*

Tomás threw himself into his studies with more zeal than ever.

"Good eye for detail," his professors wrote.

He found it hard to deal with the sick and infirm. It bothered him somehow that healthy parts were attached to a sick limb or organ. *If only there were no body attached to this fatty liver, it would be so much easier,* he caught himself thinking. He would have preferred to see the diseased part only, without having to deal with the probing questions, the begging eyes, the need to be comforted or reassured.

Although Tomás did not broach the subject of his mother's escapades, this was not reciprocal. She made snide remarks about the girls he took out for drinks or a meal. At first he felt hurt, but then he started hiding his escapades from her. And yet, she always seemed to know about his adventures, and seldom approved of his choices. She made comments on their language, the way they dressed, the families to which they belonged.

"That girl I saw you with yesterday, she looks like a crane, or no, a stork rather, all legs and a tiny head." Or: "I heard that her grandmother came from Niquinohomo. That explains the awkward manners, I presume." Tomás rarely acknowledged her sneers, but often, from the moment his mother made a comment, he lost interest in the girl. He realized that he was seldom attracted to girls his own age – their giggles made him feel nervous and insecure. Instead, he looked for older women, and they seemed to look for him. He felt comforted by the absence of coyness that was replaced by a bluntness of purpose that did not expect him to prove himself.

He started sleeping with a prostitute, and after a while realized that sleeping with her made everything easier. There was no explaining to be done, no need to justify his acts. It was clean, as clean as a newly whetted scalpel. After the third encounter, while watching her dress, he asked for her name.

"Lola," she said.

"Lola? Unusual name."

"I'm an unusual girl," she said. "But you can call me whatever you want. Some guys call me mama, others call me *puta*." She shrugged and put the money inside her bra.

"Aren't you afraid it will fall out?" he said.

She looked at him as if trying to decide whether he was mocking her or genuinely concerned. Then she bent over and kissed him on the mouth.

"Thank you for caring about me, baby," she said.

He did not go and see Lola again. There was no need for it, he realized. Once or twice, never more than that with the same woman.

Don't give them time to remember me. Don't give them time to remember who I am or what I have said, or give me a name. A total stranger, that is easiest. And since he looked for older women, he soon realized that there was an endless supply of women about to leave the business, and this suited his purpose perfectly. *I'm tricking time,* he thought. *I'm tricking time into believing that I will grow old as my putas grow old, but the truth is that I am outliving them all!*

In the dry season that followed his graduation, Victoria told her son that Fausto was leaving for Guatemala, "on a special mission."

"I'm on loan," Fausto told him. "Believe it or not, I'm on loan like a stupid library book." He laughed, a shrill laugh.

The week after, Tomás read about the coup in Guatemala. Somoza's newspaper ran glowing editorials praising the country's return to democracy, courtesy of the democratic forces of Guatemala, and assisted by troops from the equally democratic armed forces from neighboring Nicaragua and El Salvador. The paperboy sat with him and chewed on a mango pit. Slowly, until the pit was dry and hairy. The boy accompanied him until he had finished reading, and meanwhile held his own paper upside down, looking at letters he did not understand. When Tomás finished reading he gave the paper back to the boy, and half a córdoba, "to get yourself something to eat," he said. The paperboy walked away into the sun, and the heat did not bother him.

Chapter 12

If there was one thing Fausto learned in Guatemala, it was that power, real power, comes not from men wielding guns but rather from a mind relentlessly chipping and hacking away at a person's sense of belonging. Others would have called it torture perhaps, but Fausto's masters called it control. Learning this had been a revelation. For the first time he felt that he owed no explanations, no justification for his acts. He was free to do whatever he wanted, with no arbiter other than himself. A room had been opened in his mind, a room he had not known existed. It was dark and windowless. He had been let in and a lamp had been switched on for just one second during which he had realized that somewhere in the recesses of his mind there was unexplored territory vaster than he had ever imagined. In this room, he waltzed around a person who had a name and a face, and looked up at him with trust and expectation. But soon the expectation disappeared, and then the trust, and eventually the person ended up naked: a faceless body tied to a chair. He enjoyed the sight of the slumped body. Not for its nakedness, but for the surrender it represented: a bag of bones no longer possessed of a will or a sense of purpose. He controlled the exits. He knew where the doors were, and where the light switch was. The knowledge that he was in full command became an ephedrine trigger, a wild and violent wave of pleasure that washed over him like a breaker wave.

When the light in this room was turned off again he felt hungry, and wanted nothing more than to see it again, be in it again. If finding the key to this room meant lying, so be it. If it meant hurting, so be it. Accepting this was not something he had thought about and decided — it had simply happened to him, because it could. He had stopped asking why things were done, and each question that was not asked brought rewards. Colonel Castillo, his new boss, gave him an order and saw the question forming in his young charge's head. And then he saw it die, and knew that Fausto had banished the thought. He was told to arrest troublemakers, people associated with Arbenz's alleged band of communists. And he did, arriving at a house in the early hours of the morning, telling his men to kick in the door before any rooster could crow. It was disciplined and planned, and Fausto kept from this a lifelong discipline for daybreak raids. He cherished the moments when he sat in the jeep while the night receded and the first glimmer of day dawned on the horizon. He learned by doing: he stood outside the homes and surveyed the ravages, and saw that it was good.

"Now," he barked, and his men rushed in, as if they had been waiting for this one word to unleash their aggression, a jealously guarded shibboleth. They broke down the bolted doors that were meant to keep the sleeping bodies inviolate. The women, used to the cries of babies and children seeking their mothers' presence, were always the first ones to wake up when the soldiers burst in. They ran in nightgowns that flowed behind them, and locked themselves into their children's rooms. Then the men rose, drunk still with the drug of sleep, and reached for the machete they kept leaning against the night table, or the revolver in the drawer.

It was always too late. Fausto's men were well trained. They were men themselves, and knew how the deepness of a man's sleep makes him an enemy of the day's early light. Fausto's men kicked and shouted, they snarled like tigrillos. They took the men and the boys, sometimes the women too, and were out again in minutes.

Fausto never went inside himself; he always left the work of kicking in doors to others. Hundreds of people were rounded up and thrown in prison this way, often on the whim of a neighbor who had an ax to grind, land to grab, or a business to destroy. Colonel Castillo and his new government asked few questions.

"Where there's smoke, there's fire," Castillo said. "Let God sort them out."

He was sent to escort the former president on his way into exile. Jacobo Arbenz was holed up in the Mexican Embassy, where he had requested asylum, and for a while the *putchistas* toyed with the idea of not letting him out, and putting him on trial instead. Castillo talked to some of the other brass, and he made some long-distance phone calls. Then he called in Fausto: "I have a job for you, Fausto."

"Yes, sir, Colonel."

"I need for you to accompany Arbenz to the airport. But rough him up first. The soldiers will do it if you don't feel like it. And I need pictures taken."

"It's fine, sir. I will do it.

"Do what, Fausto, take the pictures?"

"No, sir, the other part, sir!"

Castillo lit a cigarette. His eyes became dark mirrors as he watched the young lieutenant in front of him. "Do you enjoy this, Fausto?"

"Sir?"

"Do you enjoy roughing up prisoners, Fausto?"

"They are prisoners, sir."

Castillo stared at him. "I can see why General Somoza has taken a liking to you." He flashed a grin.

"All right then, Fausto, but make sure he keeps that pretty face of his. We don't want the press to think we torture people here. So just get him out of here tonight – there is a plane waiting at La Aurora, to take a whole bunch of those *comunista*s to Mexico. Make sure he's on it. And take pictures. We'll show the world how we deal with comunistas down here. Eisenhower will love it!"

Fausto took a fire team over to the embassy. When the convoy reached the airport, a small group of journalists had already assembled. Fausto made a sign to the soldiers who were with him; they pulled Arbenz out of the car and into the terminal building using a back door, while the journalists were being herded into the main building. The Mexicans protested that he was under their protection, but Arbenz himself did not pip a squeak.

"Don't worry," Fausto told the Mexicans. "We'll get him back to you in a short while. A security check in the VIP room, that's all." They closed the door while the embassy staff was escorted into the main building. Inside the VIP room, Fausto motioned for Arbenz to sit down, and the two soldiers positioned themselves behind him. Then he motioned for the airport staff to leave.

"Señor Presidente," Fausto said. Arbenz had been in the military his whole life, and knew what was coming. He was like a goalkeeper deciding which way to fall – left or right. Fifty percent chance to get the right side, half that again for watching carefully where the striker is shifting his eyes. *Shifting left, he'll shoot right, shifting right, he'll shoot for left. Educated guesswork.*

"Young man," Arbenz said. "Have you ever read this book? It's a classic." He held up a thumbed book with a scratched and dog-eared cover. *The Art of War*, it read, in large red letters.

"I'm not interested in books, Señor Presidente," Fausto said. "They all look the same to me."

Arbenz was barely forty, but his hair had started graying around the temples. *He looks like a banker*, Fausto decided, *like the banker from Chinandega who was too chicken to stand his ground.*

"I was wondering," he said, "I was wondering why you gave up so easily. Castillo only had a couple of hundred men; you had thousands. Why didn't you fight?"

Arbenz gave him a cold look.

"You're not Guatemalan, are you?" he said. "Let me guess: Nicaraguan? Did Castillo bring you back from Nicaragua? I hope he pays you well."

Fausto pulled out his bowie knife and held it in front of the other man's face.

"What's this?" Arbenz smirked.

"It's for you."

Arbenz' face twitched as Fausto let it rest against the mole on his cheek.

"I don't need a knife," he said. But he did not laugh again. "Did Castillo come up with this?"

"No," Fausto said, "no, this one is mine. Since you're a coward, I thought I would give you a second chance. But I guess I was wrong. Cowards don't get second chances."

He felt like playing with this man. *Amazing*, he thought. *This man was the president of a whole country only two months ago, and now he is a coward sneaking out of his own house at night. Just because we told him to.* He blew on the knife and sheathed it.

"I heard about you," Arbenz said. "You're the knife guy, aren't you? Castillo sends you out on dirty jobs, right?" He shook his head and clicked his tongue.

"As you wish," Fausto said. "I made you an offer, but if you don't want it, we can do this differently." He made a fist and landed it on the other man's upper arm.

"Drop the fucking book," he barked. "You won't need a fucking book where you're going."

Fausto turned to the soldiers. "Hold him," he said, "and take off his shirt." When the two were holding Arbenz, then and only then did Fausto start knocking him in the chest and the stomach, and ultimately in the groin. It made him furious that the man had refused the knife. *Coward,* he thought, *if there's one thing I have no patience with, it's cowardice. Why the hell didn't you fight when you had the chance?* The more furious he became, the harder he hit the man. He almost forgot to breathe while he jabbed and knocked the wind out of him, until the man finally hung slumped, wheezing and gurgling.

"Enough classics for you, Mr. President?" he yelled. "Now let's see what all this book reading is good for, eh? Now let's see who's doing the thinking here and who's doing the doing!" He was panting while the two soldiers were holding Arbenz by the elbows and shoulders. He whispered something, so Fausto lowered his ear until it was close to the other man's mouth.

"What?" he said. "What are you saying?"

"Widow's son," Arbenz whispered. Fausto shook his head and shrugged.

"Whatever," he said.

"You're going to travel, Señor Presidente," he continued in a low voice, "so we want to make sure you're dressed for the occasion." He pulled out his knife again and lowered it, slowly, until it rested on Arbenz's hip. Quickly, he yanked at the man's waistband and cut through it until the fabric tore and his pants fell down to his ankles. The soldiers laughed when they saw Arbenz's long white underpants. Fausto fished a handkerchief out of his pocket to wipe his forehead and clean his hands. When he finished, he rolled the kerchief into a wet ball and threw it at Arbenz's face.

"Smile!" Fausto said. "It's time for picture taking, so smile for the camera, Mr. President. The whole world is watching you!" The soldiers propped him up until his arms were resting on their shoulders. They snuggled against him and smiled, as if they were children posing with their headmaster. Fausto took picture after picture, pulling back the lever until the camera stopped clicking.

"Let's get this son of a bitch on his way," he said. "After all there are journalists here waiting to snap some more pictures." One of the soldiers soaked a small towel into the ice bucket and rubbed Arbenz's face with it, then his arms and chest. When he could stand straight again, they pushed him ahead, into the bright lights of the terminal where the journalists and Mexican diplomats were waiting. They gasped and started talking, all of them at once. Fausto was undeterred, and did not stop for one second. He had his soldiers walk the man all the way through the terminal and out onto the tarmac in nothing but his underwear, and did not stop until they arrived at the waiting plane, a flurry of journalists and Mexican officials on their heels. Fausto saw frightened faces looking out at him through the small windows. He stood at the foot of the stairs and watched Arbenz as he climbed up and turned around once more, ready to speak. The propellers started turning, making a low whirring sound, as if two windmills were competing for attention.

Fausto fluttered his hands. "No more speeches," he said. "You're through with those, old man."

Chapter 13

Doctor Urbina was the most forgiving hospital director León had ever seen. He made the rounds twice a week, yet said nothing about the multitude of vendors who had set up shop on the hospital grounds to sell fried pork rind and battery-powered Madonna statues. But when it came to the seven-day rule he was utterly unyielding.

All the hospital beds were occupied in shifts, and the wounded and sick took turns sleeping and standing, or simply stretching out on the floors. However, no matter what their condition, according to the seven-day rule all of them were turned out of their beds on Saturday evening. Those who wanted to come back on Monday waited outside, patiently, to be readmitted, while an army of cleaners hosed down the corridors.

"Anyone can be cured in six days," Doctor Urbina would say.

"But, Doctor, there are cases…" someone would start.

"Nonsense," he overruled all objections. "Nonsense. If we cannot cure people in six days, we cannot cure them in six weeks either. It took God six days to create man and the whole world around him; I'm sure we can be just as diligent when we cure a single man! On the seventh day we all go home and rest!"

It was unusual for Doctor Urbina to set foot in the pathology lab.

"I dislike all those bits and pieces," he would say, "pieces of flesh with tags attached to them. It's like stepping into a butcher shop!" But he knew that he would find Tomás there.

"Come, my boy," he said as he started pushing him towards the door. "Come Tomás, there's something I want to show you. We have a special case, a military guy with liver problems, I'm ordering some blood work and…" He stopped as his gaze shifted towards the walls and came to rest on the vials with body parts floating in formaldehyde. "And tissue biopsies," he continued. Without waiting for a reaction he pushed Tomás out, his coattails fluttering behind him like tattered wings.

"I thought the military had their own hospital," Tomás said. "What happened, couldn't they solve the problem?"

"Why don't you ask him yourself?" Doctor Urbina said, "I'm sure he will appreciate the attention, and it will do you good to speak with patients for a change."

The soldier was a sergeant, middle-aged and with a yellow complexion, like scorched parchment.

Probably had too much to drink, Tomás thought. *That's what you get with these military types.* He pushed up the man's eyelids and peered inside.

"It says here that you are…Sergeant Solórzano, GN. Don't they treat guardsmen in the military hospital in Managua?"

"I live out in Quesalguaque," the man said. His left eye started twitching, as if it were doing the talking.

"I woke up with a terrible stomachache, and I didn't have time to go all the way to Managua. They told me to come here instead."

"OK," Tomás said, "we'll take care of you. Please take off your shirt now." The man turned slowly; each movement seemed to hurt him. When he took off his shirt Tomás noticed the wounds on his shoulder and right upper chest, just below the collarbone. They were fresh bullet wounds that had barely closed, as if the man had refused to acknowledge them.

Perhaps this man has no shutdown reflexes, he thought. *Perhaps his body is just a fighting machine that is not stopped by bullets or knives, only by a liver or a pancreas deciding that enough is enough.*

"What happened here?" he said, letting his hand float over the man's shoulder.

"Friendly fire. We were entering Guatemala City and the Salvadorans came in from the other side. Castillo's group was in the middle and God knows, I guess the commanders weren't talking to each other, so we all thought we were facing government forces and ended up shooting at each other."

"You were in Guatemala? With the invasion?"

"Yes," the man said. "I was sent home to recover but then this terrible pain woke me up this morning."

"So," Tomás continued, "so did you know Fausto Cortés there, Lieutenant Cortés?"

"Of course, who didn't?" the man said. "He is Colonel Castillo's aide-de-camp. Has quite a reputation, Doctor."

"Don't breathe now," Tomás said. He lowered the stethoscope and listened to the man's heartbeat. It was steady, a booming drone that nothing on earth could throw off course.

"A reputation for what?" He tried to sound less interested than he was.

"Well," the man said, "I know that he earned himself a nickname. They call him 'Lieutenant Knife.'"

"What did you say? Did you say '*Lieutenant Knife*?'"

"Lieutenant Knife, Doc, that's what he was called by all the men."

The man's heart rate went up in his ears it seemed, fast, until he thought the boom would burst his drums. *Is he lying?* Tomás thought.

"Why was that?" he said.

"Well, he seemed to enjoy it, Doc."

"Enjoy what, Sergeant?"

"The interrogations. Standard procedure, but sometimes you gotta be rough on them if you know what I mean. I'm sure you're not the queasy type, you being a doctor and all, I bet you get to see a lot of blood every day."

His head started spinning, but he managed to nod.

"So are you saying that Lieutenant Cortés was a skilled interrogator?"

"I guess that's what you could call it, Doc." The man started to laugh, but his laugh was cut short by Tomás's pressing down on his midriff. He was gasping for breath now but did not let out a sound.

Lieutenant Knife. It went through his head. The words sounded like the buzzing of a bumblebee or a mosquito, incessant and growing painfully loud. He continued prepping the man for the operation, but no longer listened to his babbling. *Lieutenant Knife,* he thought. *Could this be true? Fausto? There must be a mistake. All this fighting must be confusing; no doubt this man is mixing up people and events.*

But the idea had been planted, and it stuck. *Fausto likes knives. He has always liked knives, and this man Castillo, God only knows what he has forced him to do. But not this, though. Not arbitrary violence. Fausto has too much morality for that.*

He went around mulling the thought, alternatively rejecting and rekindling it, until it finally settled in a corner of his brain. One day he opened *Novedades* and saw a picture of Arbenz being sent up the steps of a plane. He squinted, looking at the face of the soldier standing on the tarmac. The picture was grainy, taken at night though clearly staged to ensure a good shot. It looked like Fausto, indeed.

He showed the picture to his Uncle Rogelio.

"Does look like Fausto," Rogelio said. "I always knew the army would make a man out of him." Tomás hesitated. He did not want to bring up what he had heard. But Rogelio had seen his anguished face.

"Come on, out with it, what's the matter?"

"I heard these stories about Fausto," he said. "Stories of rape and torture." Rogelio's face turned red, and Tomás could see the effort it took for him not to get angry.

"I haven't heard these stories, Tomás, and you shouldn't pay attention to rumors, that's my advice." He stroked his moustache. "Why don't you ask him yourself? You're friends, after all."

The occasion arose soon enough: when the troops came back from Guatemala, Fausto was promoted to captain, and Major Nolasco, the military commander of León, decided to throw a party for him.

"A rising star, our Fausto," the aunts said when they heard about the promotion. "He'll go far, our Fausto, so worthy of the Cortés name!"

Major Nolasco lived in a sprawling farmhouse, a house built for parties and parades, with a white-gravel driveway flanked by Roman statues cast in gray concrete. Tomás arrived late, and when he stepped out of the car he saw Fausto standing on the front lawn, between the statues of Mars and Mercury.

He was struck by how his cousin had changed in physical appearance: it was not just that the epaulettes made his shoulders appear broader, or that the stripes along the seams of his pants seemed to stretch his legs. *Somehow,* Tomás sensed, *somehow Fausto had outgrown his sailor uniform, his soldier uniform, and now he had outgrown himself.*

Fausto, half-hidden from view by the statues, was pulling down the sleeves of his uniform to adjust the saber that was dangling from his side. On his chest was the medal the President had given him. It was big and shiny: "For bravery," it said in big raised letters, as if to ward off doubters. Fausto pinned a small flat brooch to his breast pocket, underneath the medal; when he lifted the medal and let it fall back onto the brooch, it produced a dull clink. He groaned in appreciation and when he looked up, he saw Tomás standing in front of him, extending his hand.

"Congratulations on the medal," Tomás said, "I read about Guatemala in *Novedades* magazine." He could have sworn that he saw Fausto blush.

"Must have been difficult," he continued.

"It's my job, Tomás. I'm a soldier."

"How long have you been back?

"A couple of weeks."

"I thought you would have come home earlier."

"I am a soldier now."

Tomás thought that this explained little, but did not press the issue.

"I heard a story about this military guy in the Guatemala campaign who goes by the name 'Lieutenant Knife,'" he said. "Imagine that, a heck of nickname, no? Ever heard of that man?"

Fausto raised his shoulders. "Maybe there was such a man in Guatemala," he said. "So many guys out there, and they all have nicknames, you know."

"I was shocked when I heard it," Tomás continued. "These stories about soldiers roughing up prisoners, raping and torturing. Not pretty from what I heard. It just made me wonder if you had heard the same stories… You were there, after all…"

Fausto lifted one eyebrow. "You know, Tomás," he said, "I wouldn't pay too much attention to rumors if I were you. People hear them and repeat them, and in the end these stories take on lives of their own. And then what do we end up with? Trouble!" He pulled out a pack of cigarettes. "All hearsay, trust me. Soldiers don't torture, we're decent people." He lit up a cigarette, and slowly waved the match in front of his face until the embers died. As he leaned forward, Tomás smelled phosphorus first, then the acrid sting of raw tobacco leaf.

"Hmm," he said. "Yes, you're right. Lots of stories out there, and who knows which ones are true, right?" He shook his head and pursed his lips. "Whom to believe in the end, whom to trust?"

Fausto shook his head. "That's what I say, cousin. We shouldn't pay attention to rumors and old wives' tales. One drunk, cashiered lowlife with a quick tongue is all it takes to smear a man's reputation. Trust family, that's what matters."

"So are you saying there was no torturing going on in Guatemala?"

"I don't pay attention to rumors. I don't listen to stories. I live in the real world." He pulled on his cigarette. Hard, making a hissing sound. "What if someone told me there's a freak out in the hospital who cannot get it up with real women, but instead sits up all night surrounded by corpses and gets his rocks off cutting up cadavers? Would you believe it if someone told you there's a guy out there they call the dead-tissues doctor? You wouldn't, would you?"

"I'm not a dead-tissue doctor!" Tomás exclaimed, feeling his cheeks grow hot.

"Ah," Fausto said. "Who said I was talking about you, cousin?" He cocked his head and raised his eyebrow. "I never mentioned you. In fact, I never even thought about you. But you see how easily people get the wrong idea?" He shook his head, and then pulled up his pant legs so Tomás could see the knife strapped to his shin.

"See," he said. "Old habits die hard – I am a knife guy, I admit it. Doesn't make me a criminal or a sociopath." Grinning, he bent down to undo the clasp and pull out his knife. Holding it under his nose, he closed his eyes and inhaled, deeply.

"Smell," he said, stretching out his arm towards Tomás. "Smell and you tell me if this smells like the knife of this Lieutenant Knife to you. To me it doesn't. It's just steel, clean steel."

Tomás winced. "No need for this, Fausto," he said, pushing the knife away. "I do know what blood smells like."

"Look," Fausto said, grabbing his arm. "You and I, we are more than cousins. We're blood brothers; we go way back. Don't listen to any stories, Tomás. We're stronger than all this, trust me. We're family."

"Yes," Tomás said. "Yes, we're family. That I know."

Fausto grinned. "You first, me first," he said. He squeezed his cousin's arm and walked away, the clink of his medal keeping pace with his footsteps. He ticked off the statues one by one, until he reached the bright lights of the veranda where people were waiting to shake his hand.

Tomás looked at him from the shadows. *He has changed,* he thought. *Even if he is not this Lieutenant Knife, he has changed.* He looked up and saw his cousin wave at him, just once.

Ana was pregnant before a year had passed. When they heard the news, his fellow guardsmen slapped Fausto on the back with greasy hands.

"Best sharpshooter in all of Nicaragua!" they all bellowed. Fausto remembered his Aunt Elvira telling him once, when he was a boy: "a girl stops being her mother's daughter the day she becomes a mother herself. But a boy – ah, it's one of life's great mysteries when a boy ceases to be his father's son. You're all different, and some of you never grow up." He had disliked those words, and so had Tomás, but neither had been able to find an answer to the enigma. *It was upsetting*, they thought, *harsh and unfair*. But Aunt Elvira just laughed when they complained.

Ana's waters broke early, and Fausto was not there, so her housekeeper came knocking on Tomás's door.

"Doctor," she said, "Doctor, please come, Ana has asked for you." It was three in the morning. *The devil's hour*, he thought, but years of night shifts had conditioned him to wake up in a snap.

"Where is Doctor López?" he said. "Why isn't he there?"

The housekeeper said she did not know – she had just been sent to ask him to come. When they arrived at the house Ana was sitting up in bed, pale and sweaty.

"Where is Fausto?" he said. Ana said nothing, and her mother laid a long finger across her mouth.

"Please help us, Tomás," she said, "Doctor López is out of town, and we need you."

He was nervous. He had not attended a delivery since his early days in medical school, and had become unaccustomed to the wait, to letting nature run its course. But his reflexes had stayed with him – the counting, the auscultation, the lifting and turning – it all came back to him without the need to think. The nurse led him, and his mind knew where to follow. Ana endured eight hours of pushing, but she barely cried, and not until the end. In between contractions, the room was silent, except for the nurse shuffling about to serve water, and Ana's mother arranging pillows and holding her daughter's hand. The nurse handed him the knife, to tie the umbilical knot.

As he was holding the baby, Tomás felt its warmth – the strength that was already powering this tiny but perfect machine pulsating in his grasp. He made it gasp for air, then cry, cleaning out its nostrils and mouth. *Her child,* he thought. *Her child and his. It could have been mine, if I had wanted to.*

He handed the baby to the nurse, to clean it and lay it on its mother's breast.

"She looks like her father," Ana said. "So her name shall be Adriana, after Fausto's late mother." The baby fell asleep against its mother's breast, snug and warm in a world of certainties.

Ana's mother left, and the nurse drew the curtains open, just enough for the sunlight to come in, and then she left. Tomás bagged the placenta to send to the lab. He looked at Ana and her child, and saw them both asleep. But when he was about to leave the room she spoke.

"Tomás?"

"Yes," he said, without turning.

"You made me cry again," she said. "And her as well. But this time it was good." She looked at her baby and smiled. He turned around now. A chocorrón was perched on the headboard behind her. It was moving slowly, lifting up one leg at a time.

He bent his head and walked back to the bed. Slowly, as if the air had rarefied and he was having trouble maintaining his balance.

"Don't leave, Tomás. Stay with me. With us."

Chapter 14

On the day the general was shot, Milagros had been rehearsing her songs for many days. When she finished singing the general pulled her up onto his knees to ask her the kind of questions to which a seven-year-old has no answers.

"You have sung for me before, haven't you?" he said. "I never forget a pretty voice. You sing well, very well." He rubbed his sweaty chin before continuing:

"One day you will be a great singer. But you must go and find your voice first. Italy, Paris, one of those places where they train pretty voices." He bellowed on while she looked at him with wide-open eyes, fixing her gaze on the coffee stain that had formed on his chest pocket. She started breathing faster and tried to wiggle free. Her father approached and spoke to her, but she could not understand what he was saying. She watched the beads of perspiration form on her father's forehead, a forehead that went on forever all the way over his pate. He was whispering to the general now, and she felt the man's hands tighten around her waist. She wriggled, and he set her down abruptly. Her father took her by the hand and led her back to where her mother was sitting. She looked worried and spoke to her father in a hushed voice as he pulled out his kerchief and started patting his forehead.

"Daddy, who was that man?" she said.

"It's the general himself, chiquita, the President of the Republic."

"What is a President? Does he have children?" Her father did not answer, and instead whispered something in her mother's ear. She put her hand on his arm, and smiled. The band started playing, a bolero first, then a waltz. She saw the President move among the ranks, shaking hands with men who were sticking fingers under their shirt collars in the muggy September weather. The women were dolled up in imported silk and muslin dresses, clouds of feathery tulle sprouting from their waists, like a flock of ostriches.

The general invited a young woman to dance with him, and then another. He thought of himself as an excellent dancer.

"I out-dance all of you young guys anytime," he often joked with his bodyguards.

The band played "Santa Barbara," one of his favorite tunes, and he turned and swung like a young man in spite of his flab, his stubbly cheek tightly pressed against his companion's. He was waltzing close to another couple now, a girl and a young man sporting a scraggly beard. When the general was so close to them that they might have touched, the young man suddenly swept back his coattails and pulled a revolver. He took aim, a broad aim that took in all of the other man's belly and torso, and fired five shots. Blood sprayed at the bystanders as the bullets hit the presidential body. The white marble floor of the Casa del Obrero quickly turned a slippery red.

People screamed and tripped over each other, trying to get away from the scene before more shots could be fired. The young man stood still, revolver in hand, and made no attempt to move, staring instead at the body convulsing in a pool of blood. Suddenly his body wavered back and forth as if he had been pushed, first from the back, then from the front. When a bullet punched his atrium he spit up blood. The gun slid from his hand as he fell down, face up and with outstretched arms. Six bodyguards were on top of him now, holding guns to his head and chest while one checked his jugular vein. Others had hoisted the general on top of the head table, shoving aside the floral arrangement that had been carefully put together by young girls from the orphanage earlier that day. Somoza looked his bodyguard in the eye and gurgled:

"I'm a goner, Lucho, I'm a goner. Gonna kick the damn bucket."

All the doors were being closed shut, fast and loud, and soon the ballroom swarmed with military knocking over tables and chairs, and driving everyone to the back of the room. The ladies asked to sit down, but were shouted at:

"Get up, old fart: it's because of you people the boss is fucked." When an elderly man protested, the soldier knocked him in the teeth with the butt of his gun. Everyone screamed and shouted, some of the ladies fainted, and urine ran down the floor, as León's finest were unable to control their nerves and bladders.

Tomás was among the guests. When the soldiers shouted for a doctor, his neighbor poked him in the ribs:

"Tomás, you are a doctor!"

He did not react, so the man fluttered his hand towards an officer standing nearby. "Here's a doctor," he screamed, both hands up in the air now.

"Who's the doctor here?" the officer growled. "Is it you, asshole?"

"No officer, it's him!" the man said, pushing Tomás forward.

"You a doctor?" the officer barked once more, the gun pointed at Tomás's ribcage.

"Yes, I am," he said. His voice was shrill, as if his lungs were unable to draw in enough air. *He patted his coat pocket, looking for the outline of the case with the vial inside.*

"Come with me," the officer said. "Now!" He pushed Tomás ahead of him while he screamed and waved his gun to make room until they got to the table on which the big body was lying. Somoza had lapsed into unconsciousness, but his chest was heaving regularly.

"Look here, Doc, the boss is badly hurt," the officer said. "You gotta keep him alive until we get the helicopter in here, you understand?"

"Yes," Tomás said, "helicopter in here, yes." The old dictator's hair was caked with blood, sticky and mask-like, while small shards of glass had lodged in his cheeks. Blood was flowing from two wounds in his side and one in his stomach. *Hypovolemia,* he thought. *He will die soon if nothing is done to stop the bleeding.* With the officer watching, Tomás pulled open the bloody shirt.

"I need alcohol," he said. "And something to stop the bleeding; a cloth, gauze, and a knife to cut open his clothing." The officer reached for his calf and brought up a knife. He grabbed the general's shirt by the buttons and stuck his knife behind it, ripping the cloth in one long movement that sent two buttons flying into the air. Then he turned and walked to a group of soldiers to bark an order.

My chance, Tomás thought. *It's another chance, and no one will know, no one will need to pay or suffer. This is the man who killed your father. You can end it now; you simply let him bleed to death, the damage is already done. Just press in the right place to keep the blood flowing. Press harder, until he bleeds out — who will be able to tell?* His hand rested on the femoral artery, his thumb moving up. His other hand rested on the man's abdomen, purple and bloated, and slowly moved towards the spleen. *It would be so simple, an act of mercy almost.* His hand pressed down on the spleen, softly at first, then harder. The President groaned, but he was too far gone to lift his arms.

Sábado, Tomás thought, *today is Saturday, and today this piggy is going to market.* He felt his jaw tighten and the muscles on his neck swelled but before he could press hard enough the officer was back, carrying a bottle of rum and a ball of gauze. He looked at Tomás's hand lying on the general's belly while the old man groaned. Tomás kept his fingers pressing into the man's spleen, thinking that any sudden movement might set off alarm bells.

"Is he going to be OK?" the officer said, as he held out the gauze. Tomás looked at the bundle of gauze as if it were an intruder, a spoiler sent to rout the hopes of an entire nation. He knew that he had no choice but let go of the spleen and receive the bundle the officer was holding out. *Damn you,* he thought, *damn you for interrupting me. I was so almost there.* When he unrolled it, he saw that it was a large swath of tulle cut from one of the ostrich dresses. He winced and cut the cloth in strips with the knife the officer handed him. Then he wound the strips around the man's head and torso, going into automatic mode, not thinking, simply applying the rules he had been taught. The officer did not leave his side again. He watched Tomás, watched his hands intently as they moved across the fat man's body.

He barely noticed when the helicopter landed in the yard and soldiers took the body away. There was a gust of wind blowing dust into the ballroom as the helicopter lifted and disappeared above the rooftops, and he was brusquely pushed back with the others. They were falling over each other, falling and standing up again in a room that smelled of spoiled food and spilt whiskey mixed with urine and vomit. It smelled of fear. The military kept everyone in the Casa del Obrero for many hours, deep into the night. Not until the rooster crowed were the exhausted guests allowed to leave their unexpected prison cell.

When the shots rang out and screams filled the air Milagros tried to hide her face against her father's tuxedo, but she was too short, and so it was her mother's polka-dot dress that blotted out the screaming and shouting. The three of them sat on the floor, Milagros hiding her face in her mother's dress, and her mother covering her ears and caressing her hair. Milagros cried until her ears were popping.

She did not forget that day. She would remember it for the stench of urine, the pushing and screaming all around her, for the volleys of gunshots that ripped through the air. That day she decided to never sing in public again.

A curfew was imposed on the city, and no one was allowed in or out until further orders. Once they identified the assassin, his relatives were rounded up and dragged off to the Hormiguero prison, where Somoza's henchmen tortured them until they confessed anything. But anything was not good enough. It was a bitter pill to swallow for the Guard. No big-time conspiracy was unearthed, only threads of lies and half-truths that were pulled out of the conspirators and their families with the help of tweezers and meat tongs.

"The information they're giving us is useless, gentlemen," the commanding officers told Somoza's sons. "It's stale. These people admit to anything when we tighten the screws on them."

"There is no bad information, Colonel," Anastasio yelled back. "There is 'information,' and there is 'no information.' All information is good: anything we don't know yet but know we need to know is good compared to not knowing that we don't know it. Just dig deeper." The net was cast wider, so anyone suspected of being in disagreement with the government was rounded up, as were many who had ever been fingered by a zealous neighbor or a jealous friend. This lasted for several weeks until, eventually, the general died in a military hospital in Panama. His two sons succeeded him: one as President, and the other as commander of the National Guard. A good arrangement, seamlessly executed. The senators fell back in line, unconditionally supporting the new rulers: "The General is dead, long live the General!"

Tomás had expected to be elated when the news broke. But he was not. *I didn't do it,* he thought. *Or did I? Did I hasten his death somehow?* It bothered him, and he spent hours reliving the scene, looking for clues that his fingers might have pushed the pig over the edge. The groans, the bleeding, the strength of his fingers that had pressed into the man's belly and spleen – he remembered them. What bothered him was not the thought that he might have killed him. It was the thought that he would never know, and would have to live with his doubt.

Thief, he thought, *you rotten thief. First you stole my father, and now you steal my dignity.*

Chapter 15

Anastasio Somoza the younger, barely thirty years old, now commanded the National Guard with the rank of general, while his older brother Luis was President. Fausto had been called to Anastasio's office; he knocked and waited, hearing a radio being switched off inside. When the door opened, a young corporal came out, saluted Fausto, and walked away.

"Come, Fausto," he heard Somoza's voice from inside, "come sit with me." He beckoned Fausto to sit down in a brown cowhide armchair, pockmarked with small and larger holes that were perfectly round, and scorched at the edges.

"Watch out for the cigarette holes," Somoza joked. "These chairs were my father's; he used to take one of them with him even when he was on the road for a couple of days. He said he would die while sitting in these chairs! Ha-ha!"

Fausto smiled dryly. He was unsure whether to laugh or get up and out of this dead man's chair. The general slapped his thigh and stood up. When Fausto started to get up as well, Somoza pushed him back into his seat.

"Sit, Fausto, sit. We have much to talk about, you and I." He walked away, but turned around after a few steps.

"What do you want from life, Fausto?" he said.

Fausto raised his eyebrows. "Sir?"

"Yeah, what do you want from life? We all want something. What's your thing? Money? Power? Women?" He paused after each word, and lowered his eyebrows.

"Some of us want to play God. Do you want to play God, Fausto?"

"I believe in God, sir, I do not…"

"I'm sure you don't," the general cut him off. "I'm sure you don't."

Somoza was leaning against the wall now, a long cigarette clutched between his thick fingers.

"Do you know where the cigarette holes in these chairs come from, Fausto?" He raised his eyebrows, but his posture indicated that he had no intention of waiting for an answer.

"My father was a real son of a bitch. Does that surprise you?"

Fausto scratched his chin. *Why is he asking these questions?* he wondered.

"He had this special room; they called it 'the Sewing Room.' Ever been in there?"

Fausto shook his head this time.

"One day you will," Somoza said, "one day you will. Anyway, my father would have prisoners brought in, especially those who had been with the Guard, the rejects and traitors that got booked on some charge. You know: the liars and the ones who had disobeyed his commands, or the ones who had stolen from him or from the Guard. 'There are rules for everything!' he would scream at them, 'even for stealing!' And then he talked with them, schmoozed them up and made them believe that all was forgiven. They already saw themselves going home that day, seeing their children, drinking a double shot of rum and having a good meal, sliding between clean sheets under the crucifix hanging from the bedroom wall, and getting laid by their wives perhaps. And then, when he had this guy all mellow and thinking this was the end of his ordeal, he would light a cigarette and suddenly stab at the man's hand or whatever piece of skin was nearest." Somoza was grinning, seemingly enjoying the retelling.

"You see, Fausto, a tense body expecting a lash or a blow, now such a body receives the burning tip of a cigarette with anger!" He made a sputtering sound, the sound of a perfectly marbled flank steak being slapped onto the griddle.

"That burst of adrenaline that is released before the body starts hurting is enough to shut down the brain. Your teeth are already clenched, your muscles tightened, your skin is taut and your brain is bracing for nerve cells to be slashed and for your flesh to be ripped open and seared before your blood can start flowing out. But…an unsuspecting body, now that's a completely different story!" He grinned and waited for his words to sink in.

"And then my father would poke around the guy. Left, right, holding the cigarette real close to his skin, stab at the chair perhaps. I was here once when he did this to some sonofabitch, a sergeant who had stolen money from the pension fund." He shook his head, up and down, like a pump jack. "And you know what, Fausto?"

"Sir?"

"I learned more from this than from anything else my father ever taught me. Not the pain itself, hell no – I'm no sadist, Fausto. It was doing the expecting for him, anticipating the hurt and the pain. It was waiting for the look of surprise, and then the sudden dawning of knowledge even before the pain had reached his brain; knowledge that there would be no bus ride home, no children's embrace, no rum and no dinner, no wife fucking him. It was the knowledge that my father could do with him what he wanted, and that his sole reason for doing what he did was making sure that guys like him knew this. That he could tear their minds apart and put them back together again. A great lesson. The kind you won't find in any history book."

Somoza leaned back into the chair, letting his fingers run over the armrest until they found the cigarette holes. He stuck them in the way one would gouge out an eye, corkscrew-wise.

"Do you know what they did to Trujillo's chief of staff after they foiled an assassination attempt on the old man?"

Fausto shook his head. "No," he mumbled. "No, I don't."

"They sewed his eyes shut. Literally. And they left him like that for four whole months while they went into his brain to pick and dig around as if it were a goddamn vegetable patch. That was industrial, real industrial. My father looked like an amateur by comparison." He chuckled and drew on his cigarette again, watched as the smoke wafted up in the air, and then looked back at Fausto with a glint in his eyes.

These men were fathers, Fausto thought. *As I am now. What would I give to go home if this happened to me? Would I scream? Would I anticipate the pain and hold my screams?*

Somoza raised his eyebrows and scratched the big mole under his right eye.

"Doubt is the greatest ally we have, Fausto. Because doubtful people fear. The doubters are on our side – they just need to be pummeled into more fear. It's the zealots we must watch out for, the true believers. They are dangerous, and infectious to boot." He drummed his fingers on the armrest again, and leaned back.

"Some people may think we kill for pleasure, but they're dead wrong. Killing is a terrible business strategy. Sure we break some eggs, but…that's how omelets are made, right?" He looked at Fausto without waiting for an answer.

"There are rules for everything, Fausto, there are rules for everything. We get the fear of God into those bastards so they don't get the wrong idea, because it's good for business. The rest is just process. Boring stuff, but necessary. Nothing works if the bureaucracy doesn't."

Fausto licked his lips. The general continued to blow out billowing clouds of smoke that drifted out through the window and became part of the big blue skies. He half-closed his eyes and sat down again, in the second chair. Then he stomped out the cigarette in a small ashtray, with a delicate movement of his fat fingers.

"Now then, Fausto," he said, his voice coming from the back of his throat. "Tell me what you want, and I will tell you who you are. And if you don't know what you want, I will make you want things. In the end, all men want the same." There was a twinkle in the general's eye, a twinkle Fausto had not seen there before. Somehow Somoza seemed to have grown taller, his glasses thicker, his nails longer.

Leaning towards him, Somoza said: "I think you should go back to school, my friend." Fausto's face must have shown surprise, because Somoza laughed.

"Don't worry, Fausto. We're not sending you back to kindergarten. We're sending you to Panama, to a special school for soldiers like yourself. For men dedicated to our country and our values. To freedom and democracy!" He stopped to taste his own words. Fausto could see how he was pressing upper jaw against lower jaw, in a upwards movement that pressed some of his flesh between his milling jaws, and created a look of drawn-in cheeks, as if the man were ruminating, slowly digesting the value of his own words.

"Democracy," he said again, when all the other words had been swallowed. This single piece of cud had remained stuck to his palate: a stubborn word, one that refused to go away. He burst out laughing: "Ha-ha-ha, we're all democrats now, Fausto! Why, even Khrushchev, that son of a bitch, calls himself a democrat!"

At the School of the Americas, Fausto learned how effective it was to threaten a man with raping his daughter when you needed to turn him into an informant. All Lieutenant López needed to do was whisper his daughter's name into the man's ear. Then he would stand back, and say it. And again. No other words.

The list of techniques was endless. Fausto read through the manual the way he had never read any book before. He stopped only to go back and make sure he had understood correctly. When he finished reading, he closed the book, rested it on his chest, and stared at the ceiling. He thought of Guatemala – he saw the windowless room in his mind, and sensed that this book, this school, might help him find the keys.

His instructors were experts. They spoke from experience, and finalized Fausto's map of the world. Everything had been written up. Well documented, and illustrated with photographs and drawings carefully chosen and arranged. One of the diagrams mapped out how many steps to take when you stormed into a room with four or six or eight persons around a table; how to take turns shooting whom; how many bullets were needed; how to make sure that they were all dead; and how to finally leave the room again, in what order. Fausto read through the instructions and closed his eyes. He saw himself storming into a room. He smelled the occupants' fear, and saw himself taking aim and shooting one, two people, then his companion taking aim at two more. The third man: two more! And then he himself, taking out the remaining ones. They all shot the bodies closest to them once more, the ones that quivered and throbbed still, resisting the metal and unwilling to die. Then they left the room, walking backwards. His companions first, and finally he himself. It was like a page out of a manual to learn to dance: slow slow quick quick, left right left right.

By the time he graduated, he was a different man. He felt that the world had fallen into place: what had been shades of gray, had turned into stark blacks and brilliant whites.

"What do you think this whole thing is all about?" Somoza said. "Come on, go for it. I don't want guys in my guard who question everything, but I sure do want them to be able to tell their elbow from their asshole."

"Politics?" Fausto tried.

"We don't really care. That's for the newspapers, but between you and me, that asshole Castro is not all that different from us. Try again."

"Money, then? We must be in it for the money, aren't we?"

"Getting close. Money is important. Money buys more power. It's like getting three wishes from the tooth fairy and using the last one to wish for three more wishes." He laughed out loud. "That's why money is important. To screw over the tooth fairy." His laugh was gone, and he peered at Fausto while stroking his chin. "You give up, right? Let me tell you then. It's about taking away people's sense of control. Power is a means to an end, but it's also an end in itself. We decide on stuff. The rest – the money, the army, the medals and the baseball games – that's just to make sure everyone gets with the system. Try it, Fausto. You'll see that you like it, trust me. You'll see that controlling people is better than sex – in fact, you'll sell your grandmother once you find out how good it feels to fuck with someone's head. And once you, Fausto, figure that out, there won't be any holding you back. I know a killer when I see one."

Chapter 16

Nothing had prepared Fausto for becoming a father. When Adriana was born, he thought that the curtains had been drawn open, and light had been let into his life.

"Thank you, Ana," he said. "Thank you for this beautiful gift. He took his daughter riding on his horse, holding her with one hand while steering the horse with the other.

"She looks like him," everyone said, and he laughed.

"Yes, she does," he said. "Thank you, Ana."

Then small things happened. Or rather, they did not. Her head stayed large while her body grew only slowly. She slept more, and longer, than other children did, and when she finally learned to walk, she often stopped dead, her movements frozen in midair while she stared at nothing with pouting lips. At times it seemed as though she would stay like this forever. Her eyes never learned to move in step with her mouth, as if she were talking to an unseen audience, people who rushed left to right, invisible to all others. It had not mattered much when she was a child, and strangers had written it off as shyness. However, as she grew older it drove home the unmistakable message that she would forever be her mother's child.

The sight of Adriana scared him. He saw in her the accidents caused by genetic switching. She reminded him of human frailty, of the imperfections and weakness that had entered his house. He had wanted it perfect, a perfect child born of perfect adults.

Once, he got drunk, and screamed at Ana: "I have no monsters in my family! We have no diseases, we are strong people, healthy people. There are no blots in my bloodline! This comes from that mother of yours!"

"Don't be ridiculous, Fausto," she cried. "We are cousins, how can you say these things?" He grumbled and groaned, and stumbled his way into the bedroom where he fell down before he could reach the bed. He coughed, and vomit drooled down his chin. When he had fallen asleep, Adriana came into the room and stuck a flower behind his ear.

He woke up later that night, with a splitting headache. He staggered into the bathroom to rinse out his mouth, and wiped his chin with the back of his hand. When he looked at himself in the mirror he saw the flower behind his ear; it looked as if it had sprouted there all by itself while he had been sleeping, a newly grown and inseparable addition to his anatomy. He made a fist and the flower was inside of it, scared and breathless. It died before it reached the ground.

More and more often Ana found herself alone at night, and the few kind words he spoke were not enough for her. She felt like the promise of a flower that had wilted before it had had time to blossom.

Her aunts told her not to worry. "He's a very busy man now," they all said, "just be patient with him, he will open up his heart to you again, be patient."

It did not happen.

She fell ill. Fevers and vomiting, cramps that made her feel as if a sword had been stuck in her belly. She moaned and grunted, dragged herself to the bathroom where she coiled up around the toilet bowl and fainted while a trickle of blood spread between her legs. The maid who found her was old, and did not panic. She sent for Tomás. He sat with her while she spoke in her sleep, but he did not hear her. Instead, he watched the ceiling and wondered if the spiders had had time to build a web. Then he fell asleep in the rocking chair standing at the foot of her bed. Fausto never knew.

Her mother and aunts were quick to tell her to forget about it. "It is part of life," they all said, "it happens; you'll get over it, best to pretend it never happened." But she could not. It was as if she had lost part of herself: a lowly small toe or a useless extra rib, the parts we might never realize were missing if it were not for the violence that accompanied their parting.

One night, while the rain pounded the asbestos roof and hundreds of rain flies entered the house and clung to the mosquito net around her, she cried herself to sleep. In her dream she was young once more. She was standing over a hammock where a young boy was asleep, and tickled him with the tassels until he woke up. Then she saw them both, him and her, as they shored up a pelican nest that had appeared in front of a beach house. She was twelve perhaps, and he was slightly older – a boy who had stayed small and a girl who had started growing. The nest was sagging dangerously, after the storm that had passed that night. It was close to dropping altogether, and two pelicans sat motionless on a nearby rooftop while the children stood looking at them from below.

"They are afraid," the boy said.

"Of us?"

"No. They know what might happen when you upset a nest that has become unstable."

"So are they waiting for a miracle?"

They found the ladder in the barn, where it was kept for removing the spider webs that formed around the rafters. He climbed up before her, because "that's how it should be," she insisted. Inside the nest were two eggs, large and speckled. "Don't touch," she said, "if you touch a pelican's egg it won't be able to fly."

"Eggs don't fly," he teased, but she hushed him. They pushed the nest back up against the tree trunk, shoring it up with ropes and planks.

"Do you think it will work?" he said.

"We'll see."

She woke up when the rain stopped. Nothing is sadder than the silence that follows rain at night, broken only by the slow drip of water onto broad leaves and into puddles not deep enough to flow over. The creaking of wet tree bark expanding in the dark, of trees unfolding their branches, and the traipsing of an army of insects hauling in the raindrops under cover of night. The silence that follows rain at night is beguiling and treacherous, but Ana basked in it, drank from it the way Isolt had drunk the potion. She fell asleep again just before dawn, and dreamed no more. When she awoke, she remembered only the happiness she had felt as a girl on the beach. She wanted to hang on to it, desperately. Wanted her unhappiness to be absorbed by it, to be burned and scorched by it until it was no more.

It was Rafaela who invited them to tea.

"Mama Mica is having tea with me this afternoon, why don't you come and accompany us?" she told her. Fausto was away, on one of the campaigns to rid the mountains of insurgents and bandits. To get to Mama Mica's quarters she had to walk through the hallway, then the drawing room, the two places that were always filled with Cortéses of all stripes and colors. Her aunts came up to her to greet her as she entered, but she knew it would make her late, so she rushed through the drawing room and lost one of her pumps. She stopped and turned, finding a hand that held out her shoe.

"Tomás! I hadn't seen you!"

"I know. I hope I didn't scare you." She laughed, holding on to a chair while she slipped her foot back into the shoe.

"I am having tea with Mama Mica."

"So am I."

"Really? Payita didn't tell me."

"It doesn't mean much. I hear she does this all the time. We are cousins, aren't we?"

Mama Mica was sitting upright in bed when Ana walked in.

"Tesoro," she said, and held out both arms. "*Tesoro, vieni qui!*" Ana saw from the corner of her eyes how Tomás had stopped in the doorway, without greeting Mama Mica. He sat down against the wall, but the old lady never once looked at him. As if he had been there all along, as part of the furniture. Only Payita glanced at where Tomás was sitting from time to time.

"How is the girl, *cara mia*?" Mama Mica said. "I hear she laughs a lot!"

"Yes," Ana said. "Yes, she laughs a lot. We are blessed."

"*Ecco*, so you are. Laughing children, what more could you wish for? Have you ever tried this, child?" Mama Mica held out a cup of steaming liquid, yellowish and slightly reminiscent of chamomile. Ana raised her eyebrows. "What is it?"

"*Yerba de la pastora*, from my own garden." She pointed through the window, to a handful of small yellow flowers.

"Drink up, child, it's good for you. It takes away sadness and helps with heavy hearts." Ana took the cup and drank. It reminded her of chamomile, with a hint of sweet figs. They talked, and after a while the old lady fell asleep. When Ana got up to leave, Tomás approached the bed, and held the old lady's wrist to take her pulse.

"She's fine," he said, "she just needs to rest."

"Why were you so quiet?" she said.

He did not answer. Instead, he said: "They call it 'old woman's broom.'"

"What?"

"The damiana," he explained. "They did give me some to drink as well, in case you wondered."

He stepped back just as Rafaela approached the bed and covered Mama Mica with a sheet. She put a long finger over her mouth and turned to Ana.

"Shhh," she said. "Let's let her sleep, yes?"

Ana nodded and walked out. Tomás was right behind her.

"You are not working today?" she said.

"No, I took the afternoon off. I told you Mama Mica invited me over, didn't I?"

She nodded. "Why don't we drive to Poneloya?" she said.

It had come out without thinking. Without fore or afterthought. But he did not seem surprised. He drove fast, and they spoke little on the way.

It was Wednesday, and the house was still locked up. The caretaker was an old man with a hump that shifted as he walked, so he lifted one shoulder to keep the hump from slumping to one side or the other. He shuffled into view when the car stopped in front of the courtyard gate.

"*Buenos días*," he said. "Nobody told us you were coming, so you must excuse the mess. We are not really prepared for your visit."

Ana waved his excuses away. "Thank you, Pablo," she said. His fingers went through all the keys on the big ring, turning it slowly until they found the one he needed. After he opened the front door, he stepped back.

"Shall we bring you some juice?" he said.

"No," Ana said, "no, we are fine. We won't be long in any case." Pablo shook his head and shuffled away.

They went upstairs and sat on the balcony overlooking the ocean. She rested her hands on the balustrades, feeling the paint chip off at the slightest touch of her hand.

"If ever there was a time when I was young, it was during summer," he said. He closed his eyes, listening to the ocean's roar.

"Last night I dreamed of summer," she said. "Do you remember the pelican's nest?"

"The mice," he said. "I remember the mice that pushed down the nest we had raised in the barn."

"The other one," she said. "The one outside. The one where the pelicans laid their eggs." She stretched out her hand and touched his.

"Come now," he said, "it will be night soon, we must get back." He got up, but she did not let go of his hand. Instead, she pulled him towards her, until his face was close to her own.

"You don't want this," he said. "Let's return before it is too late."

She dropped his hand. "Does it mean that little to you, Tomás? Is there no love left for me?"

"Don't ask such things. You know better than that."

"Then why do you reject me?"

He looked out at the sun setting over the ocean with the unforgiving speed of the tropics.

"You married someone else."

"And you know why."

His face turned red. "There were so many things I did not understand. I was wrong."

She walked behind him, and put her arms around his chest. Then she closed her eyes and waited for the smell of juniper.

"I don't love him. I know now that I never loved him. Never have," she whispered.

"And this will solve that?"

"I don't know. But I want you to finish what you started."

He undid her arms and walked back into the room, towards the darkening corner where a bamboo bed was waiting, unmade. He picked up a book of matches and lit the dusty, lopsided candle standing on the night table.

"One candle is enough," he said, "tonight this room should not have too much light. One candle is enough, with gentle light."

"Will you come for me?" she whispered as she hid her face against his chest. "Will you come for me and take me away?" But he did not answer, or perhaps he did but her head was clouded by the old woman's broom, so she may have thought he did.

Chapter 17

After his son was born, Fausto returned to her, or so it seemed. *A new start*, Ana thought. *He was sent to me to make everything whole again. And his name will be Simón.*

Fausto was aloof at first, but as Simón grew, he watched him speak, then walk and run. He relaxed – his son was healthy and strong. He wanted to make up for the years he had been away, and found time to play with him. *I will be a better father than my own father was,* he thought. *I want my son to remember me when I'm gone.*

"Let's go to the Tamarindo River," he told Ana one day. She was surprised, but grateful.

"Yes," she said, "yes, let's go, Fausto." They all went, and spread their chairs among the rocks and boulders lining the riverbed. *We have become a family after all*, she thought.

She remembered that day for a long time. *It's the day Fausto came home*, she thought. *The day that he became a father.* She sat back among the shadows thrown by the giant boulders left behind by ancient hands, and watched how Fausto played with his son. When Adriana joined them, Fausto said nothing.

He saw how close his children were: she was her brother's nanny and his friend. But as Simón grew older, the roles were reversed – he would guide her around the market, the movie theater, and explain those things to which she could only nod and smile. Their bond was a mystery to Fausto. *How can this be?* he thought. *My healthy boy and this idiot monster? How can they see each other as brother and sister?*

One day he saw the children sit next to each other. Her arm was wrapped around his shoulder, and he was moving her finger below the letters in the book opened in front of them.

"What are you doing, Simón?" he said.

"I'm teaching Adriana to read, Father. Mother told me to teach her everything I know. She's just a little slow sometimes, but she learns well."

He was called by Somoza – "I need you to take charge of the garrison in Bluefields," the general said.

He asked to be stationed closer to home. "My son," he said. "I want to spend more time with my son, and Bluefields is far." Somoza looked at him the way he had not looked at him for many years: silently, his fish eyes magnified by thick horn-rimmed glasses.

"Simón," he said, nodding. "Simón, yes?"

They stood facing each other for one whole minute. *There would be a car passing by my house,* he thought. *One day when I'm not there a car will pass by, and stop around the corner for just a few minutes, or an hour. No matter, time would not be important.*

"Of course, general," he said. "I will go to Bluefields."

After Bluefields came Jinotega. The roads were bad and long, and he came home less and less often. His son grew up without him, as his daughter had before him. He realized that he had stopped missing his son, although he did think about him. And one day he stopped missing the thought itself. He resigned himself to accept the missing as part of him, as the part that wanted to go back to a time before he shot the buck, to the time that he received a dagger from his father, with his name engraved it.

One day he came home earlier than expected, filthy and tired after days in the mountains. When he had showered and dressed he walked out onto the porch where the children were playing with Martita, their nanny. It had started raining: a drizzle at first, noiseless and slow, and then it became thicker, denser, faster, as if someone had shifted the gears of the water mill, and it had become a thunderous wall of water. With the rain came the smell of wet earth, and hundreds of slender-bodied flies. "Rain flies," Martita called them, that landed on your hair, your clothes. They were slow and blind, born for this one moment, as if sent to them by the god of rains.

They had not heard him; the sound of the rain had drowned out his steps. When the thunder clapped the children screamed and turned, and saw their father sitting against the wall. They both ran towards him, holding hands. Simón was seven now, a child who had not yet learned to be a boy and did not try to hide his fears. He buried his head in his father's chest, but when Adriana leaned against him, Fausto curved his back, keeping Simón hidden inside his embrace. She turned away from him, and when he looked up, he saw her in profile. *That nose line, that turned-up lip. She looks so much like my mother.*

He reached out. His hand was close to her shoulder, but then she turned, and he saw the large eyes that had trouble focusing. His hand fell, and he squeezed his son harder. Adriana walked away, fluttering her hands, to the edge of the red-tile porch where she sat down and stuck her feet out into the thick rain that came pouring down from the roof gutter.

Ana came out and watched them, all of them, from the doorway of the darkened house. She sat down behind her daughter, swung her legs around her and pulled her back until their bodies had become indistinguishable. She felt the cool rain on her feet as they rested on the grass. Adriana never stopped humming. When Ana looked over her shoulder she saw that Fausto had not moved, and the boy was still hiding his face in his father's lap.

"She is just a girl, Fausto," Ana said, "and she is your daughter."

He did not answer. He brooded and gazed at the rain coming down. After a while he stood up and went inside, taking Simón with him. He showed him his gun and his knife, and photographs of himself with the general. He showed him his medals and other things made of metal and glass.

Ana sat outside, watching the rain became thicker until it was a dense curtain hanging in front of her, a curtain she could not possibly see through. Her feet were wet, and then her dress got soaked as well, but Adriana was still humming in her arms, playing with a red hibiscus flower. Ana thought that this must be her punishment: to be left behind, to have become a chair or a table, no more than furniture in her own house – seen but not wanted. She cried, because no one could see her. No one would hear her. There was rain enough here, and darkness to hide in, and the steady pouncing of water on an asbestos roof.

That night she dreamed of a boy holding a butterfly net. He was nimble and barefoot; she could not see the color of the butterflies he was chasing. *Perhaps there are no butterflies*, she thought, *perhaps he was only chasing his own past.* She woke up screaming, choking on her own saliva.

Her hair was sticking to her face and her hands felt hot and clammy. It was early still, and when she switched on the lamp, she noticed that the bed was empty beside her. He had been there; she could see the outline of his body still, the image it had left against the sheets. *To remind me of his absence.* The thought scared her — the thought of a future in which she would be living with the memory of a body only. She felt like a flower growing by the side of a busy passageway, and each time the market vendors came by they brushed it aside — annoyed by its presence, by this flower that kept growing back towards the path, waiting to be seen and touched. To be wanted and desired.

The bruising became more frequent, until she decided to resist him.

"Ana, get the boy ready," he told her, "I'm going to take him practice shooting." Ana did not like guns — her father had been the only man in the family not to have guns about the house.

"No," she said.

Fausto was almost out the door, but he turned when he heard her say "no." He tried a smile first, but when Ana said "no" again, his face tensed up.

"I'm not asking you, Ana," he said. "Get me the boy. Now."

She did not answer. He stepped forward and hit her in the face, hard, with the back of his hand. She reeled from the blow, staggering backwards. He grabbed her forearm before she could fall, a vise grip that numbed her senses.

"Get me the boy," he said, pushing her ahead of him. Martita looked on as Fausto pushed his wife towards the boy's room. She crossed herself and shook her head, but did not dare interfere. Suddenly Fausto felt something pulling at his arm, and when he turned, he saw Adriana. He grunted, tried to shake her off. He let go of Ana to undo Adriana's grip when the door to Simón's room swung open. Fausto tried to step forward, but had not reckoned with the strength of a determined woman and a fearless girl holding him back. He looked like a captured bull roaring and bellowing at the unyielding skies. He took one uncertain step and fell, taking Ana and Adriana with him. Simón screamed and ran, grabbing hold of his father's sleeve.

"Get off!" he yelled as he thumped him in the chest. "Get off them, I tell you!" His fingers touched something cold, and when he pulled hard, it ripped the fabric and came off. He fell backwards with the force of his own strength, while the medal slipped from his hand and skidded away until it came to rest against the wall.

Ana stood up and pulled Adriana to her. Fausto was lying alone on the floor now, his uniform showing a hole where the medal had been ripped out. Then Ana saw the blood dripping from Simón's hand.

"What's that?" she screamed. "Simón, let me see your hand!" The cut was deep. She poured alcohol on the wound to disinfect it, and pressed Fausto's shaving crystal onto it to stop the bleeding. Simón screamed as the crystal bit his hand.

Ana heard the door slam shut, and then the engine of his jeep. He did not come home for one whole week; when he did, Simón closed the door to his room as soon as he heard the jeep pull up to the gate. Fausto said nothing, and Ana did not ask.

Chapter 18

Fausto showed up at his cousin's house on a Sunday morning. He was not wearing his uniform, which was unusual. Instead, he was wearing a white *guayavera*. Tomás was sitting on the front porch reading the paper, and the paperboy was sitting in the backyard, where Juanita had served him a plate of *gallo pinto* – rice and beans with fried cheese.

"I am going to the cockfights in Nandaime," Fausto said. "You care to come?"

"No," he said. "You know I don't fancy cockfights."

"I think you should come. I want to show you something."

Fausto looked tense, so he decided to indulge him.

"Fine," he said, and stood up. "Juanita, I will be gone," he screamed towards the kitchen. Juanita came walking out with a big blue plate in one hand and a drying cloth in the other.

"*Sí*, Doctor," she said. "So you will not be back for lunch?"

"No," he said, folding the newspaper in four. "When the boy finishes eating, give him back the paper, and here is his *córdoba*." He left an unfolded córdoba on the table.

"You still rent newspapers?" Fausto said.

"Yes. It's easier that way. The boy makes some extra money, and I don't want to keep all those old newspapers. What for, so they will end up burning down my house one day? And in any case I don't need to be reminded of all the disasters taking place. Once things happen they are behind you, aren't they?"

Fausto looked at him with raised eyebrows. "Maybe," he said. "Let's go now."

They spoke little until they reached the outskirts of Managua. There were two ways to get to Nandaime from here: the winding mountain road that led through the cool plains above and around the city; and the stuffy and congested road through Masaya.

"Let's take the high road, what do you say, cousin?

"Fine," Tomás said. "Whatever you say."

When they got to Nandaime, the cockfight had already started. The front row was a circular pit dug into the ground around the fighting pen, where the men could get so close to the roosters that they were almost at eye level with them. They found seats in the second row, on a wooden bench. The men cheered and jostled as the two birds kicked up clouds of red dust and pecked at each other's eyes. Fausto tossed a young boy a bill and pulled two bottles of beer from a bucket with cold water.

"I love cockfights," he said, as they were sipping their beers. "These damn birds fight until they die, they just never give up. That's what armies should be made up of!"

One of the cocks was lying on its back, panting and covered in blood and dirt. A young man raised an orange marshaling bat, and the fight was over. Both owners picked up their birds, and a third man stepped into the pen to clean the low wall with water and a brush, raking off the caked mud and blood that had spattered all over it. The men who had won their bets were cheering, and went over to a corner in the back where an old man kept tabs and made the payouts. While the pen was being cleaned two boys stepped in, each holding a fresh rooster that they ran between their legs, forcing it to simultaneously walk and fly. When the roosters started pecking the boys folded back their flapping wings and held them in the air, poking them at each other. The speakers hanging in the back of the bleachers started blaring *pasodoble* music again, and the band of sweaty men rushed back to their seats, all at once.

Fausto finished his beer and belched. "I'm going to put some money on that white cock," he said. "Be right back."

The bookmaker was an old man. They were always old men, but never the same ones for very long. The skin on his face was hanging in thick folds, wave after wave, as if it were a briefcase in which he was hiding things. Fausto pulled a wad of banknotes from his pocket and started unfolding them. The old man looked vaguely familiar to him.

"I know you from somewhere, don't I?" Fausto said.

"You should," the old man replied. "You worked for me once."

"Worked for you? How so?"

"Figure of speech. But I do like to think that everyone worked for me once. I taught you about hunting garrobos when you were a boy. Don't you remember?"

"That's it," Fausto said, tipping his forehead. "Yes. I do remember. But I thought you were dead. Everyone did. You just left one day, so everyone thought you had died."

"Do I look dead to you?"

"Maybe not. Although who knows, dead men never look dead at first. So why did you leave? Didn't we treat you well?"

"Now that you're asking…in fact I think I got tired. Tired of teaching more and more people the same thing. Over and over, kinda boring in the long run, you know."

"So that's all? You just got bored and left?"

"Good a reason as any, isn't it?"

"And now you're a bookmaker at the cockfights. Less boring, I guess?"

"It's easier. I don't get involved, and I don't take sides. The pay is good. And it's one helluva spectacle, I can tell you that."

"So which one you think I should put my money on?

The old man raised his shoulders. "It's your choice," he said. "To me it's all the same. It's all money."

The jeering and cheering started once more at the arena, as the new cocks were being pitted against each other.

"I'll put fifty córdobas on that white sonofabitch," Fausto said, slamming a crumpled wad of money down on the table.

"Fine with me," the old man said. "I don't give any advice. Not any more, learned my lesson." He counted the money slowly, in front of Fausto, separating the bills and straightening them one by one.

"It's all there," Fausto said. "Don't you trust me? I wouldn't cheat on an old man, you know."

The old man chuckled. "That's what they all say. But when it comes to money it's everyone for themselves – brother against brother." Before Fausto could say anything back, the old man raised his arms and pointed at something behind him: "Look, more visitors," he said, "good for business." He grinned wide. Fausto looked where the man had pointed and saw a full motorcade coming to a stop: ten motorcycles, half in front and half behind a shiny black limousine.

"The general!" he exclaimed. "Does he come here often?"

"Quite often." The old man paused. "He has a bunch of roosters in the fights as well. But he doesn't place his bets with me." He wrote up some numbers on a smudgy piece of paper and handed it to Fausto.

"Aren't you going to wish me luck?" Fausto said.

"Luck has nothing to do with it," the old man said. "Luck is a really bad basis for making any decision concerning either money or love, if you ask me."

"So I guess I'm not asking you then." Fausto grabbed the betting slip and went straight to the general, who was being seated in the front row. When he saw Fausto, he waved him closer and patted the seat beside him. "Fausto," he said, "what a surprise to see you here. Didn't know you fancied cockfights."

"From time to time, General. It relaxes me."

"You place any bets?"

"As a matter of fact, I just placed a bet with that grumpy old bookmaker sitting back there." He pointed at the man sitting at the low table.

"Ah, him." Somoza looked over his shoulder. "Wouldn't trust that shithead with my money. He's been cheating people out of their property for years. Promises you heaven on earth, but when it's time to pay up he always comes up short. 'Tomorrow,' he'll tell you, 'I'll get you the money tomorrow.' Pray you lose, Fausto, so you won't have to deal with the agony. If I had something on him I would run him out of town, but..." he threw up his hands here, "you know I'm a man of peace, and what harm can an old man cause after all?" The general slapped him on the shoulder and handed him a beer. Then he leaned into the ring.

"That one is mine," he said. He was pointing at a black cock with a green chest and a fiery red comb and wattle.

"That cock is yours?" Fausto felt queasy all of a sudden.

"Yeah, that's my boy," the general grinned. "Hasn't let me down yet, that much I can tell you."

Both cocks had razor blades tied to their legs, which glittered as their handlers took off the strips of cloth that had covered them. The handler took the black bird straight up to the general, who petted it and whispered into its crazy eye.

"You don't shave off the comb and wattle, General?" Fausto said.

"Son," Somoza said, "this cock is such a sonofabitch, that's not gonna bother him. Any cock going for its crest, it'll just peck its eye out." The referee came into the ring and measured the razor blades with a wooden yardstick, then sloshed half a bottle of rum over the taut legs, particularly the razor blades.

"They're clean," he declared, "same size, no poison." The handlers took off the blindfolds and set down the cocks on either side of a plank. They lifted the plank, and the birds ran to each other in a whirlwind of feathers and dirt. Blood splattered the white wall, as the razor blades slashed through feathers and skin. And above all of this was the choir of three dozen sweating men – screaming, yelling, and spilling beer and rum into the ring. After seven whole minutes of ferocious bloodshed, the bell rang, and the men erupted into even more heated debates. Some sought to cut their losses, fearing for the worst now that the general's cock was in the fight. The owner of the white rooster was desperately trying to fix up his badly bruised animal. He ruffled its feathers and slickened it with oil. Then he opened his mouth wide and stuck the rooster's head inside. He closed his mouth and pumped his cheeks for ten whole seconds. When the rooster's head came out again it looked as new.

"Can it see, can it see?" the owner yelled at his assistant. When they were fully satisfied that all blood had been sucked off the champion's head they signaled to the referee that they were ready again. At once, the birds were back at each other. *As if they had been enemies all of their short lives,* Tomás thought. *Yet for all we know they may have grown up together. Could it be that these animals fight to the death without a reason whatsoever, just because someone set them up to it?*

The bench sagged when Fausto sat down next to him.

"So did you place your bet?" Tomás screamed, trying to raise his voice over the clamor.

Fausto sighed. "Unfortunately, it seems I'm betting against the general," he screamed back.

"Someone has to bet against him; how else would he make any money from this?"

"I don't think he depends on cockfights to get rich," Fausto shouted back. They watched without talking, while the cockfight went on. The crest on the black-and-green rooster was hanging on by a thread, the wattle a bloody lobe. It had lost many feathers, and its chest was crisscrossed with empty patches through which its skin was visible, eerily white with red streaks all over.

The white rooster was in even worse shape. It was lying on its back, panting and snapping, its scrawny neck turned sideways.

"Looks like you lost your money, cousin," Tomás said, shaking his head. Fausto opened another beer and looked over to where the bookmaker was sitting. The old man was handing out wads of córdobas, and at some point turned his head and looked straight at Fausto, as if to mock him. As if to say: "Ye of little faith." But his face did not betray any pleasure at having made money on this fight, or on any of the fights. No gloat, just indifference.

During the trip back Fausto was tense.

"What happened to you?" Tomás said. "It's not that money you lost, is it?" Fausto did not answer. Instead, he put his foot down on the gas pedal and gritted his teeth. The car started swerving and almost veered off the road.

"Ho-ho-ho," Tomás snapped, "what are you doing, are you trying to get us killed?"

"That would solve a whole lot of problems all at once, now wouldn't it, cousin?" Fausto snapped. "But then again, what would happen to poor Ana?" He kept his foot on the gas pedal, slowly pressing down on it.

"Ana talks in her sleep, you know."

Tomás felt a cold hand gripping his forearm. He rubbed his triceps, warming the muscle until it stopped aching from the imaginary grip.

"Do you deny it?"

"What on earth are you talking about?"

Fausto slammed on the brakes, and Tomás felt his body lurch forward as the engine stalled. He was suddenly aware of the sound of grasshoppers.

"I think you know. Don't insult my intelligence."

"It's not true," Tomás said. "And even if it were, what's it to you? You don't love her."

"Maybe not," Fausto said. "Maybe not. But that doesn't give you the right to sleep with her. Couldn't you just have stuck to your old whores?" Tomás felt his cheeks turn on fire.

"You took her away from me."

"Last time I checked she was my wife, not your girlfriend. So don't go all holy on me." Fausto looked fully awake now, leaving Tomás to wonder if his cousin's demeanor had been no more than a ruse. When Fausto unbuttoned the clasp over his pistol and pulled it out, Tomás panicked and pushed himself back against the door, putting up his hands.

"Don't worry, cousin, I'm not going to drag you out into a field and be done with it. Not my style, you should know that." Fausto slammed the pistol down on the cover of the gearbox, exactly midway between them. It looked like a shiny, gleaming fish.

"First one who feels like shooting the other," Fausto said. "Fair is fair."

He turned the key once, and the engine turned over.

"Was it just one time?"

Tomás eyed the gun. He had not fired one since the days of his childhood.

"You know that it's not true. You're drunk; you don't know what you're saying."

"I'm not drunk. And I know exactly what I'm talking about. And so do you." A herd of cows was climbing out of the low ditch, egged on by three horsemen on mules. The car stood still with the engine humming quietly.

"You went out to the beach house, didn't you? Thought no one would see you, didn't you? But you're forgetting one thing, cousin." He was shaking his head and pouting his lips, like a fish on dry land.

"It's my business to know everything. E-ve-ry-fuck-ing-thing. Anything that goes on in this goddamn town is my business. And that includes my wife. And it includes you." Tomás felt his cousin's index finger poking at his sternum, slightly deeper with each word. He pushed Fausto's finger away.

"You're crazy. Always have been. There's nothing between me and Ana."

Fausto started laughing, a hysterical laugh that only stopped when he started coughing.

"You know something?" he said when the coughing had stopped. "I could have accepted whatever lousy story you came up with. Something about your being jealous, an old flame. Shit, I would have accepted any story, basically. But flat-out denying it? You have balls, cousin, huge ones!" He reached for the gun and pointed it at Tomás.

"Lost your chance," he said. "Cowards never get second chances."

"You're crazy, Fausto, stop this nonsense!" He was perspiring as he stared at the gun pointed at him less than two feet away. He felt the gripping hand around his throat that told him he would be coughing and panting for air. He reached for his pocket, for the pouch with the needle and the vial of epinephrine. The car had become engulfed by a sea of cows, and rocked wildly like a boat on the waves. Fausto cocked the hammer. He grinned and slowly pulled the trigger. Tomás closed his eyes and waited for the pain. But all he heard was Fausto's laughter as the pin hit the empty chamber.

"Ha-ha-ha," he laughed. "Got you, didn't I?" He blew on the barrel and put the gun back down.

"You really thought I was going to shoot you in the face, didn't you?"

"You asshole. What the hell did you that for?"

"Just messing with you." He punched Tomás in the shoulder, and the smell of beer was upon him again, like a wave of seawater.

"Just messing with you, cousin. Can't you take a joke?"

Tomás pushed his cousin's fist away, furiously, and they spoke no more during the rest of the trip. Fausto chuckled and yanked the car from left to right from time to time, mumbling to himself. When they reached León, he pulled six bullets from his belt and dropped them into the chambers, one by one. Then he let the cylinder spin, and pushed it back into the casing.

"For next time," he said.

Chapter 19

He was surprised when Manolo called. "I need to talk to you," Manolo said. "Can we meet this afternoon?" He barely waited for an answer before hanging up.

Tomás wondered about the sudden call. Manolo had been his only friend in medical school, but then he had become a doctor with the Guardia, and they had lost contact. He closed the lab early and sat down in a café overlooking the Plaza. He noticed that the stone lions in front of the cathedral had grown black and shiny from the many hands that had touched them. Glancing at his watch, he wondered if Manolo had forgotten the place. Then he saw a mustachioed man waving at him from another table. When he did not wave back, the man walked up to him.

"Tomás!" he said. "It's me, Manolo!"

"That moustache!" Tomás exclaimed. "I barely recognized you!" They hugged and patted each other's bellies.

"Still not married?" Manolo said. Tomás grinned.

"Look, this is my son," Manolo said, opening up his wallet. "He's already twelve now." Tomás saw the face of a boy too serious for his age, looking away from the camera.

"He looks like you," he said. "Serious." Manolo smiled and put away the picture, zipping up his photo wallet as if it were armor.

"Can we go somewhere to talk?"

"The cathedral," Tomás suggested. They sat down in a pew towards the back of the chapel. Manolo wasted no time.

"Last week I was called in to pronounce a man dead who had supposedly died by accident." His voice was husky, seeking refuge in Tomás's ears.

"His skin was stripped off with a razor. His body was bloated and engorged."

"What?" Tomás said. "What happened to him?"

"Salt. They sprinkled the body with salt before he died. They rubbed it in until it looked like pickled fish. When I told Somarriba that

I could not write up a death certificate without mentioning what I had seen, he looked at me with those crazy eyes and laughed at me. 'Why not?' he said. 'What's it to you?' 'I'm a guardsman,' I told him, 'but I'm a doctor before anything else.' He laughed a little more and told me to get lost, that he would take care of it in any case." While he spoke, Manolo was staring at the ornate paintings and frescoes of the central nave.

"They hoisted the body on a pickup truck and drove up to the rim of the Santiago, to dump it in the crater." His eyes were red and small now. Tomás looked around, worried about listening ears, but there were none near.

"The family has been asking about the man; he was a guardsman himself. And the Guardia have been saying that he simply disappeared, that no one knows his whereabouts."

Manolo looked straight at Tomás. "I am going to tell the radio stations what has happened," he said.

Tomás shook his head. "Why would you do such a thing? Do you realize what will happen to you?"

"Does it really matter? Anything is better than letting this go on."

"You must think of your family. They will be in danger. Don't expose them." Noise was coming from outside, swelling until it was very close: drums and lira and *triqui-traqua* rattle sounds, and finally the unmistakable motley whirlwind of the Gigantona and her suitor. They came dancing onto the Plaza and stopped in front of the Social Club, where Somoza senior had been slaughtered like a pig.

"If only you had seen the body."

"I have seen corpses. I see them every day."

"No, Tomás. You see a corpse. I see what's left of a man I used to know." His lower lip had stopped trembling, and he stood up, fast. Tomás rose, too.

"Two months ago, I was up north, near Ocotal, in the offensive against the guerrillas. We went up a hill, and suddenly a shoe landed in front of me. I looked up at the helicopter, and saw the soldiers pushing out this blindfolded chap. He was kicking, trying to stay alive. But in the end..."

"Don't do crazy things, Manolo," Tomás said as he grabbed his friend by the shoulders. "Don't throw away your life, and don't sacrifice your family – you have a son, think of him."

"How can you accept that these things happen, Tomás, and say nothing? Doesn't the truth mean anything to you?

"The truth can never be worth a life!"

There was a glint in Manolo's eyes as he looked over Tomás's shoulder, into a distance where the Gigantona was nothing but a cloud of color now.

"The truth?" he snorted. "You want the truth? Would you believe me if I told you that there is a special room in the bunker called the Sewing Room, with meat hooks cemented into the ceilings? Would you believe me? Because that's the truth." He shook his head.

Tomás swallowed hard. "Yes," he said, "yes, I would. I wished I didn't, though." Manolo nodded and put his hand on Tomás's shoulder.

"I never thought of myself as political," he said. "And I still don't. We promised to be doctors, didn't we? Heal the sick and wounded, remember?" Tomás nodded, twice.

"And I tried. I thought this was just a job. I would still be a doctor, after all. But then…it was just getting worse. Stealing is one thing, but killing…I guess you can't forever pretend that things are just fine, can you?"

Tomás said nothing. He thought of Fausto, who had drawn a gun on him, as a joke. Would he have shot him with live rounds? *Not Fausto*, he thought. *Fausto is an asshole, but he has honor, like Manolo. Fausto would never hurt me.*

"Why did you come to me?" he said, emphasizing the last word.

Manolo smiled. "Looking for the devil's advocate," he said. "They're easier to find than good men these days."

Tomás saw the image of his father in his mind's eye. *What would my father have done?* he thought. *"Brave but stupid," my uncle called him. And look what it brought him. The inside of an urn.*

"Let it be, Manolo," he said. "Just let it be. Think of your family. Others will speak out, surely. You must think of yourself now. Of your family."

They walked back to the Plaza, and hugged.

"Now I know why I came to you," Manolo said.

Tomás was surprised. "But I didn't convince you," he said.

"Oh, but you did." Manolo shook his hand and smiled. "You did exactly that."

Manolo went to the radio station, as he had said he would, and denounced Somarriba out loud. The parents of the boy whose body had been dropped in the crater were somebodies, and they pushed and prodded until a military tribunal was convened. It duly sentenced Somarriba to ten years of house arrest. But with his old buddies in charge of enforcing the verdict, the convict literally laughed his head off. So two years after he had dumped a pickled body in the crater of an active volcano, Angel Somarriba's car was parked on a short and straight stretch of road between León and Managua, where cane fields formed a wall of silence. When a brown Cadillac passed him, he switched on the engine and followed. Inside the brown Cadillac, Isabel noticed that her husband was growing nervous.

"What's the matter, Manolo?" she said.

"Nothing," he said. "It's just that this car has been following us for the past fifteen minutes. I wonder why he doesn't simply overtake us."

"So slow down, then," she said. "Just let him pass, we're in no hurry. Today is Sunday." Manolo took his foot off the gas pedal, and barely had he done so when the other car overtook him and ran away, fast and angry. Manolo looked sideways when the car passed them, and started shaking. He had recognized Somarriba in the speeding car, but said nothing to his wife. He slowed down until their car had come to a complete standstill.

Neutral, the word raced through his head. *It's in neutral.* The other car drove off the road and turned around. It faced them, the sun gleaming off its black top. *Like a bull ready to charge,* Manolo thought. There was a sharp clap, and when he looked down, he saw blood running down his chest, and a shattered windshield lying in his lap.

"Jesus," he said, "I thought they had locked him up." His jaw dropped, then his head, and Isabel started screaming. The bull came closer. Humming, huffing, and shuddering in the heat. It stopped so close that the two hoods could have touched. Somarriba stepped out and yanked open the door on the driver's side. He pushed up Manolo's head with his gun and let it fall back so he could see the open eyes, big, wide-open paper eyes pasted onto his face. Then he charged his shotgun once more and shot Manolo through the chest.

Isabel had been frozen in her seat while the man opened the door. But splattered with her husband's blood she found her voice again, and screamed until she ran out of breath. Somarriba offered her a handkerchief to wipe her tears and blow her nose, a white handkerchief embroidered by the peasant women of Grenada.

"Keep it," he said, and made a dismissive gesture with his left hand while he slung the gun over his shoulder – then he walked to his car and drove back to León.

Manolo's body was delivered to the morgue in León. It came to Tomás, as they all came to him. He pulled out the two bullets lodged in Manolo's chest, and dropped them on a metal plate; it was the only sound heard in the hospital that day.

He looked at Manolo's face. "Why did you do it, my friend?" he said. "Why did you not just wait this out? You could have." He stuffed the intestines and lungs back inside the ribcage, without the need to think which part went where. *Where are you now, Manolo,* he thought. *Where are you, where is your soul amid all these bits and pieces?* He zippered up the body with the Hagedorn needle, tagged it, and shoved it into a deep metal drawer. It made no sound as it closed.

"Something else you did not tell me," he mumbled. "Or perhaps you did, but I could not hear you. You were right, Manolo, the parts don't make a person."

He walked up to his lab and drew the shutters. He pushed wet towels under the door, so he would not hear the footsteps of nurses and students passing by the next day. He drank a bottle of rum and lay down on the folding bed. His eyes felt heavy, his tongue felt thick, and he fell asleep among the livers and spleens, the embryos and brain lobes serenely suspended in giant jars towering over his supine body.

It was late in the morning when the phone rang.

"I didn't see you last night," Victoria said. "Where were you?"

"Manolo was killed," he said, "by one of those murderous bastards." She told him to hold the line, and he could hear her call Sofía, telling her to bring the newspaper. There was a long, rustling sound, as of pages being unfolded and turned.

"I found it," she said. "It's under obituaries, not on the news pages. You know I don't read obituaries." There was silence while he heard her hem and haw.

"Very sad," she said as she spoke again. "I remember him as a nice boy. How did this happen? Why didn't he ask anyone for advice?"

"He came to me," Tomás said.

There was silence at the other end.

"I tried, but he didn't listen."

"What did you tell him?"

"To let it go. To think about his family and live his life. Isn't that what you have always told me people should do?"

He heard his mother sigh. "Regretting a decision is a terrible thing for a man, I know that. But not making a decision is even worse."

"I should have persuaded him to let it be. At least he would have been alive today."

"You and I, we are not very good at persuading, are we now, Tomás?"

He was surprised. She had not mentioned the two of them in a single sentence in a long time.

"Did he have children?"

"A son. He's fourteen."

"Go see his widow then. And talk to her son."

He did as his mother had suggested. Isabel received him in the garden. Her eyes were swollen. *She must have cried this morning. Probably just before I arrived*, he thought.

"Where is your son?" he asked. She pointed back to the house.

"He doesn't want to see anyone," she said. "He doesn't understand. He thought his father had done the right thing, that's how we raised him." Her eyes started tearing, and she pulled out a kerchief to blow her nose. He touched her arm.

"I'm sorry, Isabel. I wished I could have stopped him."

She shook her head. "I know you tried," she said. "He told me he went to see you and what you told him. But he wasn't that kind of man."

What kind of man was he? Did I know him? Or did I only know the boy I went to school with, but never the man he had become? Isabel walked out with him, and when he was about to climb into his car a boy walked out of the house. Tomás recognized him from the photo Manolo had shown him. *The same deep-set eyes, the intense stare, and the beginnings of a moustache pulling away from his chin.*

"My mother said you were his friend." The boy looked at him the way he had not looked at the camera, without flinching.

"Yes, I was his friend."

"Then you should have this." He handed Tomás small leather pouch. It felt heavy.

"What is it?" he said. The boy did not answer, so Tomás unrolled the bag and saw a switchblade knife.

"He gave it to me," the boy said. "But I never used it. I hate knives."

Chapter 20

Three guardsmen jumped into a jeep to make their way to the Military Club.

"Not a moment to lose," the one driving said. "There's a cold beer with my name on it waiting at the bar!" The cobblestone streets were still slippery after the rain that had fallen that morning. In the Sutiava neighborhood, on the long narrow street that went from the Plaza to the outskirts of town, three children were playing. They jumped in and out of the muddy puddles and dragged a small dog along. It had a dirty pelt, black streaked with gray and white, like a pinto bean.

The three soldiers were laughing and telling jokes.

"You see that fat guy crapping in his pants?" the bearded one sitting next to the driver said. "These guys are unbelievable. One moment they are big shots, the next moments they crawl on all fours."

The children were walking a plank that was laid across the puddle. It sagged in the middle, but if they tiptoed over it, the water could not reach them.

"Come, César," they cheered. The dog growled and bared its fangs when they tried to push it. But it was small, and they were three, and determined. They pushed and pushed against César's butt, until at last the dog stood with three legs on the board and one in the water.

The driver and the bearded guard turned their heads to look at the lieutenant telling his story. They did not see the board, the dog, and the three children pushing the dog. And when they did it was too late.

"*Cuidao*," the storyteller shouted.

"*Mierda*," the driver yelled. He tried to yank the wheel around but it was too late, and the jeep slammed into the wall of the shoemaker's store. The wall caved in and the tin roof came sliding down, eight feet of undulated sharpness looking for a place to land.

The driver's eyes remained wide open as the roof lodged itself in the softness of his neck. Dazed, the other two crawled out while people gathered around them. They blocked the soldiers' way as they tried to stagger away, squinting like drunkards in the timid morning sun. The lieutenant pulled his revolver and waved it at the crowd.

"Step back now, everyone," he yelled. "You all keep your distance now, y'hear?" The soldiers had not seen the front of the car, where it had slammed into the wall. They had not seen that something was wedged between the car and the wall, something small and barefoot.

They were more than fifty men and women, closing in on the two soldiers.

"Murderers!" they shouted. "*Asesinos malditos!*"

"Step back!" the soldiers shouted back, and fired. Two people fell dead, and for one second it seemed as if the crowd were falling back: a heaving sea of bodies that seemed to hesitate. But then it lurched forward, undeterred, a mighty monster of the deep determined to get its revenge.

"It was an accident!" the storyteller screamed.

Fausto was at the scene within fifteen minutes. "Round up these people," he growled, "all of them, I want to know exactly what happened here!"

"They're dead, Captain," the sergeant reported back, "all three of them."

"That's not what bothers me," Fausto said. "Those three were sacks of shit, probably drunk behind the wheel. What I want to know is how it was possible that two guardias were beaten to pulp in my district! No one touches the Guard without my permission!"

They lined up everyone against the walls, on opposite sides of the street. Fausto stood in the middle, arms akimbo.

"I want to hear what happened here," he spat, "and the stories had better be the same."

So those on the sunny side of the street told their story, and those in the shadow told their story as well. And as generally happens in such cases, each time it was a different story. *No two stories are ever the same*, a young boy sitting on the curb was thinking, puzzled by the stories his neighbors were telling, stories that did not add up.

When the storytelling finished the soldiers pulled aside eleven men and one woman. Fire spat from their guns, and Fausto drove away. Some of the neighbors called themselves lucky as they hauled away the bodies that had slid down the walls. The bodies were on both sides of the street. The boy peered at them from inside his father's house, which was now missing part of its roof. The Guard drove off with the wrecked jeep in tow. The two dead guardsmen had been dropped back into their seats, and the third one was still lying slumped over the wheel. It looked as if they had drunk too much, nothing else, except for the small red stain on the olive hood.

After everyone had left, the dog came out of hiding. It had run when the jeep was upon them, just before it smashed into the girl and then the wall.

"Come here, César," the newspaper boy said when he saw it. "Come here, boy. Good boy." The dog was limping – one of its front legs was bloody and swollen. It yelped and bared its fangs when the boy poured water on its paw and swaddled it with a strip of fabric he had torn off the Gigantona dress kept in his father's storage room.

"They won't miss it," he said. "It's just a small piece, they won't miss it; she has such a long dress." When he finished swaddling the pinto bean paw he lifted the dog and carried it away. Not like a cat, not even like a baby. Like a sheep, like a lamb before it has learned to walk, slung over its shepherd's shoulders.

That evening he watched as his brother and two other boys left town for the mountains, looking for the elusive guerrillas who had promised they would change the world, starting with Nicaragua. They climbed onto the back of a pickup truck, each carrying a small cardboard suitcase. They could have been mistaken for students returning to boarding school.

"Where are they going?" he asked his father.

"Up north," Elías grunted. "Soon we'll have no grown-up boys left. So you'd better get ready to play the dwarf this year. Now help me stick this tarp under the rafters. Unless you want to get wet tonight."

The bodies were delivered to the morgue that evening: the Guardia had needed little time. A mere formality, but bureaucracy mattered – every person dead of unnatural causes was to go the morgue. Tomás gasped when he pulled back the sheet covering the girl's body. Apart from a small bruise above the left eye, her face showed no sign of death. He often felt that the faces of adults exhibited a stoic peace – as if their skin had relaxed, and relinquished the suffering that had been stored in its folds. The faces of children, however, looked anguished, as if a bitter taste had managed to hide under their tongues while their lives were being robbed.

This girl is different, he thought. *As if she were sleeping. As if her skin had not had time to wake up and recognize the pain that was about to take her.*

"What happened?" he asked the diener. He uncovered the body, and saw bruises, the signs of massive hemorrhage, but few cuts.

"An accident," the man said. "A car accident."

"How old?"

"Nine."

"And how do we know this was an accident? What if someone did this on purpose?"

"Well," the diener said, "we don't give those opinions, Doctor. We never do. We just write up what we find."

We write up what we find, he thought. *And what if we are looking for the wrong things? Then what do we find?*

He put on his gloves and mask. The diener had put a scalpel and enterotome on a small tray, and hung the rib cutters from a hook. He turned to pick up the body block and was ready to shove it under the girl, but Tomás stopped him.

"Wait," he said. "We may not need this." He bent over to examine the hemorrhage extending from below her ribcage. He saw the paint, smeared out as if it had become liquid again and had sought to hide in her skin.

"It's olive drab," he said. "Olive paint. Who buys an olive-colored car?"

"Willys," the diener said. "Only the Willys jeeps are this color."

Hmm, Tomás thought. *So I guess we'll never know if this was an accident.* He told the diener to clean up the body and return her to the drawer.

"Won't you open it, Doctor?" the man said.

"No. I have seen everything I need to see. What was her name?"

The diener flipped over the cardboard card. "Amparo," he said. "Amparo Suarez."

Tomás nodded. "Let's give Amparito back to her parents, then." He signed the certificate. Cause of death: "organ failure due to violent impact by military vehicle."

The next morning someone called.

"Doctor, it's someone from the Guardia," Juanita told him.

"Why did you write this, Doctor?" the man inquired.

"It's my job. I'm supposed to write up my findings."

"It's your job to write up the cause of death. Not why you think this happened or who might have done this. We ask you to be a scientist, Doctor, not a novelist."

"But the parents," he sputtered. "This was a child – this calls for justice."

"We'll take care of everything, Doctor. And I advise you to find different outlets for your creative impulses."

He did not let go. "But," he said, "will the soldiers be punished?"

"I said we'll take care of everything." There was a click on the other end of the line. He kept the horn pressed to his ear, waiting for the man to speak again, but all he could hear was a distant crackle.

Chapter 21

The backyard of Fausto's home was a sprawling sea of grass and fruit trees. There were prickly lemon trees, thick-trunked explosions of low-hanging mango, and a great tamarind tree that shot up to heaven. Two avocado trees with gnarled branches stood leaning together like old men whispering in each other's ears.

It was Sunday morning – early, but the air was already hot and stale, as if the heat of the previous day had never abated. Adriana and Simón had gotten up before the roosters could crow, and Martita had dressed them and fed them breakfast. Now they were playing in the garden while Martita was at the front gate chatting with the young soldier standing guard.

This guard is different from the previous ones, Martita had decided. He was young – the gun slung over his shoulder looked ridiculously old on him. But he looked handsome to her, with his one gold tooth that shone bright and full. He leaned into the towering bougainvillea and cut off a twig, roughing up the thorns with his knife until they fell off. With his best smile he held out the flowers for her to take. She blushed and stuck the small bouquet in her hair, standing close to him and laughing until there was only her smile and his gold tooth that chattered through the silent Sunday morning.

In the far corner of the garden Simón climbed up the avocado tree, and Adriana followed him. They climbed past the gnarled, thick branches, and soon were near the top, close to a lonely bunch of avocados shaped like giant green light bulbs. When Simón moved up a little more to get that one avocado just out of reach, he heard a flutter of wings, and turned.

The branch broke without giving warning. Martita heard a scream and two dull thuds, one barely after the other, as if two falling coconuts had been competing to beat the pull of gravity.

Simón was lying in a small red puddle spreading from the back of his head. His eyes were wide open, as if he were seeing something of which he did not want to lose sight. Adriana was lying next to him, her head on his thigh.

"*Dios mío*, what happened?" Martita cried out, and pushed the soldier away from her.

Ana was still asleep. She had not heard the thud, but she did hear Martita's screams. She jumped and ran out the garden door barefoot, ran until she reached the tree where the servants were standing in a small circle. She saw Adriana sitting against the trunk of the other tree, rubbing her eyes as if she had just woken up.

"Thank God," Ana said as she knelt down and held the girl's head. "Thank God my girl is safe." Then the small circle of people opened up and Ana saw a limp body. She took one step, but her knees gave out. As she crawled through the grass, her hands touched something red and sticky. She gasped for air. Her breath became shorter and shorter, ever shorter until she thought that her lungs would stop pumping and her heart would stop beating; as if her heart were seeking a way out of her body – through her mouth or her eyes; until her face started popping, and her skin started stretching and there was nothing left but the steady, unstoppable contractions of her heart clawing its way out of her body. *Let it go*, she thought, *just let it go and be done with it*. But then a belfry started ringing in her ears, bursting her skull. She snapped, and her heart sunk back into the emptiness of her chest. The belfry fell silent, and she wailed.

"Go," she yelled at the soldier. "Run and get doctor Delacorte!"

The soldier dropped his gun and ran. People turned their heads to look at the gun-less soldier running through the streets with his shirttails flapping behind him – an odd sight on a Sunday morning. When Tomás arrived at the scene, he felt only the faintest hint of a pulse.

"Fast," he barked. "Help me get him into the car." They hoisted the limp body into the car while Ana sobbed and patted the boy's cheeks.

"*Amorcito*," she cried, "wake up, wake up, I beg you, amorcito, please wake up now, please."

He called Doctor Urbina. He begged him. And for the first time in many years, the hospital gates swung open on a Sunday. The people waiting outside were surprised. They gasped and thronged silently, thinking that perhaps, just this one time, the rule had been relaxed. But as soon as the two vehicles had entered the gates were shut again, and the chatter outside resumed with renewed intensity. Inside, a generator was cranked up; it ripped through the silence, waking up a sleeping building.

Simón died just before midnight, as if all his days had been counted and spent. When there was no more pulse, Tomás bent his head, and it filled with a numbing sense of loss. It was as if the room had been emptied – as if all thoughts had been sucked out when the small body inside it stopped quivering. The other two doctors shook their heads and patted him on the shoulder before leaving through the scrub room. He was alone now with Simón's body, and the nurse who was cleaning it. He noticed how she looked at the boy, biting her lip. She sat up the body to clean off the clotted blood, but he was too heavy for her.
"Can you help me, Doctor? There's no one else."
He nodded.
"Hold him," she said, "he's only barely gone; you can still hold him as you would hold a child." He lifted the body and held it in his arms. He felt the wet hair clinging to his coat while the nurse cleaned the boy's back.
"Now lay him down," she said, "lay him down softly, it will be his last time." Tomás tightened his hands around the boy's body. It was warm, and the beating of his own heart drowned out the silence that came from the limp body resting against his.
"His name is Simón," he said.
The nurse smiled at him. "It's all right, Doctor," she said. She undid his grip, gently. He lowered the body onto the table, and the nurse wrapped the ends of the bed sheet around it, covering it completely until only the face was still visible. She nodded at him and left the room.
Now I must tell her, he thought. *God, how can I tell her this? I was there when this boy was born. How cruel that I should be the one to tell her this.*
When he opened the door, Ana rushed toward him. He said nothing. He did not want her to see his eyes, did not want her to see

the emptiness that had filled him. So he held her while her body shook. Not to comfort her, but to hide the emptiness inside himself. Then he walked her into the small room that had been robbed of its thoughts.

"*Ayy mi bébé, mi bebecito*," she sobbed.

They took the body away, and then Ana left as well, and he was alone in the room again. He sat down and looked around: a bed, a chair, a small window glued to the ceiling. The emptiness became so heavy that he fell asleep in the chair, and dreamed he had become a dwarf with a water head who danced around the Gigantona. He danced until his head was spinning and close to bursting, and he thought he would faint. But even though he stopped dancing, the Gigantona did not for one moment pause, and instead waltzed away in a cloud of whirling color. An old woman appeared, carrying firewood. Her back was as horizontal as an ironing board.

"Having problems, little man?" she cackled.

"Yes," he said. "I feel dizzy. I don't know what I'm doing in this body. This is not my body."

"Hmmphmmph," she sneered, "that's what we all say. Look at me; do you think I was meant to be carrying firewood?"

He felt ashamed. "No, I hadn't thought of that."

"What do you want, young man?" she said. "Maybe I can help you."

"How could you?" Tomás said. "How could you if you cannot even help yourself?"

"Says who?" the old woman scowled. "And in any case, don't jump to conclusions. Do not assume that I cannot help others just because of the way I look. All you need to do is ask."

He took a deep breath. "I want to court the Gigantona," he said. "She is the only one I have loved in all my life. I have danced for her, I have sung to her, but she has never noticed me."

The old woman hemmed and hawed. Then she poked him in the chest with a bony finger.

"Since she is tall, she thinks the world is home to faraway places only. But to you, as you are short, the world is a place of details so small that they have become meaningless to anyone but yourself." She reached behind her and pulled up a burlap bag.

"Take this," she said.

"What is it?" he said, but she waved her hand. He opened the bag and peered inside.

"Don't ask, just eat it." She laughed out loud, and he saw that her gums were blackened from years of chewing sugarcane. Inside the bag were what looked like slices and slivers of dried apricot.

"Eat them," she said. "Eat them, and you'll see how dreams come true."

He nibbled at one of the slices, and when he had chewed it down, he felt how his legs started stretching, then his arms, and his feet and fingers. Every single long bone in his body grew longer yet, so much that it made him nauseous. *Now I can catch her*, he thought. He moved his legs, but it felt like walking on stilts, on wobbly beanstalk stilts.

"Beloved," he shouted as he ran after the whirling cloud of color. "Beloved, wait for me, I am worthy of you now." He ran past her to block her path. She stopped and faced him, but her face was a mask still and so was his. All they could do was stare at each other with glassy eyes that were not their own.

A crowing rooster cut short his dream, and the Gigantona receded into the distance as a jeep pulled into the hospital courtyard, the sound of its screeching wheels echoing through the hallways. *The Eighth Day*, Tomás had time to think.

"Where is my son?" Fausto shouted. "Tomás, where is my son?"

Tomás sighed deep and hard, and stepped into the corridor, closing the door behind him. He squeezed his fists inside his pockets to bring back the circulation in his fingers, waiting for the inevitable. Two hands grabbed him by the shoulders and dug into his skin, until he lifted his head and faced the question.

"Where…is…he…Tomás?" Fausto's face was contorted and flushed, as if undecided between anger and pain.

"Fausto, there was nothing I could…there was nothing anyone could have done." There was a grunt, and he was banged against the door.

"Not…my…son," Fausto said at last. "Not my son. I don't deserve this." Tomás tried to push him away, but Fausto clutched even harder now, until he had his cousin pinned against the door.

"This was not supposed to happen, Tomás."

"What are you talking about? There is nothing anyone could have done, Fausto. I am truly sorry."

"Nooooo." It was a low wail, the sound of air being sucked from the deep recesses of his body. Fausto shook his head, slowly, from left to right and then back again.

"You should have saved him, Tomás. The girl should have died, not my son!"

His jaw dropped, and he stopped breathing. "What?" he said, finally. "Are you saying that you would have wanted your daughter to die instead? Are you insane?"

"Goddamnit, Tomás, my son died because she fell on top of him. He should have been the one to have been saved, not her."

"This is not about saving, Fausto! It was an accident!"

"He should have been saved!"

Tomás struggled to undo the vise grip on his arms. "Adriana is your daughter, Fausto! How can you say such a thing?"

"She serves no purpose in life. She's an idiot! You should have saved my son."

"I can't bring him back to life, Fausto. I don't have the power to bring the dead back to life. I wished I did, but I don't. You must accept that this was his fate."

"Screw you, Tomás, and screw fate!"

Fausto spat out the words, pursing his lips as if he had just tasted the bitterest of jícaro fruit. He pushed Tomás against the wall once more and grunted. Then he turned and walked back the way he had come in. Exactly that way, tracing back his steps as if they had been laid out for him, an invisible path for walking backwards out of a room where murder has been committed. He walked until he reached the jeep with the engine still running, and raced out through the gate.

While Ana instructed the maids to meticulously fold her son's clothes and arrange them in the closet to be ready for school, Fausto got drunk beyond redemption that day. Honking hard, he rammed his jeep into a herd of cows blocking his path, until it was a mass of bloodied, stampeding meat. When he was through, he drove the jeep into a ditch, a narrow canal that kept the rain from causing mudslides, right where it flowed into the Rio Chiquito. Here the jeep stopped, and Fausto fell out. His hat flew off, his jacket ripped, and his shoes walked away all by themselves. When his wallet rolled away, it landed under a lonely pochote tree standing guard, under the spiked pochote tree which the campesinos call the gladiator tree.

With Simón's death, emptiness moved into Ana's house. She dreaded the stillness hanging in the rooms, the clock ticking through the silence, ticking ahead, putting time between her and her boy. She had pleaded with Fausto not to punish Martita, but he was beyond himself. He had the girl locked up in her room, and he himself sat brooding in Simón's room for hours on end. The guard with the gold tooth was never found – he had run away as soon as the car carrying Simón had left for the hospital. The neighbors said he had run so fast it seemed the devil was on his heels – he had even thrown his uniform pants into the bougainvillea, where it sat on the colored leaves like a piece of molted snake skin. Fausto sent a squad to look for the boy at his home in Masaya, but no one had ever heard of him there.

"Fake address," the captain told him, "that should teach us a lesson. Too many rejects entering the Guard." Fausto brooded a bit more, tried to remember the boy's face, but he could not. He remembered there was a gold tooth, but when he told the captain, this one just raised his shoulders. "Half the farmers in this country have gold teeth, Colonel. We're not going to catch him with that kind of description."

The two avocado trees were cut down. Before long, the garden was littered with gnarled trunks and chunks of avocado tree, until they had all become unrecognizable pieces of wood.

"Look," the gardener said. "They're hollow inside, what did I tell you!" And it was true – the termites had spent years hollowing out the branches, until they had become little more than empty shells filled with air, and lighter than straw.

Fausto asked to be transferred to the town of Rivas, where he commanded one of the regiments. He came home to León less and less frequently, avoiding the company of a house full of women.

Simón's death touched Tomás more than he had thought would be possible. *Is this what a parent feels?* he wondered. *This constant, nagging fear that something terrible might happen to one's child? And being left with a nauseating, numbing sense of loss when it does?*

A month after Simón's death Ana had prayer cards sent out. Inside was a picture of the boy, taken only days before he died. The boy was laughing. *Unaware of the disaster that was brewing,* Tomás thought. He touched the portrait with his fingers, letting them run over the boy's face, from his forehead down over his nose, to his mouth and chin.

"Goodbye, Simón," he said as he placed the picture on his desk. "You will never grow up. You will always be your mother's little boy."

Chapter 22

Victoria lived her life as if it would never end. Pilar, her sister-in-law, asked her one day if she thought she would live forever, in the accusing tone of a fifty-year-old who suddenly realizes that some people their age can still see perfectly well without eyeglasses, yet badgers them about the need for eyeglasses until the two-eyed finally concede to the four-eyed, buy the damn glasses, and so become one of them, forever seeing the world through eyes made by others.

When she heard the question, Victoria stared at Pilar as if she were wearing a clown's costume, or worse: as if she weren't there; as if the air itself had whispered something funny in her ears, the perfectly good ears she was perfectly able to hear with. Then she started laughing, a hysterical laugh that cut through the hibiscus-scented air like a knife through butter. Tomás had gotten used to her laughter. It was the same laughter he heard when she came home in the early morning hours, smelling of rum and middle-aged men who spread around their smitten prostate smell like dogs pissing up barkless trees, scorching them with the sourness of their ketone-laden piss. He told her often that the drinking and smoking would get to her, that she would end up with a bloated liver. But since he only told her when she came home drunk, and avoided her when she was not, the message never sank in.

"Convenient," Sofía said.

While his mother might have thought that she would never die, life thought otherwise. Her hair started falling out, and then her skin turned yellow.

"You need to get tests done," he said, but she shook her head. The yellowing of her skin made her look older, and she no longer spent weekends in Managua. As if all of a sudden life was catching up with her.

If Victoria had been stoical and detached during her life, she became stubborn towards the end of it.

"Talk to her, Sofía," Tomás said, "she'll listen to you for sure." Sofía did not ask what the tests were for, or why they were needed. But she did get Victoria to agree to go to the hospital.

Tomás decided to run the lab tests himself.

"I can get someone else to run them," Doctor Urbina offered.

"No," Tomás said, "no, this is my lab, what's the difference? It's just a tissue sample to be analyzed."

Doctor Urbina shook his head. "It's your mother, Tomás," he said. "Aren't you concerned?"

"Yes," he said, "yes, of course I am." He pushed the old man out and closed the door behind him.

"It's your liver, Mother," he told her. She raised her shoulders.

"Liver, lungs, heart, what difference does it make? I've lived my life, darling, what else is there? Things are just the way they are."

A week before his mother died Rafaela came to see him. He knew she had come on behalf of Mama Mica.

"Payita," he said, "what a surprise. What brings you here? Please, come in and sit with me."

"No, Tomás," she said, "I'm here to pass on a message, no more. Mama Mica wants to talk to you." He went over later that morning, feeling awkwardly small and young again when he entered the house. It felt empty and large, a shell of dark hallways and humid patios. Dizziness came over him, forcing him to steady himself against the wall. It was as if the house had grown blind: no longer guided by eyes capable of gauging its own true dimensions, it had become a shape without form, connecting wing to empty wing, and to rooms surviving only as appendices to its intestinal tract.

Rafaela was waiting for him in the kitchen, and led him to the back room where Mama Mica was resting. The scent of lavender, distinct but faint, met him when he entered.

"Come, Tomás," she said, patting a rattan chair that had been pulled up to the bed. "Sit here, my boy, sit with your grandma now." He was stunned by how small she was. *Small and frail, so unlike the image of veiled plumpness I had preserved of her throughout the years. Must be close to one hundred years old by now.* Mama Mica stretched out a wrinkled hand and touched his face.

"Your father died when he was twenty-eight," she said.

I know that, he thought. *When I turned twenty-eight myself, I stopped counting the years. It was unfair that I should grow older or taller than my father had been.*

"You look like him," she said. "This is how he would have looked had he lived longer." Brown and freckled, her hand felt warm on his wrist. He could feel her pulse against his own, and swallowed.

"Did you know, Tomás, that a child looks like the man its mother loved when she conceived it? If she truly loved her husband, her child will look like her husband. If she loved another man, then her child will look like the other man, even if the child is her husband's." He frowned, but said nothing.

"Your mother was very much in love with your father, *hijito*. She was heartbroken when he left, and she could not understand why. She was angry with him, she felt abandoned and betrayed." Tomás reached for his kerchief to wipe his forehead.

"Has she ever spoken to you about your father?

"No," he said. "No one ever has, except Uncle Rogelio, when I was a child."

"He was an extraordinary man. Everyone who knew him admired him."

"Until he made the wrong choice."

"That did not stop them from admiring him. They admired him for his courage. For the strength of his convictions. A man who acts on his words – this is no mean feat." She smacked her lips and fluttered her hand, so he passed her the juice. When she had drunk, she closed her eyes for a few seconds.

"Ana came to see me last week," she said, her eyes still closed.

"Yes," he whispered, grateful that she could not see his face.

"She says she will never get over losing her boy. That losing him made her realize the mistake she has made."

"What mistake?"

"She doesn't love him."

He rested his forehead against his hand, shielding it from view. "They are husband and wife," he said. "They had children."

"She loves you still, Tomás."

He blushed behind the hand that hid his face. Mama Mica's hand reached out for his and squeezed it. He felt her bony fingers press into his skin, sizing him up.

"What did you do with the present you were supposed to give to Ana when she turned fifteen?" Her grip was strong, not like anything he would have expected of a woman this frail.

"What do you mean?"

"Did you give it to her?"

"I don't remember."

"Yes, you do. Just think harder."

He closed his eyes. The twilight was back, and the voices of people long gone were in his ears, but in flashes, rushed and as if the words were spoken backwards. He saw himself giving his gift to Ana, and then walking back to where he stood thinking, deciding between a book and a flask of apricot essence.

"You gave it to Fausto, didn't you?"

He swallowed. "I think I did, yes."

Mama Mica sighed. "We cannot undo what has been done," she said. "Things happen for a reason, and nothing we do can change that. You may all think Rafaela and myself are witches, but we're not magicians; we only nudge along what is supposed to happen anyway." Her hand loosened its grip on his wrist. "Ana has accepted her mistake," she said. "But she blames herself for her son's death. She thinks it's her punishment."

"It wasn't her fault," he said. "It was no one's fault. It was just an accident, a terrible accident, nothing else."

"What was?"

"Simón's death."

She cocked her head. "There are no secrets in this house, Tomás." With blood rushing to his face, he felt like a schoolboy being apprehended, caught in the act of stealing *marañon* and mangos from the neighbor's trees.

"I have outgrown games," he said.

"Games or no games, I see you unhappy, *figlio mio*. You are… how old are you now, Tomás?"

"I am thirty-eight," he said, ruefully.

She chuckled. "You know that when I was thirty-eight I was a grandmother already! Yet you are still not a father." The chocorrón was clawing at the veil like a sailor working the halyard, lowering the sails in time for the storm.

"Help your old grandmother, please, Tomás," she said. He stood up and reached behind her to arrange the pillows. He felt the warmth of her face, the prickliness of the white hair that flowed out from under the knot behind her head. When he moved back, she held his arm, and spoke close to his ear.

"And what about your mother?" she said. "You should not hate your mother, Tomás. Life has not been generous with her, and those who never received love cannot easily give it. So make your peace with her before it is too late. Remember her for what she did, not for what she failed to do."

He stayed silent and sat down again.

"I am not asking you to love her," she said. He jerked his head, afraid she might have read his mind.

"I am asking you to remember her." Before he could open his mouth, she had laid her hand on his arm.

"Remembering people is loving them. It's just that we often do not realize this until it's too late. We do not remember what we do not love, Tomás. Those we hate, their memories fade. It's life's way of easing our pain. And nothing is more terrible than not being remembered, believe me."

"I have learned to live with not being loved, Grandmother."

"That's what you say, but your mouth and your heart are saying different things." He looked at the freckled hand resting on his wrist. When she spoke again, her voice sounded tired: "These things come to people in their own time. Do not think that I have not known loneliness, *mi hijo*. You may think that with so many children, grandchildren, and great-grandchildren, I have not had the time to be lonely. But I have had my share, like all people." She patted his wrist. "Now be a good boy and pass me a glass of water, will you, Tomás?"

He walked to the dresser where a carafe was standing with one glass, covered with an embroidered napkin.

He gave her the glass, and she drank. Slowly and measuring each gulp, as if drinking too much of it would be a waste. *Or a sin perhaps,* he thought, *a wasteful sin, or the sin of waste itself. Was there such a sin?*

She lay back in the vast expanse of cotton and lace.

"Now then," she said, as she handed him back the glass, "how's the hospital these days, Tomás?"

He huffed, and said: "They call me the dead-tissues doctor." She cocked her head, and looked like a bird now, bony and saurian, a small bird perched in a leafless tree.

"Do you mind?"

He raised one shoulder: "At first I hated it, and when I found out I kept the door to the lab locked for one whole week, coming in before anyone else, and leaving after all the others had gone home."

The bird head was still cocked, so he continued: "Yes, I did mind. Of course I did. I mean, who wants to be called a dead-tissues doctor?"

"And are you?"

"Am I what?"

"A dead-tissues doctor?"

"These people don't know what they're talking about. Pathology is a highly specialized skill…"

"Which allows you to stay away from people, doesn't it, Tomás?"

"It's different, it's…"

She had pouted her lips, the way his mother used to, many years ago.

"Shhh," she said, "shhh. You don't need to convince me, Tomás. I'm already gone from this world. Convince the living instead."

The funeral was short, but Tomás was surprised at how many had come to pay their respects. He could not help but think that they had come out of habit, because of his mother's last name and her endless socializing. The day after the funeral, he sat at his desk, sifting through the papers that his mother had accumulated in her lifetime. *This is now the only proof that there once was a person named Victoria Cortés de Delacorte,* he thought. *That she was born and lived her life and had a son and died. Here are the letters and the photos; here's the proof in case anyone doubts her passage on earth.*

Sofía shuffled into sight with a large shoebox filled with more photos. She looked wrinkled and frail now. Her hair was no longer gray; it had turned pure white, which made her arms look darker than they were. The lazier of her eyes had giving up on trying to see altogether.

"Sit down, Sofía," he said. He got up to take the shoebox from her. "You shouldn't be carrying heavy things, let Juanita take care of them." She sat down without letting go of the box, and put it on her lap instead. She rummaged through it and held up a dog-eared photograph with serrated edges.

"Do you remember this, Tomás?" she said. He took the buckled print from her, holding it at arm's length. A small boy was sitting on a chair, dressed in a sailor's outfit. His eyes did not look at the camera. Instead, he looked up at the woman standing next to him. She was tall, wearing a chiffon stole that had been draped across her shoulders. Her gaze lost itself beyond the camera's eye. *In love with the camera,* he thought, *always in love with whoever was not in the picture.*

"Yes," he said. "Yes I do remember that day. I was five years old and told her I would marry her when I grew up. After the picture was taken she ran off again."

Sofía touched his shoulder. "Just because she did not tell you doesn't mean she didn't love you. Don't remember her that way, Tomás."

He closed his eyes.

"I will be leaving tomorrow," Sofía said.

"Where will you be going?" he said. "This is your home."

"This is just a house, Tomás. It's not my home."

"But you've lived with us forever. Why would you want to leave now?"

"Because my job is done."

Thinking that it was a joke, he grimaced: "I grew up a long time ago, Sofía, so if that was your job, why didn't you leave before?"

"Perhaps that wasn't my job then."

He winced. "Where will you go? Who will take care of you?"

"Ay hijito, I have four children and fifteen grandchildren, and I don't even know how many great-grandchildren I have by now!"

He thought the joke had gone far enough. "Sofía, I am talking to you as a doctor. You cannot go back to the coast. You need to take your pills; you need to be looked after. They can't do that there."

"Don't you worry so much about me, Tomás. I'll be just fine – I'm seventy-four, you know. If I've come this far, I'm sure I'll be able to hang on a little longer." She stood up. Her arms were no longer the strong tree branches that had sheltered him when he was young. They were just two thin arms now, tired of folding clothes and combing hair.

"I will leave tomorrow," she said. "Farewell, my nuunik antuka." The hair on his arms stood up inside the goose bumps that had formed in spite of the noonday heat. He had not heard the words in many years.

"What did you say, Sofía?" He took hold of her hand.

"You don't remember, Tomás?" She laughed. "Well, I guess some things are not meant to be remembered." She squeezed back harder than he thought was possible for her frail hands. "You'll be fine now, Tomás. From now it will just be you and your choices." She undid the clasp of his hands onto her own, and walked away.

"You were always the stronger one, weren't you, Sofía?" he said, but she had already shuffled out of sight.

When he arrived at the breakfast table the next morning he saw two large brass keys lying next to his plate.

"What's this, Juanita?" he said.

"They are Sofía's, Doctor."

He guffawed. "Go tell her to stop this joke," he said. "Or no, I will play along: tell her I will drive her to the bus station myself!"

Juanita hesitated.

"What is it?" he said.

"She left already, Doctor."

"What do you mean, she left already?"

"She left very early this morning, before dawn. A man came to look for her, with a pickup truck."

Sofía's departure hurt him more than his mother's. And he resented her for having left in the night, before the rooster had crowed. At first he played with the idea of going to look for her, but then he realized that he did not even know her last name. And the more he thought about it, the more he became convinced that Sofía might not even have been her real first name. *Someone lived in my house for thirty-nine years,* he thought, *and no one ever knew her real name or where she was from. And what else is there really to know about people? That's all your papers say: your name, where you were born, when you were born. Without this, you are nobody, an unknown cadaver in the morgue.*

He had not set foot in his mother's room since he was a boy, not even in her last weeks, which she had spent in the hospital, far from "that house I never loved," as she had called it. He looked at the door every day, when he walked past it on his way to his room. First he thought of sending in Juanita, but he knew that there was no escaping it. After weeks of dallying, he went in one Sunday, when Juanita was at Mass. The door creaked and he felt the hot stale air that had been preserved for weeks, the air that had been in his mother's lungs once. The curtains were half-drawn so the morning sun fell on the night table and part of the massive mahogany bed. The covers, pulled back, had been left where they were when Victoria left for the hospital. She had put on her make-up and had walked out, as if this had been just another day of shopping and socializing. He opened up the glass blinds and felt the fresh air streaming in. There were pictures on the dresser that he had never seen. Old pictures, from the time when his mother was young. There she was, in sepia, holding hands with a young man.

He took the picture of his mother and father, so young they could have been his own children by now, and held it at arm's length while he sat down on the bed. Then he laid down the picture on the starched and ironed pillow on the unused side of the bed. He curled up and buried his face in the pillow that had been his mother's, inhaling deep and hard, as if given ether.

"I will forget you," were the last words he said before falling asleep.

When he woke up it was past noon. A cloud had blocked out the sun, and the room had darkened.

That afternoon he told Juanita to clean out the room.

"Take everything out," he said. "Put all the pictures and trinkets in the storage room. Just give me the jewelry in a wooden box."

"What shall I do with the furniture?" she said.

"Why don't you take it?" he said. "Don't you have relatives who need a bed or whatever else is in there? And take out the curtains as well. Take everything. I want it bare."

Three days later, he stepped inside an empty room. The shutters were open, and the outside air flowed freely over his skin. The walls were bare and freshly painted. There was not a single sign to betray the presence of what or who had been. This was a sterile room, virgin and barren. Made barren once more. He tuned the handles of the glass blinds until they gnashed against each other, forming a tight seal.

"I want this room locked at all times, Juanita," he said.

Because there is no remembrance of former things, he thought, and knew there was more, but he could not recall it.

Chapter 23

The little girl who had sung birthday songs for the old dictator was the daughter of a senator, and her name was Milagros.

She was strong-willed but silent, and her eyes retracted deep into their sockets when she did not want people to read them. The Largaespadas had grown to prominence in the country when the first Senator Largaespada endeared himself to Somoza in the fight against Sandino's bandit army. Milagros's grandfather had been a tall and lanky man with thin cheeks and a protruding chin, and he had not been queasy about what to do with a bunch of rebel peasants whom he found hunkering in a sheep shed in the far northern corner of his property. Panchito, his caretaker, alerted him to the "invasion."

"How many?" the soon-to-be senator growled. He puffed up his cheeks and stuck out his chin.

"Ten or twelve perhaps, Don."

"Armed?"

"Machetes. I think I saw a gun as well. Shall we send for the Guard?"

"No," the Don said as he walked towards the gun cabinet and fished for the key in his pants pocket. "No use waiting for the Guard, Panchito. I'm sure we can take care of this ourselves, don't you think?" They mounted their horses and trotted off: Señor Largaespada ahead, ramrod straight, and Panchito right behind him, his horse panting and sagging under the weight.

The rebels were a threadbare bunch. But they really were rebels, that much was clear: they had felled some trees to build a makeshift shelter, and were roasting two poached rabbits when Señor Largaespada and Danilo appeared.

Justice was swift. He sent word to Somoza the father that he had twelve rebels on ice, and what did the general wish to do with the bodies? The general had just the right use for them. They ended up sitting on León's street corners the next morning, leaning against walls and high sidewalks. They all had one ear cut off, a bullet hole in the back of their head, and every trace of blood carefully wiped off. Everyone seeing the silent shapes in the early hours of dawn had their own opinion on the subject, but the few who really knew kept their mouth shut. And Señor Largaespada soon became Senator Largaespada.

Milagros grew up in a world protected by tall walls around a large mansion, with mango trees in the back and royal African palms out front. From the time she was small, piano and singing classes had been de rigueur, and she had gained a reputation as a singer by the time she turned five. Her mother, Eugenia, was a rare beauty, tall and tan, whose choice of hats and shoes had become legendary in León's social circles. This was how Milagros said she wanted to always remember her: as the elegant woman wearing high heels and big hats who went dancing with her father.

But then, when Milagros was ten years old, her mother started dropping things, or forgetting where she had left them. They were small things at first: a set of keys, or her sunglasses. Soon it became a pattern and Amparita, the girls' nanny, walked behind Eugenia most of the time, to make sure things were found.

"It will pass," the senator told himself. And then again: "It will pass." And a third time, as if words could turn desires into reality.

Eugenia sat on the veranda for hours, gazing out and mumbling to herself, rolling her eyes at the sight of zopilotes and vultures landing in the fields behind the house. She was unaware of the stares, or the talking of the daughters who came to her and held her hands.

"She has tasted the bitterness of the other side," Amparita said. "It has turned her face dark and loveless."

One Sunday, when Milagros was twelve years old, they were having dinner. Her father looked away in embarrassment as her mother stuffed the food in her mouth using her fingers only. She closed her eyes and spied around the table while shoving the remaining food inside a napkin: rice, beans, chicken, and plantain slices, everything rolled into a single cotton napkin. She spied on the others once more and put the bulging napkin in her lap. Then she pushed back her chair and stood up, without taking her eyes off her husband and daughters.

Walking backwards, she took two steps towards the door before she stumbled.

"Eugenia," the senator cried out, and rushed to her side. The children were too frightened to move and started crying at the sight of both parents down on the floor.

"No!" Eugenia screamed, pushing him away. "Stay away from my food! You can't have it. It's mine, all mine!" She gathered the rice and beans, which had scattered all over the marble floor.

"*Moros y cristianos*," she cried, "Moors and Christians, come back to me, I will keep you safe, all of you."

The senator backed away, on his knees, his napkin still stuck between the spotless collar and the swelling carotid vein.

"Valeria, go get Amparita," he said. Valeria stood up and walked backwards as her mother had done: slowly, without taking her eyes off the miserable creature on the floor. Then she turned and ran into the kitchen where Amparita was arranging plates.

"Amparita, please come, Mama is not well," she said in a trembling voice.

"*Dios mío*, what happened?" Amparita knelt down beside Eugenia and grabbed her arm.

"Please, Doña Eugenia, please let me help you," she said. Clutching the food to her chest Eugenia cast a suspicious glance. But when she saw Amparita, she relaxed.

"Ah," she said, "it's you, Amparita. Yes, you may help me. You are not hungry, I know you are not hungry." She lifted her head towards Amparita and whispered: "You are not like these beggars here who want to steal my food from me." She glanced at her husband and children. No one moved. Then, suddenly, recognition broke through her face.

"Oh," she said, her eyes opening wider as she looked down at her hands, filled with rice and beans mashed up into a smudgy pulp. She looked up again:

"Valeria," she said, "Valeria, Milagros, why are you staring at me?" She started sobbing and hid in the big arms Amparita held out for her.

"Shush, it's all right now," Amparita said. "It's alright now; I will take care of you, Doña Eugenia."

He stopped going upstairs, and Eugenia no longer came down. For the children it was if an invisible line had been drawn through their home. As if two houses had been created where there had been one, just like that, without remodeling or moving a single piece of furniture: with the stroke of a pen and the pronouncement of a single word. So now, there was a downstairs, with a library full of maps and books where a man told stories about a mythical past in a faraway land; and an upstairs, ruled by Amparita, and by the screams of a woman whose name was no longer Mother, but had become "she." And one day, no one referred to her as "she" any longer, because "she" had become part of the furniture, the fixtures, and the ghosts that lived among the furniture and fixtures, haunting the living from time to time, reminding them that they had not yet left, and that those who do not want to be forgotten make sure that forgetting does not come easily.

There was laughter sometimes, streaming out through a crack under the closed door, floating downstairs like a taunting fog. And sometimes there were songs, hummed and whispered in a steeplechase of remembrance. Milagros and her sister put their hands over their ears when the songs escaped from under the door. They closed their eyes and clenched their teeth.

"It was a ghost," Milagros told herself – the mother with the sparkling earrings and hair tied up in a raven bun left long ago.

Tío Payo, the senator's cousin, was also the family doctor, and twice a week he stopped by the house to check on Eugenia. When he came downstairs, Milagros was leaning against his car.

"Hóla, Milagros," he said as he took leave of her father.

She looked at him sternly. "What's wrong with my mother, Tío? When will she be better?"

He raised his eyebrows. "Don't worry, Milagros," he said. "Leave the worrying to us grown-ups; there will be time enough for you to worry." She did not like the answer. When the doctor had driven away, she went to see her father in his study.

"I want to talk to you," she told him, but he just nodded and continued reading his paper.

"You're not listening," she said, and hated him for it. He put his newspaper back onto his lap.

"I am listening now," he said.

"What is wrong with Mami?"

"We don't know yet."

"I overheard you and Tío Payo."

He was startled, and not good at concealing it. "What did you hear, Milagros?"

"I heard you say something about where Mami came from, and that we don't know anything about her past."

He sighed. "How old are you now, Milagros? Thirteen?"

She was both surprised and hurt by his question. "No," she said. "I turned fourteen in February. On the fifteenth of February."

"Ah," he said, "fourteen already, yes." He looked at her and noticed that her knees were no longer wobbly, her cheekbones were jutting out, and her eyebrows were sloping downward towards the narrow space where her eyes met her temples.

"I met your mother when she was not even twenty," he said. "She came recommended by Father Pío, to work as a secretary in my office. 'Here's an honest woman,' Father Pío told me, 'honest and not afraid to work long hours.' But when I asked him where she was from, he was evasive. 'Managua,' he said, 'she went to school in Managua.' So I told him that she should come in the next day, for an interview. And she did."

Milagros did not move. She had never heard this story, had always heard a different story, the one she had believed, the one that had to be true because it fit in with reality.

"She worked with us for some time," her father continued, "and then," he grinned sheepishly, "and then, well, then the things happened that always happen between people. I fell in love with her. Or perhaps she fell in love with me, but that's a detail, and I cannot speak for her. I asked her out one day, but at first she refused. 'Why?' I said, 'what's wrong with a date?' but she said that it wasn't right. Surely there were other girls I might ask out. But I asked again and then once more, until finally she said yes. And when we started talking, I discovered things." Milagros looked up again, away from the lizard she had been studying, the one basking in the sun on a rock by the gate, off the driveway.

"What did you discover?" she said. Her voice was low and thin.

"When I asked her about her family she said nothing. She changed the subject. When I asked why she used one last name only, she laughed and changed the conversation again. All I learned was that she had come from Managua, and that she had been to a school run by nuns. I became curious, and asked my assistant to do some research. And then I found out that this school was a school for orphans."

"You spied on her?"

"She told me nothing. What else could I do? I asked her about the school on our next date. She said that she had never known her parents. That she had stopped worrying about it, and had accepted her life the way it had come to her, like this. That this was enough for her. She told me all this in a single breath, and all the while she looked at me without batting an eye. *There would never be enough,* I then realized. *She would never be finished, and I would never be finished with her!* It was then that I realized that I loved her, and that I would never stop loving her. In that long breath I saw my life unfold, my life with her. I saw her and me. 'You and I,' I told her, 'I and you.'"

"Did you see me too?"

He laughed. "Yes, I saw you. And your sister. We were all there, minuscule people in the eye of a giant storm. I saw us aboard a raft made of balsa wood, tossed about and no land in sight." He smiled, and Milagros managed to undo the knot in her eyebrows.

"So that's it?" she said. "That's what we know about where Mami is from?"

"Does it matter?" he said. "Does it matter to you that she was not born to a good family?"

"No. I had always wondered why we had family on your side only. But why did you need to hide this from us? Why not tell us the truth?"

"My family," he said, "my family and the expectations they had of me. I could not be married to someone without a past, without a name. Names mean so much to people."

"It doesn't matter to me, Papa," she said. "She's my mother, I love her no matter what." He held out his arms and she came to him.

"You are so much like her," he whispered. "I can see how you will be one day. So strong, so much like her."

The car accident happened while he was traveling back from Managua, just before arriving at La Paz Centro. Milagros was playing the piano when the news arrived. It was the rainy season, when mold formed in the closets, and people took out the things that had been hiding there, to stuff them with new mothballs. She had been practicing the Minuet, from the French Suites, but the lower C was stuck and made a muffled thud as she pressed it. It always happened during the rainy season, when the humidity found its way under the cover and hid behind the dampers.

It was Valeria who answered the phone, just as Milagros was getting angry at the key, the piano lessons, and the piano teacher, and at the piano itself, lodged inside buckets of sand and water to keep the termites from invading. Then Valeria started crying: "Millie, Millie, Daddy is dead!"

The senator lived, but his legs would not. And so he became the first Largaespada to go back to spending most of his time in the company of a cart.

"You should get a wheelchair," Tío Payo said.

"A what?" the senator asked, because there were no wheelchairs in León in those days.

"It's a chair on wheels. You know, like they have in the U.S. and Europe."

"A chair on wheels? What for?"

"They'll push you."

He retired from politics, and after a while wondered why he had waited so long.

I became a senator because my father had been a senator before me, he thought. *Tradition, I guess.* But he no longer believed that politics would solve any problems.

"One day," he told Somoza, "one day we'll all wake up and our servants will be gone. They will all have gone to the mountains, leaving us to cook our own food and clean our own toilets."

Somoza did not laugh. "We had that already, José," he said. "And my father got rid of that bastard Sandino thirty years ago, remember? We'll keep them in check, don't you worry."

Chapter 24

"I will send you abroad," he said, "to study." His voice had been that of an adult speaking to another adult, and perhaps it was true that the events had made him see her in a different light. Perhaps this was why she thought he looked younger, because she herself had aged that day.

"You will go to a boarding school in France," he continued. "You will be safe there."

She was sitting in her room with the shutters closed. Sitting in the white wicker rocking chair that had been there for as long as she could remember; the chair in which her mother used to rock her asleep. It was missing a few strands of rattan, and she remembered when each one had broken off. She could smell the milk spilled on the headrest, the thick *pinol* drink that had lodged itself inside the wickerwork maze, leaving a smell of cocoa and cornmeal.

She had been told to stay in her room, and had eaten dinner there. Not even her sister had been allowed to come in. She had stopped crying, and no longer saw the outline of a body lying in a red puddle that meandered without haste or afterthought, out onto the white tile floor until it reached the front door.

"Can I come in, *amorcita?*" she heard her father's voice. She opened the door, and the two attendants wheeled him in. He took a deep breath.

"Do you know what happened this afternoon, *hijita?*" She saw the body once more, and panic gripped her. The woman had not screamed, although her mouth had been wide open, and the surprise on her face had stayed there. And then the blood, rich and dark red. She did not want to remember it; she wanted to think that it had all been a dream from which she would awake, that she would find the doll sitting in the rocking chair, and find the servants busy in the kitchen and Amparita upstairs making sure wet towels were pushed against the base of the bedroom door.

"Something bad happened, Milagros," her father said. "An accident, a bad accident."

There it was, she thought. *There was the reminder. So it really did happen then. It was not a dream.* She listened without looking at him. *An accident*, she thought. *He says it was an accident, so why am I being sent away?* She held on to the wicker chair, and cried.

He had spoken to the Guard – "don't bother with the morgue," the guardsman said, "we'll take care of it."

The pistol that had accompanied him for years was stored in a drawer of his desk. "I was cleaning it," he said, "an accident, it was dark. The maid's relatives will be paid."

They all nodded; no more words were needed.

"Gentlemen."

"Gentlemen."

While her father was taking his siesta, Milagros went looking for a ruler in his study. She opened every drawer of his desk, until she came upon the shiny black gun. It felt heavy as she lifted it with both hands, and aimed at the stuffed deer head and the paintings on the walls, taking aim: "P-taff! P-taff!" she imitated the sound of gunshots. When she heard a shuffle at the door, she turned. Her finger pressed the trigger, the bullet left the barrel, and the looming body of Amparita fell to the floor. Silently, as if not wanting to give the girl away.

Many years later, she told her friend Socorro that in that precise moment, when her father told her she would have to leave their house, she felt as if she were floating. She saw herself rising from the wicker chair: ten, fifteen feet perhaps, until she could see her father clearly from above, and her own body sitting motionless, frozen, and listening to him. She rose even further, until she could see the courtyard, and the roof of her house, and through one of the windows she saw her mother lying on the bed while Amparita arranged her pillows and sang to her. She saw the stables and the stableboy sitting in front, tying knots in ropes without knowing if they would ever be used. Far beyond, she saw the road leading to her house, and on it a cloud of dust announcing that the piano teacher was arriving for her sister's class.

Valeria came to her early the next day.

"Wake up," she said. "Wake up, Milagros, it's time to get ready." She sat up and rubbed her eyes.

"We'll come to visit you," Valeria said. "Don't worry, you'll be fine. We'll wait for each other." They held each other in the still-dark room so they could not see each other's faces.

Her father was waiting for her on the porch, drinking coffee with Tío Payo and his wife. He tried to stand up, pushing at the handlebars with both hands, but fell back on his seat.

"Come now, my daughter, and receive your blessing," he said, banging on the wheelchair with both fists. He kissed her, and she stepped into the waiting car. Tío Payo and his wife were talking to her father, and then they shook hands. She looked up, at the window with the shades that were always drawn, and imagined that just this one time they might be up, or perhaps slightly open, enough for a curious pair of eyes to peek through.

"Speak but one word," she whispered. "Speak but one word, and I'll stay. No matter what happens, I'll stay."

The shutters remained closed. Not even the wind made the slightest attempt to move them. Looking through the rear window she saw her father's white guayavera becoming smaller as they drove out, until he was dwarfed by the fence posts, and then the trees that grew larger and larger as she drove through the gate.

The road to El Rama was as bad as they came in those days, and driving the three hundred miles from León to El Rama took all of a day. They slept in a guesthouse, the only one in town. Water bugs crawled over the floor, and the bedposts were set in buckets of water, to keep the bugs from climbing up. She spied the ceiling for flying ones.

"No flying roaches here in El Rama," the toothless owner said as she stood in the door, grinning. "They all left for Managua years ago!" The buckets reminded her of her piano, a big monster soaking its feet in sand and water.

The next day they boarded a paddleboat that took them down the Escondido River, to Bluefields. The town had once been destined for greatness, expecting the hundreds of canal builders that would put it on a par with Panama, digging the elusive canal connecting the Atlantic Ocean with the Pacific that obsessed an entire nation for nearly one hundred years. Milagros and her chaperons spent the evening at the rectory, waiting for the next boat out. She went out into the garden and sat below the giant traveler's trees.

"They have all descended from a single bright blue seed brought from Africa by a slave who had hidden it inside a slit in his skin," the parish priest told her. "And this is how everything started – with a single seed that spawned a forest." They looked at the trees towering over them, their leaves lined up in perfect north-south formation while the trade wind tugged at them, enticing the blue seeds to travel back across the wide sea. She tasted the wind, tasted its brine and wildness on her tongue. *This is my last evening at home,* she thought. She was surprised that it did not make her sad. A parrot flew up, a streak of fire blinding her in the darkness before disappearing behind the tree line.

They boarded the steamer later that evening, just before midnight.

"A strange time to board a boat," she said to Tío Payo.

He raised his shoulders. "Why tell you I know the answer if I really don't, Milagros?" he said, smiling. "But in any case there's only one boat out of here, and when we have no choice we tend to not ask questions."

They went to Jamaica first.

"It's exactly one thousand kilometers from here," the sea captain told her. "Lots of zeros, and you could just add more zeros in front of that lonely 'one' at the beginning, and it would make no difference." She stood at the railing when they steered into Kingston Harbor, and noticed how the waters changed colors, from turquoise ocean side to a murky khaki inside the bay. A flock of pelicans flew towards her in tight formation, but when they got closer they separated and flew her by, left and right. When they walked down the plank way, off the small steamer, the captain waved at her. He made a zero with his thumb and forefinger and held it up at her.

"The zeros don't count," he shouted, "only the ones."

The ship that took them to Liverpool was so much larger than the steamer that had taken them out of Bluefields. And there was no captain to talk to. In fact, she wondered if there even was a captain, or if perhaps this enormous ship had a brain of its own. It was a long trip:

she started counting the days, but after one week she gave up and stayed below deck, leaving her cabin only to eat.

One day she went outside. The cold air hit her in the face and chest like a wet hand. She gasped and breathed in, gingerly, slurping between her clenched teeth to taste this new air, like a cosmonaut taking off her helmet on a newly discovered planet. *It tastes cold*, she thought, *but otherwise the same.* When she exhaled, the air came out as a small cloud, fine and thin. It dissipated fast, so she tried again and again until she was breathless and feeling dizzy. The next day Tío Payo told her that she had a cold, a bad one, and that she had better learn how to dress for cold weather because it was nasty and inhospitable, but this was the weather she would call home in the years to come.

After Liverpool there was a short boat ride across the Channel, the train to Dordogne, and the hired car ride to the convent. She finally stepped out onto a bed of dried leaves and squashed quinces. Tío Payo and his wife stayed only one night, in the nearby town, and the next day they came by to bid goodbye. She saw them off, thinking *now I belong to a different world.*

The convent was built of old stone and brick, overgrown with red and green moss, and vines that stretched up to the highest gables. The convent rambled without sprawl, long and drawn-out with endless corridors all extending in the same direction. The few hallways that intersected did not invite gatherings. Her classes were long, and tedious; there were few smiles and even fewer moments of laughter. She wrote to her father religiously, and he answered promptly. When he wrote that her mother had not left her room in five weeks she cried, and her impulse was to run all the way back, no matter the long and sickening ocean crossing.

In time, she no longer heard the gunshots, and the memory of the falling body receded to where she could no longer guess its existence, even if she wanted to. There were alcoves in her mind, set back from the endless halls and pathways that tied her to her past, and where she might shield painful memories from the prying eyes of the present.

One day she wrote to her father that she would not return to Nicaragua. She cried when she wrote it. She erased it and wrote it again, until the letters had formed an imprint on her retina, and she saw them everywhere she looked: "I will not go back." She went to bed that night seeing the words burned into the empty air, against the whitewashed ceiling, but when she woke the next day, they were gone.

She never sent the letter, and from that day on did better in school. Three years passed, and then it was spring again, and there was nothing more the nuns could teach her. Her father wrote that he kept two new dogs about the farm, a red Labrador and a black mutt, a Belgian shepherd.

"I named them Cain and Abel," he wrote, "because they help me forget, and make me want to believe in the future."

"Do they fight much?" she said, but he wrote that they were never together.

"They avoid each other; the Labrador stands guard by the front gate while the black dog chases rabbits around the cotton fields. I see them from afar," he wrote. "Sometimes I see only streaks of color amid the green: a red bolt and a black stripe. When I see them I think of all the tomorrows yet to be lived."

Then there was Paris. She left her provincial boarding school to enroll in law school, and found a garret room on Rue Cherche-Midi. She had to walk up five flights to her *chambre de bonne*. Slowly, with rungs creaking under her feet. The building smelled of old people who had locked themselves into boudoirs without knowing why; who had long since forgotten that once they had been young and had felt desire. *The death of desire*, she thought when she looked out through the window carved out of the low mansard wall. The moon looked like a frumpy dowager from an era long past. She covered herself with the sheets, all the way up to her eyes, so the moon would not see her.

The faculty walls were dirty, from the thousands of hands that had touched them, and the slogans painted by students clamoring for change. An elderly woman was busy washing them down. *She looks Portuguese*, Milagros thought. *Stooped and shrunk, and not wearing gloves. Just a pair of wrinkled hands scrubbing down illusions.* She stopped to read one of the slogans sprayed onto the wall in thick, irregular letters. They started forceful and deliberate, but drooped towards the end, as if the author had become tired halfway through, or lost faith or interest, finishing the sentence out of a sense of duty, rather than conviction.

This is where she met Roberto. He was from Montevideo, he told her, and she repeated the word a hundred times, making fun of his accent. During her years in Paris, Roberto became the brother she never had. They took up studying in each other's company because, she said, "you understand my silence." Often, he looked at her while she was lost in her books and papers.

"There is an aura about you, you seem to glow," he told her, surprised by his own admission.

Paris was home to a large community of Latin American exiles, and Milagros soon found a friend in Socorro, a woman from Guatemala. They met at the goodbye party of a Chilean friend, a journalist.

"An accident," Roberto said when she asked about a woman sitting in a wheelchair. "Or some disease perhaps, why don't you ask her?"

"Let me help you with that," Milagros said when the woman bent sideways to adjust a lever.

"You've done this before," Socorro said, watching as Milagros fixed the lever.

She nodded. "My father. I learned to flip the switches and pull the brakes many years ago."

"Not many people can do this," Socorro said. "Most people stay away from wheelchairs. And from the people sitting in them. Must be they are afraid it's contagious." They both laughed.

Socorro had been an official in the government of Arbenz, and the years of exile had not been kind to her.

"These wrinkles," she said, "it's not just my skin, it's my whole head. We grow older, and what we do not realize is that our countries need us less than we need them. One day they will tell us 'come home,' and when we do, we will be looking for things that are no longer there. We will be looking for people who have died and houses that have crumbled. We will realize that our countries did not wait for us, and that will be the rudest of all awakenings – a punishment more cruel than exile itself."

At the wedding of a friend, Socorro told Milagros about the invasion of Guatemala. They were sitting in the garden of a half-timbered country house near Rambouillet, built in Alsatian style. It was a house Socorro said reminded her of her home on the shores of Lake Atitlán, where she had grown up.

"It was an Austrian house," she said. "You know we had many Austrian immigrants in Guatemala; so many had come just before the War. The country appeared to be a haven of tranquility to them." She paused and looked around, squinting.

"I was on a list," she said. "They had lists of everyone in the government, everyone who had ever attended a rally. There were two lists: one for those to be disposed of, and one for those to be exiled. It was well organized, well prepared. We knew who was behind it. And all that for bananas." She laughed; a dry and distant laugh.

"They roped us in at night," she continued. "They broke down my door and took me to the barracks, where I was held with other women. This is where the torture started, and the raping. When they were through raping us, they brought us back to our cells and threw a stack of tortillas at us, as if we were dogs. My friends thought I would die that day, because I had passed out during the interrogations and the torture. When I came to, they clapped their hands; they told me I had gotten another chance, a new lease on life. 'Now you have two lives,' they said, 'one to live, and one to give away.'

"It was only because some of us had relatives with money and contacts that we were released. Five of us were taken to the airport and put on a plane in the middle of the night. And while we were sitting on that plane, handcuffed still, one of us glanced back through a window and shouted: 'It's the President!' When we looked out we saw how the president was standing in front of five soldiers. We had not expected to see him alive, and were surprised and relieved. They laughed at him, and pushed him when he did not move fast enough. He walked up the stairs of the plane that took him into exile wearing only his underwear. A soldier was snapping pictures and another one shouted, 'Look at the emperor and his new clothes!'"

Milagros looked away, at the trees and the children playing with the dogs, and thought: *how can I pretend to be innocent? Even though life goes on, in seemingly endless circles, as if it had not taken note. As if it did not care.*

"Why are you here, Milagros?"

She was surprised. No one had ever asked her this question.

"Why are you here, Milagros?" Socorro said once more, turning towards her. Her expression was blank: all her emotions were folded back into the wrinkles that held her face together.

"I know, it's not a fair question," she said. "But it's just not enough to know where you are. You should also know why you are where you are." She sighed, and patted Milagros's hand. "Exile is different for each one of us," she said. "For some of us it's because of what we did back home, and for some of us it's for what we didn't do. And for others yet…" She shrugged. "Well, for others it's just that they needed to run away and put an ocean between themselves and the ones left behind."

"What if we do not even have that?" Milagros whispered. "What if we do not know why we are not elsewhere?"

Socorro shook her head. "The most terrible of fates, if you ask me. The fate of a vegetable. Even animals have a sense of where they are going. Whales, elephants, they look for love, for a place to die. They don't need maps, they just know."

"But I have done something, Socorro, and I cannot go home."

"What might be so terrible that you cannot go home?"

Her lip started trembling, and she tried to stop it with her hand. She held her lip, then her chin, waiting for the trembling to stop, while Socorro's hand rested on her shoulder.

"Do you want to talk about it?"

She shook her head and wiped her face.

"No," she said. "How could I? I have tried to forget it for so long."

"But you didn't, did you?"

Milagros shook her head and bit her lip.

"Hmm. It's when we remember, that we become truly human. When we acknowledge our fears and accept our shortcomings – this is who we are. Remembering is painful, but it helps us heal. And when we're done healing, we can finally start loving."

"How can I do this?" Milagros sobbed.

"By forgiving yourself. I forgave my torturer, and only then could I have peace. So you, my little Milagros, must forgive yourself, because you are your own torturer. And you'll see, after that you will become the woman you have always wanted to be.

"Come now," she said, opening her arms. "I have a life to give away, remember? And I'm giving it away to you."

One day Socorro asked Milagros if she could brush her hair. She took the brush and raked it through the other woman's long hair.

"*Coquito*," she said, "your hair is so brittle, why don't you cut it?"

"I have not cut it since the day I left Guatemala."

"Why not?"

"It's one of the few things I have left that I can decide by myself. When everything else has been decided for you for so long, you need something that is all yours; something that depends on you alone. So you do not give up hope."

Milagros twitched. "Hope," she said. "It's what remains when all else has gone, isn't it?"

"Yes. And it never leaves."

Her life had few distractions. She was content with Roberto's and Socorro's friendship, and felt little need for the company of others. Once, in the midst of winter, she met a boy at a party, and went with him. He was tall and tan in spite of the wintery bleakness, but she did not remember his name, nor the room they had entered. Perhaps her mind had refused to name the witnesses of their encounter, keeping them forever clueless the way Ukrainian peasants carry their dead out of the house: feet first, so they would not remember the way back home and return to haunt the living. She remembered only that it was winter, and that the trees had seemed shrill and lifeless as the door slammed shut behind her, and she walked into the formless night.

The next day, as she was walking up the stairs to her room, the concierge opened up the creaking door to her downstairs apartment.

"Mademoiselle," she called up behind her. "Mademoiselle Largaespada, a gentleman called earlier today."

"A gentleman? Who was he?"

"He said he was your father, Mademoiselle." The concierge managed a thin smile. She was a woman with broad hips, a mother surely many times over, although Milagros had never seen any children playing in the yard, *but perhaps they had stayed behind in Portugal,* she thought, *or perhaps they had died. Yes, perhaps they had died, why not? Children die all the time, so why not Madame Dos Santos's children also?*

"He said he would call back later today."

Milagros said nothing, so the concierge said: "I will call you."

"Yes," Milagros said, "yes, thank you, Madame Dos Santos. Thank you."

Her mind spun. Her father had never called her before. She sat on her bed and stared out the window until it had darkened around her. Finally, the call came from below: *"Mademoiselle, venez vite, c'est vot' papa à l'appareil."*

She was breathless by the time she reached the phone.

"C'est là," Madame Dos Santos said, pointing at the phone sitting on a small wooden table. The horn looked as if it could turn into a snake any moment. She stretched out her hand. It felt heavy and cold, and she almost dropped it. When she held the receiver to her ear there was static at first, and then a sound as if someone were breathing under water.

"Hello," she said, "is that you, Dad?"

"Hija!" the horn answered.

Her voice sounded deeper than he had remembered, and he tried to imagine the young woman to whom it belonged.

I have only myself to blame, he thought, *I sent her out of my sight, why should she have stayed the child that I sent away?* She told him about her friends and her classes. When she ran out of things to tell him she waited, but he remained silent.

"What is it, Daddy?" she said, but she knew already; she knew before he spoke the words.

"Your mother," he said. "She had an accident."

"An accident?" Her voice was hoarse. "What... How...?"

"We found her in the field this morning. She must have gotten up early and walked out, because no one saw her leave the house. My black dog found her lying by the riverbed. She must have been there for hours."

"So..." she said, "so how is she?"

She heard only the crackle of static at first, and then her father's voice, every other word he spoke hijacked by the static.

"Oh," she said, "is she...?"

Madame Dos Santos saw how the girl started trembling, and pushed a chair against the hollow of her knees.

"Your Uncle Payo says it's a snakebite. Perhaps this was why the dog was so upset. It yelped and refused to get near her."

She sat down and took the horn away from her ear.

"Do you want me to come home, Papa?" she said at last, because it was the only question she had left.

"I can't ask you that," he said, "I sent you away, how can I ask you to leave everything behind a second time?"

She sat looking at the moon that evening, and the moon shone back on her. *Exile is a place of apple trees,* she thought.

The next day she told Roberto: "I will finish this term," she said. "I have learned enough about the laws, enough from books."

"I will come with you," he said.

"Why?" she said. "It's not your country, why go there? Things are falling apart."

"It does not matter," he said. "Things could not possibly be falling apart more than where I am from."

And so it happened that soon after, as the flaming Malinche trees were bowing their heads under the fullness and fury of the Nicaraguan summer rains, Milagros, and shortly thereafter her friend Roberto, arrived in Nicaragua, just as many others were getting ready to leave it.

Valeria was at the airport with a new driver, a burly man Milagros did not remember. As they drove through Managua, the city that had been ravaged by an earthquake a few years earlier, her sister pointed out the places that were no more:

"This is where the soda bottling plant used to be," she said, "and here is where department store such-and-such used to be." Milagros saw only empty shells, skeletons of buildings with bed sheets and colorful T-shirts fluttering from clotheslines strung between pockmarked pillars. Children were scampering up the three or four stories that had barely any flooring left, with planks precariously stretched across the chasms. Here and there she saw olive-green tents pitched inside a building, and where the green canvas had worn thin, plastic tarp had been sewn onto it, to keep out the water.

"My God," she said, "the earthquake was three years ago. I thought they would have rebuilt by now."

Valeria pursed her lips, and pouted at the driver before speaking: "The government tries all it can, but you know that there simply isn't enough money." The city was crawling with military, more than she remembered. Or perhaps she had never noticed before, because it was not a thing she had cared to notice.

"It's nasty," the senator said when they were having dinner that night. "I always knew it would come to this, although I hoped we would remain civil…" He paused and looked at the shadows they were casting, by the light of a single light bulb dangling from the porch beam.

"I am happy that you came back, Milagros, you know that. I have waited for you to come back for the past ten years."

"No," she said. "Eleven. They were eleven. Your counting has not improved with age, Papa." She leaned over and kissed him on the cheek.

"But…" he looked at her sternly now, "but you must promise me that you will leave again soon. And that counts for you too, Valeria."

"Dad!" they both exclaimed. "Why? Why should we leave?"

"This country is going down the drain. It's hard not to notice there are guardias on every street corner, is it? Roadblocks, raids – every week I hear about another family that has sent its children elsewhere. The rich send their children overseas, while the poor send their kids to join the damn guerrillas! There won't be room for anyone who wants to remain neutral. Some prospect!"

Milagros shook her head. "So perhaps we should not be neutral then, Papa. We think that being neutral will protect us, but perhaps that's what has gotten us into trouble in the first place." The senator was surprised by the fierceness of her words, but before he could say anything Valeria said: "What will you do, Father? Will you come with us?"

"No, Valeria," he said. "You know me better than to ask that question. We Largaespadas have lived on this farm for a century and a half."

"I will stay with you, Father," Milagros said.

"If Milagros stays, I will stay also," Valeria said. She laughed to hide her nervousness, and then they all laughed, a laugh that drifted out into the garden until it reached a red dog and a black dog sleeping on opposite ends of the lawn. They perked up their ears to listen, but soon went back to sleep.

Chapter 25

A horse and rider came trotting towards him, leaving deep prints in the soggy sand. When they stopped in front of him, the instant coolness of their shadow made him shiver.

"So, Doctor," the rider said. "Are you here to see the beast?"

"Aren't we all?" Tomás said, raising his eyebrows.

"Yes," she said. The puzzled look on his face made her laugh.

"You don't remember me, Doctor? I'm Milagros, Senator Largaespada's daughter." She bent down and held out her hand to him.

"Of course," he said. "I did not know you had come back. It's been many years since you left. How many…eleven, right?"

She was surprised. "Yes," she said. You have a good memory, Doctor."

"Anatomy," he said. "Anyone who has had to study anatomy must have good memory. Counting bones. Making sure not one goes missing."

She smiled. "On the way in this morning I saw lots of pickup trucks crowded with people. I heard the beast is less than a mile from here, just north of the lagoon. Shall we walk up?"

"By all means. And please don't call me Doctor – it makes me feel old. Call me Tomás, please."

She laughed and pulled at her hair band. He saw how the reluctant knot became a wave of hair hugging her shoulders as she moved. She dismounted and let go of the reins, and the horse followed without straying. Alongside the rocky pier that jettisoned out into the ocean, a fishing trawler had been pulled ashore by a dozen fishermen who were unloading the catch of the night into large wicker baskets. When he bent down to look at the fish, Tomás suddenly felt something wet pressed against his ear. Instinctively, he pulled away.

"It's just a seashell, Doctor," she teased. When he turned, he saw the conch shell in her hand.

"Listen," she said. "Listen please and tell me what you hear." Her hand pushed up the hair along his temple, and he felt his ear being encased by the shell. At first, there was silence. Then, without warning, a deep rustling sound that reminded him of the shifting sands he had imagined inside a clay urn, long ago. Slowly, she moved the shell away, and while at first he heard the noise grow stronger, it eventually died down.

"What did you hear?" she said.

"The blood running through my ear."

"How prosaic." She put the shell against her own ear now, and closed her eyes.

"I hear the ocean," she said. "I hear my heart beating in synchrony with the ocean lapping at the hull of a ship. They seek each other, you know, our blood and the oceans – they are cousins, bound by salt." She laughed, and took the shell off her ear.

"When I was a girl, my father used to take me out fishing. He used to say that the ocean takes care of each wave until it reaches the shore."

Now Tomás laughed too. "It sounds like something out of a book!" he exclaimed.

"It probably was. You know that my father is shameless when it comes to quoting others without acknowledging the source."

Past the first of the rows of prickly pear that girded the lagoon, they saw people run toward the shoreline, brandishing spades and hacksaws: men, women, and children, yelling and shoving each other aside as if their lives depended on getting to the beast before anyone else could.

The whale was enormous indeed. But it was not its size that struck Tomás; it was the eyes. In them, he saw the sadness of the traveler who has arrived at the wrong port, and realizes the naked, cruel truth of his mistake. But the people were not interested in its eyes; they were hacking away at the quivering mound of flesh, and rolling up thick swaths of skin to get to the blubber beneath it, part of their unstoppable conquest of the agonizing giant. Children were selling fried plantain slices, while further away, under a lonely jícaro tree, a woman with thick arms had fired up an oil drum filled with charcoal, and was hard at work grilling slabs of whale meat.

Tomás pointed at a man standing by the whale's head, taking measurements.

"Let's ask that man," he said. "He's from the Biology Department.

"How did it end up here?" Tomás asked the man.

"We don't know," the biologist said. "They swim past here twice a year. This is a young male, the kind that swims hard and fast to get to the breeding grounds before the older bulls arrive. Maybe this one had something wrong with its compass, who knows? Wrong time, wrong place perhaps. If it happens to people it can happen to whales, can't it?" He grinned. "And maybe, just maybe, this whale got its love songs wrong and called it quits. Those things happen too, you know."

"How do you know it's a male?" Milagros said. "I didn't know you could tell fish apart."

"It's not a fish," the biologist said. "If it were a fish it would be dead already."

"The irony," Milagros said. "So are you saying a whale could drown?"

"Of course it could. Whales can't breathe under water any more than we can."

"Well," Tomás said, "male or no male, fish or no fish, it's here." He patted the rough black skin, and suddenly the whale shuddered, sending the Lilliputians scrambling. The biologist opened his backpack and brought out an oversized stethoscope, which he pressed against the whale's skin, close to the eye.

He shook his head. "It's finished," he said.

Once the word was out that the big fish was dead, the people no longer felt any restraint. They hacked and sawed a path through the bloated underbelly that had swelled in the hot tropical sun. A big woman with a red kerchief tied around her hair was in the breach, puffing and stabbing the whale with a machete. When she punctured the stomach it exploded like a giant balloon, and a wave of sour water came out, knocking her off her feet. When the waters receded, the people closed in, sticking out noses and wanting to have a look at the things that had come out of the fish and were lying still between the big woman's naked brown legs.

It was a pair of shoes. Badly damaged by gastric acid and encrusted with barnacles, but shoes nonetheless, with tangled laces tied into the tightest of knots.

"Go get the expert," a man in a uniform jacket told a young boy. He twisted the boy's ears to make sure the seriousness of his command was understood.

"Go tell him to come, tell him we found something inside the fish."

The boy came to a halt in front of the expert. "The guardsman says you should come," he shouted. "They found something inside the fish." The boy tried to run back, eager not to miss any of the action, but the expert hit him over the head.

"It's not a fish," he yelled. Turning to Tomás and Milagros, he tipped his baseball cap. "Duty calls," he said. He turned on his heels and waggled out behind the boy.

The big woman was still sitting with her legs apart, brushing off the barnacles on her clothes.

"Shoes," she mumbled, making an angry face. "Dirty old shoes!"

"What?" the others said, the ones closest to her. And the ones behind them started asking too, in ever-expanding ripples reaching the people standing behind them: "What did she say, did she say shoes?"

"Yes, I said shoes," she yelled. The crowd hushed now, all at once, and they all looked at the expert kneeling beside the woman. He dangled the shoes by a tangled pair of laces, as if he were swinging a thurible filled with hot coals and incense. Even the women frying plantains had stopped stirring the boiling oil and had come closer to hear what this was all about.

"Well, don't all look at me," the expert said. "I'm a marine biologist, not a soothsayer! This is human stuff! I don't know where these shoes come from any more than you do!"

Milagros and Tomás were still standing by the whale's eye, watching the scene.

"What do you make of this, Doctor?" she said.

The expert seemed to have gotten the exact same idea. "Why don't we ask the doctor here?" he said, raising the shoes up in the air. He held them as if they were a trophy that was being surrendered. They dripped seawater on the children that stood nearest, and they shied away, afraid perhaps that they would get stained or burned. The expert made his way through the throng until he stopped in front of Tomás, and held out the dripping shoes. *Am I supposed to say something?* Tomás thought. The expert shook the shoes again, and more stomach water sprinkled on the bystanders. The children scurried away, and mothers pulled their children to themselves.

"Yes, well, I guess we'll take care of this," Tomás said. He held out his hand to take the tangled mess.

"Good," the expert said. "We all know that you can never have enough shoes in life, Doctor!"

And that was all the people needed to hear. The woman with the red kerchief was back in the whale's entrails, knee-high, carving out square chunks of meat that were swiftly carried away, until the whale resembled a brick wall through which a cannonball had been shot. A fleet of pickup trucks were waiting where the sand turned into a mud road, and were quickly being loaded with whale bricks, to be sold on the markets of León and Managua. No one would know that this was not a fish.

The expert was busy taking out tools from his backpack: a hacksaw, rubber gloves, and a scalpel.

"Looks familiar, right, Doctor?" he grinned from under his thick glasses. "Let's see what we can preserve for science here."

Tomás fumbled for his watch. "I must go now," he said, "I am expected at the hospital soon."

"Yes, I suppose you are," Milagros said. "That's where doctors belong after all."

He blushed. "Are you mocking me?"

"Wouldn't dream of it. And please let me accompany you back to your car." They found a stick, and he hung the shoes up on it before slinging it over his shoulder, to keep the shoes from dripping on them. The horse walked behind them, licking salt off the shoes, and nudging Tomás on with its nose.

"Easy, Xiomara," Milagros said. "You're going to knock the doctor off his feet if you keep this up!" But the horse did not let up until they reached his car. Tomás put the shoes down on the seawall bordering the beach and looked at them.

"Strange," he said.

"What is?"

"They're not the same. They're not a pair."

"How do you know?" she said.

He pushed them together, matching the soles. "Two left feet," he said.

She laughed. "So how did they end up in a knot?"

He shook his head in puzzlement. "I don't know."

"I wonder what else that whale might have been carrying in its stomach – so much else the rivers carry to the sea."

He nodded. "A sign," he said. "My nanny would have called this a sign. But she called everything a sign." He laughed, but this time she did not.

"What if it really were a sign?"

"For what?" he said.

"Not for what. For whom."

They shook hands. "Goodbye, then," he said. "Thank you for accompanying me."

"We'll meet again soon," she said. "I know we will." He watched her as she tied up her hair once more and mounted the horse. Then he sat down on the low wall and took off his shoes to empty them. Black volcanic sand blew into the wind, and some of it turned around and clung to his hair and lips. When he looked up again the horse and rider had become a single figure against an angry, rising sun.

There were no roadblocks on the way back to León. *Thank God,* he thought. *For once. Let's hope we can have a few days without gunshots.* His car followed the meandering streets until he reached the hospital, and he parked outside. He had to elbow his way in among the stalls selling soda pop and plastic flowers, all parts of a world that went on living, stubbornly, in spite of the faraway drone of artillery fire. When he arrived at his lab, he dropped the shoes on a table and flipped open the window slats. There was smoke up north. Big, billowing swirls of yellow smoke, the kind that comes from adobe houses burning to the ground.

Chapter 26

"There is a woman who could use some company," Uncle Payo said. "Would you mind spending some time with her?" Milagros looked up from her book, surprised by her uncle's request.

"Who is it?" she said.

"Ana," he said. "Ana Cortés. Her husband is now the military commander here in León again. You know that she lost her son a few years ago, don't you?"

"No," she said. "No, I didn't. What happened?"

"He fell from a tree. An accident. Termites. A stupid accident caused by a rotten tree." He sighed. "Her husband is always away, and even when he is not he doesn't talk to her. She is a lonely woman wasting away in a room. She could use some company."

"I will go," Milagros said. "Please tell her I will stop by."

They did not remember that they had met before, and it might have taken many conversations to put the pieces together. But Ana did not want to speak about that past. She had locked that part inside her, where she thought it would be safe and would not die.

She asked about Paris. She wanted to know how the rain smelled, and if the grass in the Bois de Boulogne was kept short-cropped still.

"I don't remember," Milagros said. "I always thought about coming home; I never tried to remember those things."

"Did you go to the Luxembourg Gardens? We used to live near the Gardens, rue de Fleurus. On Saturdays we strolled in the Gardens, and on Sundays Papa took us to the Eiffel Tower. We took the Metro — what an adventure! Papa used to tell us to walk back to the Champs de Mars Metro station in case we got lost. 'When you see crowds of people, trace back your steps. Always best to go back to where you came from,' he said."

Milagros laughed. "That was good advice," she said.

One day she was presented to Fausto.

"My husband," Ana said, and the two shook hands. Milagros did not recognize him from the wedding picture in the living room, much less from her own memories. In the picture he looked young and relaxed, a man looking forward to being married, to having a family and living his life. But the man who was introduced to her was impatient, as if every minute spent in conversation was a minute lost. He looked tired to her, in spite of the broad shoulders, the straight back, and the steady, low-pitched voice. Later, she saw him walk out and into the backyard where a moss-covered tree stump stood guard in front of a garden house. He bent down to lift a small rock hiding a key. Ana stood behind her as she looked through the window.

"Forgot his key again, she said. "That's why we keep a spare under the rock. He often takes a nap in the afternoon," she continued. "He says he sleeps sounder in the garden house than anywhere else."

"Can you read to me, Milagros?" Ana said. "We have so many books here; why don't you read to me?" Milagros was glad to oblige. Reading to Ana made her think of the afternoons she had spent with Socorro, and Ana did not ask questions.

The list of books was endless. Milagros read while Ana sat back and listened. Sometimes Ana closed her eyes, but when Milagros stopped reading, thinking she was asleep, Ana shook her head. Adriana came in at times, and curled up against her mother.

They read as though the books were scheduled for burning, and needed to be read before they were consumed by flames. When they were through with the books in Ana's house they asked Rafaela for books from the Cortés mansion. Rafaela passed by herself, bringing along a large leather trunk.

"Mama Mica has picked most of them," she said. "No one in our house has time for reading anymore, so she is happy that you asked for them." The new arrivals all had smells to them — coriander and peppermint, coffee and vanilla, as if each one of them had lived a story seeking to entice and seduce a reader. Near the bottom of the trunk was a dusty notebook bound in thin but supple leather. When Milagros opened it, the deep, earthy smell of cacao entered her nose. Her nostrils flared, but the sweetness of the nut that followed calmed down her impulse to wince.

"It's a diary," she said. "Old and hand-written." She slid her hand over the first page, caressing the flourish that marked the start of someone's thoughts, committed to this notebook. *A hopeful flourish*, she thought. *Hopeful and not afraid of life.* She turned the page, and then another.

"It says 1929," she said.

"Is there a name?" Ana said.

Milagros shook her head.

"Read it, please," Ana said. "Mama Mica does everything for a reason, and if this diary is in the box it is probably worth reading." Milagros flipped back to the first page and started reading.

Her name was Aurora, and *in the beginning*, she wrote, *there was a beggar scavenging through a garbage pile, and he found me. I was found on a garbage pile in the city of Valencia, when I was no more than six days old. He told the priest that he had heard me cry, and found me lying on a bed of chicken bones, naked and cold. He wrapped me in the newspaper under which he had been sleeping, and when he held me to his chest I stopped crying, and fell asleep. This is what I have been told.*

My early years I remember as if in a dream. The orphanage was a place of discipline and order, with little room or time for thinking back about an imagined past. The sisters gave me a diary to keep, and I filled it with my thoughts, without ever turning back the pages. When I turned seventeen, I decided to become a nun. The sisters asked me to set out across the ocean, to bring God's Word, His Love and His Promise, to the Indian tribes living on the eastern seaboard of the Central American isthmus. A school had been set up by the Church and was in need of helping hands to teach and take care of the children. Wild Coast, Mosquito Coast, the words meant little to me when I boarded the ship that would take me on a long and sickening voyage. In the spring of 1927 our ship moored in the Bay of Belize. An elderly priest was waiting for me at the end of the ladder; he greeted me and bowed — no one had ever bowed his head to me. "I am Father Juan de la Selva," he said, flashing a smile that revealed two gold teeth. "Welcome to the Wild Coast, sister."

There were two men to carry my bags, two men with naked torsos who were browner than any men I had ever seen. We mounted a buggy while the two men hauled the trunks onto the back rack. One of them sat in the driver's seat, and the other one had jumped on top of the trunks and bags piled high, holding them down with the weight of his body. When he leaned forward, I smelled his body, a deep scent of musk and mold, and a hint of metal and juniper when his breath ran out to me. He was so close that I felt the air warming around me.

At the Church of the Immaculate Virgin the rest of my instructions were revealed: I was to travel on a banana boat to reach a settlement on the Mosquito Coast. The day before I was to sail, Father Juan came in with a young man dressed in a cotton shirt and smudgy white pants. His skin was dark, and his hair was short and frizzy. It is not safe along these coasts, Father Juan said, so Esteban will come with you, to protect you.

We sailed south along the coast of Honduras, and reached the mouth of the Coco River. The captain told us that this was Cape Gracias a Dios, where Columbus had run into a storm that had not calmed down until they decided that one man would be tossed overboard. The sailors made the sign of the cross as they rounded it, even though they had heard the captain's tale many times before. Three pangas pulled alongside, and young men and boys carried up baskets of fruit and diced meat. The captain gave them a few coins, which the young men breathed on and rubbed with their loincloths. One of them sputtered and argued, pointing at the coins. I watched as the sailors formed a circle around him. What is it? I asked Esteban. He is saying it's the wrong coin, Esteban said. He is saying that he wants the coin with the old woman's face on it; that they are trying to cheat him out of his money. And are they? I asked. He said that they were trying to give the boy a coin with an old man's face on it, and with mountains, and a sun, and he did not want it. The men were saying there was a new country, with a new chief. That the old woman was dead, but the boy did not believe them.

The sailors pushed the boy back to the railing, forcing him to take the coin, but he threw it back at them, saying there was no other country, no other chief. That there was only the old woman, and that we were crazy, all of us, talking about a country that did not exist. They steered their pangas into the mangrove forests, and were swallowed within seconds. I shivered at the thought of a life spent amid the green jungle lurking behind the shoreline.

The morning after we rounded Cape Gracias a Dios, I took out the papers I had been given. And this is where it happened. Coffee, dark and strong, spilled, and blotted the letters until the ink and the paper had become almost one. My heart *sank; my destiny was sealed inside tiny lumps of brown, wet paper. I could make out only two or three letters that had remained: B...L...I.*

Esteban suggested I ask the captain. Bilwi, the captain said. It's Bilwi. I thought Father Juan had said something else, something that sounded like Boolfill, but who was I to ask? Do you have a map? I wanted to know, but he only repeated that they were sending me to Bilwi.

Two days later the captain stretched out a hairy arm to the coast, and told me we were mooring at Beelfee. Boolfiil? I asked. Is that Boolfiill? And he said that yes, it was Beelfee, right there.

There was no one waiting for us at the pier. I looked at the seventy-five houses and huts set amid the palm trees, and thought that it could not be there, but when I turned around, I saw that the men were lifting my two trunks onto the pier. The trunks clicked when they touched land, as if they were magnets touching metal, acknowledging their true destination. They told me this was Bragman's Bluff, and that next-door was Bilwi, the Indian settlement. We trudged through the muddy streets, looking for the orphanage. Then we went to the office of the Standard Fruit Company, which owned the boats and the port, and the roads that led to the port, but the clerk said there was no orphanage there. He was a sweaty man with a ruddy face; when I told him of my suspicions he said, "Blewfields," which sounded much like what Father Juan had told me. But the rainy season has just started, sister, he said, so there won't be any boat going that way for the next few months. I sent a telegram to the orphanage priest in Blewfields, and another to the Jesuits in Belize, but no response ever came.

We stayed at the guesthouse of Standard Fruit, and Esteban found a job diving for pearls. He was good at it, and the boat owners fought among themselves to get him on their team. A score of girls were always waiting for him as he returned, giggling when he walked past them. Early one evening I walked to the beach and saw how the pearl divers were setting up a maypole, while young girls were grooming each other, getting ready for the dance. It had stopped raining, and for a brief moment the sun was back, a window in a wall of clouds and smoke billowing up from the fish smokeries. Then the sun set, fast, and I watched from behind a tree as the dance started. It was a whirlwind of brown skin and colorful cloth jumping and crawling against the moonlit sky, until they were a single, giant mass of arms and ribbons, and legs jutting out towards the evening sky, kicking the moon. I saw Esteban among them; he was laughing, and the moon reflected on his teeth.

That evening, he came to the cabin late. I was lying awake and staring at the ceiling, the image of the maypole dance still on my retina. I heard him shuffle around in the small kitchen, drinking water, and then the familiar sound of cane toads was back.

I was grateful when a family of Moravian farmers offered to take us in, while we waited for the next boat. The couple was in Bilwi to buy provisions, and about to return to their farm some forty miles inland. I met them at the general store, where I went to buy soap. Horst was an elderly gentleman who spoke English with a strong German lilt, and only broken Spanish. He had come from Moravia after his wife and children had died, he told me, in the great flu epidemic that had killed more people than the war itself. Ilse was his second wife: stout and sturdy, she was born near Bilwi to missionaries who had landed there before there were banana plantations and telegraph poles.

The trip from Bilwi to Horst and Ilse's farm took one whole day by horse and buggy. Sitting on the backseat, I saw how the buggy's wheels cut slick furrows in the muddy tracks that closed up fast again. The farm stood in a large clearing among plots of neatly tended farmland, and just beyond it I saw the tree line of a green jungle. Horst showed me an avocado sapling standing in front of the main house. It was six feet tall, and he told me that this was the first tree he had planted after he arrived on the farm.

I asked him if he had always been a farmer, but he said that, no, he had been a bookbinder before. But then his wife had died, and so had his two daughters, and he said he had wanted to die himself.

But he did not. He could not. Instead, he crossed the ocean, where he found Ilse, and then, he said, he himself was found. Do you remember them? I asked. Do you remember your first wife and your children? He smiled, and said that they were the reason he was still alive. We must remember, he said. We are alive so we may remember. It is not their gravestones that will keep their memories alive. It is us… He looked younger when he told me this, in spite of his wrinkles. His face looked like a book, I thought, like a living book.

I have been staying with Horst and Ilse for nearly five years. It has been as if I were living a dream from which I cannot awake. It is as if here, in this clearing in the middle of a green wilderness, we have shed all knowledge of the cardinal points that make a round earth flat. No need for a compass in this place — there is no west from here, no north, no south. There is only here, only now. Horst has given me a handcrafted notebook, and I have started keeping a diary once more. But it is different this time, and I sense that my words no longer reflect the anguished thoughts I had when I was a child. I now accept our imperfect world, accept that it may never be anything more than that, because that is how it was created. Not out of desire, and not out of chaos. Out of nothingness.

My last habit tore when I was out collecting firewood, and today I found one of Ilse's long skirts and a blouse draped over the chair in my bedroom. When I put them on, I realized how long it had been since I stopped wearing such clothes. Ilse and Horst were sitting in the kitchen, eating breakfast, when I walked in. They looked up as I stood in the doorway. "Gut," Horst said, and laughed: "Now I see the Aurora that was hidden from me." I washed the torn habits one more time, and put them away in my trunk. I never opened the second trunk, with the two hundred Bibles.

Esteban has learned to work the land, he who grew up a son of the sea. He now digs up yams and yucca, instead of turtle and lobster. I often wonder why he has stayed with me, even though he was sent to accompany me to Blewfields. I imagine that, in his eyes, I must have abandoned my mission so easily.

I have strayed so far, and don't think I can ever go back. Today started hot and humid. We were working in the fields when Esteban took off his shirt. His skin is the color of burnt umber, and it glistened in the morning sun. He has stopped cutting his hair, and it curls down his shoulders in unruly waves that seem to protest the pull of gravity. When the heat became unbearable, just after noon, we walked back to the house. I went inside, and Esteban went around the back and hauled up water from the well under the nispero tree. He held the bucket high with one hand, and with the other tipped it, slowly — I heard him neigh when the cold water lashed his burning skin. I heard him as I stood in front of the desk where my diary lay open, waiting for the events of my life to run their course, so they might be seen and heard, be recorded and not forgotten. How foolish I had been until today, thinking that events were random flakes of dust that had landed on my path. They all had meaning and purpose. And consequences. All the events in my life have been consequences. Consequences born of thoughts, and thoughts born of desire. And had I feared the thoughts or the desire? Desire is a red-green mango begging to be picked. Desire is what I felt inside this small bedroom where I thought I was safe, sharing my thoughts only with a lamb gut diary. Where I saw how glittering water ran down a man's skin and then away in thick droplets, fast, as if chasing demons hurrying

"Stop here please, Milagros," Ana said.

Milagros put the book down. The maid had come in to announce there was a blackout, and had lit candles. The flame flickered near her face, and Milagros could no longer see Ana, half-hidden in the darkened room.

"There is more, Doña Ana," she said. "The diary is not finished."

"I want it to finish. Here. Please."

Milagros closed the notebook. The smell of cocoa had filled the room while she had been reading, and when she licked her fingers, it tasted bittersweet.

"Of course," she said. "Would you mind if I take it home with me? I will return it."

Ana nodded. "No," she said. "The rest may be for you, or someone else. For me, the story ends here."

Chapter 27

Senator Largaespada had invited a small group of friends and acquaintances "to discuss in confidence," the way they could no longer do at the Social Club. No one called it civil war yet, and the well-to-do in particular resisted thinking of the conflict in those terms, but that was what it had become.

"I imagine you must be happy to be back," Fausto said. "Remind us, how long were you away, Señorita?"

Tomás noticed how Milagros shifted the position of her hips, arching her back.

"Eleven years, Colonel," she said.

"Must have been difficult to live so far from your family." He leaned back into his chair, and continued without waiting for her answer. "May I call you Milagros?"

She nodded.

"Well then, Milagros," Fausto continued, "and forgive me my curiosity, but…they don't like us very much in Europe, do they now?"

"That depends on whom you ask, Colonel."

"How so?"

"We have many friends over there."

"Friends?"

"Yes, people who wish us well. People who have our interests at heart. Our real interests."

"And which would those be?"

She shrugged. "Why would you want to ask me? You are a colonel in the Guardia."

Fausto raised both arms and clasped his hands above his head. "It never ceases to amaze me that so few people answer the questions you ask them," he said. "Somehow, people love answering a question with another question."

"I don't hide behind questions, Colonel."

"Then I'm sure you would not mind indulging me." He laughed, and so did the others in the circle. "What are our 'real interests,' as you call them?"

She stared back at him. "Justice," she said. "It's about justice."

"Ah," Fausto said. "Justice." He smacked his lips, and sucked on an imaginary piece of meat stuck between his teeth. He draped his leg over the armrest of the rocking chair, until his boot was swinging towards her.

"You see, Milagros, we are not so concerned with justice. But we are with order. And with security. All this talk about justice – order is what people need, and justice will follow. You'd be surprised, in fact, at how many people are willing to give up those vaunted little freedoms in return for order and stability. In return for the promise of a walk at night without being mugged at gunpoint."

The senator scraped his throat. His neck had been twitching, and his scars were contracting until he felt as if his skin were choking him. "I think we'd better have some more coffee," he said. "Luisa, coffee, please."

But Fausto did not let up. "I am intrigued, Milagros," he continued. "Please indulge me. Someone who spends three years in a convent and then decides to become a lawyer… What happened?"

"Why should that be so strange?"

"You tell me. I never had an itch to become a lawyer. Or a priest, for that matter. I never had such a choice."

Her hands rolled into fists, and he saw them. "We all have choices, Colonel, and most of us make them. The law…the law is imperfect, but better than nothing."

The senator felt that his skin had itched enough, and jumped in: "Tell me, Fausto," he said, "I heard reports of rebels thirty miles out of León. Shouldn't we be concerned? I even heard about guardsmen uniforms being found behind gas stations!"

"No such thing as defectors in the Guardia, Senator. But there are cells that have infected our institutions, like viruses, that much is true. And then there are these young people, kids from good families who get caught up in this political business all of a sudden. They read the wrong stuff, listen to the wrong people. Then they start doing stupid things: smuggling weapons or money, or providing safe haven for rebels. We don't always know who they are, but they're careless. All people become careless when they think no one knows what they're doing. So sooner or later we will catch up with them, and on the day the game is up…"

Milagros snapped. "So that's how you bring back order? By torturing people?"

Fausto did not blink. He continued rocking his chair, and when he spoke his voice was steady and deliberate: "We don't torture, Milagros." He looked at her the way a schoolteacher would, surprised and hurt by his pupil's attitude.

"We're not barbarians! We're patriots. True patriots, who realize that our country needs defending. Now, if that means breaking some eggs, well…" His hand made a dismissive movement and came to rest on his knee. "But torture, now that's a big word. A very big word. So big I would be careful with it."

She was unfazed. "And the maimed bodies that turn up in the streets every morning – where do they come from?"

"You tell me!" There was laughter from around the table, but Fausto continued looking at Milagros only.

"Really, you tell me. You see, in spite of what you may think, the Guardia does not control everything in this country. And that dead-man-propped-up-against-the-wall trick, that one's been around for quite a while, right, Senator?" He flashed a smile and glanced at the senator.

"We know for a fact that the communists have sympathizers all over, and that includes even people in the morgues," he continued, looking around the table. "My own theory is that there are people who work on some of these bodies at night. You know, make some ugly-looking cuts and all, and then prop them up outside, before dawn, to scare the bejesus out of ordinary folk. Just to make them believe that the Guardia is all a bunch of monsters. But we're not, you all know we're not."

He leaned back and pointed a finger at Tomás. "Ask my cousin here," he said. "He practically lives at the morgue. Ask him what he thinks." He laughed.

Tomás felt blood rushing to his cheeks. "There's nothing irregular going on at the morgue," he said. "I don't know who spreads these lies around, Fausto. I wouldn't listen to all these lies if I were you."

Fausto grinned. "You sound like me, cousin," he said, wagging his finger. "You sound like me. So then what do you think is going on with these corpses?"

"Who is interested in scaring people?" Tomás said. "If you answer that question you have your answer, don't you?"

"Yes," Milagros said. "You said it yourself, Colonel. This scares ordinary people out of their wits. And we all know who stands to gain from that." Fausto stopped laughing. He looked from Milagros to Tomás, and then to the other people sitting around the table, until his gaze rested on the senator.

"We all have a job to do," he said. "And we don't always ask why. My cousin here once tried to save the life of the President's father, did you all know that?"

"Yes," the senator said. "Yes, I remember that very well. Not a day I would forget easily." Milagros looked at her father, then at Tomás.

"What happened?" she said.

Tomás shook his head. "Why do you need to bring that up, Fausto? The man is long dead, and I didn't save his life. So why bring it up? Don't we have enough dead people already?"

"Why get so upset, cousin? You did the right thing then, didn't you?"

Tomás shrugged. "A medical oath is not like any other promise. It requires you to always do the right thing. Blindly, no exceptions."

"Maybe," Fausto said. "And maybe we all see different things. Or see things differently. But courage and honesty are different things, just so you know it."

The sound of chirping cicadas had been swelling sharply, until it was a wall of sound standing guard two feet from the torchlights. They all sat without speaking, and had it not been for the blind priest, they might have been mistaken for highway robbers with daggers half-drawn, waiting for the least sign to throw themselves at each other.

Fausto broke the silence first. "You know," he said, "we're all family somehow. We're all sitting around the table here, so these discussions, they're good. They clear the air. But let's not forget whose side we're on, and where our interests lie. We all make omelets here, all of us!"

The rest of the guests remained silent, so Fausto looked around once more, laughing. "Look," he said, "this is just a game of chicken.

No one wants to get hurt, and yet... No one gets hurt who's not in the wrong place, you understand?"

A rumbling swelled in the distance, and then there was a heavy clap, as of thunder. Some of the men ducked their heads, a reflex after years of heeding sniper warnings.

Fausto jumped to his feet. "Damn it," he grumbled. "Can't even have dinner in civilized company. Do these rebels ever let up?" He shook hands with the senator and rushed out, without taking leave of the others. Soon, the remaining guests took leave as well, until only Doctor Payo had stayed behind, to accompany the senator.

"I have nowhere to go so fast," Doctor Payo said. "What's the difference: sitting here or at home?" The two cousins sat for a while, drinking rum and discussing how far away the explosion had been. Finally, Payo pressed the senator's elbow and got up to leave. On his way out he passed in front of the library. The door was wide open, but no light was on inside. He peered in, and saw the outline of a lone figure prostrate on the tile floor.

"Milagros?"

"How did you know it was me?"

He sighed. "I know everyone who lives in this house," he said. "I daresay I know some of them better than their own parents know them. And that includes you."

She smiled, but it lasted seconds only – a reflex, no more.

"I had not been in this room since coming back."

"Hmm." He sat down in one of the visitor's chairs. "On purpose?"

She sighed. "I don't know. Purpose is something that we always assume but know nothing about, if you ask me. Maybe there is no such thing. Maybe everything is really random. Unstructured. Unintended."

"Then why avoid places?"

"Because of what they remind us of – they always seem to remind us of loss."

"The story of mankind."

"I guess."

"But we're not doomed to relive our losses every day of our life, nor pay for them, are we?"

She laughed. "That only happens in stories, Tío!"

"So live your life, not a story. Not bad memories. Life is what we make it, Milagros. It is what we want it to be – the good and the bad. It's not only about loss."

"No?"

"No. So laugh."

She woke up early the next day. The sun had risen fast, throwing hot rays of light that snaked into her room. Sifting through papers on her desk, she found the notebook. When she opened it, the smell of cocoa warmed her nostrils once more. She turned the pages to where she had stopped reading to Ana, and with every page she turned, her fingers felt warmer.

Yesterday we went to Bilwi, with Horst and Ilse. We bought canned food, soap, and candles. I walked to the port, and Esteban walked two steps behind me once more, as if he were a servant. We passed by the Standard Fruit Company's office, where the telegraph was, but I did not go in. I glanced at it once and walked on to the port. Perhaps the fat man is sitting there, clutching a telegram in his sweaty hand, I thought, a telegram covered with dust, from the priest in Blewfields, or even the Jesuits in Belize or the order back in faraway Spain. A telegram wondering where I am, arranging for me to be picked up and taken to Bluefeels where I will continue the mission that was laid out for me. I wonder if God has changed my course. Perhaps I was never intended to be a nun. Perhaps I only took the habit out of a sense of gratitude towards the kind sisters who saved me from a hard bed of bones. Standing by the port, spying on the pelicans flying above the crests of the breaker waves, I decided that I would not go back, and that I would not go on. That here, halfway between where I had come from and where I had been told to go, was where I would stay.

On my visit to Bilwee, an old woman stood in my path and waved me down with a dappled hand. She looked so old, I thought, she must have been older than the town itself. Her back was bent into a perfectly square angle, and her head and limbs stuck out as if from beneath a giant turtle shell.

Your hand, she cackled, give me your hand. She pulled a handful of herbs from a bag dangling from the rope around her waist, and rubbed it into my hand. I withdrew it as soon as I felt the sting, but she held on, tracing the grooves in the palm of my hand with a long bony finger. Esteban was standing behind me, his long hair smelling of juniper berries, and I felt how the warm static of his skin made the hair on my arm stand up. What is this herb? I asked him, and he told me it was old woman's broom.

There was so much more. Pages and more pages. Milagros imagined how for this woman who spoke to her through the vastness of time, the days must have slowed down until they came to a standstill, binding yesterday and tomorrow into a single sentence that defied the nauseating pace of her own today.

I never pictured myself as a mother. I stopped playing with dolls when I was five, and never went back. As if nature had prepared me for other tasks. Now that I am pregnant, the thought of Blewfields is receding yet more, like a shadow overcome by cloudy skies. Neither Horst nor Ilse are surprised, and if they are, they do not show it. And they do not judge me, or Esteban.

I am going into labor. I do not know if this is my sin or my destiny. Have I fallen this much, that I can no longer distinguish what I must do from what I must not? I want this child; want it with all my heart.

There was a space, and then the whiteness of waiting pages. The last writing was uneven, scrawled across a random page. Hastily, it seemed, as if its owner had raced against nightfall. In unapologetically large letters it read: "*Oh, but to have loved.*"

Milagros turned the page, and then another one, until she found one more entry, a single sentence. The handwriting was firm and even, and spoke of austerity and discipline: "*Aurora has died while giving birth to a girl.*"

Dizziness came over her, brought on by the smell of cocoa stinging her nostrils. *Bittersweet,* she thought. *But it's a story. I'll return it to Ana tomorrow.*

Chapter 28

"These shoes are too tight, Humberto," Tomás said. He put the shiny new shoes on the counter that cut in half the minuscule cubicle where Humberto was busy fixing footwear. The store smelled of strong glue, so much so that Humberto's own wife told him she got drunk just from getting near him at night. He took the left shoe and peered into it with one eye, the other one clamped shut.

"Too tight, eh, Doctor?" he said. "*Está bien*, just leave them, I'll have one of my shoe tamers walk them in." There were still shoe tamers in León in those days, because there were still shoemakers who made shoes. They bought the leather off the cow's back, and worked with deerskin, alligator, and sometimes snakeskin as well. This pair of shoes was made of garrobo leather, the best-looking iguana you could find, with a magnificent sheen. Garrobos fetched a handsome price, and were rapidly turned into the most elegant pairs of shoes and ladies' handbags León had ever seen. Most of the garrobo leather ended up on Humberto's bench. He was the best shoemaker in town, and rarely received complaints. He knew that his clientele were exclusive and demanding but loyal, so he had shoe tamers, *amanzadores,* for every size and width: reliable people who would walk the shoes until they had stretched just enough, without sullying them or damaging the leather. The amanzadores rarely wore shoes of their own, and their feet were broad and wide, browned by the sun on top, and reddened by the earth underneath, just as Mother Nature had allowed them to grow.

When Humberto arrived, the man who was to walk in Tomás's shoes was sitting in the doorway of his house. He was painting a new mask for the enano cabezón his son would be wearing.

"Elías," Humberto said, "that looks like a good mask. You haven't lost your touch yet from what I see." He lifted the brown paper bag he had been carrying and shook it, as if there were a baby's rattle inside. "I have a pair of shoes for you to break in, Elías," he said.

"Yes, Don Humberto," Elías said, "when do you want them back?"

"Five days," Humberto said. "Five days, no more. I need them back on Thursday, you hear?" He shook his bony finger. "The doctor will need them for a wedding. So, Thursday?"

"*Ayayay,* Don Humberto, that's very fast. I'm not sure I'll be able to walk that much in so few days!"

"Then walk more, Elías. Take them everywhere, not just for afternoon strolls. These shoes need to have lived before I give them to the doctor. But be careful with them; the last pair you did got banged up so much, I had to replace the vamp."

"I'll be careful, Don Humberto, trust me," Elías said. Later that day, he climbed inside the ten-foot-tall Gigantona doll, and shook the torso to make the arms sway and swirl. His son was wearing the new enano mask, banging the drums and singing the song that all boys learn by heart. Underneath the Gigantona's immaculate dress, two garrobo leather shoes danced and stamped, holding two brown feet firmly prisoner even though they screamed and begged to be released. For the next three days, the shoes of Doctor Tomás Delacorte Cortés danced the breadth and width of the streets of León.

Every Wednesday evening, Elías went out to drink with the other men in his neighborhood, and this Wednesday was no different. The shoes were still tight on his sore feet, but he knew he had little time left, so he kept them on, and after a few shots of rum he almost forgot about them. It was past midnight when all five friends stumbled out of the cantina, and staggered along until they came to the narrow bridge that spanned the Rio Chiquito. Rainwater ran here in the wet season, taking with it dead dogs and other garbage that no one wanted, until it threw itself into the sea.

Elías stopped and brought his finger to his lips. "Shhh," he said. "I saw something down there."

"So why are you shutting us up, brother?" his companions said. "If you saw something you should go and check it out, not shut us up!"

Elías leaned over the low railing of the concrete bridge, and peered out into the dark. Then he swung his leg over the side, and the two shiny shoes that were expected at a wedding were suddenly hanging in the air, and then took their master with them, sliding down to the bottom of the flood channel amid stinking *güiligüiste* branches and rotting cornhusk.

When he crawled to his feet, he saw the wallet. It had no name card inside, no driver's license. It was really just a wallet with money in it. Lots of it, almost five hundred córdobas, he counted. His excitement rose with every bill he saw. He stuck the money inside his shoes, under his sweaty feet, leaving just fifty córdobas in his pocket. Then he saw the other pair of shoes, stuck in the thick black mud, hidden under a güiligüiste branch.

"More shoes," he said, looking at them with appreciation. "Now Elías has shoes of his own."

When he climbed out of the ditch, his friends had left. He looked around, breathing heavily. The street was deserted but for two stray dogs.

"Some friends you are, all of you," he mumbled, before making his way to where the ladies of the night plied their trade.

"Elías," one of them said, "what are you doing here?"

"I've got money," he said, "lots of it. I'm a rich man now."

Two of the ladies got closer and sniffed at him. "You should go home, Elías," the older one said. "Go home and sleep it off." She pushed him back into the street with both hands.

"No," he said, "no, I have money, and shoes. I want you to listen to me." He set down the muddy pair of shoes on the pavement, pulled out the fifty córdobas he had in his pocket, and waved them in the air. The two women looked at the money, and then they looked at each other, raised their shoulders and laughed.

"Come with me then, Elías," the older one said, the taller one with the bleached hair. She led him away to a house on the corner where a one-eyed man stood guard for her. When she closed the door behind them, Elías started laughing and wheezing.

"What's the matter?" she said. "What's so funny all of a sudden?"

The alcohol was losing its grip over his mind, as if a veil had been lifted. "Nothing," he said. "Should there always be a reason?" She raised her shoulders and pulled up her dress.

"I just want a little perfect hour," he said, "a perfect hour to forget about these Gigantona dresses. I hope you understand that." She lay down on her back, her dress lifted all the way up to her eyes.

"No," he said, "no, pull it down. I need to see your face, your lips." He dropped his pants down to his ankles and fell on top of her.

"Don't you take off your shoes?" she said.

"No," he mumbled, "not today. I can't take them off today, not even tonight. They will go to a wedding soon."

Chapter 29

"These guerrillas are a laughable outfit," Fausto thundered. "A ragtag band of rabble-rousers and misfits. No ideology, just a whole lot of air and guns, but too chicken to put up a real fight." But they were there, in the mountains and the cloud forests, stoking up unrest with wild tales about taking over the country. As time went by, the rumor took on a life of its own. The market women talked about the giant Gigantona in between sales, as they ironed out smudgy one-córdoba notes with their hands, one by one. The maids who came shopping were drawn into the rumor mills, and told their mistresses. The next week the mistresses came themselves, and before long, the market had become a milling crowd of people who spent less time shopping than talking.

It was rumored that the guerrillas would take the city of León coming in disguise, at night. They would take the city before the Guardia could wipe their butts and pull up their pants. They would overrun the whole place and shoot up the Guardia with their pants down and crapping all over themselves. The rumors became wrapped in ever more graphic details as days went by. Fausto did not mind much the talk about the guerrillas, but he did mind the rumor about the Trojan Gigantona. No one knew anything beyond this rumor. Who was building it: a secret. Where it was being built: a secret. When would it be ready: another secret.

When the noise level grew to such heights that it sounded like a revolution brewing, Fausto called in his lieutenants.

"What's with this Gigantona business?" he said. "I don't like secrets, especially secrets I have not been let in on. Go find out what this is all about!" They sent out a spy, a woman selling sodas. She came back with the story of the giant Gigantona.

"It's going to be the largest ever built," she told Fausto. "And there will be eleven dwarves. Not just one, but eleven. And the dwarves will be larger than grown-up men."

"So who was building this thing?" Fausto wanted to know. "It could not possibly be just one person, there must be a small army working on this, surely." The woman had no information on this. He became agitated, and started seeing enemies everywhere.

"With all this talk of the guerrillas planning a move, something must be brewing," he said. "I'm sure this is it, this is how it's going to happen: a Trojan horse." He brooded, imagined the guerrillas streaming out from under the Gigantona dress, an army of dwarves throwing off their masks and taking over his city.

"Where was it being built?" he demanded.

Again, there were no details. *So why the hell did I send this woman?* Fausto thought, but he controlled his impulse and anger, because the last persons in the word he wanted to vex were his informants. He sent out more informants. They asked around the fabric stores, inquiring who was buying up large quantities of sash and cloth; they asked around the barber stores, to see who had been trying to buy up the hair that the barbers collected to be bleached and fashioned into wigs. And so on and so forth. They did a complete analysis of all the parts and pieces that needed to bring a giant Gigantona to life, believing that this would lead them to the secret mutineers. But that most important body part of all they did not know, and even if they had known, they would not have known where to look for it.

"It's the heart," the woman selling purple soda told him. "If you want to know who's building the thing, find out who is building the heart."

"What?" Fausto snapped. "What on earth are you talking about?"

"Yes," she said, and came closer to his desk, until she was standing so close he could smell the rancid niff of spilt beans.

"I know what I'm talking about, Major," she said again, and frowned until her forehead seemed to have split in half. He felt the impulse to tell the lieutenant to give her water.

She's nothing to me, he thought. *Just another worm ready to sell out her own kind. God, these people have no sense of honor whatsoever, little more than animals.* But he thought the better of it. *She had more to say,* he decided. *She's a good informant, just how I like them: unobtrusive, with a sharp eye and an ability to chat up anyone she meets.*

"The lieutenant will pay you," he said, and shoved her out the door.

"Who is spreading all these rumors?" Fausto asked his men.

"People," they said, and shrugged.

"People!" Fausto sneered. "I don't know of anyone by the name 'people.' Every rumor starts somewhere; every story starts with someone. I want you to find out where this one started. I want names, you hear, even it means you go all the way back to Adam!"

They brought in a man in rags, and put him away for a couple of days, "to soften him up." They had picked him up while he was visiting a prostitute in a house of ill repute.

"Rabble-rouser!" they yelled when they pulled him to his feet and slapped him in the face.

"Your grandmother!" he screamed back. "I've paid for this, have you no shame? Leave a man his pleasure!" The Guard was in no mood to joke around, so they put him in the slammer, and on the fourth day they took him to see Fausto.

"Who's this?" he said.

"It's the guy who's been spreading rumors about the guerrillas coming to town," the captain said. Fausto lifted a crooked eyebrow. It was the one characteristic that still tied him to Mama Mica.

"What's your name?" he said.

"Elías," the man said.

"And what do you do for a living?"

"I sell newspapers," the old man said.

"My men here tell me that you also make up some of the news yourself from time to time."

"Well, do you?"

"Do what, Don?"

"Make up the news yourself. Especially when it concerns the guerrillas?"

"No, Don."

He was getting angry now. "Why is it that I find that hard to believe?"

"What's wrong?" Tomás said to the paperboy, seeing him downcast.

"My dad is gone."

"You mean he left?"

"No, he never came home. He's been gone for a week now."

"Whatever is the world coming to?" Tomás said, shaking his head. "What's your father's name?"

"Elías," the boy said. "Like me."

"So where are you staying now, Elías?"

The boy shrugged. "In the house," he said. "My brother Elvis came home last week."

The Gigantona that came dancing towards Colonel Cortés's house was no different from many of the others that were being paraded through the streets of León that day. She had an orange dress with broad white ruffles in horizontal stripes, powdery pink cheeks, and flaxen hair. If Tomás had been there, he might have thought she had stepped right out of his childhood. And yet, not one was a copy of another, because the Gigantonas did not live long. Like dogs, their years were counted seven-fold.

What was unusual about this Gigantona was the presence of two dwarves. Not that it had not happened before – there had been Gigantonas with two, three, and even four dwarves whirling around her, like moths around a flame. However, each dwarf also needed to eat, and the good people of León were no longer as prosperous as they once were, courtesy of bad harvests and the need to keep not one but two competing bands of armed men content and well fed. So the pickings had become slim – the Gigantonas attracted on-lookers and dancing children, but ever fewer citizens to donate the money and food that would keep her and her dwarves in business.

This particular troupe did not seem to mind. They walked fast, and stopped nowhere to perform and ask for money. The dwarf beating the drum got tangled up in his drum straps, but after fruitless attempts to disentangle himself seemed to give up altogether, hoisting the drum on his back to pick up the pace.

It was an odd sight when they rounded the corner of the Calle Poniente, and came in full view of the Cortés house. The Gigantona was leading them, her torso and head swaying as if she were a giant ship being tossed about on the high seas. The two dwarves came running right behind, holding on to masks that had shifted so the cutouts for their eyes no longer lined up. When they came to a stop in front of Fausto's house, the drummer pushed his mask into position, and started beating the drums:

It did not take long before one of the maids walked up to the gate, accompanied by Adriana, and asked them to come in.

"Doña Ana would like to offer you some food," she said. Adriana did not take her eyes off the Gigantona – she walked up and caressed the long dress, then squeezed the ruffles between her fingers before bursting into laughter.

"Come now," the maid said, and led the three visitors to the outdoor kitchen while Adriana held up the Gigantona dress as if it were a bridal gown. When they came to the kitchen, the Gigantona bent her head, and some strands of her hair were caught in the telephone cable that was sagging across the backyard.

"Don't lose your hair," one of the maids said. She pointed at where a strip of ruffle had been torn off: "You already lost part of your dress," she said, and the maids all laughed. Meanwhile, the dwarves put down their drums and maracas, and stood by, waiting. When the cook put three plates of rice and beans on the table, the maid beckoned for the guests to sit down.

"And you can take off your masks now," she added. The dwarves looked at each other and shook their heads in unison, while the Gigantona stood silent.

"We can't," one of the dwarves said in a high-pitched voice. "But we'll take the food with us." The maid shrugged – *what good would it be to argue with two dwarves and a Gigantona?* She motioned to the cook, who shoved the gallo pinto into a plastic bag and put a knot in it. The inside of the bag quickly steamed up, and when the cook handed it to one of the dwarves, drops had formed on the inside, and were quickly running down onto the rice. One of the dwarves tied the bag to his belt, and dropped the tunic back on top of it.

"Bathroom," said the dwarf who had spoken before.

"All three of you? At the same time?" The maids laughed and pointed towards the outhouse that stood in the back of the garden.

"Strange folk," the cook said to the maid. The maid raised her shoulders. "What's strange about them?" she said. "Probably just a bunch of kids trying to make ends meet."

"But did you see the shoes on that Gigantona?" The other maids bent over to catch a glimpse of the shoes.

"Look expensive. Wonder where they found them."

Fascinated by the orange ruffles, Adriana had followed the three performers as they walked to the garden's edge. She saw how the drummer reached under the Gigantona's dress to pull up something long and black, and how the other dwarf was holding a small black fish. They did not stop at the outhouse; instead, they hurried towards the garden house where her father lay sleeping. When they reached it, one of the dwarves peered through the window and saw Fausto, asleep. The Gigantona positioned herself in front of the door, her back towards the cabin, holding a long gun at knee-level. The dwarf wielding the crowbar moved to pry open the door, but his companion gestured for him to stand back, and instead moved a rock to uncover a small key. He turned the key in the lock, and slowly pushed on the door. At this moment, Adriana snuck in between the Gigantona's legs, and threw herself onto her sleeping father.

"What?" Fausto screamed, startled. "What's happening?" Instantly awake with the onrush of adrenaline, he saw two dwarves in ill-fitting costumes at the foot and the side of his bed. One of them was pointing a gun at him, while the other was holding a crowbar to his thigh. The door war was blocked by a sea of flowing tulle, orange, and white.

"Time to die, asshole," the dwarf wielding the crowbar said. "Our time to give you water now." Fausto reached for the pistol he kept under his pillow, but the weight of his daughter did not let him. He felt something sharp and heavy rip the muscles of his calf, and screamed. When he looked down, he saw blood staining the sheets, and the black crowbar resting on his leg.

"Shoot him, Che!" the dwarf with the crowbar said. "Shoot him, quickly!" The other dwarf aimed his gun, but each time Adriana was there, covering her father's torso.

"Can't get a shot," the dwarf said. "Pull the girl off him!" The other dwarf dropped the crowbar and tried to pull Adriana away, but she did not let him, and held on to her father with ever more force.

"We need to go; just shoot the bastard already, doesn't matter where!"

Adriana had held on tightly, and closed her eyes. When the shot fired her whole body jolted, then stiffened. But she did not cry; she squeezed her eyes shut until they hurt. Then she felt a hand on her head, and her neck. Briefly, softly.

"The girl is fine," someone said. "Let's go now, quick." The two walked backwards, and before leaving the room the one with the gun lodged a bullet in Fausto's foot. The three ran out through the servants' gate, and quickly disappeared in a cloud of dust.

"You'll live," Doctor López said. "Lost a little blood, but the bullet grazed your temple only. There's swelling, and you'll have a headache for some time. Your foot though…the bone is splintered; you'll need time for it to heal."

Fausto growled.

"Adriana saved your life, you know," the doctor said. "If she hadn't been there I don't think they would have missed their shot."

"Damn amateurs," he said. "These were amateurs. They could have shot me dead but they didn't."

His lieutenants had crammed into the hospital room, but were keeping a safe distance from their commander.

"In my own house!" he yelled at them. "In my own house! If they can pull this off, they can do a lot worse. Go find the bastards and bring them to me!"

"We found a trail of wet rice and beans leading from your house to the Church of the Redemption," one of them said. "But from there, nothing."

"Nothing? Hasn't anyone seen these amateurs run away?"

"It's Gigantona time, jefe, lots of them all over town these days." Fausto saw how the lieutenant hesitated.

"What?" he bellowed, "Out with it!"

"We found a shoe," the lieutenant said. "One of them lost a shoe." Fausto felt his head explode, the blood rushing to his throbbing temple.

"And you want me to go out and find the owner of a shoe?" he hissed. "Who do I look like to you? Prince Fucking Charming? Now you go and find every single Gigantona in this town, and that's how we'll find these *insurgentes!* Every single one of them!"

When Fausto arrived home from the hospital, Ana was waiting for him on the porch. Adriana was sitting on the floor, playing with a ragdoll.

"I am leaving you, Fausto," she said, once the men had left. "And I'm taking Adriana with me."

"Why?" he said. "Why now?"

"Do you need to ask? People came into our house and almost killed you. Almost killed her" – she pointed at Adriana with her chin.

"Adriana," she continued, "go to the kitchen, honey bear, and tell Maria to give you *atol.* Would you like that?"

When Adriana had gone inside, Ana turned back to Fausto. "Do you expect me to wait for my second child to die as well?"

"That's not fair. I loved Simón as much as you," he said, raising his voice.

"Perhaps," she said. "I don't know if you ever loved anyone in your life. I even wonder if you ever loved me."

He was silent. "The boy," he said. "I wanted him to be…"

She shook her head. "Always Simón," she said, squinting her eyes. "Why don't you love her? She is your daughter, and she's still alive. If it hadn't been for her, you would have been dead. Doesn't that mean anything to you?" She shook her head and watched the ceiling fan before continuing: "Mama Mica once told me that a child looks like the man its mother loved when she conceived it. I think she was right. And you never understood that."

"Understood what?"

"You call her a monster."

"What are you saying?"

"If you call her a monster, what does that make you? You are heartless. Cold and heartless. You always were, but I refused to see it for so long."

"Maybe," he said. "But I never cheated on you the way you cheated on me."

"What?"

"You think I don't know? I never said anything, but I always knew you loved Tomás more than me."

"That was a long time ago. We closed that chapter."

"You did. Or you think you did. You never asked me what I thought."

She sighed. "It doesn't matter anymore," she said. "I will be leaving."

He got up to hit her, but the crutches slipped and his leg gave out.

"I won't let you," he said. "I need you here."

"I am not asking you, Fausto."

"You cannot take her with you."

"What? What do you mean?"

"I won't let you take her."

"You don't need me here. You don't need anyone. You don't love either one of us, so why keep us here? Everyone here will die, don't you see it?" When Fausto said nothing, she shook her head. "I guess you can no longer see these things," she said. "You're lost, Fausto. Everyone will die, and you're part of those who make it so."

Tomás went to see her. She looked pale and frail, as if years had been added to her life in a few days' time. He was surprised to see her dressed in boots. A felt hat too warm for the rainy season was sitting on the couch besides her, waiting for a command, for a sign to be gone. He sat with her but did not know what to say.

Strangers. We have become strangers. Yet once we were so close. Where did our friendship go? Was it all sucked up into that empty room?

"I will be leaving this place," she said. "I will go to Paris."

He had not expected it. "Why?" he said.

She turned her head, sharply. "Need you ask? Do you men all forget your promises?"

He blushed. "But how…is Fausto going with you?"

"I am leaving him. And you. I am leaving two dead men and my little dead boy. You are dead, all three of you, in your different ways, but only my little Simón did not ask for it. Why should I spend the rest of my life with dead people?"

She lifted the hat and stood up.

"Goodbye, Tomás. I hope you find what you are looking for. There must be some chance at happiness left in you."

When Tomás was about to step into his car, Adriana rushed towards him. She buried her head in his chest and put her arms around him. A lithe young woman, she was almost his height now. He patted her back, stroked the long hair that reminded him of Ana when she was young. She broke their embrace, and pulled him along until they got to her room. In the middle of the room was a heap of dusty objects. He spied a wooden train, a few toy plastic soldiers, and a dented tin flashlight.

"Where did you find all this, *muñeca?*" he said. She moved her lips and looked towards the door, as if someone had just entered. He recognized Fausto's old hunting knife, and pulled it out from a scuffed leather sheath, slowly. The blade had turned dull and blunt, no longer the mirror it once was. He sniffed the blade, but it smelled of rusty iron only. Adriana pulled out a notebook, and held it out to him.

"Book," she said. "Smells like chocolate. Pretty. For you."

He smelled the bitter ripeness of cocoa beans, and a hint of vanilla that promised to lessen its bitterness.

"Thank you, muñeca," he said, and kissed her on both cheeks. "Take good care of your mother."

They left that same evening. Ana pulled out three of the four suitcases lying at the bottom of her closet, and as they were opened the smell of naphthalene filed the room. She unfolded and refolded the clothing inside, repacked the suitcases and closed them again. One of them held her winter clothes, and an old guidebook to Paris. The second suitcase was packed for Adriana – it had been filled and emptied, replaced and repacked many times, reminding her that time did not stand still. The last one had remained unopened.

She said goodbye to the servants, told them to take care of Fausto while she was gone. From the back of the car, she looked one more time at the porch from which she used to watch the sunset, and the garden where her children had grown up. Then it was gone, hidden behind a Malinche tree standing guard, its flamboyant red and orange blossoms swaying in the wind.

Juan drove them to Corinto. The fishing trawler that had moored there was at least fifty years old. Adriana read out loud the name that was painted on the hull, in large yellow letters: *El Arcoiris.*

Nothing moved throughout the trip. The sky was empty and serene. At noon, one of the crew members came by and offered them food, and they ate the rice and beans scooped into plastic plates. When they disembarked that evening, in a small Salvadorian port across the Gulf of Fonseca, the sailors handed them back their suitcases. One of them was ripped open by a rusty nail in the cabin wall.

Chapter 30

When Tomás came by the shoe store on Friday morning, Humberto was all apologies.

"We lost your shoes, Doctor," he said.

Tomás gave him a look of surprise. "What do you mean?" he said. "How could you lose my shoes?"

"My amanzador," Humberto said. "He said he wore them every day except Wednesday. He left them at home that day, and when he came back he could not find them again. What can I do, I am terribly sorry."

"I need my shoes, Humberto. I'm invited to a wedding. I can't very well go without shoes, can I?"

"I will give you a different pair, Doctor, until we find them. Here," he said, putting a pair of iguana leather shoes on the counter. "Finest garrobo, already walked in!"

Tomás looked at the shoes. They looked expensive, although slightly beat-up at the caps.

"I guess they will do," he said.

"I fixed them up this morning, they're in mint condition. And your size, Doctor." Humberto pulled a brown paper bag from the shelf behind him and dropped the shoes inside it. When Tomás pulled out his wallet, Humberto refused.

"No," he said, "it is I who should pay you, Doctor. I am terribly embarrassed that we have lost your shoes." Tomás put away his wallet and reached for the paper bag. At that moment, Humberto looked around furtively, and in a voice that was conspicuously lower than before he said: "Doctor, could I bother you with something?"

"Of course, what is it you need, Humberto?" He thought that the man might want a prescription, or free medicines perhaps.

"I have been asked to provide some storage space for this Gigantona," he said, "by one of my walkers. But I myself have no space. Look around you; this store is much too small. And my home, well, let's just say that my wife's tongue travels far." He hesitated, and Tomás frowned.

"I was thinking, perhaps you could store this Gigantona for a couple of days, Doctor?"

"I don't know," Tomás replied. "I mean, it's kind of an awkward request, really."

"I know, Doctor, but this man, he really needs a place to store it for a few days, that's all. He's a good man, but very poor you know, trying to make ends meet…"

"All right then, I guess a couple of days won't kill me. Tell your friend to drop it off later today!"

That evening, he found the Gigantona lying on his couch. The ceiling light made her stoic face look whiter than ever. Juanita had gone home for the weekend, and the rest of the house was only dimly lit. He saw two dwarf masks sitting on the chair beside her. *What are we going to do with you?* he wondered. In his head, he ticked off the rooms of his house to figure out where he could leave it. He stopped when he got to an empty room, and shrugged. "Why not?" he said.

The key was in a small drawer inside the cabinet where he kept his rum and rat poison. The key felt heavy in his hand, cold and smelling of acrid rust, but the lock opened as if it had been oiled all along for the past seven years. Inside, the paint had started chipping and showing signs of mildew. The air smelled stale and moldy. He pulled a bed sheet from the closet in his bedroom and spread it on the floor of the barren room. Then he went back to the living room where the doll was lying patiently. He carried her into the empty room and abruptly dropped her on top of the sheet. The two dwarf masks ended up hanging on the crank ax used to open the glass blinds. He locked the door behind him and went to bed, thinking no more about it.

The next day he went into the storage room to look for a hammer. Boxes and crates were piled high, and the toolbox was nowhere in view. He was about to give up when his eye was caught by a mouse sneaking into a rattan trunk. "Vermin!" he snapped, "I'll get rid of this right away!" But when he opened the trunk he did not find the mouse. Instead, he found a horsehair blanket, and under it a red-brown urn. His heart skipped a beat as he saw himself as a boy again, hiding the urn at the bottom of his closet, holding on to it, shaking it, talking to it.

He stretched out his hand, half-expecting to get burned. But the urn was cool to his touch. The clay had hardened, and no longer gave up its redness without a fight: when he looked at his hand, he saw that it had remained unstained.

"Might as well put all useless things together," he said, "so we get rid of everything at the same time. I don't know why I've been keeping this thing for so long." He carried it to the Gigantona's room, where he put it down in one of the corners.

He went to the wedding of a distant cousin that afternoon wearing the garrobo shoes Humberto had given him. They felt good, so much so that he ventured out onto the dance floor, which he had not done in many years. He whirled and spun like a young man, until he felt breathless but happy. He was still humming when he got home, but when he passed in front of his mother's room he stopped abruptly. There were voices behind the locked door: whispered, in the way of lovers, or conspirators.

"What on earth?" he exclaimed, and rushed to get the keys. But when he opened the door everything was exactly the way he had left it, and the room was silent. He walked around the long dress stretched out on the floor, watching the pale face and long yellow tresses. His hand trembled as he opened the blinds and the hot night air streamed in. He lifted one of the masks off the handle and put it on his head. It was dark inside, and the smell of glue and rubber boots filled his nostrils, making him dizzy. The cutout eyes were set too far apart, as if trying to take in all of the known world – not just that part that they had been allowed to see, but all of it: the trees, the gardens, the rivers, and the hills far beyond them, until they crossed the mountains that had been set between them and happiness. Tomás strained to see through them, to see the tamarind tree that stood outside his house, its leaves rustling evenly in the night wind. Hot and perspiring he pulled at the mask, hard.

I can't breathe, he thought. He reached for the syringe, and panic struck him when he realized he had left it on the table on his way in. Then, suddenly, his breathing slowed, until it was his own again. He no longer felt the weight of the mask, as if it had become part of him. When he looked down at the Gigantona he saw her the way he had never seen her before: he saw the great beauty that comes from being able to run away.

"I am free," the Gigantona said. "I am my own woman, I choose my own companion."

The words echoed in his ears, and he clawed at the mask until he had ripped off the cardboard ears, and his hands had turned red.

"Then choose me!" he exclaimed. "Then choose me, damnit. How come you never choose me?"

His own words startled him. *Am I crazy? Am I crazy or is this the only thing that makes sense in this whole damned universe?* He was sweltering, and took off his shirt. Fast, ripping buttons. He dropped his pants down to his shoes until he stood naked in the moonlight. A trickle of sweat ran down his back and then his left buttock. Nothing moved in the room.

He beat his chest, once. And again. Slowly at first, then faster, until it hurt.

"*Bomba, bomba,*" he barked. "*Yo soy el enano cabezón.* I am the dwarf with the water head. I have loved you forever but you care not for me. Your eyes I do not dare meet even in my dreams." His chest was burning now, but he did not stop: "*Bomba, bomba,*" he continued. "Your lips I would kiss, if only you let me. Your hair I would caress, if only you told me." His voice felt dry and sharp, like wind being slowed down by tall grass. He inhaled and stopped there, leaning against the other mask hanging from the window, his lungs filled with burning air. When he let out the air again his voice was a whisper:

"Remember me. Forget you not. Remember me. Forget you not. Remember me. Forget you not."

He repeated the words until his lungs had been emptied. Wheezing, he dropped his arms to his sides until the burning in his chest had faded to a dull reminder. Then he took off the mask and threw it onto the Gigantona.

"Dead," he said. "Both of you. Dead."

Chapter 31

They were being rounded up from every low-roofed and thin-doored house, like so many tumbleweeds.

"Get those Gigantonas, and take down everyone's name." Those had been Fausto's orders. Soon, however, they realized that it might not be so easy to find the one that had been used to try to kill Fausto.

"They all look the same, jefe," his men told him. "They all have long dresses and yellow hair; how do we know which is the one they used to get into your house?"

Fausto mulled it over. "Just get all of them. At least they won't be able to pull off this trick again."

When people objected, they were told off at gunpoint: "Do you have a problem, *india?*" the soldier said, pointing his gun at her.

"But this Gigantona, it's my livelihood," she protested, "this is what my husband does for a living, and my son plays the enano. If you take our Gigantona we'll be ruined. You're leaving us in the street!"

There was no negotiating. No buts, no ifs. Fausto's orders had been so strict that no one dared slack on this one; no one dared take money or favors in return for turning a blind eye. No exceptions: only the slaying of every single Gigantona would do, whether innocent or guilty. They went through the Indian neighborhoods and then through the slums and shantytowns. It was the most colorful razzia ever seen in all of León, with tens of Gigantonas being hoisted onto olive-green army trucks and driven to the barracks. They were stacked up until they resembled a maypole reaching up to heaven, with arms and hands stretched in all directions, pointing accusing fingers at their henchmen.

"Are they all here?" Fausto wanted to know.

"We combed through every house and hut," his commanders bragged. "Unless you want us to search the houses of the bourgeois as well?"

Fausto stared back at them. "So?" he said. "So go look for them. I don't care which house you get into, just bring me those damn dolls!"

He stuck out his chin and slipped his right hand between the buttons of his jacket.

The commanders knocked on thick and solid doors this time.

"What is this?" the bourgeois cried, indignant. "You have no right!"

"Says who?" the guardia snarled, shoving them aside with hairy arms. They found no Gigantonas of course.

When they came knocking at Tomás's door, he was not home. Juanita opened up and was met with growls:

"Move aside, woman, we need to get in and inspect." She was wise enough not to argue with guardsmen. They went through every room, uncovering bedspreads and the pile of clothing to be ironed in the backyard. One of the soldiers turned the doorknob of Victoria's room.

"What's in here?" he barked. "Open up! Now!"

"This room is not in use," she said.

"Now," he yelled, "I said 'now.'"

"I don't have the key," Juanita said. She cowered against the wall, breathing heavily. "Only the doctor has the keys."

The comandante came in, together with two more soldiers.

"What's the problem?" he said. "What's in this room?"

"I don't know," Juanita said. "I don't have the key, only the doctor does." And this was true.

"Open that door," the commander beckoned. The two soldiers locked arms and took one step back. Their boots crashed into the door, at midriff level, but it did not open. It was slightly warped around the lock but resisted the kicks, stubbornly refusing to give up its secrets.

"Sonofabitch," the commander spat, "I want that door broken down right now!"

One of the soldiers shouldered his gun and aimed at the wood around the lock. The shot blasted a hole in the air, the wood split and splintered, and a gentle push was all that was needed after that to dislodge the door from its frame. The soldier stepped back and the commander entered the room, pistol drawn and two soldiers peering in behind him.

"God in heaven, what the hell is this?" the commander exclaimed.

Inside the room, in all its splendid womanly glory, a Gigantona was lying on a bed sheet. Her hair was ruffled, her dress was crumpled, and the stilts lying against the wall looked awkwardly much like broken crutches. A silent dwarf mask with big empty eyes was snuggling up to her, while another one was hanging on the wax pin that operated the blinds.

"What kind of freak lives here?" the commander said, as he turned around to Juanita.

"Doctor Tomás Raúl Delacorte Cortés," Juanita said. She pronounced each of the words with much emphasis, assuming that they would sink in separately, each one holding its own. As the commander made no sign of deference at hearing the magical words, she added: "I have not seen this door open in many years."

"Well," the comandante said, "in any case it's a Gigantona, so we'll take it."

"What about the dwarf masks?" Juanita said. "Will you take them too?"

"Hell no. I have no instructions to take masks, only Gigantonas." He noted down Tomás's name in a notebook, with a description of the Gigantona's dress and the two masks. The soldiers dragged the Gigantona out, but they were tired after a whole day of hunting dolls. They pulled too hard at the fabric, so the head came off and rolled away until it came to rest against the urn. One of the soldiers ran after it and positioned himself behind it.

"Ready?" he said. He kicked the head back to his companion but missed his aim, and the head bumped against the urn instead. The urn was brittle by now and its molecules too tired to resist. So it broke into a thousand pieces, and released its long-held contents onto the tile floor.

"Stop clowning around, you two," the commander said. "We have more work to do; let's get going!" The soldiers pulled out the headless doll and tossed it onto the truck, where more Gigantona carcasses were piled up high. Before the sergeant left the room he bent over and picked up the battered pink head. Shaking off the ashes, he looked at it.

"Nah," he said, and dropped it. Then he lit a cigarette and snapped his fingers.

"Step on it, you guys," he said. They drove away fast.

That night, with two days to go until Christmas, all the guardsmen not on duty had gathered in the central courtyard of the barracks to gaze at the mountain of colorful dresses and rivers of yellow hair. When the last truck had come back, Fausto gave orders to set the pyre ablaze. The soldiers cheered and applauded as the flax-colored hair zinged and sparked, and the many-colored dresses burned and flew away as wisps of smoke. It was a short-lived fire, a fire that would not have lasted long enough to cook a pot of beans. Fausto looked at the blaze but felt no pleasure at the sight. He was leafing through the notebooks given to him by his commanders, all twenty-three of them filled with the names and addresses of people from whose houses the Gigantonas had been taken.

"Well, well," he said, when he saw Tomás's name. "Doctor Delacorte Cortés has strange hobbies indeed. And two masks. Well, well."

When Tomás came home that night, Juanita said nothing. She served him dinner, closed up the house, and retired to her room. Walking to his bedroom with a bottle of rum, Tomás saw the splintered door, and frowned. He pushed it open, slowly, as if expecting a lion to be lurking behind it. But there was only a mask hanging from a nail in the wall, and the other one lying next to the torn head of the giant doll, covered by a heap of ashes and shards of clay. A dirty band of red wax pointed in his direction like an outstretched finger, and when he walked towards the window, he felt shards lodging in his soles. He was surprised to see how uniformly gray the ashes were.

So that was all then? he wondered. *Just a heap of ashes, nothing else?* He pulled the mask from the nail and threw it down where the other two heads were lying. He went to get matches, poured rum on top of the pile, and lit it.

"Fuck everything," he said, "what good is it to have a dwarf mask without a Gigantona? Now that the old whore is gone, might as well get rid of this one as well." The flame was low and dim, no sparks. It left a bright red spot on the white tile floor but he did not notice it under the coat of gray ashes. He finished his rum and went to bed.

He did not hear any noise outside his house that night. No drunks singing, no boys telling lies to girls, and no beggars asking for a

Christmas bonus. But in the street outside his house a man was sitting against the wall, his head stuck deep inside his jacket, so he might have been mistaken for a *chismoso, a* Peruvian gossipmonger.

Juanita's hand was trembling when she served him breakfast.

"What is it, Juanita?" he said.

"There is a dead man sitting outside your house, Doctor."

"What?" he said. "Outside my house?"

"Yes, and one of his ears is cut off."

He was speechless. *Why against my house?* he thought. Juanita went to the kitchen and came back with more coffee.

"Anyone we know?" he said.

She shook her head. "People say he was a day laborer from Chinandega. Everyone thought he was sleeping, but when someone pushed him, he tipped over. And then there are his shoes, Doctor."

"What about them?"

"He had only one shoe on, Doctor."

He leaned back. "He must have lost the other one," he said. "People lose their shoes all the time, what's strange about that? I lost two shoes recently myself."

'Yes, Doctor. I know, Doctor. In fact…"

"What, Juanita?"

"He was wearing your shoe, Doctor."

"What? You mean one of the shoes they lost last week? But how? Are you sure?"

She nodded. "I saw him, Doctor, and I saw the shoe. It was yours."

His mind raced. *What does this mean? Am I being set up? Is someone trying to frame me?*

"What happened to the man?" he said. "Is he still there?" He did not wait for Juanita's answer, and instead moved to the door. Outside, towards the far end of his house, a large group of people had gathered. When they saw him approach, they stepped back. He bent down and touched the man's neck, then his eyelids. The belly felt unyielding to the touch, like dough kept in the crisper of a refrigerator. The laceration on the side of his head showed no jagged edges – a single slicing movement had done this, without spilling blood on the man's shirt. *Has probably been dead for a day,* he thought. *But no putrefaction yet, even in this heat. Whoever did this knew how to keep a body cold.*

He now saw the shoe. It was his, without a doubt. It was clean, and kept the foot firmly wedged inside it. He pried it off, saw how the top of the counter had pressed into the flesh so much that it had ripped the skin.

That's a big wound, yet very little blood, it went through his head. *They must have put that shoe on you after you died, my friend.* He told three men to lift the dead man and carry him into his house. Juanita spread a bed sheet on the floor, and the men laid down the body.

"Call the Guardia, Juanita," he said. "This is not our business, it's theirs. And serve these good men some refreshment, please." When the men had left for the kitchen, he pried off the shoe and pushed it away, under a low table.

When the Guardia arrived, they asked him questions. "Who had found the body? When did it arrive? Why was it there?"

"I don't know," he said. "When I went to bed last night it wasn't there."

"Do you have enemies? Any idea who would do this to you?"

"I have a big wall," he said. "I can barely see the end of it when I stick my head outside. How would I know? And who says that this was for me?"

The lieutenant's face was blank. "It's your wall, isn't it, Doctor? And you live here, don't you, Doctor?" He snapped his fingers, motioning for his men to move out, and turned back to Tomás.

"We're at war, Doctor, in case you forgot — we don't speculate any longer, those days are gone."

The lieutenant told him to not leave town until this was cleared up. When they had left with the body, Tomás took a deep breath and wiped his forehead. *This is crazy*, he thought. *I haven't done anything, so why these questions? Is Fausto behind this? But why?*

The morgue called him when he was at the lab. The Guardia had just left a man, NN, No Name.

"Big gash in his left foot?" he said.

"Yes," the receptionist said. "How did you know?"

"Doctor's instinct," he said. He hung up.

"This man won't tell me much either," he mumbled. "Maybe I've been talking to all the wrong people."

Chapter 32

There was a knock on the door of the lab.

"Go see who it is, Juan," Tomás beckoned to his assistant. The boy opened the door just enough to stick his head out and see a young woman leaning against the pockmarked wall.

"Yes?" he said, "What do you wish?" Tomás could not hear their conversation, but soon enough his assistant was back, standing halfway between the door and the examination table.

"It's a Miss Largaespada for you, Doctor." Tomás cocked his head, opening his left eye slightly more than the right one.

"Tell her I'll be there in a couple of minutes, Juan."

When he had finished slicing through the brain tissue, he washed his hands. Thoroughly, as if he were going in for surgery. Then he stepped outside. Milagros was dressed in a cotton tunic and sandals. *Too masculine almost,* he thought. They shook hands.

"Doctor, I was in the neighborhood and decided to stop by. I am not disturbing you, I hope? Since it's lunchtime I almost thought I wouldn't find you here."

"No, absolutely not. In fact I often forget to eat lunch."

"Perhaps you would like to have lunch with me, Doctor?"

He was taken aback by her directness. He touched his chin, half stroking it and half hiding his mouth. "I'm not sure that would be appropriate. I mean, your reputation and ..."

She cut him off. "I have been thinking about something you said at the dinner party last week. Something I would like to discuss with you, Doctor."

He did not know what to think. A medical problem? He was hardly the kind of doctor to make house calls, or even examine patients. In fact, he had not touched a sick person in years. She stepped forward, and he moved back until they were standing on separate sides of the threshold. She laughed.

"Doesn't this remind you of a movie, Doctor? Perhaps I'd better come, in, yes?" When she stepped past him, he smelled jasmine.

"Ah," she said as she looked around, "this reminds me so much of my biology classes!" She stopped in front of a large jar filled with formaldehyde and a single pair of ears floating inside. She thought they were both turned her way, as if listening to her. The assistant was looking at Milagros with a curious expression in his eyes.

"Juan," Tomás said, "you may go now. We'll finish this up after lunch." The boy left, but not without looking back with a wide grin on his face.

"So many," she said. "Why do you keep all these specimens, Doctor?"

"Please call me Tomás," he said. "And to answer your question, perhaps I shouldn't. They take up space, and no one claims them. People don't really care what happens with the bodies of their relatives once they are dead, you know. In the morgue we sew them back up, and people do not ask what's inside. Or even if any parts are missing. So things end up here in my lab. Unclaimed property we would call this, and as everyone knows, whatever is not claimed has no value. Everything needs to have an owner, don't you think?"

She laughed. "Yes," she said, "I agree. Everything needs an owner, whether it's a body part or a brainchild. But what if something is claimed by more than one person?"

"I can hardly think of more propitious circumstances," he replied. "Nothing increases the value of things so much as multiple claims." She laughed, and walked to the window. Peering through the shutters, she turned the axle, to let in more light.

"This must be the tallest building in all of León," she said. "And do you see that building out there? The white one, all the way out of town, sort of half-submerged?"

He peered out. "No," he said. "What is it?"

"The Fortín," she said. "It's where the political prisoners are held. And even though they can't see us, we know they are there."

They went to a large restaurant frequented by students and teachers. It was a rowdy place, but there were quiet corners if you looked for one. A fat woman waggled up to them and rattled off the choices: "*vigorón*, boiled yucca with cabbage and pork, roast chicken and shredded beef, everything with rice and beans." They made their choice, and almost immediately a second woman came around with their orders.

"I like these student hangouts," Milagros said. "They are so... full of energy, don't you think?"

"Very different from Paris, yes? May I ask you what made you decide to come back? It's hardly a good time to start a law career in Nicaragua."

She hesitated, and looked at the milling crowds outside, the women selling soda pop and oranges, the outsize Cadillacs and the soldiers leaning against lampposts.

"That doesn't bother me," she said. "We all have a role to play. Anyway, one day all this will be gone."

"What is it you wanted to ask me?"

"What?" She looked puzzled, but then she remembered. "Oh yes, I wanted to know why you challenged your cousin. You asked him 'Who spreads those lies, and who is interested in scaring people?' You did not answer the question though."

"Should I have? It was my question, wasn't it?"

"Yes, but since no one answered it, I was wondering..."

"I have a lot of questions, and every day I have new questions. This war...things were easier before."

"Others are asking the same questions, Doctor. I mean, Tomás," she added quickly. He glanced left and right, but their closest neighbors were sitting ten feet away. Two bored soldiers were chewing on sugarcane near the entrance of the restaurant.

"I hope you're careful with these words," he said in a low tone. "A dinner party at your father's house is one thing; a public place is something else entirely. I hope you understand where these words might land you."

"Being careful has not done us much good so far," she said. A group of yelling schoolchildren crossed the street in front of the restaurant, and they remained silent until the children had passed. When she spoke again he noticed how her jaw line had hardened.

"Why is it that just about everyone in this country seems to think that this mess is not their business?"

"I can't speak for everyone," he said.

"But you can speak for yourself?"

He shrugged. "Not everyone is born a hero. They don't live long."

"Is there anything between a hero and people who live long, then?"

"Yes," he said. "Me. And thousands of people like me. My father…" He stopped and looked down at his hands, his fingers. White and cold, unused to sunlight and rough surfaces.

"My father was a hero," he said. "Or at least he was fearless, if I am to believe what many people have said about him. Others have told me that he was a fool. The only thing I know is that I never knew him."

"I think all of us fear, whether we admit or not. It's just that some act, and others don't."

He wrung his hands until they looked rosy.

"I went to see the son of my friend Manolo the other day," he said, without looking at her. "Manolo was shot in the chest in front of his wife. Not pretty." He took a sip of water and continued: "I sat here with him, at this very table. And two years later I performed an autopsy on his corpse. It felt as if we were continuing the conversation we had started two years earlier." He paused, deliberately controlling his breathing.

"His mouth was still open, and I had to force the jaws shut. As if he hadn't finished telling me something." Milagros's hand stirred slightly, making the ice cubes clink. In a flash she saw the shadow of Amparito falling to the ground with a scream on her lips that never became a word.

"What did he tell you?" she whispered.

"Nothing. Absolutely nothing. Our minds play tricks on us, you know, but our bodies know how fragile we really are. They know how easily bent and torn we are. Our minds – they want us to forget that we are prisoners of our bodies. But we can't really ever forget this."

She leaned forward. "So do the dead tell us anything at all?" she said.

"Just that," he said. "And that we need to remember those who died."

She nodded. "I understand that," she said. "But remembering is hard. It hurts."

"Manolo had a son," he said. "He's a very brave boy; he wants to remember his father. But soon his memories will fade, and then he will have only regrets. And in time, his regrets will turn into rancor."

"It's because of men like your friend that we have hope for a better future," she said.

He smirked. "Maybe," he said. "But does a fourteen-year old understand this? Did we ask him what he wanted? Did he have a choice? Why him? Why not someone else's father?"

She shook her head. "I have stopped asking those questions," she said. "It doesn't really matter whether our parents made those choices themselves or whether they were made for them. It mattered to them, but it should not matter to us. We live our own lives, and all that matters to us is whether their deaths had any meaning."

"Do you think it's that easy to forget the past?" he said.

"Not forgetting. It is whether we allow it to rule the present."

The cathedral bells started tolling. Timidly at first, and then louder, as if the hand of an acolyte had been joined by that of a veteran rope puller. He looked up, shielding his eyes, and saw a young boy hanging on to the rope as if his life depended on it. He was standing between the two statues flanking the copper bell, making it swing until it reflected the noonday glare in hues of green and red.

"I must go back now," he said. He pulled two banknotes from his pocket and left them on the table.

"Wait," she said. "I wanted to ask you something else."

He turned to her, curious.

"Why did you suggest the whale might be a sign sent to us?"

"Did I say that?"

She nodded.

"A joke surely. I must have made a joke."

"How do we recognize signs that are real?"

"I wouldn't know. I don't think I have received many."

She burst out laughing, and so did he.

"I enjoyed our conversation, Milagros," he said. He felt the blood rise to his cheeks. "And I enjoyed your company," he added.

"I enjoyed it too, Tomás."

He called on her a few days later. The senator was sitting on the front porch and pointed at one of the rocking chairs:

"Sit down, young man, what's new?" Tomás was well into his forties, and had long since stopped thinking of himself as a young man.

"May I ask you something, Senator?"

"I think it's still a free country." He laughed. "You may, but I cannot guarantee that I will give you an answer."

"Why did you leave politics?"

"Perhaps I should tell you why I got into it in the first place."

"And?"

"I don't know the answer. So quitting wasn't that hard either." He sighed. "We do so many things because they are being thrust upon us. It takes guts to make your own decisions, and act on them."

Milagros came walking out, dressed in riding boots.

"Hóla, Tomás," she exclaimed. "What a surprise to see you here this early!"

"I see you are getting ready to ride out. Beach or meadow?"

She let out a laugh.

"My daughter always rides on the beach, Tomás," the senator said, taking hold of her hand. Milagros bent down and kissed her father on the cheek.

"You must excuse me," the senator said, "I need to be taken care of now – they will perform unspeakable torture on me." Tomás raised his eyebrows.

"Nail clipping," Milagros explained. "If it were up to Papa, he would grow long claws, like an eagle." They watched as the senator was rolled inside by the two silent young men.

"Do those two ever talk?" he said. "I have never heard them say anything."

"No," she said, "my father picked them because they are mute and deaf, both of them."

"What for?"

"He said he was tired of having to argue about everything. 'That's what you get from a life in politics,' he said."

"How do you know they're deaf? Mute perhaps, but deaf?"

She looked at him, puzzled. "No one has ever asked that question."

He laughed. "Doctor's instincts. You never take anything for granted. I guess not all deaf people have their ears cut off."

"But those with cut-off ears are surely all deaf?" she said.

He shrugged. "Not according to science. What we think of as an ear is really not much more than the horn of a phonograph."

She was speechless at first, but then she burst out laughing. "No one ever thought about that," she said, "we always just assumed they were deaf because they were mute."

"Second opinions," he said. "Always ask for a second opinion."

"Yes," she said, "I like second opinions."

She looked at her watch, then back at him. "I must go now. Will you walk with me?" He nodded, and they walked to the stables. But when they got there, it was empty.

"Where's the horse?" he said.

"The horse is in the meadow," she said. He raised his eyebrows.

"Fresh meadow air is better for her. And besides, I need the room for something else." She lifted a canvas tarp to reveal five wooden crates.

"What's in there?"

"Things," she said, "things from the future."

The next day Tomás was back at the senator's house. And the day after and the one after that. He rushed through his biopsy cuttings and shavings during the day, just so he could be with her. His assistant knew that by 4 p.m. no new samples were to be tabled.

They drove to the beach, to watch the sunset, or had dinner in quiet places. She was gone often, and for days in a row. On those days he felt cranky, and lashed out at his assistant, who grinned and whispered behind his back. When she came back from one of her trips she brought a young man with her.

"Tomás," the senator said, "meet Roberto, one of Milagros's student friends from Paris. He is visiting Nicaragua for a couple of weeks on his way back to Uruguay." The boy and the man looked at each other suspiciously, like two dogs eyeing a bone.

"Funny time to come visiting here," Tomás said. "I mean, with the guerrillas and all that, we don't get a whole lot of tourists."

Roberto shrugged. "I'm not really a tourist," he said. "More of a student, I would say. Or an observer."

Tomás took an instant dislike to the young man. *He speaks of the world as if he had been around it on a motorbike. Twice. Cocky and pedantic little fart, who does he think he is?*

"He's my friend," Milagros said.

"I don't like him."

They were sitting under the mango tree that gave shade to the front porch. She rubbed her shoulders and upper arms and looked at the sun that was setting fast.

"You don't need to like him," she said. He had expected a different response, defensive perhaps, and was disappointed by her seeming indifference.

"You're just jealous," she continued.

"What?" he said.

"You don't need to be jealous, Tomás. Not with Roberto. But I like that you should be jealous."

Roberto stayed several months. Each time that Milagros went off for a week, or sometimes a day only, he was gone as well. Until one day, he did not come back with her.

"Where did he go?" Tomás said.

"Why would you care?" she said. "You must be happy he left, yes?"

And he said that yes, he was happy now; he had never liked the boy.

A week later she called him, late in the day. He dusted off his satchel, and went to her house.

"He has not stopped vomiting all day," she said as she led him to the guest room. Roberto looked very pale; his eyes were watery and popping out, and his skin was glistening like a pig's. He shivered as Tomás placed his hand on the burning forehead.

"When did the fevers start?"

"Two days ago."

Roberto himself said nothing. He looked from Milagros to Tomás and back again, and pulled the covers over his face.

"Where has he been?" Tomás said. "You don't get dengue in León. He must have been in the bush."

"Dengue? Is that what he has?"

"Seems like it, as far as I can tell. We'll run tests tomorrow. Meanwhile I'll give him a pill, to knock him out – I imagine he has not slept for days." He rifled through his bag and brought up a small flask with pills. She pushed one between the boy's lips, then lifted his head and gave him water.

It took only minutes for the pill to take effect. The shivering stopped and Roberto's head fell to one side. Milagros and Tomás stood looking at each other.

"Is your father here?" he said.

"Asleep," she said, "everyone in this house is asleep."

"Except for us."

"Yes!" She laughed. "Yes, except for us. May I invite you for a drink? We have pomegranate juice."

They sat on the veranda, and she offered him a glass, and he drank.

She scraped her throat: "I didn't think he would come back," she said, "I thought he had gone to the mountains, that he had stayed there."

"How did he get into this?"

"He started driving me around," she said. "I asked him to accompany me on visits."

"Visits where?"

"Up north. East." She shrugged. "Places."

"This boy has never been exposed to tropical diseases; you're lucky he has not died from it. You should have known better than to drag him into the bush."

She frowned. "I did not force him to come," she said. "He came because he wanted to."

"And these visits…how often?"

"Depends…two or three times a week perhaps…sometimes less. We deliver food to poor farmers, clothing too."

"He won't be able to accompany you for a while."

"I realize that. It's…a problem."

That was how it started. He offered to accompany her. There was a crate in the back of the car, with a canvas tarp draped over it, and tied down with thick ropes. The first house was half a mile outside of a small town, a farmhouse southeast of Estelí, surrounded by a wall of bougainvillea and lemon trees. Two men came out of the house as she honked the horn. They eyed him suspiciously.

"A new driver?" one of them said. "What happened to Roberto?" She shook her head.

"Nothing," she said. The men ignored him and hauled the trunk from the back of the car. After that they went back inside the house and shut the door.

"What was that?" he said.

"What was what?"

"What just happened out there?"

"If I didn't think you would guess I never would have brought you along in the first place."

When it dawned on him, he got upset. "This is not a game," he said. "You're playing with fire. Do you realize what could happen if you got caught?"

"Are you afraid?" she said. "Or merely annoyed?"

"You're playing dangerous games."

"They're not games."

"No, they're not. And I wished you had told me before."

"You didn't ask. You said you would go with me wherever I needed to go, didn't you?"

"What was in the crate?" he said when they were back on the main road again. She did not answer, feigning concentration on the road ahead of her. But he did not let up.

"What was in the crate?" he asked again.

She braked suddenly, and his body lurched forward while his mind held on to the seat, stubborn and resentful. She rested her forehead on the steering wheel and let out a deep sigh.

"Damnit," she said. "Damnit, first you get upset that I dragged you into this without telling you what it was about, and now you want to know what was inside that crate. What for? You're a spectator, Tomás, you have told me that yourself."

"I figure that if you are going to endanger my life you might as well tell me for what."

"The less you know the better. Trust me."

"Why are you doing these things?"

"Because I believe in them. Don't you believe in anything?"

"I don't want anything to happen to you, Milagros. That's why I come with you. That's what I believe in."

She shook her head.

"You're a doctor," she said. "You're sworn to ease suffering. Don't you believe in justice?"

It did not stop there. The next time he accompanied her he no longer pretended he did not know what or why. He accompanied her wherever and whenever he could, to villages and farms in the north, the west. He visited places he had not known existed. There was always a wooden crate in the back of the car, with a canvas tarp covering it. She knew when to avoid the open roads and take dirt roads or muddy tracks to avoid roadblocks.

"How do you know where to go each time?" he asked her once, but she raised her eyebrows and pouted her lips.

Coward, he thought. *Don't pretend you don't know. You either get out right now and forget about this girl who has come and upset your world, or else you jump in and join her.*

"They have their networks and we have ours. They have informants; we have peasants. The difference is, we don't need to pay the peasants to keep us informed."

One afternoon, near Malpaisillo, they stopped at a turnoff where the asphalt turned into a dirt road covered with black volcanic ashes. A woman was sitting under a guanacaste tree selling soda pop, and they bought two drinks from her. As she lifted her arm to empty the bottles into small plastic bags that she tied into a knot, they noticed that the woman was nursing a baby. It was hanging on by its gums, clinging to her breast by sheer gum power it seemed. It was swaddled in a swath of cotton running in brown and yellow stripes that were tied around her shoulder and down her waist. Tomás's eye was drawn to the brown nipple flopping in and out of the baby's mouth. Every time the woman moved, he heard the grunts of the child as it was being smothered, and protesting when the nipple was being withdrawn.

"Where are you headed?" the woman said.

"El Jicaral," Milagros said, and went back to sipping her soda. Then she pointed at the baby. "Boy or girl?"

"A girl," the woman said. She opened up the swaddle to reveal a brown bundle of pudginess.

"She eats veeeeeery well," she hollered, revealing a set of blackened teeth. *Sugarcane,* Tomás thought.

"I'm lucky I have a lot of milk. Some of the women in my village give their babies lemonade, or cane water."

"That baby is so big, it will chew off your breast," Tomás said.

The woman laughed. "She'd better enjoy it while she can, Don. She'll know what hunger means soon enough."

As they drove the last miles to San Nicolás, they spoke little. When they reached a house surrounded by thick rows of deep green cornstalks, she put her hand on his arm.

"It's here," she said, and reached for a backpack lying on the backseat. The cabin was built of cypress wood, the type that grows taller than all other trees. Cypress trees make hissing sounds at night as the winds race through them, bending the tall branches to the breaking point until they sweep back, bursting with resentment.

In the early years of the century, German immigrants from Baden-Baden had settled in the region around Matagalpa. They had loved the high grounds, which were cool and reminded them of the Schwarzwald back home: the dimly lit undergrowth where dusk turned to twilight away from the harsh light of day, and the sound of pine needles being crushed by deer hooves was all that disturbed the sleep of giant spruce. They felled the tall cypress trees and fashioned them into cabins, built them at forward positions on the mountainside so they could tend to their coffee plants while dreaming of mansions in the valley. And when the mansions came, the cabins were abandoned.

"There's no one here," he said.

"Surprised, Tomás?" She stepped out of the car and opened the trunk, told him to take out a horsehair blanket from under the canvas tarp. They heard gunshots, and the low drone of artillery fire in the far distance. But gunshots had become part of the background by now, and only their absence was cause for pause.

The cabin was empty but for a table and four chairs, and a wooden cot against the wall. A dusty set of deer antlers was hanging from the wall. Milagros looked at the knotted cypress wood that was all around her. This was the cabin she had been looking for. No one had lived here in a long time: it was an empty shell, indifferent to the people who passed through it. This house would not bother taking in their smells or their thoughts and making them its own, as if to say: "Why bother? There will be others. There will be people who will set down their suitcases without unpacking, and drift in and out of each other's lives." So it was true perhaps that when Milagros took Tomás's hand and placed it on her breast, when she kissed him and pulled him onto the cot with the horsehair blanket, the house did not look on. As if it had decided to not hold on to any memories of this, so there would be no consequences, no changes in the web of time and laughter.

But Tomás would remember. He would remember the wooden cot that drifted away from the wall, and the smell of resins that had stayed strong and pungent in spite of the spider webs hanging from beams and rafters, a smell that might last a thousand years. She closed her eyes as he entered her, and not a word escaped her mouth.

Then you will know, as you yourself will be known. The words raced through his head, but he could not remember where he had heard them, although he remembered how they continued: as a thin line of scared-looking words that danced away through the sky: *For a man in the embrace of a woman who loves him will no longer know the difference between self and other.*

"You make me whole again," he whispered. She opened her eyes, slowly, as if awakening from a dream that had taken her far and away.

"What?" she said. "What did you say?" He dared not repeat the words.

"Nothing," he said. "It's nothing. I love you, Milagros." Saying it was less difficult than he thought it would be – how easy it was, after all, for love to be reduced to a string of words. Her smile was broad and deep, so unlike he had known her to smile before today. It was no longer the smile of a woman walking on the beach while shells were exploding within earshot. Her smile came from inside, as if a mask had fallen and she had become a woman once more, rather than a rebel in a nauseating war. He saw her again as he first saw her, saw how all of her masks had been shed until it was she, Milagros, whose face was revealed to him in a cabin made of whispering cypress wood.

In that one moment, the outside world ceased to exist for him. Or perhaps the world itself had become part of him. For the first time in his life, he felt that the world had no bounds or limits, that he himself had become the map he had not found in others.

The dull thunder of artillery coming in from across the mountain had settled into a pattern that synchronized with his heartbeat. *It is not enough for feelings to dwell in a man if he does not dwell in his love,* he thought. But the flash of insight was gone almost as fast as it had arrived.

Fleeting and taunting, the promise of wholeness that had been dangled before his eyes had left. He saw himself as a man again, nothing more and nothing less: a vessel for blind fears and boundless hope, a wanderer in the land of Nod.

Lying behind her, he let his fingers walk down the small of her back, until they reached a brown birthmark, in the shape of a bird's wing.

"My mother had one just like it," she said, as if she had read his thoughts. "But it was inverted: white against her tan. We used to laugh when I was a child and my nanny gave me a bath. My mother would come and sit with me, point out my birthmark in the mirror, and roll up her skirt to show me her own. 'See,' she said, 'we are birds of a feather! We will always be together, because a bird needs both wings to fly.'"

Tomás lifted his finger, and let it hover above the birthmark. "It does look like a bird's wing," he said. He could not see her face, and thought, *does she expect more questions, or is she happy when I do not ask for more?* He looked at her back, a landscape that lay motionless but for the clockwork heaving of her shoulders, and the impulsive rippling of her skin.

"Marry me, Milagros."

Her body shivered slightly, or so he thought, but it remained still. She did not turn when she spoke, nor did any of her muscles tighten.

"You know what I do, Tomás. Don't ask me this."

"But I love you."

"Since when did love overcome all obstacles, tell me? Why can't you love me just now, just here?"

Her words bounced off the walls, and their bleakness reminded him of his mother's, years before, when he was a small boy and had walked in to find her passed out among empty bottles and shattered portraits. "Remember Noah," she had said, "remember when Noah's son found him uncovered."

"I can't," he said. "I need more than this. I cannot love a shadow, a ghost who drops in from time to time. I need to love a living being, someone who reminds me that I am alive, that my loving her makes me human. A second chance – call it a second chance. Don't you believe in second chances?"

Her body shuddered and her skin contracted into goose bumps.

"I do," she said. "If you knew me at all you would know that second chances are what I most believe in."

"So what are you running from?" he said. "What is it that you need to prove?"

"That's not fair," her voice came back. "You know that's not fair."

He nodded. "Maybe not. And maybe it would make it easier to accept. Knowing, that is. Perhaps…"

"Don't ask me to be your savior, Tomás. I cannot trust my right hand to know what my left hand will do tomorrow. I can never give you security."

"I am tired of losing things," he said. "Tired of losing people. They walk into my life and out again. Why is it that no one stays? All I have is dead people."

"Maybe it's you who has walked out of their lives." She stood up and got dressed.

Fast, he thought, *the way soldiers dress.* He watched her, watched her reflection in the cracked mirror covering the wardrobe; she looked distorted, larger than the mirror itself.

Her nakedness has now become part of me, he thought. *It has become part of my shame and part of my desire. I will never be able to let go of her, because her nakedness has enveloped us both.*

When she finished dressing, she sat down next to him, and took his hand. "You men meet life head on, as if you were a hurricane making landfall – furiously, blindly. We women, we don't live our lives that way. We discover life little by little. We learn to love it, not as we would like it to be, but as it has come to us."

"Is this what you have learned in Paris?"

"I could have learned it anywhere else just as well," she said. "The only thing I have learned is that what we do is more important than what we do not do. And we must love what we do. Those are the things that really matter."

He shrugged. She gritted her teeth. "Don't, Tomás. We make decisions every day, but so many of them are about what we won't do, and so few about what we will."

She offers me nothing, he thought. When he looked at her, dressed in her riding boots and underwear, he saw half the soldier and half the woman. He saw her winding her way back into the cocoon that would

take her away from him. She was not begging him to let her go, and
not expecting him to insist she stay. He sensed that she stood there in
the full realization that there would be many tomorrows, but that she
did not know what any one of these had in store for her, or for them.

They spoke little on the way back. He drove, and she sang songs.
After three songs she started pushing his hip.

"Sing with me," she said. "I need someone to sing with me today."
He resisted at first, but when she started singing louder he relented,
and joined in.

"See?" she said. "See, it's not all that hard. Do you feel happy
now?"

"Yes," he said, and laughed. "In fact I do."

"You are a terrible singer, I must say. But at least we know that
now."

"You, on the other hand, sing very well," he said. "But come to
think of it, I have never heard you sing. Why is that?"

She fell silent, and stared out the window. "You have heard me
sing, Tomás. You just don't remember it." He thought about it, but
could not recall any moment or event.

"I give up," he said. "When was it?"

She shook her head. "It's not enough to have memories. You must
also be able to forget them."

He nodded. "Yes," he said, "I understand that. And then what?"

"And then you must be patient enough to wait for their return."

When the sun had set she fell asleep. He slowed down the car until
the engine and her breath were in tune, and the car felt like a giant lung
powered by her breathing.

We're far from the ocean, he thought. *So far from the ocean, and yet here I
am inside a seashell, inside a woman's lung. But it will not always be this way. One
day all this killing will be over, and we will live a life together, on the outside.* In
his mind's eye he saw Milagros riding her great brown horse on the
beach. Towering, bridging the space between the foaming water
breaking itself on the sand, and the rolling clouds above, moving fast as
if in a silent movie.

Milagros's thoughts were elsewhere. They were floating around on
great billowing cloud fingers. Not in straight lines like his, but circular,

or mandala-shaped perhaps, and they were not with Tomás only, although he was there. But today they were mostly with Socorro, on a sun-drowned meadow at a French peasant wedding, and the shape of a motionless body in a darkened doorway was with her no more.

Chapter 33

A Malinche tree in bloom is the closest most people will come to seeing a flaming sword. It hovers eighty feet tall, and dominates the landscape from far away. In the early days of May, the Malinche tree springs into bloom, filling the air between its branches with clouds of deep orange. Its roots spread out far and deep, solidly anchoring it in the moist earth. It was in the shadow of two Malinche trees with full canopies reaching out to each other across the Pan-American Highway that a patrol of guardsmen had set up a roadblock. Tomás was waved down by a captain, while three young soldiers pointed their guns at him.

"Where are you going?" the captain inquired.

"I am a doctor; I have been called to attend a patient."

"Strange time for a house call," the captain said. "It's Saturday evening." Tomás said nothing.

"What's in the bag?" the captain said, pointing at his satchel. He showed them.

"I'm seeing a sergeant in Quesalguaque, a Sergeant Solórzano. Do you know him?"

"Of course we do," the captain said. "Old liar, should have been cashiered years ago. No one ever trusts a word he says. You do realize, Doctor," he continued, "that the rebels are operating nearby? This is neither the time nor the place for house calls."

"They called for me." He felt his scalp turning prickly with sweat.

"Will you be traveling back tonight?"

"I…I don't know yet. It's a complicated case; I may have to spend the night."

"In that case, Doctor," – the officer rolled the "r" until it sounded like a drum being beat – "I advise you not to leave again until after dawn." He ticked his hat and waved him through.

The trip was uneventful after that: miles of sugarcane flowed past, some of it flowering. *Why has the sugar not been brought in?* he thought. *It's way past harvest time; it'll all go to waste.*

He arrived in Chinandega just before nightfall. The absence of soldiers in the streets was striking. He parked his car behind the cantina and ordered a meal. It was brought in fast, but he ate little. He unfolded the newspaper he had brought with him: "Idi Amin accused of massacring another 20 of his fellow Ugandans in cold blood," it read. Amin had personally cut off their testicles while they were still alive, and stuffed hem in their mouths. It was from this newspaper, tucked away in the international news section, that a paper had slipped out that morning. It had floated gently down to the floor, as if on wings of its own. He had bent over to pick it up, to find that it was a page from a child's notebook, neatly folded into four sections. He had smoothed the creases and read the message: "Friends of yours have fallen ill. Please come to Chinandega on Wednesday. There is a small taverna opposite the photographer's shop. I'll be waiting for you there. M."

He brought the note to his nose and inhaled. Nothing. Just the faint smell of wood pulp and the metallic taste of black ink. He could not smell the hands that must have written it, carried it, and stuck it inside his paper.

It was almost ten, and he was the only patron left when a young couple entered the cantina. The man was dressed in brown pants of a thick and coarse make, and a shirt that must have been beige once. His companion was smaller. *Mouse-like, a nervous mouse with a twitching nose and whiskers to take in the surroundings faster than with eyes alone.* They both looked at him, and the woman said something under her breath. The man walked up to him.

"Doctor Cortés?" he said.

"No," Tomás said, "It's Doctor Delacorte. Cortés is my mother's last name."

The man did not react. "Please come with us," he said.

Tomás got up and called the bartender. "How much do I owe you?" he said.

"Twelve córdobas and fifty centavos," the bartender said. When they were outside, Tomás started for his car.

"You won't need your car, Don," the woman said. "You can leave it parked behind the cantina." He hesitated, but then realized that there would be few roads where they were going. They walked in a single file, and within a couple of minutes they reached the outskirts of town. The night air was filled with the chirping of cicadas, more than he had ever heard. The man signaled for Tomás to follow him down a ditch, where three horses were standing under a eucalyptus tree. Tomás recognized Milagros's brown mare.

"That one is yours. I take it you do ride, Doctor?" the man said.

"Yes, of course."

They went through large expanses of sugarcane, and after a few hours they had rounded the volcano and come to the foothills of the Cordillera de los Maribios. The air was thick and dark, and a dense mist was flowing down the volcano's flank, blotting out the moonlight.

"We will stop here, so the horses may rest," the woman said. They dismounted, and soon the two started arguing in hushed voices. Tomás noticed how the woman shook her head in disapproval several times, but each gesture of disapproval was countered by more arguments and gesticulating by the man. He occasionally looked at Tomás, who had stretched out against a mango tree. The reason for the quibble became clear soon enough, when the man approached him with a kerchief: "I will have to blindfold you," he said.

"What is this?" Tomás protested. "This is not necessary."

"Maybe not. But there are lives at stake."

"If you think I'm a spy you should never have brought me here. I'm a doctor, I cure people." The man looked at him patiently, holding up the blindfold with both hands. Back on the horse and blindfolded, Tomás found it hard to maintain his balance, and soon felt seasick. His body swayed while his legs were spread out over the mare's ballooning barrel. *She is with foal. I can feel it lapping at my shins, like ocean waves.* His heart started pounding, and he felt as if he were floating, upside down and tumbling backwards. His legs were tingling, so he shook them energetically, careful not to kick the mare. When he retched, the woman pulled up beside him.

"Chew on this," she said, as she shoved some leaves in his mouth. The peppermint was strong, but it did clear his dizziness.

After another two hours he heard the tinkle of running water. *A river*, he thought, *or water springing from a rock*. Soon there was the dim clunk of cookware, and someone helped him off his horse. Nimble fingers undid the knot in the kerchief, and he covered his eyes against a determined sun climbing over the horizon.

"Thank you for coming, Tomás," he heard a familiar voice. "There is much need for your skills here." Milagros kissed him on the cheek. "Breakfast?"

There were little more than a handful of ramshackle huts, with roofs of plantain leaves held together by sisal rope. They walked to a makeshift table where two young men were sitting behind big plates of gallo pinto. One of them was the man who had brought him in, and he was not surprised to see Roberto, who was busy opening a radio set while eating.

"You know Roberto and José of course," she said.

"Roberto I know. And it's good to hear that this young man has a name, too."

"Hello, Doc," Roberto said. José said nothing, and instead glared at him with hard eyes. No one spoke much during breakfast.

"Please walk with me," she said when they finished. "I will show you why we need you here."

She walked ahead of him. "Are you nervous?" she said, without looking back.

"I was yesterday," he said. "Now I am mostly tired. Spending a whole night on horseback with a blindfold on is not my idea of an outing."

She laughed. "They do not trust you, Tomás."

"That is obvious."

"Can you blame them?"

He thought about this. "I'm a doctor," he said. "You called for me because I'm a doctor."

"To our people you are one of them. And your cousin is their henchman." She stopped and turned, looking down on him.

"You asked me what I learned when I was away. This is what I learned. I learned to see myself as a person not separate from others."

"I have little sympathy for these rebels, you know that."

"I do. Nobody wants war, Tomás. Nobody wants to die. We didn't ask for this, but they have left us no choice." She turned again and they moved up the path.

"There was a dead man sitting against my house the other day," he said. "These things mean something, you know."

She stopped. "Are you saying the colonel is on to you?"

"I don't know. Who puts these dead bodies out in the street? I am in charge of the morgue, I would know if bodies were missing."

"Only if they came from the morgue. What if they came from the Sewing Room?"

He had heard of the Sewing Room. Everyone had heard of the Sewing Room. Manolo had told him about it.

"Does it exist?" he said.

"There are many Sewing Rooms," she said. "There must be one in every town and city in the country. And they are being used for only one thing. You have one outside your window, and you tell me you don't know what it is?"

"What is?"

"The Fortín. Acosasco. That's where the dead people come from that sit against your wall."

"Fausto and I grew up together. He would not do these things — this was all done on someone else's watch. I accused him once, years ago, but without proof."

"Maybe the proof sits outside your house in the morning," she said. "It's not us, that I can guarantee. So if they're not from the morgue either…"

Fausto would not do this because of the rebels, he thought. *He must be cross because of something else. Didn't he say he knows everything that happens in León?*

"I'm sure he knows about your accompanying me," she said. "The man has spies everywhere, because he pays well. How far do you think he will go?"

"I don't know. He's my cousin."

The moment he spoke the words he regretted them. Not because he had not meant them. It was because he was no longer sure he could believe them himself. *Why did Fausto never act on his threat when he suspected me and Ana? Why didn't he ever have me picked up? Why didn't he harass me, as he would have done with others? If the Guardia had Manolo killed — what makes me think I am safe? Just because Fausto is my cousin?*

"There are puppet masters behind the puppet masters," Milagros said. "For all we know your cousin knows where you are right now. He may have informants in our ranks. You yourself, or even me. Now you know why they blindfolded you."

"But I wouldn't…" he started.

He noticed that her eyes looked tired. "We all say that, Tomás. Do you really think there are people who don't scream while their ears are being cut off?"

When she saw how his mouth sagged, her expression softened. "But I have faith in you," she said. "Maybe I'm the only one among my comrades, but I do have faith in you."

"Being branded physician to the rebels is not going to help."

"I realize that. We could use a good doctor, but don't worry, we won't publicize your coming here. You are more useful to us alive than dead or in jail. At some point though, they will connect all the dots and might come for you, and they will try to break you. The few people who were in a Sewing Room and lived to tell the tale said it was not pretty, so the less you know the better. Now, shall we go to the lazaretto? We had a nurse…"

The last stretch before the top was lined by a single row of green bamboo stalks hiding the valley below from view. People were walking up and down the path, some leaning on makeshift crutches. A few looked back when they saw him pass. The lazaretto was a crumbling, abandoned chapel, with a nave and two wings. The walls were made of straw and mud, with cow dung to cure it and hold it all together. In spite of the darkness, he could make out twenty or thirty bodies. He saw a young man clutching a *petate* beneath him, gasping and blue in the face with pneumonia.

"You must bring them out," he said. "All of them. I will examine them here, in the daylight, under the trees. Do you have any medical supplies?"

She nodded. "We have tetracycline and alcohol, and some other antibiotics as well." One by one, the sick and wounded were brought out. They squinted at the harsh light, but no one complained. Two women went into the chapel carrying big plastic buckets that must have been yellow once, with a logo printed on them of a company that had left the country long ago.

"How long since the nurse left?"

"Two months."

"And no one else here knows anything about medicine?"

"Not really. We invent things when someone is really bad. Often things go wrong."

He sighed. "All right," he said, "let's get to work then."

Among the wounded was a young man with a pale face. His feet were badly cut. He kept looking at Tomás while Milagros cleaned his feet and applied ointment.

"What's your name?" Tomás said.

"Elvis," the boy said. "I think you know my brother, Elías. He says you buy newspapers from him and then you give them back."

"Yes," Tomás said. "Yes, I do know your brother. He's a good boy, always comes in on time. What happened to you, Elvis?"

"We tried to kill the colonel. And when we ran away I lost my shoes. One in the street, and the other one when we crossed the bridge over the Rio Chiquito. There was glass on the street."

They worked into the night. There were people with gunshot wounds and stab wounds, young men shuddering with malaria and break bone fever, and broken bones that were badly set. It was as if all of God's tribulations had descended upon this small band of outlaws. As if they had found Pandora's Box and opened it, unaware, or without regard for consequences. He broke bones that had been broken before, and set them with splints. He ground up the antibiotic tablets, and applied the powder directly to the wounds. He scratched and wiped through layers of grime and caked blood, but in the end he could offer little more than rum to clean out the wounds, and endless strips of cotton to swathe and bandage. *Cotton and rum,* he thought, *that's what we know about.*

They did not complain. They said "thank you" as he finished with them and moved on to the next one.

"You give them hope," she said.

"Why?" he said, surprised. "I've done so little."

"They know who you are. It's not the medicine you give them. It's you."

It was night by the time they finished. "Let them stay outside tonight," he said, "until you have cleaned out the place. The night air will do them good." He collapsed against a tree and remained there without moving. He saw her as she moved from one person to the next. She spoke to them, softly, touching a hand or a forehead. *She is so alive,* he thought, *and so are all of them, even those who are close to dying. They cling to life; to the miserable life they have — bitten and hunted, cornered by dogs and infested with lice. Like deer facing the hunter.*

She sat down beside him, and when a cold breeze arrived she moved closer to him, and dropped her head on his shoulder. He felt the warmth of her body, felt her hair sticking to his stubbly chin like the angel hair Sofía used to drape on the Christmas tree. So close she was, and yet so far away. He brought up his hand, caressed the tresses falling off the side of her head. She did not stir, and had he not felt her heaving chest against his, he might have thought that she had simply slipped away.

"It's strange, isn't it?" Her voice was low and small.

"What is?" he said, hoping that she would not move her head. His feet felt heavy, as if made of wet sand.

"Strange how we float in and out of each other's lives," she whispered. "Somehow we all live our own life, only our own. We visit with others, we say we love them, but are unable to build our house inside theirs." Her head sank until it was resting on his chest, and he saw her lips making small movements, ever smaller, as if she were whispering to herself. He bent down, straining to listen, holding her as if she were a child. Then her breathing became regular, and deeper, as if a veil had been lifted, and her breath had taken flight.

When he woke in the early morning, her head had slipped and was resting on his legs. He carefully slid out from underneath her, placing his jacket under her head. She did not wake up.

He worked through the day and did not see much of her until the early evening, when they met for dinner.

"We will escort you back after nightfall," she said. "It will be best for you to return soon, the Guardia might become suspicious."

"Will I be blindfolded?"

"Yes," she said. "Blind men are not afraid in the dark." He slept a few hours, left instructions for tending to the sick. Before leaving, he saw her again, but she showed no need for privacy.

A soldier, he thought, *she behaves like a soldier who lives for war.*

He arrived back on early Tuesday morning.

"Call the hospital, Juanita," he said. "Tell them I'm not well, please." He slept through the day, and arrived at his lab the next morning before dawn. Opening the shutters, he saw the sun rise quickly. He squinted and strained his eyes to see the low white building not far from the river, on the opposite bank. It was not trying to hide, yet he had never seen it before.

She came home two weeks later. Tall in her planter outfits and riding boots, she seemed so sure of herself, so certain that no one would betray her.

He admired her. *Does she not fear?* he wondered. *Or does she simply refuse to be ruled by it?*

Chapter 34

The morning brought rain, the kind that washes torrents of mud from mountainsides, and swells the waters of Lake Managua until they flood the shantytowns built on its shores. Tomás was still in bed when he was roused by the sound of a car stopping in front of his house, boots jumping into puddles of water, then a knock on the door.

"Juanita, go see what they want," he shouted. The knocking turned louder, until it made the doorframe shudder like a horse that has been running for too long and needs to be dried down. He heard screams, and the sound of metal on metal, claps and clips banging against rifles. Juanita removed the bolt holding the two doors in place, and opened up one side to reveal the face of an angry lieutenant with two soldiers behind him.

"We've come for the doctor," the captain said. "Call him now!" Tomás got dressed fast and came out to the front door. The captain stood halfway inside.

"Yes, Lieutenant, how may I help you?" he said.

"Captain," the man corrected him, "I'm a captain, not a lieutenant."

"Captain. Please tell me what brings you here."

"I have orders to escort you to the Cuartel of the Guardia," he said. "You are to come with us, at once."

It was as if a cold hand were gripping his neck. His voice was hoarse when he spoke again.

"What is this about?" he said.

"I have my orders, Doctor. You are to come with us."

"There must be some misunderstanding. I will make a phone call," he said. "Excuse me one second."

The captain shifted his feet. "No, sir. My orders were clear, sir. You are to come with us at once."

"But surely…"

"No, sir."

"Let me call Colonel Cortés, he will straighten this out."

"My orders come from Colonel Cortés, sir."

His mind raced. *This could not be true,* he thought. *Fausto would never have me arrested. On what charges?*

"Are you arresting me, Captain?" he said.

"Please come with us now, Doctor." The captain was patient but insistent.

"Fine," he said. "I'll come with you."

"Juanita," he shouted back into the house, "bring my umbrella please."

They led him past countless closed doors, until they opened one with well-oiled hinges. The room was small, with a wooden table placed in the middle, and some chairs that had been left unpainted. When he looked up he saw a ceiling fan and a single light bulb, and next to it a meat hook that had traveled into the ceiling and anchored itself there without the need to explain or apologize. Straight beneath it, inside the concrete floor, was a small drain. And in between the meat-hooked ceiling and the cloaca floor was empty space where molecules still tasted of sweat and pheromones, the pungent scent of fear that dogs smell so well, and snakes. But to Tomás's nose, the air smelled of little else than staleness.

They left him to himself for two hours, and during those two hours he tried not to look at the meat hook growing from the ceiling. Finally, a young lieutenant came in, carrying a manila folder. He looked at the ceiling and turned on the fan. Then he sat down at the opposite end of the table.

"Doctor Delacorte," he said. He looked at him without blinking. "Do you know why you are here?"

"No," Tomás said. "No, I don't know why I am here." Shifting his weight, he felt how his muscles pulled at his collarbone.

"You seem to be very friendly with Senator Largaespada's daughter, Doctor."

"Is that a crime?"

The lieutenant needed no time to think. He leaned over, a faint smile playing on his lips: "Look here, Doctor, we all like to go for a little roll in the hay, especially with a pretty young thing. We're not moralists, you know." He pulled his body back, and the smile was gone. "However, if we find that your involvement with her is —

different – more than a *cojería*, then we do become interested, and concerned."

"I don't know what you're talking about."

"Come now, Doctor. The car trips, the visits to abandoned houses. Did I leave out anything?"

"You are an intelligent man, Doctor. A learned man. You're nobody's fool."

"I don't know what you're talking about."

The lieutenant's head was nodding like a pump jack: "Shall I refresh your memory, Doctor?" Tomás shrugged, and the lieutenant opened the manila folder lying in front of him, in a single, determined motion. He scraped his throat and started reading: "On September 11, Milagros L and Tomás D were seen driving on the road to El Jicaral. On September 25, Milagros L and Tomás D were seen entering a house belonging to a former coffee planter, Wolfgang Gunther, known collaborator, less than ten miles from the front lines." He stopped reading and looked at Tomás.

"Tell me something, Doctor," he said, pausing to inhale smoke from an imaginary cigarette. "Why would an established man like yourself drive out into guerrilla territory and be gone for two whole days?"

"I am called to complicated cases sometimes. Are you a doctor yourself?"

The lieutenant shook his finger. "That's a good one, Doctor. I admire your loyalty, if that's what it is. God knows we need more loyal people in this country. But put yourself in my position for one second. What would you think of a doctor doing the kind of things you have been doing, the things I have just been listing for you? Would you like for me to continue reading?"

"No, I see that you have quite an extensive network of informants."

"We run this country, Doctor. We make sure things run, so that our citizens are able to sleep at night. Citizens like yourself, Doctor, law-abiding citizens loyal to Nicaragua."

He is taunting me, Tomás thought, *what else could it be?*

"Are you politically involved, Doctor?" the lieutenant continued. "A member of any party, any group?"

"No, I'm not." He felt his skin stiffen. "I'm not, as you surely know already." His voice sounded like a crow cawing, he realized, hoarse and shrill. The lieutenant pursed his lips and nodded, the kind of nod that meant neither yes nor no.

"Was your mother politically active, Doctor, that you know of?"

"No," he said, "she was not." The nod continued, unflinching.

"I understand that your father harbored political ambitions."

Tomás's mouth fell open. "My father died forty years ago. What on earth do you mean?"

"Are you surprised that your father was politically involved?"

"I am surprised that you should bring up my father who's been dead for forty years; yes, I am surprised by that. What's this all about?"

"Did you hate your father, Doctor?"

"I never knew my father."

"You're not answering my question."

"That should be an answer."

"It's not. Did you hate your father?"

What game is this man playing? he thought. *Why is he asking about my father?*

"It's better for you if you hated your father. There's no shame in that, Doctor."

"I don't understand why you're asking these questions."

"We can ask any question we want. We're the law, didn't you know?" They sat in silence. Tomás looked at his shoes, and the young lieutenant stared up at the meat hook.

"Here," the lieutenant said, and stood up. "I want you to listen to something." He walked to the far end of the room and opened the door. A strong smell of sweat and urine danced into the room, and Tomás instinctively curled his upper lip and nostrils. The lieutenant did not seem to smell it, and if he did, it did not bother him. He stuck his head out, cocked it with one ear facing Tomás and the other stretching out into the corridor. Then he turned and looked at Tomás again. "You hear?" he said. "You hear that noise?"

"No," Tomás said, "I don't hear anything."

The lieutenant looked genuinely surprised.

"Something wrong with your ears, Doc," he said, and closed the door. "These guys are making such a racket it would wake up the whole town if we had not boarded up all these windows. Hell, it would wake up the dead if we were close enough to the cemetery!" He laughed and walked back to the table.

"I am curious," he said. "What happened to you, Doctor? I hear you were a regular guy. Good family, country club, lucrative jobs. Why risk all that? Why risk all that for a girl?"

"Unless there is something else you want to tell me?" The lieutenant pulled out a Swiss army knife from his pants pocket and started playing with it. Tomás glanced at it from the corner of his eyes. He saw the bright red shaft with the silver cross on it. It was flipped open, then closed, open, closed. Each time it snapped shut there was a dry noise, as when a camera shutter clicks. The lieutenant yawned and stretched his arms.

He now saw the lieutenant for who he really was: a young man, almost a boy still, who had been given a toy to play with, and as the boy grew up, the toy had grown up with him. *Is this what happens to all boys? Do they all grow up without realizing that their toys have grown up with them? That the games have become more than a game, and they can no longer go back?*

The boy lieutenant said: "Colonel Cortés tells me that you are cousins. He says you practically grew up together. Amazing, who would have thought that?"

"Why is that so surprising?"

"The colonel doesn't have friends outside the Guardia. The Guardia is his life."

"Has he told you this?"

"The colonel tells me many things."

With every word, Tomás saw the lieutenant grow younger: first he saw him without his uniform, then in his schoolboy outfit. And then, finally, he stopped growing younger, and Tomás saw him climb an avocado tree and open up his knife to cut an avocado for his father.

The boy had stopped asking questions, and Tomás had started asking them: "When did you start working with Colonel Cortés, Lieutenant?"

"I was posted here six months ago. Was in Boaco before."

"So where are you from, then?"

"I'm from Rivas, but I grew up in Managua."

"And were you there when the earthquake happened?"

"No," he said. "But my mother died at the hands of a looter."

The avocado fell. The boy was still sitting in the tree, but he now looked at Tomás with the eyes of a grown man once more.

"You may go now, Doctor." He kicked back his chair. "Guard," he shouted, and the door opened. "Escort Doctor Delacorte out. Goodbye, Doctor." He did not extend his hand.

Tomás was breathing heavily, and he patted the case inside his jacket. *You didn't need it after all,* he thought. When he stepped outside it was still raining, but he decided to walk. By the time he reached home, the rain had slackened. He knocked, but no one came. *Juanita must have gone out,* he thought, and checked his watch. A raindrop fell on it, enlarging the numbers so there would be no mistaking them. He fumbled for his keys and struggled with the lock as the metal pushed back at the key, or perhaps it was the force of small insects seeking shelter from the rain, crawling over each other in search of a dry place, refusing to be dislodged so soon. He pushed the door open to a screeching stop – it was dark inside, and humid. As he found the light switch and turned it on, he saw the mountain of books and papers. He should have expected it, of course. If anything he should have been surprised that it had taken this long to happen. *But what had they been looking for? This is not a war between ideologies or competing visions of this world or the next. It's about power if anything, about money at most. If they were looking for writings incriminating me on that account, what might they possibly have considered incriminating?*

He was careful not to step on the papers as he made his way to the kitchen, thinking that he would pick them up, rearrange them, and put them back in their familiar places. The books had been turned open and held by the spine, like rabbits held up by their ears, and shaken until they release their secrets.

Maybe the interrogation at the station was a joke, he thought, *a distraction, a ruse to keep me away from here while the others rifled through my papers.*

His feet touched glass, and when he looked down he saw a broken frame with small shards still stuck under the edge. The woman in the torn photograph no longer smiled at him, as if her mouth were covered by a veil. He picked up the frame and peered at the eyes that were staring into a distance of which he was a part no more. He felt like coming home after a long absence, when once-familiar objects, neatly arranged side by side in a mental image, need to be reordered to make sense once more, and be allowed to learn to breathe again. He shook his head and abruptly dropped the frame back on the floor.

The lock of his liquor cabinet had been busted. Empty bottles of rum were lying on a nearby counter, but a single half-empty bottle had remained standing. The box of rat poison stared at him as intact as it had been on the day he first saw it. He poured himself a glass of rum and threw it back, in a single shot. The alcohol burned his throat and nostrils; he closed his eyes until the dizziness passed.

The next morning, as he shifted through the broken glass and shattered papers, he found the notebook. Or perhaps it found him, drawing him in with the deep smell of raw cocoa that makes one hungry even while it satisfies. The notebook was thick, and bound in tight calfskin leather. He sat down and opened it, slowly, his head still aching from the rum.

The voice that spoke to him from across the years was so clear that he looked up and around, suspecting the owner to be present in the room. The loneliness of the life that was being hurled at him, and the soul that had not looked for love but had found it where there was little else – *so much like mine*, he thought. He imagined the place where there were no road signs, no roads, and where the illusion of love itself had become a woman's home. Her words spoke of now and nothing else, of a boundless desire to believe in today, with no fear of tomorrow. He envied her for the love that had blossomed where all of the world's conventions had been ignored; where the universe had been made whole again, and the apple had been returned to the tree, uneaten.

It is love that makes you whole, he thought. *Not fear. Not vengeance. Only love, and believing in it.*

He closed the book and held it by the spine to read the letters engraved on it. A yellowed square bit of paper slipped out and fluttered away. Slowly, as if hesitating; a bird or a butterfly released from its cage after a long sleep. When he turned it over, he saw that it was a photograph, in drab sepias. It showed two young women of pale complexion, one with dark hair and the other a blonde. Both were wearing long and shapeless dresses. An older man with a sallow face was clutching a broad-rimmed slouch hat. No one smiled: they all looked away from the camera, and in different directions. *Perhaps they had been frightened by this newfangled machine,* he thought, *or had been told by the photographer to look stern, so their children and grandchildren would remember them for their discipline.* "Brown Photographers" it read on the back, in a stamp that had faded little. There was no year.

He studied the people in the picture with the keen eye of a pathologist: a cheekbone here, a less-than-perfect symmetry there – the telltale signs of genetic dispositions, the things you cannot give away even though they are yours alone.

He felt the way a bystander must feel who is suddenly drawn into an afternoon ball game, or a roadside accident, or the birth of a child in the busy market square. He saw the ball landing in his lap, the car that stopped in front of his house, and then the baby cried.

When he looked more closely at the dark-haired woman he saw a dark spot on her left arm, the one that was dangling aimlessly, as if she had been robbed of something valuable. He scraped a fingernail over the spot, an instinctive movement to see the picture as it must have been in its original state. But the delicate film of silver oxide revealed nothing but the paleness of egg white-coated cotton. No secrets were lying beneath the picture, only cotton. White and virgin cotton unseen by the sun, and the butterfly that had been flew away.

Chapter 35

She called him at the hospital.

"I need to talk to you," she said. She sounded hushed.

"I will meet you in an hour," he said, "at the Capilla de la Virgen Milagrosa."

The chapel was on the outskirts of town, on the road to Chinandega. He could barely see her against the blackened walls, by the light of a handful of candles. Her body tensed against his, and he stopped himself from kissing her.

"When did you come back?" he said.

"Three days ago." She looked away.

"León is no longer safe for you."

"They must have been suspicious from the start," she said. "These hangmen have good informants."

"Then why did you come back? Why risk it?"

The candles were flickering wildly now, as if someone had started breathing on them.

"I am pregnant."

His knees started shaking, and he covered his eyes with one hand. She looked at his face, waiting, but he did not speak.

"Don't you want to know?"

"Know what?"

"If it's yours."

He saw her again as he first saw her. He saw her trembling lips, and wondered if they were trembling for him. He remembered the moment she made him whole again. His side hurt as if a bone had been yanked out, violently and unannounced.

"Is it mine?"

"Yes."

She needed no time to answer. Why, then, did she want me to ask?

The church bells started tolling and her feet scraped the ground, like a deer trapped in the undergrowth.

"Marry me, Milagros," he said. "Leave this nightmare behind you. There is still time. Marry me; I will take care of you."

She shook her head. "I cannot marry you, Tomás," she said. "I will not marry anyone as long as this war is not finished."

"And once it finishes?"

"I don't think that far ahead. I don't have that luxury."

"You could if you wanted to. Everything else can be arranged."

She shook her head. "You are selfish. You're not asking this for my sake."

"You call me selfish? How can you be so blind? Look around you. If you are going to have this child, think of the world you are bringing it into!"

"I can't run away from this. There is no meaning to my life until this is over."

"It will never be over. Human beings are cruel; they will never stop hurting each other."

"Even if that were the truth…"

"It is the truth. It's the only truth we know. Everything else is lies."

She looked up at the nave and licked her lips. "The place you are in must be terribly lonely, Tomás. I only wished you understood why I am doing this. If you did, you would stop being selfish."

He shook his head. "I can arrange something. A friend…it would be safe."

"No!" Her eyes grew wide. "You don't understand. How could you think I would not want to have this child? Damn you!" She banged the pew with her fist.

He could see through the half-open door, where rows of sugarcane stood still in the noonday heat. *So then end it,* he thought. *Just say the words. There are so few of them — there won't be time for them to hurt, they will just fly out and be gone. Just like that, just some more words on their way into the world.* But he didn't.

"I cannot leave you, Milagros," he said instead. "If that makes me selfish, so be it."

"Words mean nothing, Tomás, you must mean them. And you must make them mean something." He took her hand, and felt her breath. He wanted to remember how it was when she had rested her head on his lap at the rebel camp. But her breath was faster this time, harried and restless, as if life had caught up with her before it had had time to teach breathing lessons.

Chapter 36

He woke up panicking, the mosquito net tangled around his legs. He had dreamed he was returning from a party, with a woman he had never seen, and he was insisting he carry the children into the house. She shook her head, soundlessly but determined. He had bit his lip until he tasted the blood in the sides of his mouth, slowly mixing with his saliva. Finally, she sighed and handed him a pair of men's shoes wrapped in thick cotton cloth. He lifted the tongue, and saw the heads of two minuscule wrinkled children, sound asleep.

"My children," he said. "My children, I will take care of you." He walked behind the woman as she opened the door and disappeared into the house. He did not see the brick on the pavement, and when he lost his balance one of the shoes dropped from his hands and rolled over.

"Let them be all right," he said, "let them be healthy and alive." He crawled after the shoe and turned it over. Then he put the other one next to it and pulled aside the cotton flaps.

The shoes were empty. Both of them. Empty.

"But," he heard himself say, "but what happened, where are my children?"

At that moment he woke up. He thought about the dream over breakfast, and could not get it out of his head. *I will drive to Poneloya*, he thought, *to get some fresh air.* On the way out, he drove past the Cortés mansion. Mama Mica had died three years before, "from an allergic reaction to a spoonful of honey," everyone had said, although this had not been established by science. The full family had stood around the ballooning ninety-nine-year-old body lying in state, and looked at Tomás with accusing eyes as he suggested an autopsy, to eliminate any doubts.

"What for?" they all said. "It was the bad honey, what part don't you believe?"

"Shame on you," Aunt Elvira had screamed. "Shame on you, Tomás, for suggesting this. How dare you even think about laying a finger on her? Mama Mica was practically a saint! Have you no respect for sainthood?" She spat on the floor and turned around.

"I'm just saying, maybe it was something else," Tomás sputtered, but the looks on all the Cortés faces were enough to shut him up. Aunt Elvira stood guard in front of the corpse, ready to defend it with her life.

"…dead-tissue doctor…" he heard someone mumble. "Only happy when he can cut open cadavers."

Rafaela was sitting outside during the row, sucking on a piece of cinnamon bark. She was still thin, and her face showed few wrinkles, although her short-cropped hair had started graying.

"So," he said as he sat down next to her, "do you think she died of bad honey, too?"

She looked straight at him. "She may have died of bad honey for all I care," she said. "Although I somehow suspect that she did this on purpose: leaving just before turning one hundred. She probably had enough of it, and figured that everything was going down the drain."

He stood up and started towards his car, but turned back before he had taken two steps.

"Did you know my father?"

"Took you forty years to ask that question."

"Maybe I never wanted to know before."

"So why now?"

"I never knew him. Everything I know about him was told to me by someone else."

Rafaela looked at him with one eye closed.

"I loved your father."

He was aghast. "What?" he said.

"Heavens, Tomás, there's no law against that, is there?"

"Before…"

"Your mother and I were the same age. I loved him first, but it did not last."

"But why?"

"Why what? Why I loved him? Or why he left?" She raised her shoulders. "I loved him because he was free. And I wanted to be free like him. For me, love has no limits. I would have followed him."

"So what happened?"

She threw away the cinnamon bark and stood up, brushing off the brick dust from her dress. "You know the rest," she said.

With Mama Mica's passing it seemed as if all the good luck of the Cortéses had turned to dung. At least that's what Doña Elvira said, because soon there were no more Sunday classes to teach the young ones about the Ancestor. With Mama Mica gone, the last umbilical link to the Ancestor had been severed, and their past had now become less palpable, as it was no longer embodied in a quivering mass of mammalian flesh.

As the guerrillas advanced, and violence became so visible that it could no longer be ignored, many of the clansmen and women left the country, not wanting to witness the march on their mansion by the great unwashed. They expected to be able to come back one day, clean out their mansion, and pretend it never happened. *An interlude*, they thought, *part of the pendulum of history*. And so, one by one, the wings of the great Cortés house emptied, as the offspring started their next voyage of exile. At first, they were quickly replaced by more distant branches of the family – uncles and cousins more than twice removed, eager to spend some time at the Forefather's fortress, so that all of León would see them and recognize their birthright.

"Ahaaah, so you all are Cortéses after all!" people would say. But soon they realized that the Cortés house had become an empty shell, a facade for past glory, and all that had been desirous when they were on the outside, lost its shine and shimmer now that they were on the inside. They realized that this was just another dilapidated house with a leaking roof. Living in a world defined in terms of what they wanted, and not in terms of what they had, these Cortéses in the third degree, now robbed of their illusions, started leaving as well, and no longer thought of their forefather as the Forefather. Adam had become adam, and adam had become man no more – de-capitalized, de-hyphenated, and ultimately humanized to the tenth degree.

The south wing was boarded up, and then the west wing, until at last there was just the east wing left where Rafaela was living on her own, although perhaps there was still the spirit of Mama Mica keeping her company, for she never spoke of loneliness. The garden from where Mama Mica and Rafaela had harvested bitter roots and pungent herbs, and the ripe flesh of fruits that had stoked the passions and fortunes of the Cortéses throughout a century of procreation, had long since become overgrown, and there were parts where no one had set foot for the longest while now, since the days when gardeners started becoming scarce. So with no more gardeners around, Rafaela had taken it upon herself to clear the entry to the front door, *based on the simple truth,* Tomás thought, *that no one else would beat a path to her door on their own account.* She stood in the doorway of the house as Tomás drove past. He waved at her, and she waved back at him while the sun glittered and bounced off the machete dangling from her other hand. The door was open behind her, and he imagined the coolness of the dark corridors flowing out, caressing her ankles until it formed a low wall of air for her to stand on.

The beach was deserted. No fishermen, no lovers, and no lone horses knowing their way home – only pelicans scooping into the breakers. The carcass of the whale straddled mid-beach, where the palm trees could not give it shade, nor could the pull of the ocean draw it back into a watery grave. All that was left were five immense vertebrae and chevron bones jutting out from the sand, and a full row of ribs bitten and blanched by the sun and the salty mist. He saw someone sitting inside the ribcage, someone who had draped freshly washed clothes over the neatly curving bones. Where the sand was dark and wet, two children were playing with a gourd, the tough and bitter fruit of the jícaro calabash tree that thrives on sandy soil and brackish water, growing where nothing else can. The children came running towards him as he sloughed through the sand that was sucking at his feet, and flashed small, pearly teeth while they pulled at his coattails: "*Don, porfa Don, cinco reales, Don.*" He fished out some coins from his pocket and gave them one each.

"*Gracias, Don,*" they screamed and ran away again, holding the coins up in the air. The woman sitting amid the laundry turned around when she heard the screams. He came closer and leaned against one of the bones. When he stroked it, he felt how rough it was, pockmarked by hundreds of small insects drilling their way in.

Like a corset, he thought. *Like a corset for a giant woman who has forgotten that she was wearing it, and went dancing away over the hills in pursuit of pleasure.*

"What are you doing here?" he said.

"I watch the laundry, Don," she said. "They pay me to make sure that nothing flies away and nothing gets stolen by any of those scoundrel boys." She pouted her lips in the direction of the children playing in the sand.

"So whose clothes are they?"

She raised her shoulders. "People in the big house," she said, pointing to one of the fenced-in houses. "They told me to watch the clothes, Don, that's all. They pay me, and I watch the clothes. I don't ask questions."

He sat on one of the vertebrae sticking out of the sand, and took off his shoes. Emptying them slowly, he watched as the trickle of sand blew away in the wind. *That's how simple the world is*, he thought. *They pay us, and we don't ask questions. And why should we, after all? All these questions just get us deeper into trouble.* But he continued asking anyway: "Where are you from?" he said.

"From here, Don."

"And have you always lived here?"

"As far as I know."

"And those children? Whose are they?"

She was becoming annoyed by his questioning. Or perhaps it was just nerves.

"Someone's," she said, "someone's in the village."

He did not press on. *What for? It makes no difference, will not make any difference. She will not give any answers, and if I expected to get clarity on the beach, I was wrong. "Things are just the way they are, Tomás," my mother told me.* He sat down on the sand, and let it run between his fingers. *There's no end of it*, he thought. *What is it when all those who loved us are gone, and when those we love are not within our reach? What is it when all we have are those we do not love?* How was it that Milagros had said it? "We float in and out of each other's lives." He had not wanted to float out of hers. Had not wanted her to float out of his.

And what would his father have said? When the lieutenant mentioned his father, it had not stirred anything. It had been something outside of him, something that did not involve him. But he did remember the urn buried in his wardrobe, and how it had moved to a wicker suitcase, and eventually to a bleak and empty room.

The woman had taken down the clothes, and finished folding them into a large yellow basin. He looked up to see her stand in front of him, holding out a bottle of water.

"You're sweating, Don," she said. "You look red and hot. Please drink some water."

He took the bottle and drank.

"I am in love," he said. "But she does not want to marry me."

The woman laughed, and sat down on another vertebra.

"How long have you known this woman, Don?"

"All my life. Would you believe it?"

She shook her head. "You are a very patient man, Don."

Or a stupid one, he thought. He gave her back the water.

"My father was a brave man," he said. "He believed in what he did. Just like the woman I love. But he died before he could tell me this."

The woman opened her eyes wide, and raised her shoulders. "Your problem is very complicated, Don," she said. She stood up and lifted the wash basin, held it pressed against her waist, and trudged away through the sand.

"Adios, Don," she said. "I hope you will find each other."

The jeep was waiting for him when he parked in front of the morgue, the captain leaning against it, impatiently. Tomás felt calm, calmer than he had felt in a long time. When he got out of his car the captain opened the door of the jeep, and Tomás got in. He did not ask questions this time.

They took him to the white building he had seen from a distance. He looked at the landscape without seeing it, and only remembered that they crossed a concrete bridge over the Rio Chiquito, and that small boats were moored on the riverbank below. Dug halfway into the ground, the bunker was much smaller than he had expected. The central courtyard smelled of fungus, and through the penumbra he saw the distinct redness of lichen growth creeping up against the walls. He was led into a small room, with a table and two chairs. There was no hook screwed into the ceiling beams. Instead, a picture of Somoza was hanging from the wall, grinning at him. He stood waiting for a few minutes, hearing boots walking and running outside the room. The door opened, and the young lieutenant from Rivas came in.

"Doctor, we were expecting you. May I offer you coffee?"

"No," Tomás said. "No, thank you. I am fine." The lieutenant shrugged and left the room.

After the silence returned, Tomás started hearing other noises. There were screams, and muffled sounds, and much water being splashed onto something. There were more screams, and then they stopped, abruptly. He looked at his watch: 9 a.m. *At this time, the tortilleras will be rattling the padlock on my gate,* he thought.

He looked around when he heard voices. There was no one, but he saw that a few of the Styrofoam ceiling squares were missing. He strained his ear, and thought he recognized Fausto's voice.

"We will move three days from now," Fausto said. "Is everything ready?"

"Almost, Colonel. The scouts have been selected. We'll start from Quesalguaque at 6 a.m. We'll go around east to cut off their escape route."

"Make sure we keep this operation under close tabs. I don't want any fuck-ups with this. We'll strike fast and flush out these rebels once and for all. Especially those three that tried to kill me." There was more mumbling and then Tomás heard a door being closed.

When the door opened once more, Fausto entered. His boots and the lower parts of his pants were wet, and he was drying his hands with a dirty towel. He did not seem surprised.

"Tomás," he said, "they told me you were here." He came closer while he continued to dry his hands. When he stood in front of Tomás, he raised his eyebrows, one at the time.

"*Cómo estás, primo?*" he said. He put the towel aside, and sat down behind the table, folding his hands so that no one would know where they had been and what they had done, and he became the colonel.

"Do you know why you are here?"

Tomás sighed. "What for?" he said. "Why play games? You brought me here, so you should know why I'm here."

"What do you know about this boy, this Uruguayan that showed up in León a while ago?"

"The young man who's staying with Senator Largaespada?"

"Yes," Fausto said. "Yes, that's the one. Roberto."

"A friend of Milagros. They met in Paris."

"And why is he here?"

Tomás shrugged. "He's a friend," he said. "A friend, visiting."

Fausto pursed his lips. "Let's get something straight," he said. "There are no tourists in Nicaragua these days. There's just us now. All of us. And we're in such a goddamn awful mess that no tourists want to wet their asses in our swimming pools."

Tomás raised his shoulders. "I can't tell you things I don't know."

"So then tell me the things you do know."

"And if I don't?"

"I don't think you realize what you're up against."

"You?"

Fausto shook his head. "There's only so much I can do to protect you, cousin. Who do you think keeps these files, eh? Who do you think reads them?"

Tomás stayed silent.

"I could keep you here for as long as I want," Fausto said. "A week, a month. Makes no difference to me."

I need to leave, was all he could think. *I need to leave now, before it's too late and the damage is done.*

"What do you want to know?" he said.

When Tomás had left, Fausto called the young lieutenant.

"He'll take us there, Danilo," he said. "Make sure you don't lose him. Do we have any scouts from Malpaisillo or thereabouts?"

"I believe we do, Colonel. A Sergeant Solórzano."

"The liar?"

The lieutenant nodded.

"Alright then," Fausto said. "Bring him here."

Danilo came back with a grizzled man.

"Your name, Sergeant?"

"Solórzano, colonel, Sergeant Solórzano."

"They tell me you're from Telica, Sergeant?

"Posoltega, sir."

"Good. You will accompany the lieutenant tomorrow. He will tell you what to do. And Sergeant…"

"Sir?"

"I don't mind liars, but I have no patience with people who don't do their job."

Chapter 37

The senator's house was on the outskirts of town.

"Look," the senator said, leaning over. "This whole place is going down the crapper. I don't give it more than three months." He chuckled. "And so we're back to where we started, aren't we?"

"What do you mean?" Tomás said.

The senator poured out the last of the rum and continued: "Some of us came here a long time ago, and others only recently. And others yet, well they were here before everyone else. And while we were busy eating steak, they figured it out. We have these fancy last names, but that doesn't mean we don't know how we got to be what we are now. My grandfather made his political fortunes by scaring poor peasants off his land. And before that…for Christ's sake, the man sold charcoal off a pushcart." He made a dismissive gesture with his hand. "All this claptrap about aristocracy, spare me; they all came on a boat and could barely read and write. So they invented some fancy name for themselves and figured out how to turn a good opportunity into a fortune. Old families, what the hell does that mean – we all go back to Cain, all of us." He plunked down his glass. "You'll see, soon enough everyone will be selling charcoal off a pushcart again, fancy names or not. Cheers, young man."

"Aren't you afraid?" Tomás said.

"I am, but what good will that do me? My daughters, they will survive. They are not afraid of the future." He smacked his lips. "Now," he said, "how many years have you worked at the hospital?"

"I don't know. Since I started medical school."

"And did you ever wonder why your hospital shuts down on Sundays?"

"The seventh day," Tomás said. "It's a rule."

"Yeah, a rule. Have you ever asked him?"

"No," Tomás said. "We have all just assumed that the rule would be there forever." He thought about the one time the rule had been lifted.

"That's right. We have always assumed that everything would be like this forever." The senator shook his head. "That's where Milagros is different," he said. "She questions all the rules. She figured out that it doesn't matter how long a rule has been around – you question them all!"

Tomás nodded.

"Of course we have all been raised to accept things and not open our mouth. And who would listen to you anyway, right?" the senator continued.

"Wouldn't that depend on what you have to say?"

"It may depend even more on what the others know. Or think they know. Which reminds me of a story I must tell you: once there were two men: one blind man and one that could see. When the lights went out they were both in darkness, and no different from one another, but only the seeing one knew this, and was afraid."

Tomás laughed, shaking his head. "I think someone may have told me that one," he said.

The senator grinned. "Surely you did not come here to listen to an old man ramble on about blind men not being afraid, did you? Not with all of this" – he stretched out his hand to point towards the clouds of black smoke to the north. "More important things to take care of, right?"

"I need to find Milagros."

"Do you know where she is?"

"No, but I thought you might."

The senator shook his head. "I don't know. But I know someone who might." He waved his hand to call his attendant. "Let's go," he said. They went to the barn, where the brown mare was the only horse left. When Tomás stuck out his hand, the mare licked the salt off it, all the way up to his elbow.

"I think Xiomara will know where to go," the senator said. "She will be your blind man."

He pointed to the corner of the barn, where a foal was sleeping, coiled up onto itself. "The foal is strong now; it will survive a few days without its mother. Just make sure she comes back in one piece." He held out his hand. "Take care of my daughter, young man. I already lost her once."

"Yes," Tomás said. "Yes, I will take care of her. It's a promise."

When Tomás was about to leave the senator pointed to his shoes and said: "Good garrobo leather. Did you get them at Humberto's?"

"Yes, but they belonged to someone else; he gave them to me because his shoe walker lost mine. I rarely use them."

"Do they fit?"

"Yes."

"Then wear them. We all borrow from others in life, whether it's a horse, a name, or a pair of shoes. Some women carry a baby whose father is not the man they married. You can borrow anything in life, except courage or honor. And when you choose dishonor, you end up with war. Even an old fool knows that." They shook hands.

"Where is Doctor Urbina's office these days?" he asked the receptionist.

"Top floor, Doctor. Same as always." Tomás had not gone up to Doctor Urbina's office in many years. The doctor was retired; he just came in because it had become a habit to walk from his home to the hospital every day. Tomás knocked and opened the door. The professor was sitting behind his desk, peering over his glasses.

"So you're still here, Tomás." It sounded like an affirmation rather than a question.

"Yes, I'm still here, and so are you. You'll live to be a hundred, surely."

"But people forget about you, and once you're forgotten you might as well be dead." He struck the floor with his walking cane.

"Soooo," he continued, "any news from the pathology front?"

"No, not really. Just the usual, you know."

"Just the usual, yes." The room looked exactly the way he remembered it from twenty years earlier, except for the skeleton standing guard before a closet full of scrolls and books. When the professor gestured for him to sit down, he realized that the visitor chair was no longer there. *He must have forgotten that he no longer has a visitor's chair,* he thought. *Someone probably took it away years ago and the old sod hasn't even noticed. And why would he, if no one ever comes to visit him?*

"I've been wanting to ask you something for many years, Professor," he said. Doctor Urbina cocked his head.

"Why did you invent the seven-day rule?"

"Everything needs rules; this one is as good as any."

"The rule looks pretty crazy to most people around here."

"Do you think the rule is crazy?"

Tomás sighed. "Well…"

"What happens after the seventh day?"

"They all come back inside."

"Wrong. They start killing each other. The lot of them. Read Genesis, it all goes downhill after the seventh day. Cain slew Abel on the eighth day. The rule is not crazy. They are."

Tomás shook his head. "That's just one old story, Professor. Who says all stories need to end the same way?"

"So how do you think it should end?"

"I think that on the eighth day we stop talking to dead people, and start worrying about the living."

Professor Urbina wagged a bony finger. "You can't change the past," he said.

"I don't need to. The past is dead. It died a long time ago."

He took painkillers and antibiotics from the hospital infirmary. *How much can a mare carry so soon after she has foaled?* he wondered.

"Juanita, I might be gone for a while," he said when he was having breakfast, early the next morning.

"But you will be back, yes, Doctor?"

"Of course, why wouldn't I?"

"The neighbors left yesterday. They locked up all the rooms and left behind a caretaker with a gun."

What are they thinking? he wondered. *Do they think that once this is over they can just come back?*

He paid Juanita her salary in advance. *"Por si las moscas,"* he said. "Tough times, and worse times coming, so we shouldn't leave any debts unsettled."

She tilted her head, uncertain what to think of his words. "Come back safely, Doctor," she said. "I will be waiting for you." He nodded, and then they loaded the medicines into his car. When he arrived at the senator's house, the horse was already saddled up.

"How did you know I would pass by today?" he asked the stableboy.

"The senator told me," the boy said. "He told me to dress the horse."

"Is the senator up already?"

"No, Don, he never gets up this early. But he sends his regards."

He drove his car into the barn and transferred the medicines to the saddlebags.

"Don't tie them to the cantle," he said. "Use the pommel instead." The stableboy arranged the two bags and stepped aside when Tomás swung his leg over the broad back.

"Will you visit patients, Doctor?" he said.

He ignored the question. "Tell the senator I will bring her back soon, you hear?"

"Yes, Don," the boy said. Tomás looked up at the house as he rode out. For one second he thought he saw a pair of eyes peering through the shutters of an upstairs room. *An illusion, surely,* he thought. *Unless they carried him up, but why would they?*

The soldiers manning the roadblock waved him through without questions, and he reached the turnoff after two hours. He stopped to give the horse some rest, and drink water.

"Now it's your turn," he mumbled when he was back in the saddle. He dropped the reins, waiting for the mare to choose where to go. She scraped the flint beneath her, creating small sparks. But she did not move. He dismounted and sat down. He made noises, pointed her towards the two volcanoes beckoning in the distance. *It's a horse,* he thought. *Not a dog. Maybe the senator was wrong. This horse doesn't know any more than the rest of us. But I want to believe it does.* The mare looked at him and licked his hands. Then she walked away, towards the larger of the two volcanoes. He followed her, shaking his head.

It took six hours to reach the place where the river sprang from the rock. They had stopped only once, and it had been the horse who had nudged him on after they rested. For the last part he kept his eyes closed, and when he heard the sound of falling water he knew he had almost arrived. He had been blindfolded the first time, and now saw how narrow the path really was, and how steep the slope. When he saw the smoke he dismounted, and shouted to make his presence known.

"Who sent you?" José said, training his gun on him.

"No one. I came to warn you."

José smirked, pushing the gun closer to his chest. "Why should we believe you? You were at the Fortin yesterday, and now you're here!"

"I told them your camp was near the Cerro Negro volcano. I sent them elsewhere."

"And you want us to believe this, hijueputa?

"They knew already; they were planning an attack in three days. So when they asked me, I confirmed the location. Look, I know you don't trust me, but I am telling the truth."

José turned around. "What's in his bags?" he said. "Did you find anything? A radio? He must have something to communicate with, to tell them how many we are."

"Nothing," a young man said. "Just medicines."

José lowered his gun. "What's the trick?" he said. "What did you promise your cousin? And what do you get out of this?" He pointed the gun at his head. "Give me one good reason why I should not put a bullet in your head right now. You think you are protected? Maybe out there, but not here you're not."

"Where is Milagros?" he said. "Can I speak to her?"

José shook his head. "You're out of luck, Doc. I'm in charge here now." They tied his hands and left him in one of the huts. It was humid, and he heard the scuffle of small animals between the bamboo stalks that held up the walls.

After a few hours the door opened and Milagros stepped in. "What have you done?" she said.

He told her. He told her he wanted to be with her, and that nothing else mattered. "Brave but stupid," he told her, "that's how they said my father lived his life. But he was neither brave nor stupid. He was just a man who had made a choice."

"And now what?" she said.

"I cannot go back. When they find out I sent them to the wrong place they will come for me."

"So you want to stay here?"

He nodded.

"It won't be easy to convince them."

"In two days they will know."

She peered at him. "How did you find your way up here?" she said.

"Your horse."

"My father's idea?"

"Yes."

"What else did he tell you?"

"To bring you back."

"No, he didn't say that."

He laughed. "OK," he said. "He told me to keep you safe."

"Hmmm. Yes, that's what he would say."

She tied the horse to a tree by the brook, to a giant mahogany tree that cast its shade across the water. He watched how she scratched the horse's poll and tapped its flank, speaking softly.

When he finished tending to the sick, he was led back to the hut. José sat down outside, against a tree. "I'll keep my eyes on you," he said. "Anything happens, you'll be the first to get it."

Chapter 38

Dawn had not arrived yet when they left the bunker. A company of sleepy-faced soldiers got onto jeeps and drove off to the drone of hundreds of cane toads. The soldiers were on edge; they grunted to themselves rather than to each other, like caged arena beasts waiting for the door to be thrown open. Fausto bellowed for his lieutenant two hours into the day.

"They won't expect us coming in today," he said. "Let's keep it that way."

By noon the scouts returned. "The camp is twelve miles due east," Sgt. Solórzano reported, "in the shadow of the San Cristóbal volcano."

On the crags north of the San Cristóbal volcano wild olive trees grow. No paved roads lead there; it is a place off the maps, kept off the maps.

This morning, Milagros got up later than usual, and went to the lazaretto to check up on a wounded boy recovering from a leg shot.

"When do you think I'll be able to walk again?" the boy said. There was a dog by his side, a limping dog with a leg that hung on by a thread. *They make a good couple,* she thought, *between them they have more than enough legs to walk to the other end of the world. Twice.* She smiled and laid a hand on the ailing leg.

"Soon," she said. "Everything will be solved soon, I promise."

The first bullet lodged itself in the wall behind him, spitting up bits of splayed bamboo and dried mud. The door was thrown open, and he saw José in the opening, pointing his gun at them.

"You'll die with us," he said. "Pay the price." He pulled the trigger, and Tomás felt the bullets enter his body. The last thing he felt was José's body falling on top of him, spitting up blood.

Then there was darkness.

The small band of rebels was no match for the soldiers swooping down like a swarm of locusts. The ones in the lower huts put up resistance for as long as they could, but they were hopelessly outnumbered. Within half an hour the ones who had survived surrendered, and were quickly tied up and pushed back into the huts.

"Take only the ones on the list," Fausto said. "The rest of them, give them water."

Milagros had not brought her gun. "Stupid," she hissed. "How could you be so stupid to leave your gun behind?" She sat against the wall until the fire stopped and a small group of soldiers stormed into the lazaretto. A young soldier's boot kept her pinned to the ground — one foot up, one foot down, as if she were a hunting trophy. The soldiers laughed as they pushed the limping boy and his dog into a corner with the others. The dog bared its fangs and snarled, its tail hanging stiff. One of the soldiers cursed. He shouldered his gun and fired at the dog as it tried to stand on its hind legs. When the dog yelped again, the soldier fired another bullet, and the dog went limp.

They took her outside, along with the other women. As they were being led down the path, she heard gunshots coming from the lazaretto: a series of identical gunshots, carefully timed, one exactly like the other. There were screams, and then more shots. When she turned around she saw one of the soldiers hold a torch to the bamboo curtain.

"No!" she screamed, but the soldier behind her slammed his rifle butt between her shoulder blades.

"Keep moving," he growled, "we're not asking you for your opinion. You're lucky we're not putting you down like the rest of these dogs." Dazed by the kicks, she held on to her belly.

Fausto winked when she walked past him.

"So we meet again," he said. "No surprise to either one of us, I guess." He grinned. "You should have pulled the trigger when you had a chance, young lady. Too afraid of breaking eggs, I guess." She turned her head and spat in his face. He continued grinning.

"All a game," he said, as they pushed her along, downhill, to where the jeeps were waiting. "Win some, lose some. Fuck the rest."

Chapter 39

Silence, he thought. *So much silence. Even more than on a Sunday in the morgue.* He opened his eyes and there was only darkness.

Where is everyone? he thought. *There were tens of people here; they couldn't all have left, not all at once.* A fly buzzed, and then another. They were buzzing over his chest, but when he tried to move his arm to chase them off, he felt the weight. He pushed, but his shoulder hurt, and his side. He rolled over, pushing with his other arm, and the body slid off him. He smelled the blood. Smelled the metal that had found its way into his body. *Pennies*, he thought. *Sofía's pennies.*

He touched his body, mechanically, starting with his chest and abdomen, then his arms and head. He could not reach his legs, and when he tried to sit up the pain brought him down again. A bullet had lodged in his right side, below the liver, and another one in his shoulder. There was blood all over, but his forehead felt cool. "Muscle," he said. "Muscle and fat."

I need to get up. Dress my wounds, drink water. He pulled himself up, slowly, and finally he was out in the moonlight. As he walked down the path, he saw bodies. In his lab and in the morgue, death had been clean and clinical. Slices and slivers tagged with endless strings of numbers and letters. But not here. Here it shouted at him, wordlessly, and without apologies.

He heard a rasping sound, like a voice straining to speak through a knocked-out windpipe.

"*Veni*," the voice said. There was a shape sitting against a tree. "Come," it said once more. None of the other bodies moved, and when he came closer he recognized the face.

"Roberto!" he exclaimed. "What happened?"

"We didn't hear them come." The words were slurred and thick with blood.

"Who?" he said. "Who did this?"

Roberto squinted. "Your cousin," he said. "Who else?"

Tomás felt a fist squeezing his stomach. *How had Fausto known? Why did you think you could outsmart him?*

"Where is Milagros?" he said.

"I don't know," Roberto said. "They did not kill everyone. They had a list." The words hit Tomás in the stomach, like a hammer.

"Be quiet now," he said. "Be quiet and don't move. I will get you out of here."

The mare was where Milagros had left her. One of the bags was still there; he pulled out alcohol and gauze, and cleaned his wounds. It stung, but the bleeding stopped – the bullets had been small, and the gun had been old.

He went up to the lazaretto. It was still smoking. Among the bodies lying inside a circle of charred wood he spotted a dead dog. "A three-legged dog," he said. "Who would have thought that I would find a three-legged dog here, of all places?"

Then he saw the boy.

"Elías?" he said. In spite of the burns, he recognized his paperboy. "What were you doing here, Elías? You did not belong here."

He covered the body with rocks, and before placing the last one he pulled a half-córdoba from his pocket and stuck it between the boy's fingers.

"Go get yourself something to eat," he said. "It's a long journey."

He dragged Roberto down to the river and dressed his wounds as well as he could. Then he lifted him by the arms and slung him over the horse's broad croup. He set out down the slope on the other side, towards Chinandega, riding and sometimes walking, when the horse tired.

He arrived at Manolo's house just before dawn. He left the horse against the wall, out of sight, and stuck his hand through the metal grid to rattle the padlock. When the maid came out he told her to call Isabel. Instead, the boy came out. He peered through the darkness and approached.

"It's me," Tomás said, "your father's friend. I need your help." The boy said nothing. He turned around and came back with a key to open the gate. Tomás reached for the reins and pulled the horse into the yard. The boy gasped when he saw Roberto's body slumped over the saddle. He stepped back at first, but then he took a deep breath and steadied the horse while Tomás pulled down the body.

"He dead?" the boy said.

Tomás shook his head. "No," he said. "No more dying today. Now please help me carry him into the house." The boy looked at him when he pulled out the switchblade knife and cut away Roberto's clothes.

"Do you have alcohol?" Tomás said.

The boy nodded. "My mother keeps it locked up."

Tomás smiled, in spite of the pain that gripped him when his midriff swelled. "And you have the key, yes?"

"I will get it," the boy said.

An hour later Isabel arrived. By then Roberto's wounds were tightly dressed, and his breathing had become deeper.

"Can he stay here?" Tomás said. "He's just a boy, and I have nowhere to take him. I am responsible for him. He needs to see a doctor, someone you can trust."

"Of course," she said. "No need to ask. Or explain. We will take care of him." He nodded.

"Now it's your turn," she said. "I'm a doctor's wife, remember?" She brought out Manolo's satchel, and her hand rested on the clasp for a few seconds before she opened it.

"It's going to hurt," she said. "But you knew that already."

When the bullets were out, he slept for two days. He woke up to find fresh clothes lying on the chair, and his shoes polished to a shine. When he walked into the living room, Isabel smiled.

"I did not think I would see his shirts on any man ever again," she said. "It's good this way."

"What will you do now?" she asked when he had eaten.

"I need to go back," he said. "I made a promise."

"Hmm," she said. "Yes, the shirt fits you."

Chapter 40

"Prison number 21," it was called. The local people who dared to venture out called it *El Repollal*, the Cabbage Patch, because of the skulls strewn about, looking like cabbages. There was no gate, and the guards did not ask him any questions, beckoning instead for him to walk down the narrow walkway that led into the concrete shell. They searched him, and took away the knife. When they found the syringe and vial the captain waved his hand, and they put the case back into his pocket.

When he entered the room, the darkness blinded him. The windows were small, and the moonlight that had snuck into the room was timid, no more than narrow strips of light waiting for an object to fall on. There was a shuffle, and then the rustle of fabric or dry leaves, as if an animal were hiding in the darkness, positioning itself for the assault.

"Come, Tomás, you are here to see the beast, aren't you now?" Fausto leaned slightly forward, and a moonbeam fell on his head. It looked smaller suddenly, as if the moonlight had shrunk it, reduced it to the size of a large avocado. The shadow cast on his face was drawn out into a cowl that made his head seem never-ending.

"Why the sudden interest, Tomás? Why didn't you just live out your boring life?" Fausto stepped out of the shadows and stopped four feet away from him.

"How did you find out?"

"Come now, Tomás. Look at me. You think I was born yesterday? That little conversation with my lieutenant – you really think we don't have soundproof rooms in here? I knew you'd go to her the moment I released you – you were the perfect bait. And you did an excellent job. Now sit down." As Tomás sat down and rested his hands on the table, he felt the scars left behind by cigarette burns.

"Why did you come back here? To get your woman out and screw the rest of them?" Fausto took out a cigarette and lit it.

"I think you've gone mad," Tomás said, trying to control the trembling. "You see enemies where there are just people living their lives. How can you sleep at night, how can you look at yourself in the mirror every day?"

Fausto laughed. It was a short and hoarse laugh. "I feel nothing when I look in the mirror," he said. "And I don't lie awake at night fretting about anything." He seemed to be tasting his own words while he drew on his cigarette and tipped off the ashes. When smoke swirled into his eyes, they narrowed into slits.

"Nobody gives a damn, Tomás. Nobody here gives a damn whether people die or not. They just want this to go away, and they don't give a damn how we do it."

"People do care. People know right from wrong."

"Right and wrong? The world is not about who's right and who's wrong. It's about who calls the shots. Right and wrong: psaaaah!" He spat on the floor, where it left a dark-red stain. "It's me who decides what's right and what's not. It's me who decides who gets to take his ass home tonight." He pulled at his cigarette with hard, angry puffs, his eyes half-shut. Then he walked to the wall and stood with his back to Tomás, looking out through the small window.

"This is not your fight. You should have stayed out of it. We would have been friends still."

"I didn't ask to get involved."

"So why did you? You're a doubter, Tomás." He shook his head. "You're just like Ana – content with your life until the day you get bored with it. The two of you – you never believed in anything other than your own doubts and desires. Weak and passive, and you stayed that way. Now she" – he pointed over his shoulder towards the cells – "she believes in something. That's why she's dangerous."

The kerosene flame filled the space between them. It cast shadows on the wall behind them, and made them appear larger, yet fleeting.

"And all these dead people, don't they matter?"

"They have never mattered. Not ever, and you of all people should know that."

"If they could talk..."

"But they can't. And they never will – the dead are dead." Fausto rubbed his forehead, stroking his sweat back into the pores.

"Death owes me, Tomás. It took from me, and I want it back. And you took from me, too. You owe me for the oaths you haven't kept. You owe me for my son. And for my wife."

"Is that what this is about? People owing you? Life owing you? Nothing will bring back your son, Fausto. And nothing will bring back the past. Everyone has lost people: you, me. Why don't you make it stop? Do you want to spend the rest of your life killing people?"

"No," Fausto said. "This is not what I signed up for. But it is a consequence." He shrugged. "And in any case, what makes you such an expert on killing people, eh? Have you ever killed anyone? Do you know what it feels like? You were so close once, weren't you? More than once, right, cousin? But you couldn't." He leaned over until his stubble tickled Tomás's ear. "You know nothing about killing. She does, but you don't." He stood up and threw his cigarette away, watched as it spit sparks into the air and fell to the ground, smoldering and lighting up as the air passed through it. He leaned against the wall and crossed his arms. Then he pulled out his gun and laid it on the table.

"So do it," he said, and stood back against the wall. "Let's get this over with – I'm sure you don't need me to convince you, *hermano*. Just do it."

Tomás looked at the blue and black revolver lying in front of him. It was turned his way, so it would ease into his hand without effort.

"What is this going to…?" he said, but there was a kick against the table before he could finish his sentence.

"No more talk."

He felt the anger grow inside him. His breathing quickened, and his heart was pumping louder.

Another kick. "Do it."

He grabbed the gun and stood up, shoving aside the table. Holding the gun with both hands, he trained it on Fausto.

"Damn you!" he screamed.

"You must cock it. If you are going to do it, do it right."

Tomás pressed down and cocked the hammer. He heard how the cylinder lined up with the forcing cone as the bullet lodged inside the barrel, grinding itself into position.

"See how easy it is? Only one thing left to do now." Fausto reached behind him and pulled another pistol from his belt. He pushed in the magazine and pulled back the slide, then let it spring back in a single, effortless movement.

"Second chances," he said. He raised the gun and pointed it at Tomás's head.

"Thirty seconds, cousin. If you don't shoot before that, I will. You first, me first."

Tomás closed his eyes and saw the child's shoe stuck in the mud. He saw pelicans fly up from the roof of a beach house, and a scrawny prisoner with a badly bruised arm noiselessly screaming at him before being loaded onto a truck.

"Fifteen."

He opened his eyes and saw that Fausto had not moved. The moonlight falling into the room covered half of his face now, but the gun was in darkness. He saw the boy who had steadied his hand when he taught him to drive. He smelled the blood thickening in a folded plantain leaf.

"Ten."

The explosion was deafening, but the bullet itself made little noise as it struck the wall. He dropped the gun, and it rattled down the table onto the ground. In a reflex, Fausto touched his chest, surprised by the blood that had splattered over his shirt and neck. Then he felt the pain: the bullet had grazed his cheekbone and pierced his ear. He started laughing, but was interrupted by loud banging on the door.

"Colonel?" someone screamed. "Colonel Cortés, are you alright?"

"Yes," Fausto yelled back. "Yes, I am fine, false alarm." He took out his handkerchief and pressed it against his ear.

"I must say, I didn't think you had it in you, Tomás. I thought that one day you would simply go out like a candle, pfffffft, like that." He lit a cigarette and pulled on it, hard. "Perhaps I underestimated you. Perhaps you are not so unlike myself." When Tomás reached for his cousin's ear, Fausto jerked back his chin, sharply.

"No," he said. "I don't need your medicine. I don't trust any man to heal a wound he himself inflicted."

He kept his hand pressed to his ear, and the handkerchief quickly turned dark red.

"You need to get antibiotics," Tomás said.

Fausto ignored him.

"You know that she is pregnant?" he said.

"Yours?"

"Yes," he said. "Yes, it's mine."

"Figured as much." Fausto slapped his thigh, grinning. "I can read you like a goddamn book, Tomás, like one of those damn books that you have been living your life through. You could have saved yourself the trouble."

They were sitting at opposite sides of the table; the kerosene flame rose steadily between them without flickering, undisturbed by the words they spoke, as if they were not spoken in the same dimension.

"What will happen to her?"

"She will be tried for treason."

"But, you said…"

"That was before you sent me to the wrong place."

"You promised you would not hurt…"

Fausto cut him off: "You haven't learned a thing, have you? It's not what I say that counts; it's what I do."

"You lied to me."

"And you took from me. Twice. So now I'm taking back from you."

"Not this. She has nothing to do with it."

"She has everything to do with it. She is the reason I lost Ana. And the reason I lost you. So go now and tell her what happened, if you dare."

When he emerged into the cool night, Tomás no longer trembled. He was aware that the grasshoppers had started chirping again. Dawn was still far away, yet he could imagine the outline of the mountains, the tall trees swinging in the night breeze, and the conger monkeys perching on their branches. The rustle of a river was the loudest noise around. *The Rio Chiquito*, he thought. *It really is this near then.*

He was escorted to a cell; the soldier standing guard unshackled the big rusty padlock and swung it open. The air drifting out was musty and stale, smelling of hay and cornhusk that had been left to rot. Tomás stooped and bent his head as he stepped inside, and the door slammed shut behind him.

"You have until dawn, Doc," he heard the guard's voice from outside. "Enjoy it."

Chapter 41

There was only one person in the cell, lying on a cot in the far corner. His heart started beating louder while he strained his eyes, and his pupils adjusted to the dark. Her shirt had bunched up around a full waist, and he saw the birthmark that stood out like a blot of sepia ink carelessly spilled onto a sheet of paper. He stood in front of the cot, looking at her. With two fingers he touched her neck, then her forehead. She was warm but not feverish. A steady pulse. When he put a hand on her forearm, she opened her eyes. Not joltingly, as he had expected, but slowly, as if she were still asleep.

"Tomás? Where am I?"

She raised her body on her elbows and looked around the semi-darkness.

"The Fortin," he said. She looked dazed, and reached behind her back, where the rifle butt had hit her.

"Let me look at that," he said. She cringed as he pressed his fingers between her shoulder blades, looking for injuries.

"Where else are you hurt?" he said, touching her legs through the bloodstained pants. She gritted her teeth, but let out a groan as he pressed her knee.

"It's swollen," he said. He twisted her leg, slowly.

"But you'll be all right. Now let's get you out of here. How do your legs feel?" She shook her head dismissively.

"How do you plan on getting us out of here?"

"There are small boats moored by the river, a few minutes from here."

"We're in prison," she said. "You don't just walk out of prison."

"Leave that to me," he said.

She closed her eyes. "What about the others?"

He shook his head, and took out the leather case from his pocket. He broke the vial and filled up the syringe while she watched.

"What is this, Tomás?"

"Epinephrine." She looked puzzled, so he said: "Adrenaline."

"What do I need adrenaline for?"

He spritzed a drop out of the syringe and replaced the cap.

"It's not for you. I need to finish what I have started."

He stood against the wall next to the door, and banged the wood with his fist.

"*Raso*," he shouted, "*raso*, are you there?"

"Yes, Doc," the man on the other side answered. "What do you want, Doc?"

"I am ready here, open up now." The door swung open and a gust of cool air floated in.

"OK, Doc, come on out now," the soldier said as he peered inside.

When the head appeared inside the door opening, Tomás let the needle come down. It was resting in his hand as if it were a dagger, and lodged itself in the man's neck without drawing a drop of blood. He pushed down on it while he covered the man's mouth with his other hand. The soldier was a bull of a man, with thick muscle cords standing out on his neck, but the adrenaline swam up his veins and shot straight to his heart, assaulting it like a battering ram. His eyes popped, and the rippling veins and muscles on his neck froze as he turned pale. Tomás caught the big man's body and pulled it inside the hut. When he looked up again, Milagros stared at him with bulging eyes. He left her no time for questions.

"Lean on me," he said. "We must go now, fast." He led her into the central patio, and from there up the narrow walkway, until they were out among the trees.

It did not take long to get to river. She fell once, and when he reached for her in the dark he smelled the horsemint. Two small rafts, baskets of bent willow rods, were moored on a narrow pebble stone bank, tethered to a tree. He lowered her in and pushed the raft off the bank. The he waded into the water behind it, and pushed it to where the waters ran wild. The raft rocked and heaved without moving out further, so he groped under water. Sitting down on the rope, he started undoing the knot that kept the raft tethered while the current tugged.

There were screams, and then steps. They were five, and Fausto was among them. Five who had come running out as if someone were stealing their water. Their uniforms were unbuttoned, and the bandage around Fausto's head showed a single rust-brown spot.

"Tomás, get out of the way," he growled, training his gun at a place behind his cousin. "Don't do this, Tomás, don't make me do this! Step away now!"

He did not move. He heard Milagros gasping for air behind him, and felt the water tug at the rope with a force he had thought existed only in horses.

"Let her go, Fausto," he said. "Just let her go. Don't you believe in second chances?"

"This is not the time to argue, Tomás. This is not your fight. Now step away, you're leaving me no choice!" Fausto tilted the gun downward, his finger pressing on the trigger.

He loosened the knot behind his back, and felt it slip from him. The coracle tugged once more, and then the force of the water took over.

"Damnit, she's getting away. Fire at the raft," Fausto bellowed. The soldiers jumped forward and fired at the raft, but it had already been caught by the current, and was quickly spinning out of sight. Tomás felt one of his shoes slip off. He threw his hands in the air and tried to scream, but his voice did not obey. He felt as if someone had kicked his legs, and something had slammed into his chest. He felt his knees quiver, and the taste of metal was under his tongue. His back felt wet and cold. He reached for the vial, instinctively, and surprised it was not there. Fausto's face loomed over him, blood-streaked and angry.

"Damn fool, why?"

There were more gunshots, splashing feet and cursing men. Then the shots stopped.

"I did it, Fausto," he said, "I did it."

"Did what, damn fool? Got yourself killed is what you did!" Fausto shook him, raising him by the front of his shirt.

"You're taking from me again, Tomás!"

Fausto was very close to him now, his face becoming larger and larger, and Tomás could feel his cousin's breath streaming towards him.

"Aisa. Yapti." he said. It came out as if he were speaking under water.

No pain. No anger. Just time. Time that leads us into valleys of grace, like weary beasts. Children singing in falsetto voices, a birthday song of times long gone, and from beyond comes the splish-splash sound of a basilisk treading on breaking water walking on and on it never stops never sinks; were we led all this way for birth and death with voices singing in our ears that we were our mothers' only sons, and that she was a widow?

He saw a tall woman wearing a Gigantona dress. She wore no mask, and her features were barely visible against the blazing sun. There was a narrow turret behind her, set atop a Spanish wall holding back the sea, and traveler's trees waving in the wind. It was the trade wind, the wind that had brought so many to these shores in search of fortune. *How many had come to find love? And how many had not sought it, but found it regardless?*

The woman smiled at him, or perhaps it was the wind behind her that smiled. She opened her mouth and pursed her lips, and on her lips he read his name, the name that had been his from before the time he was born. The sea was calm, and united with the air above it.

Chapter 42

El Paraíso is the first town a traveler encounters after crossing from Nicaragua into Honduras. Twenty guerrillas were holed up here, a ragtag band of tired-looking men and boys. They had spent years in the mountains and forests, taunting the outposts of the new regime, fighting boredom and a revolution no one had ever really wanted. The commander took his lieutenant aside, a young man from Somoto.

"Danilo," he said, "walk with me."

"Yes, Colonel." Danilo followed him into one of the buildings, where a desk was waiting.

"Sit, Danilo. Cigarette?" He offered the pack of Lucky Strikes. "No, Colonel, I don't smoke. Thank you."

"Yes," the colonel said, "yes, you are right, I keep forgetting." He lit his own and blew out smoke.

"We have lost three men in the past two weeks, so we'll need some new recruits soon. And we need better intel: we've been sloppy – too many towns we walk into when the Sandinistas have barely left. Those *hijos de puta* know things before we do."

Danilo nodded: "Sí, jefe, you just tell me how many you need and we'll get them for you." This was what the colonel liked about the young man. He was swift to act, and never questioned his orders. Danilo was the only one in his motley outfit who had been with him when there was still a National Guard and he was still a real colonel, not some fly-by-night commander lording it over a marauding band of guerrilla fighters. He spread a map out on the wobbly table, unrolling it carefully and pointing out two villages.

"We'll go for Consecuencias," he said, "just west of Dificultades. We'll come in from the east, here." He let his finger come down on the map.

"*Perfecto*, Colonel," Danilo said. "The Sandinista patrol passed through the village five days ago."

"No cooperatives?"

"Not that we know of. No cooperatives this far north."

"You'll take ten men and swing in from the north, from around the river bend. The rest of us will come in from the east. There are no more than two hundred houses there – when you hear us engage, fire in the air. Don't shoot them unless you have to. Move the women and children into the plaza, round up the men on the north side. The usual. This whole thing should be over in fifteen minutes." The colonel rolled up the map and put it back into its plastic sleeve. He drew on his cigarette and watched the men outside from under his hat. *Ragtag bunch*, he thought, *what happened to my regiments? Six years, six damn years of stinking mosquitoes and landmines.*

Fausto drew on his cigarette one last time and threw it away. "OK, men, let's move it," he said. They lined up behind him and filed out of town. Two klicks out they swerved off the road, onto a cow path, and from there they went through dry forest and scrubland for three whole hours. Cactus land. It had not rained in the region for over five months now, but clouds were gathering, and it was just a matter of time before the downpour would hit.

"We are due north of Dificultades now," Danilo said, looking at his compass and pointing towards a few thin smoke plumes rising in the distance ahead of them. Fausto nodded, and they marched on, until they reached a yellowed hilltop. He raised his hand and the men fell silent. Dificultades was just across the border, and if there were border guards they would be on alert.

They reached Consecuencias by noon.

"No Sandinistas," Danilo reported.

"Fan out," Fausto ordered, and they split up in two groups, as planned. Twenty minutes later Fausto's group entered the village and started shooting in the air. When he heard gunfire coming from the other side, he knew Danilo had come in as well. They kicked in doors, screamed for people to come out with their hands above their head. Young children started crying while the older ones, especially the boys, stared at the guns with looks of curiosity. Soon everyone was rounded up in the plaza: men and older boys on one side, women and children on the other.

"Who's in charge here?" Danilo bellowed. A burly man came forward.

"Who are you?"

"Francisco Guzmán Perera. I am the mayor."

"*Bueno, hombre*, we want to talk to you. Who else is here? Teacher? Nurse? Where are the smart ones here?" The mayor looked back and beckoned left and right for men to come with him. There was one woman. The nine of them trailed behind Danilo as they entered the cantina, followed by three of the soldiers, while the rest of the peasants were told to squat in the square. The sky closed up rapidly, shutting out the few remaining streaks of blue, and a muddy drizzle soon started splattering fat drops onto the people squatting in the square.

"*Oye*," one of them said to the soldiers, "it's going to come down, at least let us take cover." He and two others got up and moved towards the portico.

"*Quedáte allí, hijueputa*," one of the soldiers barked, pushing them back with the butt of his gun. "Here nobody moves until we tell you to."

Fausto had taken up a seat inside the bar, and was drinking coffee. He pointed to a long table and beckoned for the nine villagers to sit down.

"We want to know who in this place work for the Sandinistas," he said. The men and one woman looked at each other.

"We don't know, Don," the mayor declared. "There are no Sandinistas here. We're just peasants; we're not involved in politics."

"So how come you are the mayor here? Who appointed you?"

"We are all from here, Don. All of us. There are no people from the capital. Most of us have never even been to the capital."

"Liar," Fausto snarled, "you're a damn liar. We know that the Sandinistas have installed *políticos* in every hole in the ground. Who are they? Is it you?"

The man looked at his feet, too afraid to face this angry guardia. He put the palms of both hands together and let his chin rest on his two index fingers.

"*Santito*," he said, "there are no Sandinistas here, Santito."

"Take him into the kitchen," Fausto told the soldiers. "And you" — he turned around and stared at the seven men and one woman gathered around the table — "you stay here and listen, maybe that will refresh your memory. Nothing refreshes a man's memory as much as listening to his neighbor's confession. We'll talk again in thirty minutes!"

It did not take thirty minutes.

"Farmers," Danilo said, "can't take a thing; they pass out or spill their guts at the first sign of a knife." One of the soldiers threw a bucket of water onto the man's face, but he made no noise. When one of the soldiers kicked him, his body twitched, but he did not wake up.

"He told us nothing, absolutely nothing, that sonofabitch." Danilo spat, and kicked the body once more.

"Maybe he didn't know anything," the other soldier said. "Some of these guys really know nothing."

The rain had stopped, and some of the villagers had taken off their shirts, ad hung them up to dry. A young man stepped forward, but one of the soldiers quickly pushed his gun into the man's chest. "Hey you, where do you think you are going, hijueputa? Sit back down before we blow a hole in your face!"

"Señor," he started, "I am Padre Rafael, I am the village priest."

"So where's your frock, Padre?" one of the soldiers sneered. "Left it at home? Don't like being seen wearing a dress?" Fausto raised a hand and waved for the man to step inside. The priest saw the motionless shape on the floor and kneeled by him.

"What have you done?" he cried out. "This man has done nothing wrong." Fausto looked amused, delivered from boredom for a few short minutes.

"What do you want from us?" the priest said.

Fausto sighed. "We will leave tomorrow morning. But only if we get what we need. So this can be fast and painless, or…" he did not finish his sentence. "Get me the list of *políticos*, Padre, and we'll be on our way. You know how this works.

The priest remained silent.

"I also need three young men to come back with me," Fausto said. "No, make that four."

"What?" the priest exclaimed.

"Yes, we need recruits. Life is not eternal, you know. I have lost three men in the past couple of weeks."

"But how, I cannot tell people to…"

"Come now, Padre, someone like you can tell people anything, and they will believe it. There must be young men here dying to use a gun; it's not as if I were going to feed them to the dogs." He laughed. "I'm sure there are people here who hate those Sandinista hijueputas as much as I do. And just so you know this is not highway robbery — we're giving one hundred dollars to the families of each new recruit. Got to keep the wheels well oiled!"

Now the other soldiers laughed, too.

"God will punish you for this," the priest said. "Even if there is no more justice on earth, there is justice in heaven."

Fausto snorted. "Not again," he said, closing one eye. "God. Justice. All those big words. It's just words, Padre. They don't mean anything. Not anymore, and not here. Here the only thing that matters is what we do, not what we say. I can just put these people out of their misery and nothing will happen. The earth will not stop turning. Nothing. Indifference. Isn't that what you are really afraid of, Padre, deep down inside?" Fausto turned and cocked his gun, aiming at the peasants. Not at anyone in particular, just at the lot of them, thrown together like a headless flock.

"No!" the priest screamed, but the bullet had already left the barrel. The peasants screamed, terrified by the blood on their clothes and bodies. But when they found that the blood was someone else's, they screamed for relief.

"See? There's your proof. What more do you need?" Fausto unbuttoned his breast pocket and counted out thirty ten-dollar bills. "One hundred each," he said, putting the wad on the table. "Now get me the four boys." He shoved the money over to the priest. "Go on, take it, it won't bite," he said. Then he turned around to his men. "Take these bodies out of here, Danilo."

The remaining peasants trembled as the soldiers prepared to drag the two bodies out through the backdoor.

"This man is not dead," the priest said, pointing to one of the bodies.

"Fine, give him water," Fausto said. The soldiers elbowed each other and started laughing.

"What's so funny?" the priest said. "Is it funny to look at a dying man?"

"Giving water," Danilo said. When the priest looked at him with a blank face, Danilo grinned from ear to ear. He pointed his index finger at his temple, forming a perfectly square angle with his thumb. Then he rapidly yanked his hand away, and made an explosive sound.

Fausto turned back to the cowering peasants. "I need you to tell us where those Sandinista pigs are, and what they're up to. We will come through your village once a month, and each time we pass through here we will need information without anyone else knowing. Anyone caught passing information or collaborating with the Sandinista hijueputas gets a bullet in the head — but not before we rape your wives and daughters. So what's it going to be?"

"We don't know anything," a fat man said, "we're just farmers, Señor *Capitán*."

"That's not what I call cooperative," Fausto hissed. "I don't want to hear that kind of answer. I want to hear answers that give me information, not more questions. I have plenty questions myself." His hand shot out and grabbed the fat man's ear. Then he reached for his bowie knife. It left the scabbard without making a sound, obedient and ready, and grateful for the outing. An instant later the fat man was clutching the empty space where his ear had been, and where blood was now spouting, gushing out between his fingers. His scream came a split second later, as if his mind had needed time to wake up. He fell to the floor, wailing, until his voice ran out of breath, and his wailing had tapered off into a moan. And then there was only a rocking body and a gaping mouth. Fausto cleaned his knife on his pants and threw the ear on the table. It rolled over twice and came to a rest, face up.

"Now, since God gave you ears to hear, I suggest you all start using them," he said. "Because if you don't, I guess you won't need them anymore. So start talking!"

He kicked the writhing body on the floor, and said, "Danilo, get this over with." The lieutenant and two soldiers pulled the three bodies out by their feet. Three shots sounded, and the moaning stopped.

"Anyone else wants water?" Fausto looked around him. Lined up against the wall, the remaining villagers in the bar were staring at their feet.

"You make me come all the way here for nothing!" he barked. "Fuck you, fuck all of you!" He aimed at the huddling people and emptied the clip. Then he dropped the gun and stepped in among the bloodied bodies that had slid down the wall, and sliced off an ear from each one of them. Some of the people not dead; they were moaning and screaming, and when Fausto grabbed hold of their ear, they squealed.

"Sábado," he yelled, "Sábado. To each little pig comes Saturday!" He threw all the ears on the table and leaned over them, closely, breathing on them. "Now you know what happens with people who don't listen," he yelled. "They – don't – need – ears!"

Three young men from the village joined the group of soldiers as they marched out the next day. The drizzle had turned into thin rain, and a blanket of mammatus clouds was massing overhead. Fausto looked at them disapprovingly. *Cotton,* he thought, *cotton clouds.*

"We have to get to Somotillo by tonight, if not we miss the rendezvous," Danilo told the men. "Too bad, we'll just have to get wet." Some of the men pulled out their ponchos to cover themselves, but most of them did not bother. After following the river for two hours, they reached a meadow where a herd of scattered cows were grazing in the yellow grass.

"Any Sandinistas out there?" Fausto said.

"Looks like the coast is clear, jefe," Danilo said. "But you never know of course. They just might be sitting out there waiting for us to run up that hillside – we'd be sitting ducks. We'll have to cross here, climb up the hill over there, and reach that tree line on the other side."

"And just cows, right?"

"That's right, jefe, just cows." Fausto looked at them. Some were lying down, chewing cud, slowly. *Like eating air,* he thought. *Like chewing on the damned ideas full of air that have brought us to this mess.* It reminded him of someone he had known long ago. Someone he had sold his soul to. *Damned cows.*

They advanced cautiously, a wall of flesh charging up a hill in slow motion. Fausto went first, marking a path among the grazing cows. Then the rain thickened. *There won't be enough time to reach the trees,* he thought. *Everyone will be soaked, the guns will be wet, and we'll be defenseless if we run into a Sandinista patrol!*

Suddenly, the sky was illuminated by thick veins of silver. And on its tail came the angry clap of thunder.

"Run for those trees," Fausto screamed, as he ducked between two cows. The clouds broke, and torrential rains started flogging the men. The two cows nearest to Fausto stopped browsing and walked away in opposite directions. Slipping on the sharp grass that had folded to the ground under the weight of the pounding water, Fausto lost his footing. He was on all fours now, indistinguishable from the grass in his camouflage outfit.

"This is what they have brought us to, goddamnit," he rumbled. "Wallowing in the mud like beasts. Goddamn consequences." The water ran down his kepi, and the crest of his nose. He was surprised by how salty it tasted. *So far from the ocean,* he thought. He saw the distant tree line beckoning on the hill, a flaming Malinche tree among them. His anger rose, and he stood up, raising his gun. He fired in the air and then at the cows: left to right, in one sweeping movement. Two of the cows mewed lowly, and knelt until they were standing on hind legs only and finally fell over, their big and empty eyes popping although their panting was more akin to a deer's, timid and wheezing. Fausto smelled the ozone tickling his nostrils, as if he were biting down on electric wire. The first time he had tasted the sting of ozone was in the barn where a mare had foaled. Where a red-stained butcher block had been set up for the spaying of bulls and the gutting of foals unable to stand on their own legs. These were the thoughts that went through Fausto Cortés's head while his body sizzled and fell. The gun slipped from him, cascading down the hillside until it reached the riverbank, the riverbed, and sank to the deepest darkness of the river's channel.

"He looked as if illuminated," his men told everyone back at the base in El Paraiso. "He was like a statue in church, the ones with neon candles flickering all around them."

It kept them talking for a long time, though never doubting. Doubting was reserved for other men.

www.ingramcontent.com/pod-product-compliance
Lightning Source LLC
Chambersburg PA
CBHW031321210726
48287CB00005B/1642